DEATH RANG
THE BELL

D1590061

DEATH RANG THE BELL

A Blackwell & Watson
Time-Travel Mystery

Carol Pouliot

LEVEL
BEST BOOKS

Author Photo Credit: Kevin Lucas

Cover Artist: Ella Smith

First edition

ISBN: 978-1-68512-000-9

Cover art by Ella Smart

This book was professionally typeset on Reedsy.
Find out more at reedsy.com

To Denise Donato, my best friend since kindergarten, with love and all those wonderful memories.

Praise for Death Rang the Bell

"Carol Pouliot's Blackwell and Watson make a terrific detective duo. *Death Rang theBell*, the third installment in this highly inventive series, serves up a real treat—a perfect combination of mystery, time travel, and romance."—Deborah Crombie, *New York Times* Bestselling author of the Duncan Kincaid/Gemma James novels

"*Death Rang the Bell* brings time-travelers Detective Steven Blackwell and contemporary researcher Olivia Watson their toughest case yet. The taut police procedural illustrates the constraints investigations faced in 1934, when one of the wealthiest men in an upstate New York town is murdered on his own doorstep. The relationship between the pair deepens as the twists keep piling on. Pouliot has the period details mastered, adding realism and depth to this wholly satisfying read."—Marni Graff, author of The Nora Tierney English Mysteries

"With engaging characters, a murder mystery, and a trip back in time, Carol Pouliot's *Death Rang the Bell* will keep you turning the pages all night!"—Nancy Allen, *New York Times* Bestselling Author

"In a quirk of time, present-day journalist Olivia Watson and nineteen-thirties detective Steven Blackwell share a house, a growing relation-ship, and now—with Olivia the only witness to a fatal shooting on the night of October 31, 1934—a murder investigation. A Halloween setting, a house where time folds back on itself, and a crime with deep

i

roots in the past make Carol Pouliot's *Death Rang the Bell* a joy for fans of crisp writing and twisty, character-driven plots."—Connie Berry, Agatha-nominated author of the Kate Hamilton Mysteries

"A delightfully immersive story, filled with surprising twists and turns, a touch of romance — plus a heroine you will happily follow as she jumps between decades, *Death Rang the Bell* is a truly great escape."—Alison Gaylin, *USA Today* and international bestselling author

"Carol Pouliot's Blackwell and Watson Time-Travel Mysteries provide an intriguing glimpse into life and crime solving in the 1930s. Olivia Watson discovers the veil between current day and 1934 is thin as she steps between the two time periods to help solve mysteries that occurred long before she was born. This intriguing and beautifully written series will draw you in and make you feel right at home in a time period you'll wish you could visit."—Grace Topping, Agatha finalist and *USA Today* bestselling author of the Laura Bishop Mystery Series.

Chapter One

NOVEMBER 1916 – SYRACUSE, NEW YORK

H ot coffee spilled over the rim and burned her hand. *Lillian wanted to cry. At nine in the morning, she'd been on her feet since six and had seven long hours to go. She didn't know how much longer she'd be able to keep it up. She was constantly exhausted and the struggle to breathe was worsening; some days it was nearly unbearable. She knew the disease was going to overpower her, and that moment was coming soon.*

Lillian slid around some tables and set a heaping plate of eggs and bacon, potatoes, and toast in front of Arnie McCormack, then topped off his cup from the pot in her other hand. McCormack lowered his newspaper and leered, pinching her behind as she stepped away. Rude bastard. She'd like to pour the scalding coffee over his head and dump his breakfast right in his lap.

The only thing that kept her going every day was the thought of her beautiful little boy. Well, not so little anymore. He was growing up fast, nine years old in January. She managed a smile and wiped away a tear before it became a flood. Best not to think too much about things. Especially money. Lillian knew if she didn't get the money somehow, she'd never see her son grow into a man.

And what about her letter? It had been four weeks since she'd mailed it. Surely he should have written back by now. She hadn't been unreasonable, hadn't asked for much, only enough to pay for treatment at the Little Red Cottage in Saranac Lake.

Dr. Trudeau's Little Red Cottage. It sounded like heaven. Lillian had heard wonderful things about people being cured there. Imagine, cured! The thought made her dizzy.

Lillian returned to the lunch counter, using the backs of chairs for support. When she arrived at the griddle, she was breathing hard.

Tomorrow, *she thought,* if I don't get an answer tomorrow, I'll send another letter.

Chapter Two

WEDNESDAY, OCTOBER 31, 1934

The Three Witches of Macbeth were doing a swell job. Annie, Molly, and Lilly led the parade of pirates, sailors, and fairy princesses through Knightsbridge, picking up ghosts, goblins, and a mummy along the way. Crowds of families followed the costumed children down Victoria Avenue to the entrance of The Elks Club, where, from the top of the staircase, The Three Witches hissed, "Double, double toil and trouble; fire burn and cauldron bubble."

Molly cried out, "Beware, all ye who enter here." Then she thumped a tall gnarled staff on the stone step, and Annie and Lilly grasped the thick iron rings with both hands and heaved. As the massive oak doors creaked open, the masquerading children flew up the stairs and into the community room, awash with the scents of apples and cinnamon.

Carved pumpkins flickered in the semi-darkened room, revealing white cobweb-filled corners and big black spiders and bats hanging so low that adults had to duck. Seeing colorful bags piled on black-draped tables, one little boy jumped up and down, clapping his hands in glee. A girl grabbed her friend's hand, and they did a little dance, and three teenagers slapped each other on the back. A Halloween treat awaited each of them. Eager to explore, the kids fanned out.

"Ooh! I feel like I'm ten again," said Olivia, shaking the black-and-orange tin noisemaker. "Why didn't we wear costumes?"

Steven gave her a look. "What if I had to rush out for an emergency?" he asked.

"You could've dressed like a cop." She smirked.

"Hi, Steven." Decked out in an eye patch and pirate gear, Jimmy Bourgogne appeared from behind Olivia, swept off his hat, and gave a courtly bow, bending low to the floor. "Miss Watson."

"Jimmy, you look fantastic," exclaimed Olivia. "I didn't recognize you with that mustache and goatee."

"Congratulations, Jimmy. You fellas did a swell job," Steven said.

"Thanks, but the credit really goes to Leon here."

A slender young man with light brown hair joined them. He sported a plaid shirt with a tin sheriff's badge pinned over his heart, red kerchief around his neck, and holster holding a toy gun attached to a leather belt.

"Hi, Leon." Steven extended his hand. "This is my friend Olivia Watson. Olivia, Leon Quigg is my mailman."

"Nice to meet you, Miss Watson," Leon said, nodding as he doffed his cowboy hat.

"I'm glad to meet you, too. This is a wonderful party."

Jean Bigelow sidled up to Olivia, yelling amidst the racket. "You made it!"

"Jean! Isn't this swell?" Olivia chuckled to herself. Liz and Sophie would crack up hearing her talk like a real 1934 person.

After several months, acting like she belonged here had become second nature, but Olivia Watson didn't belong here. She lived in 2014 and only visited 1934 from time to time.

This week Olivia was spending several days in Steven's time. No passport, no suitcase, no plane ticket required. All it took was a simple step across the threshold of her bedroom door into Steven's

4

Depression-era house–simple but the key to her recently discovered ability to time travel.

"What are you reading tonight?" Olivia asked the librarian.

"Edgar Allan Poe. 'The Cask of Amontillado.'"

"That's the one where the guy gets walled up, isn't it?"

Jean nodded. "I've been practicing creepy voices for days."

"Well, you look the part. I love your cape, very 19th-century." Olivia touched a fold of Jean's costume. "Ooh, velvet. I wish I'd worn that."

The organizers had packed the evening full of entertainment. Steven and Olivia watched a magician pull pennies out of children's ears and a rabbit out of his top hat, and wondered how he made the mayor's watch disappear. The kids bobbed for apples, the water sloshing out of the metal washtub soaking the floor. The younger children played Pin-the-Tail-on-the-Donkey and Drop-the-Handkerchief, while the older ones played charades and told ghost stories.

At seven-thirty, the kids crowded along the row of tables where members of the Elks handed out treats. Noses in their black-and-orange bags exploring the treasures within, they moved to the far end to select their favorite soda, handing the tall glass bottles of Hires Root Beer, Orange Crush, and Coca-Cola to Jimmy Bou and Leon Quigg, who were armed with metal bottle openers.

The evening culminated with storytelling. The village librarian, led the young children into a side room, spooky picture books in hand. The older ones gathered behind the curtain on the shadow-filled stage where Jean Bigelow waited in flickering candlelight. When they'd settled in a circle on the floor, Olivia among them, the librarian cleared her throat and began.

"The thousand injuries of Fortunato I had borne as I best could; but when he ventured upon insult, I vowed revenge...."

Chapter Three

It had been a grand evening. Everyone had enjoyed the party. He'd found himself in conversation with some interesting people and stayed longer than he'd planned. He was especially glad for the chance to watch the children. Seeing their smiling faces and listening to their laughter fortified him for his task, and reassured him it was the right thing to do. It had to be done. It was long overdue.

But he had time to kill first.

He left the Elks Club and headed to the saloon on the corner for a boost of courage. *A stiff drink ought to do the trick.* Standing at the end of the bar, listening to snatches of conversation, and nursing his whiskey, he watched the place fill up. After a time, he finished his drink, said no to the barman's offer of a refill, and left the noise behind. The streets were quiet and cold.

He turned onto the Margate Road, shivering, wishing he'd worn a heavier jacket. As he made his way along the sidewalk, a gust of wind broke through thick cloud cover, revealing a full moon, reminding him of a line from a poem he'd learned in school. "The moon was a ghostly galleon tossed upon cloudy seas." He'd loved that sentence since the moment his teacher had read it aloud to the class, and the words had never left him. There was no better description of a night like this.

In a low voice, he said the sentence out loud, the words rolling off his tongue like fine wine. He pictured a huge trading clipper dipping in and out of great cresting waves, its bow reaching for the skies, its stern getting lost in the abyss of mountainous waves. In and out, up and down. The wind whipping the sails; the crew struggling to stay on their feet. That poem, "The Highwayman," had sparked a love of poetry that had lasted a lifetime. Well, ten years anyway.

As he approached the Village Green, the lighted face of the clock in the tower told him it was nearly eleven. Although it had been a bold decision to do it at the house, this had been the ideal time to choose. Knightsbridge was a ghost town.

He continued putting one foot in front of the other, forcing himself to remember the conversation he'd overhead shortly before he'd lost his mother. He'd known then that eventually he would confront him—the man who had robbed him of a childhood filled with love and laughter. He needed to know why that man had done what he'd done so many years ago.

In the distance, someone laughed. He stopped. Boisterous conversation accompanied the merriment. Now was not the time to meet someone on the street. He held his breath and listened, waiting for the sounds to come closer. Moments passed. The sounds faded away. He exhaled deeply, slowing his accelerated breathing. *What should I do?*

Go, a little voice whispered inside his head. *You have to settle this once and for all.*

He gave one resolute nod. He crossed the street, stepped up onto the sidewalk, and walked on in the inky night.

Chapter Four

"Y"ou can't tell me you still hate Halloween. Not after the party tonight." Olivia regarded Steven, sipped her tea, then reached for another Fig Newton. "You know, these taste a lot better now than in my time."

Last winter, when time had folded over in the house where they lived, 21st-century Olivia Watson and Depression-era Steven Blackwell had learned the art of time travel, and had reached the point where they were comfortable in each other's time. As before, they spent their days working, but got together in the evening in one or the other's house. Olivia owned a business, which allowed her to spend a fair amount of time in 1934, while Steven's policeman's job limited his visits to the future.

"I admit the party was fun," he said. "And I enjoy seeing the kids in their costumes. But, you should have seen it before–pranks, vandalism, sometimes violence and assault. And if there was a full moon, it was worse. I'm still holding my breath. Something always happens on Halloween."

"It's nearly eleven. Halloween's almost over."

"Don't jinx it."

"You'll be glad to know that in my time, Halloween has been a fun holiday for decades. Dressing up in costumes, carving pumpkins and decorating your house, scaring the kids who come to the door trick-or-treating." Olivia laughed.

"What's trick-or-treating?"

She offered a brief explanation.

"I see. Well, I'm glad to hear it. The chief sent some patrolmen out tonight just in case."

Olivia took another sip of tea, then excused herself to run upstairs to the bathroom.

Steven sighed. *One more hour. Maybe this'll be the year nothing bad happens.*

A blast shattered the silence.

Steven levitated from his chair like a marionette jerked by strings. He flew through the kitchen and down the hall, grabbed his gun from the console cabinet drawer, then ran out onto the front porch. As he sped past the staircase, he yelled up at Olivia. "Stay put. That was a gun!"

Olivia had just washed her hands and put the towel back on the bar when, for no particular reason, she pushed open the curtains and peered out the window. Gazing upon the spectacular full moon riding on a cloud, she took a deep breath. *I love it here*, she thought.

Her eyes fell on a figure moving in the shadows toward the house across the street. *This town goes to bed early. I wonder who's out so late.* In the light of the winking Jack-o'-lanterns marching up the neighbor's front steps, Olivia squinted to see if it was anyone she knew.

The visitor was slender and wore a short jacket, dark pants, and a cap pulled down over his face. He mounted the stairs gingerly. Olivia watched as he rang the doorbell and waited. A light went on and a face peeked out from behind the draperies. Moments later, a man opened the door.

Olivia watched as they talked, but the conversation was brief. The visitor took something from his right jacket pocket.

Crack!

Olivia cried out, "Oh, my God!"

The man fell back onto the floor inside the entry. Olivia inhaled so deeply she felt dizzy. Chills ran up and down her arms. Her mouth agape, Olivia watched as the killer spun around and fled down the steps, bolted across the front of the house, then disappeared round the side into the darkness. She saw Steven reach the end of their front walk, threw open the window, and shouted, "Steven, go left! He's heading to the backyard. Left side!"

Ignoring Steven's order to stay put, Olivia raced out the door and out of the house. She flew up the neighbor's front steps and skidded to a halt at the entry.

A tall, middle-aged man in pale blue pajamas and a plaid flannel robe lay inches beyond the doorstep, his slippered feet near the threshold. Olivia observed one perfect hole in his forehead. She knew not to enter the house or touch anything. It was too late anyway. There was nothing to be done. She stepped off the porch and stood sentinel at the bottom of the steps. At least she could secure the scene until Steven came back.

It was several minutes before Steven returned from behind the house. Alone.

"You didn't find him?"

"It was too dark." He looked over her shoulder at the victim. "Poor Mr. Shipley."

"He's dead, Steven. I saw it happen. I *saw* the killer."

Steven grabbed her shoulders and searched her face in the flickering light. "Are you all right? That was a terrible thing for you to see."

"I'm fine." Seeing the disbelief on his face, she added, "Really. I don't know why but I *am* okay."

"Did you see anyone else?"

"No, just the one guy. He shot your neighbor then ran away."

"Can you wait here and not let anyone up on the porch? I need to check the house to make sure no one's here."

"Yes, of course. Your neighbor lived alone?"

Steven nodded. "Mr. Shipley had been estranged from his wife for a long time." He took a hesitant step, then stopped to brush a stray lock of hair from Olivia's face. "You're sure you're okay?" His voice sounded strained.

"Yes, go ahead. Do what you have to do."

Gun in hand, Steven stepped around the body and disappeared into the darkness within. Olivia didn't know where to look. Feeling it wasn't right to stare at the dead man, she kept her back to the porch and the doorway with its horrible new centerpiece and waited with her heart in her throat. It hadn't occurred to her someone might be inside the house. What if an accomplice attacked Steven while she was standing out here? Should she tiptoe to the doorway and listen to ensure he was okay? No, Steven told her to wait here. Olivia trusted him, so she waited.

Alone in the black night, Olivia stood mere feet from a dead man. She glanced up and down the street that was both familiar and unfamiliar. In her time, there would be lots of activity—costumed revelers returning home from parties, people getting in a late run with music blaring from their earbuds, and cars zipping by with the bass thumping so that it shook the chassis. Here the street was silent. She listened. An owl hooted in the distance. Dry autumn leaves rustled not far from where she stood—there were animals about. Something flew by, so close to her face she felt the air on its wings. A bat?

While she waited, Olivia ran through everything she'd seen. Using mnemonic tricks from her journalism training, she closed her eyes and pictured each scene as if in a movie. Association was the technique that worked best for her. She thought, *Slim Jim.* The killer was a slender man. She'd like to *cap off the evening with a small piece of chocolate.* The killer was dressed in a short brown jacket and cap.

She went over his movements and mimed them standing in place. She pretended to walk up the path, climb the stairs, stop and talk, shoot to kill, spin around, glance up…*What? Where did that come from?* Had he looked up? Olivia racked her brains. He spun around and flew down the steps, of that there was no question. But had he glanced up at her? Where had that memory come from? More importantly, was it real?

The dim streetlights with their foggy halos had little effect on brightening the dark street. The bathroom light in Steven's house must have stood out like a beacon and could have easily drawn the killer's attention. The glance, if there had been a glance, had lasted only a nanosecond. What would the killer have seen in that lightning-quick look? She'd been standing at the window with the light behind her—he would have seen a silhouette, nothing more. She should be safe.

Since she wasn't sure and didn't want to worry Steven, Olivia decided to say nothing for the moment.

Steven reappeared. "All clear. I called the station. The fellas are on their way. Would you do me a favor? I need my gear. It's in that leather bag near the phone stand in the hall. Can you get it for me? I can't leave the scene unsecured."

"Sure, no problem."

"Grab my heavy jacket from the front closet, too. It's awfully cold."

As Olivia hurried across the street, it hit her. Oh, no! She was a *witness.* From the moment she'd looked out the window, she had become involved in his case. How long was it going to take for everyone to discover who she was? How long until their secret was revealed?

Olivia returned carrying a small satchel and a jacket. She set the bag on the ground and handed the jacket to Steven.

"No, it's for you," he said. "I don't want you to catch cold." He held it up, and Olivia slipped into its warmth.

"Thank you."

As she zipped it up and folded the cuffs to free her hands, Olivia caught his scent. She turned her face into the collar and breathed in.

Steven climbed to the porch, took a flashlight, and aimed low, moving it to the right of the door, then to the left, the yellow cone crawling across the wooden floor.

"No shell casings. I bet the killer used a revolver. Olivia, would you hold this?"

"Where do you want me to point it?"

"The body." He extracted a notebook and pencil from his pocket and sketched the scene from his vantage point at the victim's feet. He drew the doorway with the victim lying inside, eyes wide open.

"Thanks. Now, the path and the ground by those bushes."

Descending, Steven checked every step and looked behind each pumpkin. He set his satchel on the ground and made another sketch, roughing in the Jack-o'-lanterns and outlining the feet in the doorway.

As Steven and Olivia retraced the killer's get-away route, he moved the flashlight along the edge of the path where the man had fled, sliding it over the flagstones and under the boxwood hedge. Olivia walked with him, twice reaching out to rifle the soil when she thought she saw something.

They were nearly at the corner of the house when Steven saw it. "There!" he exclaimed. Lying at the edge of a flagstone, something silver glittered. He handed her the flashlight again. "I have to record this."

While Steven drew a third sketch, Olivia bent over and peered at the find. A tiny medallion emerged in the cone of light. "Oh, it's a religious medal."

"Would you get a marker out of my satchel? They look like short sticks in a rubber band." He took back his flashlight. "I'll keep the light on this so I don't lose its position."

"What is all this stuff?" Olivia asked, rummaging through the hold-all.

"The things I need at a crime scene: my flashlight, a tape measure, tweezers, magnifying glass, different size paper bags for evidence, and a pair of gloves so I don't get my prints on things. There's a garden trowel for digging or loosening the soil around an object, tape, and my Swiss army knife."

"Interesting. Ah, there they are." She pulled out the bundle of markers and handed one to him.

He stuck it in the ground, then cocked his head. "Sirens. Here they come."

"Steven, they're going to have to question me, aren't they?"

"Yes." He stepped toward her, standing so close she felt his breath on her face. "I know you're scared about being found out," he whispered. "Don't worry. We'll figure something out. But, Olivia, this is an official investigation. No matter what, you can't lie to the police."

Chapter Five

Gray Wilson arrived first. When the dapper police photographer pulled up to the curb, Steven's jaw dropped. "Wowie! When did you get that?" A brand new cobalt blue Packard Super Eight Coupe roadster reflected the soft light of the streetlamps.

"Picked it up this afternoon. Isn't she sweet?" Gray grinned.

"Must be nice to have a wealthy grandfather."

"It is. So, what have we got? Is this the house I think it is?" Gray asked, taking his equipment from the trunk.

"Yes, if you're thinking Benjamin Shipley. Someone shot him about…," Steven consulted his watch, "…thirty minutes ago. I heard the shot."

Gray whistled. "Ooh, boy. That's one rich family." He closed the lid and handed Steven a bulging bag while he balanced his camera equipment in his other hand. "Would you mind carrying my Sashalites?" He saw Olivia. "Miss Watson, what are you doing here?"

Steven set Gray's lights on the grass as Olivia said hello on her way to check out the Packard. "She came to the Halloween party with me tonight."

Gray raised his eyebrows. "I see."

"It's not like that," Steven whispered, glad that Olivia had wandered out of hearing distance.

"But, you wish it were." His friend smiled knowingly.

Steven stood aside while Gray shot the path to the front of the house, the staircase leading to the porch, and the victim from all angles. When he'd finished, Steven pointed to the medal. "See if you can manage enough light to photograph this and around the side. That's where the killer escaped."

The rumble of an engine and squeal of brakes announced the arrival of Steven's team. His partner Sergeant Will Taylor exited the driver's side of a 1929 black Ford sedan. Officer Jimmy Bourgogne, known to everyone as Jimmy Bou, hopped out of the front seat. Patrolmen Ralph Hiller and Pete McGrath jumped out the back, hooting when they saw Gray's roadster.

"Yikes!" Ralph exclaimed. "Get a load of the butter-and-egg man."

"Did ya rob a bank?" croaked Pete.

"That is some snazzy automobile," drooled Jimmy Bou.

"We'll have some questions for you later, Mr. Gray Wilson," said Ralph, pretending to scowl and pointing a finger.

"Miss Watson, what are you doing here?" Pete noticed Olivia.

"Steven and I went to the Halloween Party at the Elks Club." She turned to Steven. "I'll wait in the house, okay?"

Before anyone could say anything else about Gray's astounding car or Olivia casually strolling across the street, Doc Elliott arrived. The lifelong smoker and his old Model T coughed and sputtered in harmony. The Oneida County Medical Examiner was a gray-haired man with the strain of decades on the job etched into his face. Steven had worked with him for thirteen years, since he'd been a rookie at age twenty.

"Sorry to get you out so late, Doc."

"Not your fault, Steven, but thanks." He groaned as he climbed the three stairs. "Oh, my goodness. It *is* Benjamin Shipley. I thought this ⟩

was his address."

"Jimmy, secure the scene, please. Ralph and Pete, stand guard at the sidewalk. We don't need any nosy neighbors. Will, would you bag that silver medal over there?"

Doc flattened himself against the doorframe and sidled into the house, stepping around the victim. As he knelt, Steven wondered which song he'd choose tonight–the ME had a habit of singing to the victims. Steven suspected the songs acted as armor against the sadness caused by this part of the job. Doc began the staccato beat of "I Never Slept a Wink All Night," a Max Miller tune that had topped the charts for weeks.

The medical examiner lifted the victim's head. "Well, that's something you don't see every day. Looks like the bullet's still inside. We'll have to wait until the postmortem." He opened the robe and unbuttoned the pajama top. "No obvious wounds here." Doc struggled to his feet. "I'd say what you see is probably all there is, Steven. One shot through the forehead."

"Thanks, Doc. By the way, I heard the shot."

"You did, did you? You and Miss Watson having a late evening?" He lit a cigarette. "I'll get to this first thing in the morning." He waved at the two mortuary attendants waiting by their vehicle, smoking and chatting. They threw their cigarettes to the ground, slid out a stretcher, and hurried up the walk.

When the body had been removed, Steven stepped back into the foyer to call the station. "We're ready for him," he said to the night officer, then picked up a set of keys from a wall console, turned out the light, and secured Benjamin Shipley's front door before joining his team on the lawn.

"All right, fellas. It's getting late. Let's take an hour then get some sleep." Facing the victim's house, he pointed to the left. "After he shot

Mr. Shipley, our killer ran along the side there toward the backyard."

"How do you know that, Steven?" Will interrupted.

"We have a witness." He paused. "Olivia."

Jimmy Bou gasped.

"What?" chorused Ralph and Pete.

"Yeah, we were in the kitchen having a cup of tea. She went upstairs and happened to look out the bathroom window as the killer was walking up the path here."

"Doesn't that beat all?" exclaimed Ralph.

"What'd she say, Steven?" asked Jimmy Bou.

Steven described what Olivia had witnessed. "I ran after him, but I was too late. And I couldn't see anything back there. It's too dark."

"He was smart to pick tonight," said Will. "Unless the wind picks up and blows an opening in the clouds, that full moon is useless. Escaping behind the house was clever, too, nothing back there but The Green. Our killer disappeared into a big black void."

"Let's find out if anyone did see something–some of the neighbors seem to be awake. Maybe we can find out which direction our killer came from and if anybody saw his face. Olivia didn't get a good look."

"The stores have been closed for hours. They won't be any help," Ralph said.

"He wouldn't have gone down Hickory when he got to Victoria. It would have taken him too close to the station," said Pete.

"But, if he went the other way, there's that block of houses across from the bank," said Will.

"Steven, I'll go over there," volunteered Jimmy Bou. "I don't mind waking people up. I'll ask if they heard the shot or saw a man running past. What do you think?"

"That's a good idea. You can go home afterwards. We'll see you in the morning."

Jimmy straightened his policeman's cap and trotted off.

"Let's divide up Chiltington," Steven said. "I'll take from my house down to the corner–I'd like to talk with Judge Randolph. Will, you take from here to the corner at Tulip. Dr. Kranken might be up–maybe he was out on a house call." Steven directed Ralph and Pete to cover the other two sections.

A black sedan pulled up to the curb as they were about to split up. The rookie patrolman rolled down the window. "Hi, Detective Blackwell. I'm here to watch the house for the night."

"I hope that's a heavy jacket you've got on. It'll be a long cold night otherwise."

"It sure is. Is there anything I need to know?"

"I've checked all the windows on the main floor and locked the doors. You can stay in the car out here in front, but I want you to walk the perimeter every 30 minutes. There's a call box at the corner if you need to contact the station." Steven indicated the direction of the emergency iron box.

Alone in the darkness of the second-floor bedroom, Olivia observed the action as if it were a silent movie. From the window, she watched Gray Wilson set up his tripod. He adjusted something on his camera and walked toward the backyard, then, using a handheld light, he proceeded to illuminate the scene as he backed up to the front of the house. *Ah, a light painting!* Olivia had tried that once in Rome and found it interesting the technology was used as early as the 1930s.

She watched two men stow the body in the back of the mortuary van, a white vehicle resembling the plain, boxy cars belonging to the police department, but longer to accommodate the stretcher. She saw Steven's team talking and doing a lot of pointing up and down the street, as well behind the victim's house, and imagined it would be a while before he came home.

Olivia had an early appointment in the morning. There was nothing

else for her to do and no more to see. Time to call it a night.
She went downstairs and left a note on the kitchen table.

> *Steven,*
>
> *I'm meeting with a client at 8:30 tomorrow morning. I know you or someone at the station will have to question me about what I saw tonight. Can we talk first? What am I going to say if they want to know when I was born and where I live?*
>
> *I can be ready by 6:00. Can you come and get me then? Maybe I can have breakfast with you before you leave for work.*
>
> *Thanks. Olivia*

As Olivia stepped across the threshold, sliding back into her own time and her own bedroom, she watched Steven's mother's Art Deco boudoir fade away, replaced by her own cozy furnishings. Evangeline's ice-blue drapes became Olivia's white gossamer curtains, and her white walls turned into Olivia's pale blue ones. Although she'd been doing this for months, every once in a while the enormity of what had happened to her and Steven—and how it had changed their lives—struck her. If someone had told her the turn her life was about to take, she'd have laughed at the absurdity of the idea.

Last winter, Olivia had awoken in the middle of the night to sheer terror. A man stood at her bedroom door. Frantic to escape her worst nightmare but paralyzed with fear, Olivia had been forced to lie and wait, unable to cry out or dial 911. The man had peered in at her then, after what had seemed like the longest moment in her life, he'd shaken his head as though confused and walked through the wall.

What was *that*? Was she dreaming? Was she losing her mind? After several more nights of these appearances and disappearances, Olivia spoke to him. To her amazement, he answered.

They discovered Einstein had gotten it right—there was no past, present, or future; all time happened at the same time.

Now, what were they going to do? Was their time-travel secret about to come out because she witnessed a murder?

Olivia texted Liz and Sophie: *Saw a murder tonight!!! Interviewed (interrogated?) by police in the morning. Yikes! Can we meet for dinner Fri.?*

Before she turned out the light, Olivia took her journal from the drawer in her nightstand and chronicled the events of this incredible evening.

Chapter Six

As Steven approached Judge Randolph's house, he forced himself to push aside thoughts of Olivia and the problem they faced. Glad to see the lights still on, he turned into the paved driveway, a rarity in 1934, and climbed the stairs to the grand entry. Stepping between fluted columns, he rang the bell and heard chimes echo in the two-story home. Judge Randolph flung open the door and beckoned him in.

"I hoped you'd stop by when you finished," said his father's best friend, putting his arm around Steven's shoulder and ushering him into a cozy study where a fire warmed the room, its flames throwing shadows on the walls. "Come sit by the hearth. Would you like a drink? How about a bourbon to ward off the chill? Look at you, out on a night like this with only a sweater. They said on the radio we'll likely see flurries overnight."

Randolph walked to a well-stocked drinks cart and splashed a generous portion of Maker's Mark into a cut-glass tumbler. The amber liquid glowed like molten gold in the firelight. "Here, get that in your belly," he ordered, handing the drink to Steven and lowering himself into the matching leather club chair on the opposite side of the fireplace. A bushy-tailed ginger cat hopped onto the judge's lap, turned around twice, and settled. Steven heard the deep rumble of purring as Randolph absently stroked the cat.

Unused to hard liquor, the whiskey burned all the way down Steven's throat, and his eyes watered. "Thank you."

"So, tell me, son. I heard the shot and then the sirens. Who was it?" The judge frowned, his thick brows forming a straight line across his high forehead.

"Benjamin Shipley."

Randolph gasped. "No!" He gulped a mouthful of his drink. "That makes what I have to tell you all the worse."

"What? Did you see something?"

The judge's face sagged, and he nodded. "A couple of minutes before the shot, I was drawing the drapes and saw a man walking up the street. He had a dark jacket on, and a cap pulled down over his face."

"Who was it?"

The judge hesitated. Steven could see he was upset. "I've only seen him once since he moved away, and my eyesight isn't good anymore at night, but there was something familiar about him. He reminded me of Ben's son, Theo."

"Theo? I thought he lived in New York City. Is he here visiting?"

"I don't know. When he left, he was so angry with his father that, as far as I know, he only came back for his grandfather's funeral. He hates his old man."

"Why? What happened?"

The judge stood. There was a loud *hiss* and an orange blur as the cat dove for the fireplace, then settled at a safe distance on the thick Persian rug. Randolph reached for the Maker's Mark and topped off their glasses, then grabbed a poker and tilted a log back onto the andiron. A shower of sparks filled the back of the hearth.

"Ben's wife Alice left him fifteen, sixteen years ago. Theo was only a kid. By the way, she's a cousin to Chief Thompson's wife."

"I didn't know that."

Randolph nodded. "Alice found out Ben had cheated on her. She's a religious girl, so divorce was out of the question. She tried to take Theo with her, but Ben chased after them and dragged the boy back here. He underestimated what it takes to raise a child. After a couple of months, he realized he couldn't do it and sent Theo away."

"That poor kid. I can understand why Theo resented him, but to kill him? Especially after all this time. Do you think Theo is capable of cold-blooded murder, Judge?"

"I'm afraid I can't answer that, Steven."

Chapter Seven

DECEMBER 1916 – SYRACUSE, NEW YORK

Somehow Lillian made it through another workday. Darkness had fallen by the time she got off the streetcar. As she did every day, she thanked God the stop was only half a block from the house. Pulling her wool scarf tighter around her neck, she paused to catch her breath at the bottom of the wooden staircase at the front of Uncle Brian's and Aunt Cathleen's looming two-story house on Tipperary Hill. The ascent looked as daunting as Mount Everest. Wheezing, she put a foot on the first step and began to climb, her hand gripping the railing, her chest heaving, her lungs on fire. She stopped on every step and bent over to catch her breath. It seemed like only last week she'd been able to make it up two steps before needing to rest. The disease was worsening.

Tipperary Hill was home to Irish immigrants. Like an immigrant herself, though she'd traveled less than two hours, Lillian had made her home on Syracuse's West Side for nearly ten years. People were friendly and if anyone asked, she told them her husband had died. That stopped their questions.

At first, it had been unimaginably hard. Pregnant at seventeen, she'd felt the bottom of her world give way, broken pieces scattering in all directions. Her father had been unable to speak to her. The disappointed look on his face sliced into her heart, leaving shredded strands that hung dead inside her. Her *mother had cried, then took pity on her and contacted Aunt Cathleen, who out of the goodness in her heart agreed to take Lillian in. Uncle Brian was a tough old bird who had seen just about everything. He had harrumphed and moved on. His only comment had been that they weren't a charity. Lillian had to pull her own weight.*

The first thing she'd done when she moved to Tipp Hill was take the streetcar into Syracuse to look for a job. She got lucky on the third day—or so she'd thought.

The waitressing job was brutal. On her feet ten hours a day, six days a week, Lillian made little money, and, although she smiled and acted cheerful, she also made few tips. Nevertheless, every Friday she was proud to hand over her wages to her uncle, who seemed to appreciate the effort.

When Lillian opened the door, the aroma of boiled corned beef and cabbage assailed her, and her stomach turned over. Lillian knew she had to eat to keep up her strength, but lately, no matter how much she forced down her throat, she was tired all the time. More than tired. There were days when she felt there were no bones in her body.

Lillian pushed the heavy oak door closed and paused, trying to get a lungful of air. She removed her boots, then leaned against the wall, panting. A full ten seconds later, she reached up and hung her coat, hat, and scarf on the hall tree.

Lillian followed the pungent odor to the back of the house and found her aunt and uncle in the kitchen, waiting for her for supper. She heard a shuffling behind her in the hall and suddenly two skinny arms hugged her tight around the middle. She turned around in his embrace.

"My darling boy!" Lillian exclaimed, brushing hair from his forehead. "How was school today?"

"Good, Mama. Our teacher read Aesop's Fables. *They're stories about animals but they're really lessons for people. I liked 'The Lion and the Mouse' and 'The Fox and the Crow.' During recess, I went to the library and borrowed a copy so I can read more tonight." His eyes sparkled with*

delight.

"You and your books," she sighed. But her voice held pride at her son's knowledge and ambition.

After supper, Lillian helped Aunt Cathleen do the dishes while Uncle Brian sat at the table with a second cup of coffee, the evening paper, and his pipe.

"You really should eat more, lass," said Aunt Cathleen. "You're fair wastin' away."

"I try but it's hard to keep it down. I'll do better tomorrow."

Chapter Eight

THURSDAY, NOVEMBER 1, 1934

S teven winced as his bare feet hit the icy oak floor. Even his nose was cold. He peeked out the window and saw it had snowed overnight. A good two inches covered the ground. *I wonder if the almanac will be right this year,* he thought, remembering Poor Richard's prediction of a long hard winter. He realized he'd been so busy he hadn't checked to see how much coal was left from last winter. *Better get that organized before the cold weather takes hold.*

He wrapped up in his flannel bathrobe, stepped into a pair of warm slippers, and descended into the cellar. He pulled a chain dangling from the ceiling and a light bulb came to life. Ducking under the heating ducts snaking across the ceiling, Steven walked to the giant black octopus furnace that occupied most of the space. The door to the coal chute on the far side was latched shut. He undid the fastening, saw the big wooden bin was only a third full, and made a mental note to call for his deliveries to arrive on an automatic schedule again this winter. Certain Olivia wasn't used to a house this chilly, Steven decided to put the heat on before bringing her into his time. He grabbed the shovel and transferred some coal into the belly of the iron furnace, then turned off the light with a tug on the chain and left the damp cellar.

Steven filled the percolator with water, spooned rich ground coffee into the aluminum basket that sat at the top of the pot, and lit one of the gas burners. While the coffee brewed, he went back upstairs to get ready.

After slicking back his hair in the bathroom mirror, he dug out his winter suit. The pure wool tweed kept him warm without having to wear long johns, even on the coldest of days. He buttoned a white shirt and slid a tie around his neck. The one he chose had been a Christmas gift from his mother, one of the last things she'd given him. Sitting near the shining tree last year on Christmas morning, she had told him how excited she'd been to find a *cravate* with Art Deco swirls in orange and gold that would complement his favorite chocolate brown suit. He knew it was silly, childish even, but somehow he felt like she was nearby when he wore this tie–almost like she was touching his shoulder. He closed his eyes and tried to remember how it felt hugging her.

Back in the kitchen, Steven got out the breakfast things: the orange box of Wheaties, bowls, spoons, cups, sugar, and a bottle of whole milk.

At six o'clock, the rich aroma of coffee filled the kitchen. Steven climbed the stairs and walked to the front of the house to get Olivia.

PRESENT DAY

It was a gorgeous fall morning. Olivia selected the streets with the most trees for maximum foliage enjoyment, and as she ran under their dazzling canopies, sturdy oaks and tall maples put on a spectacular scarlet and gold show along the way. She finished her run in record time. Sweating and breathing hard, she unlocked and pushed open the front door, kicked off her sneakers and pulled her top over her head as she dashed up the stairs.

Her respite was short-lived. As she showered, Olivia's thoughts returned to last night. Had the killer really looked up at her?

What should I do? I don't want to tell Steven because it'll distract him from his work, and the most important thing is for him to solve this case. If the killer's local, he'll find out I'm visiting Steven, so he'll know the silhouette in the window was me. I shouldn't be alone this week. I'll stay close to Steven or make sure I'm in a crowd where the killer can't get at me. If I can't do either of those things, I'll come back home to my time as fast as I can. Yeah, that sounds good.

After toweling off and blow-drying her hair, Olivia paused in front of her closet. *What am I doing today? Breakfast with Steven, Skype with Dr. Hoffman, then the interview at the station and ride along with Steven. Okay, 1934 clothes with a top that can pass for my time.*

Olivia had recently put all her modern-day clothes on one side of the closet and many of Steven's mother's vintage outfits on the other end. It made things easier and helped ensure that she didn't make any mistakes. Grateful that Steven's mother had worn her size, Olivia selected a crisp white blouse tucked in dark brown corduroy trousers and a sweater the color of tangerines.

1934

As Steven neared the doorway, he saw Olivia appear, standing near her sleigh bed.

"Good morning. How did you sleep? Were you able to get any rest?"

"Morning! I slept fine. I don't know why I wasn't upset. Maybe because there wasn't any blood, and I didn't know him. How late were you out?"

"I got to bed a little before two." He grimaced.

Steven reached out and took her hand. As he stepped back into his hallway, Olivia crossed the threshold, slipping into the past. They grinned at each other.

"This never gets old," she said.

It was one of those 21st-century expressions that tickled Steven and made him grin back at her.

They moved through his hallway, covered in navy blue wallpaper dotted with large white hydrangea.

"We have another witness," he said.

"Really? Who?"

"Judge Randolph. He gave me the same description you did."

"Wow, that's great. Did he recognize him?"

"Maybe. He thought he looked like Shipley's son, Theo."

"Oh, no. How awful!"

In the kitchen, Steven poured their coffee while Olivia checked out the photograph on the Wheaties box.

"Ooh, a sports person." Her eyes lit up at the image of Lou Gehrig swinging a bat next to the logo, *The Breakfast of Champions*. "Would you save this box for me when it's empty? Liz's husband Joe would love it for his collection of baseball memorabilia."

"A cereal box? Sure, if you want it."

"Hey, what do you think of my new sweater? I got it with the money from the magazine articles I sold. It's the first thing I bought with my own money." She struck a pose.

"Looks aces." He gave her the thumbs up.

"Thanks. As a matter of fact, my complimentary copies should be coming any day now. I can't wait to give them to the girls. They're going to be so excited to see their names in print."

Last spring, Olivia had interviewed several women about life during the Depression and, realizing it was important to talk with the next generation of women as well, she approached teenagers Annie, Molly, and Lilly, who were thrilled to be included. Olivia's first article appeared in *McCall's* in July, the second was in the upcoming November issue of *American Girl*.

At times, Olivia wondered if she was making a mistake–she had never allowed herself to be so visible when she started spending time here. For months, she'd been careful not to do anything that could change the future in even the smallest way, but at some point, she'd stopped thinking like that. Sometimes she thought what she was doing was meant to be. Because, after all, she was doing it. She wondered if she was right or if she was deluding herself by rationalizing her actions.

Steven poured his Wheaties and handed her the box. Olivia couldn't remember eating this much cereal since she was a kid. She'd have to invite Steven for breakfast in her time once in a while. She missed her Greek yogurt with berries and her egg-white veggie omelets.

"Steven, do you think the chief will still let me drive around with you this week?"

"I don't see why not. I'll check with him first thing. So, about this morning, Olivia, will you be done with your meeting by nine-thirty? I'm going to have Will interview you. I can't do it. I'm too close to you." Steven felt himself blush. He'd meant close in a professional sense, but it sounded like something else when he'd said it out loud. However, when he noticed her smile and the glimmer in her eyes, he was glad it had slipped out.

"Yes, I don't have to go anywhere. We're Skyping."

Skype was one of the many things Steven had learned about life in the future. Half of the time it seemed that Olivia lived in a Jules Verne or H. G. Wells novel. Her world was completely foreign to him.

"I'll be by the door at quarter after. Is that okay?"

"Yes, I'm having a morning update with my team and I'll want time to talk with Chief Thompson." He ate the last spoonful of cereal and tipped his bowl to drink the rest of the milk. "Now, listen, about last night…."

"Yeah, I'm worried about my statement."

"Don't be. I've thought it all out. It's helpful that Judge Randolph saw the killer. You won't be the only one identifying him. When Will asks for your address, say you're staying with me for a while."

Olivia burst out laughing. "Oh, Steven, I've been a bad influence on you. Last spring, you would never have come up with an idea like that."

His face reddened. Before he'd met Olivia, he never told lies. Now, they had a secret to protect. "Well, you have to say something. I don't like it, but since you do live here, why not?"

"If he presses me, I'll say my lease is up and I don't have a new address yet."

He rolled his eyes. She, on the other hand, was a pro at making things up. "All right, that's fine. And while we're at it, say they'll have to reach you through me."

"Right, that's actually true. What about my birth date? That's the tricky part. Will they need to know that?"

"No, only the address and phone. And *just* answer the questions. Don't embellish. Be honest and as detailed as you can about what you saw."

"Don't worry. I know that."

Steven sat shivering in his icy cold car, waiting for the engine to warm up. This was one of those times when he wished he had a car from Olivia's century–those heated leather seats, those engines that didn't need warming up.

Knightsbridge was a mix of autumn and winter this morning. Steven saw flashes of colorful leaves peeking out from under their white cloaks as the last hold-outs clung to the trees. As he drove to the station, he set his priorities for the day: contact the widow, locate the estranged son, look for a witness, get a warrant and search the Shipley house, and set up the murder board.

He pulled into the gravel lot behind the one-story brick building, pushed down on the clutch and brake, moved the shift into first, and cut the engine. Grabbing his lunch box and gear, he walked the short path around to the front and climbed the steps. Although it wasn't seven yet, the ever dedicated Tommy Forester was at the front desk.

"Morning, Detective Blackwell."

"How are you, Tommy? Do I smell coffee?"

"Yup. Got it going first thing."

"Is the chief in yet?"

"Ten minutes ago."

Steven hit the light switch in the CID room—the Criminal Investigation Division—where he and Will worked, and where the murder board was always set up. After stowing his lunch, he went to Chief Thompson's office, knocked on the frame of the open door, and entered.

"Good morning, Chief."

Chief Andy Thompson, his carrot-colored hair sticking out like he'd been electrocuted, was polishing off his first pastry of the day. "Morning, Steven. What the hell happened last night?" he growled, then took a big gulp of coffee. "You know Ben is related to me? My wife is Alice Shipley's cousin."

"I didn't know until last night. The judge mentioned it. I'm sorry for your loss."

Thompson took another swig of what Steven called *mud*, then lit one of his ubiquitous Camels. "That's okay. Don't know why I even said that. We weren't close. Alice left him years ago. After that, we never got together as a family." He blew smoke to the ceiling and bit into his second pastry. "So, whadda ya got?"

"Olivia and I were in the kitchen. A few minutes before eleven, she went upstairs to the bathroom. A minute or two later, I heard a shot."

"Just the one?"

Steven nodded. "I ran out of the house. Olivia happened to look out the window as the killer was walking up the front path."

Thompson flew forward in his creaking chair. "She *saw* him? Miss Watson saw the killer?"

"She saw everything, Chief."

"When's she coming in for a statement?"

"Nine-thirty." Steven filled him in on what Olivia had witnessed.

"I saw the report from the overnight front desk officer. What did Doc have to say?"

"Only what I told you. One shot in the forehead. It was unusual, though. There's no exit wound. The bullet stayed inside."

The chief raised his eyebrows. "Hmm."

"Will, Ralph, and Pete went to talk with neighbors where there were lights on. Jimmy Bou went over to the 300-block of Victoria in case the killer ran in that direction. Said he didn't mind waking people up."

"That kid slays me." The chief chuckled.

Steven told his boss what Judge Randolph saw. "The man reminded him of Theo Shipley but he hasn't seen him in years and it was dark, so he's not sure."

"It's somewhere to start, though. We know where the killer came from."

"Yeah, it gives the patrolmen a direction to begin asking questions."

"What about Miss Watson's statement?"

"Will should interview her. When the case goes to court, we don't want any hint of impropriety. She's staying at my house, you know."

"The whole town knows, Steven," Thompson said wryly. At Steven's grimace, he added, "Nobody cares. You know that, don't you?"

Everyone knew that Miss Watson stayed at Detective Blackwell's when she was in town, and that it wasn't proper for a single fella living alone to have a female guest stay overnight. But Knightsbridge was a small town, and folks prided themselves on doing things their own way. Besides, everyone liked Steven, and everyone adored Olivia. The citizens of Knightsbridge simply shrugged and went about their business. After all, didn't everyone have a secret or two?

"Okay, right," he muttered. "What about the article she's researching for *The Gazette*? Can she still ride along with me this week?"

"I don't see why not. The rules still apply. I told her not to get in your way or let anything about a case slip out. She strikes me as honorable. I'm not worried. And I know you won't let her interfere."

"Thanks."

"Are you going to notify Alice?"

"Yes, after Will takes Olivia's statement."

"Good. I'll get her address and telephone number for you. She lives in Liverpool with another cousin, a woman named Edith Adams." He popped the last bit of pastry in his mouth and drank the rest of his coffee.

Back in the CID room, Steven pulled the large blackboard from the corner and wheeled it into the room, silently thanking his father for passing on an appreciation of order and routine as he set it in place. He knew organization was the key that helped him do his best work. During an investigation, Steven used the murder board to keep track of the case information. He tacked Gray's photographs on the wooden frame, posted details from Doc's autopsy report, and wrote Hank's forensic conclusions in the appropriate columns and boxes. Now, he grabbed a piece of chalk and wrote:

VICTIM - BENJAMIN SHIPLEY
WHEN - 10:55 pm Wed. Oct. 31
WHERE - 12 Chiltington Rd., front door of his house

HOW - Shot in the head once. No exit wound
JOB - Manager of family business. Shipley's 5 +10

Steven boxed off the top left corner of the board and added:

KILLER
Male. Slender. Wearing short brown jacket, dark pants, cap pulled over face.
Approached from bottom of street. Exited along left side of house.
WITNESSES
Olivia Watson (13 Chiltington)
Judge Randolph (1 Chiltington)
Killer reminded JR of Theo Shipley.
SUSPECTS
THEO SHIPLEY - estranged son
Motives: 1. Hated his father.
2. Revenge for taking him from his mother when young.

He boxed off the area below and labeled it EVIDENCE. There was one item to start the list—the silver medal of the Virgin Mary. Before setting the chalk back in the tray, Steven added: *Does it belong to the killer? Is the killer religious? Catholic?*

The last thing he did was make a note that he'd found no casings at the scene. He concluded: *Did the killer use a revolver?*

As Steven settled at his desk, Will came in with Jimmy Bou on his tail.

"Morning, Steven," they said in unison.

"Fellas." Steven nodded his greeting. "How d'you make out last night?"

"Nothing for me," said Will. "Doctor Kranken was up and heard the shot, but he was in the back of his house so he didn't see anything.

The other folks I talked to either didn't hear the shot or thought it was a car backfiring."

"I've got something, Steven," Jimmy Bou said. "When your cousin Jim took the dog out to do her business, he saw two people: a man hurrying down Tulip Street, wearing a cap and a short jacket, and a fella in a coat and fedora walking along Victoria. He didn't know who either one was." Jimmy Bou looked from Steven to Will and back. "That's important, isn't it?" He delivered his *coup de grâce*. "We can map the killer's route."

"You're right. Good thinking."

He took an oversized piece of paper from his middle drawer and sketched a rough map of the center of town. He drew a large arc at the top, labeled it Chiltington Road, and added two small squares across from each other mid-curve representing his and Mr. Shipley's houses. He designated the area inside the arc as the Village Green, with Victoria Avenue stretching across the bottom. On the left, he sketched Hickory and the Brighten Road as vertical lines. On the right, Tulip and the Mohawk River Road became vertical lines as well. Steven took a red pen and formed a series of small arrows moving from the corner of Chiltington at the judge's house, up the street to the victim's, then around the back, through The Green, across Victoria and down Tulip.

He held it up. "What do you think?"

"Sweet," Jimmy Bou said.

"That's good," said Will. "The killer could have come from a house–his or someone else's–but, given the time of night, we can narrow it down to a handful of bars or restaurants where he might have been. We can do the same after he fled the scene. This is really swell, Jimmy."

"Thanks, Will." Next to Steven, Jimmy Bou admired Will the most.

"Will, would you interview Olivia? I'll get her after the briefing,"

Steven asked.

"Sure."

Steven noticed the clock. "Let's get started. The team should be waiting."

The patrol room was a crowded sea of dark blue. Uniformed men sat on chairs, perched on desks, and leaned against the back wall. Chief Thompson had commandeered the most comfortable seat in the place and was lighting another cigarette. Most of the men were smoking as well and had a coffee cup nearby. They all held a notebook and pen or pencil.

"Good morning, fellas," said Steven, weaving his way to the front. "I'm sure you've all heard that someone murdered Benjamin Shipley a few minutes before eleven last night. The killer shot him at the front door of his house. We have a witness who saw the whole thing but, the killer's back was to her so we don't know who it was."

"Who's the witness?" shouted someone in the back.

Steven felt his face grow warm and was annoyed with himself for blushing. With all the dignity he could muster, he said, "My friend Olivia Watson. She's staying with me this week."

It was a testament to the high regard in which the squad held Steven that not one man said anything. There were no whistles, no catcalls, not even a raised eyebrow. Even the resident comedian Pete and his sidekick Ralph remained silent.

Steven moved on, telling them what he'd reported to the chief. "I set up the murder board with some basic information. As always, stop in as often as you can to check updates.

"Now, about Judge Randolph's impression that the fella could be Ben's son, Theo. Has anybody seen him?" He scanned the room and waited.

Several men shook their heads.

"I don't even know what he looks like," said one.

"Me neither," said another.

"He was before my time," commented a young officer.

"Chief?" Steven turned to his boss.

Chief Thompson stood to address the room. "Some of you may know that Ben's wife, Alice, is my wife's cousin. I don't like talking about family. Who does? But, you have to know the history of the Shipleys. Ben worked all the hours there were in a day and he wasn't always faithful to Alice...."

1918

Alice Shipley had heard the rumors. She'd tried to hold her head up and pretend she wasn't mortified when Ben cheated on her, but that and his absences were taking a toll. She was having trouble sleeping, and she'd been short with Theo more than once.

Alice's marriage had been a bitter disappointment. Lonely and adrift, with no one to talk to or have fun with after Lillian left, Alice thought Ben would be her lifelong companion. Instead, she found herself saddled with a stranger who only cared about business. Cold, distant, and with a complete lack of interest in trying to understand her or what she needed, Benjamin Shipley had been a disastrous choice. Alice knew she'd made a mistake the week after they'd returned from their short honeymoon. No longer the gallant suitor who had feigned a generosity of spirit, he acted like Alice wasn't in the room. Ben left for the store early in the morning and didn't return until late at night. His empire of five-and-dimes was all he thought about.

For Alice, the only good thing that had come out of the union was her beloved son—her honeymoon child, born nine months after their wedding day. Alice doted on Theo, devoting all her time and energy to his well-being and education, and, she had to admit, on occasion spoiling him as well.

It took Alice a long time to leave Ben. At first, the thought terrified her.

How would she live? Where would she go? Then, a visit to her cousin Edith's in Liverpool changed everything. Edith's husband had recently died, and she was lonely. Although she worked eight hours a day as a nurse at one of the Syracuse hospitals, nights and weekends were hard. Alice confided her own loneliness to her cousin, and the idea was born.

Edith invited Alice to bring Theo and live with her. Her husband had done well, and Edith owned their three-bedroom home. There was plenty of room for Alice and her young son, the house was near an excellent school, there were children in the neighborhood for Theo to play with, and, the pièce de résistance, Edith thought she could get Alice a job at St. Joseph's. The hospital was expanding the admissions department and would need to hire someone in a few months.

Initially, this audacious plan shocked Alice, but as the idea grew, she became excited. Freedom was in sight. She took the time to find out what her rights were as a married woman in New York State. Finally, in the summer of 1918, while Ben was at work, she packed up their belongings, took Theo, and left.

She should have known better. It took a humiliated and furious Benjamin Shipley less than four days to discover what she had done and where they'd gone. He was angrier than she had ever seen him. When he showed up at Edith's front door, Alice feared for her life. Screaming, out of control, and threatening, his red face inches from hers, Ben told her he would never allow her to keep Theo. He pushed his way into the house and found his son. He dragged the boy into his bedroom, ranted and raged while forcing Theo to throw his belongings into a suitcase, then drove him back to Knightsbridge. Ben warned Alice that he'd tell everyone in town she was having an affair if she fought him on it.

Alice's world imploded, shattering into tiny pieces. Her life was over.

Chief Thompson wrapped up. "It was selfish to bring Theo back here. Ben didn't have any genuine interest in his son—and he didn't want to take the time for him either. He sent him to The Manlius School, the military academy and boarding school near Syracuse. It was a cruel thing to do to a sensitive boy. Theo loved to write, had a book that he scribbled in all the time. Imagine a boy who'd rather be writing instead of throwing a ball or going fishing! Anyway, he graduated from the academy and took off for New York City. Over the years, we've had some news from Alice. Theo's a professional writer now, writes for an important magazine. As far as I know, he's only been back here once."

"Until now, maybe," Steven said quietly.

Chief Thompson nodded. "Maybe."

The atmosphere in the room had shifted while the chief spoke. Steven didn't want his team feeling sorry for Theo, who was now a suspect and possible killer. He had to get the fellas back in the right frame of mind.

"Okay, men," he said, louder than usual. Everyone snapped to attention. "We've got a lot to do today. Before I give out assignments, Ralph and Pete, did you have any luck last night?"

"Nope. None of the houses had lights on by the time we started our canvas," said Ralph.

"We're going back this morning. Maybe we can catch people before they leave for work," said Pete.

"Okay, come back here when you're finished. I want you to go with Will to search Mr. Shipley's house, then you're going to figure out where the killer was before the murder."

Steven held up the map he'd drawn and explained the significance of all the red arrows. "Ray, I'd like you to get some of the patrolmen together and do a grid search of The Green. If the killer dropped the gun, that could well be the spot. After you've finished, start looking into where our killer went *after* he ran behind Mr. Shipley's house." He told his team about his cousin Jim seeing a similarly dressed man hurrying down Tulip Street. "Canvas the area here." He indicated the north side of town. "I'll tack this up on the wall near the murder board.

"Charlie, write up a request for a search warrant for Benjamin Shipley's house. We're looking for correspondence from Theo—letters, cards, postcards, anything that shows recent communication between him and his father. Also, appointment diaries or calendars. Have Chief Thompson check the paperwork before you take it to Judge Randolph. The judge is expecting you. Wait for him to sign it. When you're finished with that, I want you to find out who owns the Shipley stores now that Benjamin Shipley is dead. Start with public records, then talk with Sam Silverstone at the *Gazette*." Steven consulted his notes. "Will's going to get a witness statement from Olivia.

"Now, speaking of Olivia, one last thing, fellas. Sam asked her to write a series about different jobs in town. He calls them behind-the-scenes articles. The idea is she spends time with the people doing a certain kind of work and reports on what it's really like. We're up first. Olivia will be talking with you and riding along with me for a few days. She's got the chief's approval and understands the limits of what she can write. She's not allowed to reveal any information about the investigation and she's promised not to get in the way."

"Fellas," Chief Thompson interrupted, "this'll help the department. It'll be good for people to understand what we do for them every day."

Steven nodded. "Please welcome her and answer any questions she might have."

A murmur of approval flowed around the room.

"Swell idea."

"Maybe folks'll see how hard we work."

"It'll be sweet to have a pretty face at the station for a few days."

"Yeah, better than your mug."

"Hey, Steven, what about me? I don't have an assignment," Jimmy

Bou called out.

"I didn't forget you. You're going with me to Liverpool to talk with Mrs. Shipley."

"Olivia, too?"

Steven suspected Jimmy Bou had a crush on Olivia. *Well, who wouldn't?*

"Yes, Olivia, too." Honestly, sometimes he felt like Jimmy Bou was his teenaged son.

Chapter Nine

After the meeting, Chief Thompson visited Steven in the CID room. "Here's the telephone number at St. Joseph's Hospital where Alice works, and her home address and phone." He handed Steven a piece of paper.

Steven grabbed the phone and dialed zero. "Operator, get me number 3-6123 in Syracuse, please." While he waited for the call to go through, he wrote Alice Shipley's information in his notebook, and gave Will the slip of paper to do the same.

Will kept one ear cocked while he read—and memorized—the morning *Gazette*. His partner never ceased to amaze Steven with his ability to read something once and recall it months later. He was invaluable during an investigation and Steven counted himself lucky to work with him.

"I see. Thank you." Steven hung up the heavy receiver. "Alice Shipley took the day off to go to the dentist." He got out his map of Onondaga County, checked her home address, and planned his route for the drive later. "Will, I'm going to get Olivia."

Steven pulled the dark green Chevy into his driveway and cut the engine. The sedan was his pride and joy. Every Sunday after church, he washed and waxed the automobile, then shined the headlamps and used a special brush for the spokes on the wire wheels. When the

45

exterior was spotless, he cleaned the plush interior and polished the beautiful wood dashboard until it shone. Then he'd take her for a drive.

Steven was glad this new case was taking him to Liverpool. It would give him a chance to take Olivia for another ride, even though Jimmy Bou would be in the back seat and they wouldn't be able to talk freely. He ran up the front steps, threw open the door, and took the stairs two at a time. He slowed at the top to catch his breath. It wouldn't do to let Olivia know how happy he was to see her again so soon. As he approached the end of the hallway, he watched as she came into view, smiling, waiting for him on the other side of the threshold.

"Hi. Are you all set?" he asked.

"Yes, but I'll be glad to get this over with."

Steven felt the warmth of her hand as he held it, bringing her through the doorway into 1934. "You'll be fine. After you're finished, we're going to Liverpool to talk with Mr. Shipley's widow, Alice."

"Awesome! You know how much I love a road trip."

Steven chuckled at the now-familiar expression. "We won't be alone, though. Jimmy Bou is coming with us."

"That's okay. He's fun."

Steven opened the passenger door, and Olivia slid onto the tufted bench seat upholstered in a pale gray chenille-like material. He walked around the car and hopped in. As he turned the ignition key, the mailman walked up the drive. Steven stuck his head out the window.

"Morning, Leon."

"Hello, Detective Blackwell."

"You remember Miss Watson," Steven said.

"Yes, of course." Leon Quigg peered in and touched his hat. "Nice to see you again, Miss Watson."

"You, too." Olivia smiled.

"Miss Watson is expecting some mail any day now, Leon."

"I'll keep a lookout."

When Steven escorted Olivia down the hall to the CID room, he caught a murmur of her name in the patrol room as they passed. Although he was happy to spend more time with her, he was regretting the newspaper project. He didn't like all this attention on her. Extra attention meant people might notice something, and that was the last thing he wanted. Their secret might leak out. Then where would they be?

"Good morning, Will." Olivia greeted Steven's partner, then perched on the edge of the wooden chair next to Steven's desk.

Olivia had never been interviewed by the police and was surprised at the nerves sparking through her body. She was glad Will was doing the questioning. She and Steven had been out to dinner with him and his girlfriend, and she felt comfortable with him. She suspected the chief might observe with Steven behind the mirror, but she didn't mind. She'd spent time with Chief Thompson as well and wasn't afraid of or fooled by his gruff appearance. Deep down, under that tough exterior, he was a nice man.

Will led Olivia to a small room towards the back of the station. A plaque on the door said *Interview 1*. Okay, that got her heart beating faster.

The room was sparsely furnished—a wooden table with two steel-framed chairs on each side. Olivia glanced at the naked bulb hanging from the center of the ceiling, then wished she hadn't—spots floated before her eyes. Will invited her to sit and walked to the opposite side of the table. Olivia had watched enough cop shows on TV to know the police always positioned the suspect with his back to the door. Whatever was jumping around in her stomach was now doing a tap dance. She poured a glass of water and took a big gulp.

"Olivia, I don't want you to be nervous or scared," Will said. "You're going to tell me what you saw. That's all." He extracted a notebook and fountain pen from his jacket pocket, opened the notebook, and uncapped the pen.

"First, I need your full name and address for the record."

"Olivia Watson. I'll be at Steven's for a while. I'm changing apartments."

"That's fine. No middle name?"

"No."

"All right. Start at the beginning and take me through the whole thing. Don't worry about putting in too many details, the more the better. We'll know what's important. I'd rather have you tell me too much than not enough. We could miss something that might help."

"Okay, he was slender." Olivia took a deep breath and told him everything she saw from the window. "I didn't see his face. When I first saw him, he was walking up the path to the house and had his back to me. When he ran away, he was in and out of shadows. The light wasn't good. Plus, his cap was pulled down over part of his face."

"Do you think you'd recognize him if you saw him again? Maybe the way he walked? That can sometimes be a unique feature."

"I doubt it."

"What about a description of his trousers or jacket?"

"He had a short jacket on. It wasn't leather. There was enough light so it would have reflected. It must have been some kind of material. I'd say it was a medium brown. His pants?" Olivia looked away and tried to picture the killer. "They were darker than the jacket. That's all I can say for sure."

"Anything else? Glasses? Facial hair? Beard, moustache?"

"No, I didn't see a front view for more than a couple of seconds. After he shot Mr. Shipley, he ran down the stairs, but he had his head down. And when he went across the front of the house, it was too dark to see any details. He was only a figure then."

"How tall would you guess?"

"He was a lot shorter than Mr. Shipley. But then, Mr. Shipley was inside, so that would make him taller. There's a small step from the porch up into the house. When the killer ran in front of the hedges, his head was almost even with the top. So, however high the hedges are, I'd say take an inch or two off and you'll be close." Olivia sighed, pleased to provide these details.

"I can see the effect your journalism training had on you, Olivia. You're a good witness."

"Thank you." She took another breath as the tap-dancing changed to a foxtrot.

"Where did he get the gun from?"

"He took it out of his jacket pocket."

"Which one?"

"The right one. Oh, of course! He's probably right-handed because he held the gun in his right hand when he shot Mr. Shipley."

Will smiled. "Like I said, a good witness. Can you think of anything else? Any detail or impression even if it doesn't seem important."

"I'd guess he's fairly young because he was agile. He ran down the stairs and across the front of the house really fast. He's probably in good health and good physical condition."

"That'll give us something to think about. All right. That's it for now." He stood and finished on a more formal note. "Thank you for coming in, Miss Watson. We know where to find you if we have any more questions." He opened the door and extended his hand to guide her out, then grinned in a conspiratorial manner and whispered, "Enjoy your drive today."

By the time Steven, Olivia, and Jimmy Bou were on their way out of town, the morning sun had melted the snow and the temperature had risen to thirty-nine.

Olivia cracked the window and breathed in the crisp air. "What a perfect day," she said, happy she'd put on Evangeline's St. Moritz coat. The cream-colored garment hung to just below her knees and was beautifully knitted in a basket-weave pattern. Two large black Bakelite buttons held the collar closed, leaving the front open. With the heater on in the car, Olivia was toasty warm. "I wonder how Mrs. Shipley's going to feel about the news after being separated from him so long."

"You can never anticipate someone's reaction to a violent death, especially murder," Steven said. "Be prepared for anything."

An hour and twenty minutes later, Steven engaged his blinker and left Route 31, then continued on Route 57. He headed south into the village of Liverpool and turned onto Fourth Street. A couple of blocks later they entered a sharp curve and Fourth Street became Cypress.

Olivia counted off the house numbers. "There," she exclaimed, pointing to a modest stone house with light blue shutters set back from the road. Red, gold, and russet leaves from the maple and horse chestnut trees towering over the property covered the small front lawn. Oliva watched a bright orange leaf dance in the breeze as it floated to the ground. Scattered across the yard, dozens of dark brown chestnuts gleamed in the sunlight, mixing in with others still in their spikey green shells.

Jimmy Bou jumped out and held the door open for Olivia. Steven rang the bell, and they waited, Olivia one step behind the police officers.

A graceful woman with shining auburn hair scraped back into a French twist opened the door. "Yes, may I help you?" She had a lyrical voice.

Steven folded back his coat collar to reveal his badge. "Detective Sergeant Steven Blackwell and Officer Jimmy Bourgogne from the

Knightsbridge Police Department. Are you Alice Shipley?"

"Yes, I am."

"We'd like to speak with you, ma'am. May we come in?"

A look of confusion flashed across her face as Alice Shipley ushered them into a bright room. Steven noticed she carried herself like a dancer. She was lithe and seemed to glide from one place to another.

The room was a small library. Floor-to-ceiling bookshelves framed a plump sofa on the left, and sunlight poured in from the picture window at the front.

Olivia couldn't help herself. "Oh, Mrs. Shipley, this is beautiful!"

"Thank you, dear." Alice Shipley's hand swept over a couple of side chairs. "Please, sit down. Excuse me, you are…?"

"Olivia Watson." Olivia automatically held out her hand and was surprised when Alice Shipley shook it as though it were the most natural thing in the world.

Steven took a moment to study Mrs. Shipley as she settled across from them on the sofa. Clear gray eyes sparkled behind round glasses with a tortoiseshell frame. Her oval-shaped face was unlined, although he knew she must be approaching fifty. Long slender fingers held a book, the worn ribbon marker peeking out. She set her book and glasses on a small piecrust table, then regarded Steven and said, "Now, Detective, what brings you here from Knightsbridge? I assume this is about my husband."

"Yes. I'm sorry to tell you Benjamin Shipley was murdered last night."

"Oh, my." Her face registered shock and her hand flew to her chest. "I didn't expect that."

"What did you expect, Mrs. Shipley?"

"Well, I don't know, really. Maybe that he had finally agreed to a divorce." She glanced up at Jimmy Bou, standing to the side, taking notes, then she looked back at Steven. "I'd been asking him to make it official for the past few years. We both knew I would never go back to him."

"Why would you think the police would come to your house about a divorce?"

She gave a small, embarrassed laugh. "No, of course they wouldn't. I don't know. It was the first thing that came to my mind. Can you tell me what happened?"

"Where were you, Mrs. Shipley, last night between eight and one in the morning?"

"I belong to the Women's Trade Union League. We had a meeting in Syracuse."

"Until one in the morning?"

"Yes, sometimes we have a lot to discuss."

"And what were you talking about last night?"

Steven noticed a subtle shift in her manner; she'd become guarded. He needed a distraction to push her off balance before she shut down and refused to tell him anything. "Are you okay? Would you like a glass of water? Officer Bourgogne can get it for you."

"No, thank you. I'm fine."

"All right. Now, you were saying...about last night's league meeting?" Steven prodded.

Suddenly, the dancer looked more like a stern headmistress about to use a ruler on his knuckles. "Are you aware of the disgraceful working conditions women face today, Detective Blackwell? I can see by your face that you are not. Well, let me tell you. They're forced to work long hours with few breaks for lower wages than their male counterparts. In many cases, they must buy their own uniforms out of the meager salaries they're paid. They are rarely eligible for a raise and almost never promoted. I think that's unfair, don't you?"

"Yes, I do actually. And your organization is doing something about that?"

At the genuine concern on Steven's face, Alice Shipley relaxed and said in a less severe tone, "Yes, yes, we are. We're planning a strike at my husband's Syracuse store on Salina Street. If that goes well, we'll do the same thing in other cities. We have the support of the First Lady, you know."

"Mrs. Roosevelt is a member of your league? That's impressive. I wish you luck in your endeavors, ma'am. Now, getting back to last night, can you provide me with the names and addresses or possibly telephone numbers of some women who were at your meeting?"

Alice Shipley rose and crossed the room to a mahogany desk. She opened a side drawer and extracted a thin file folder, then copied something onto a small piece of notepaper. "Addresses and telephone numbers of our president and vice-president," she said, handing it to him, and he noticed again how lovely her fingers were. Piano hands, his mother used to say.

He thanked her.

"You're very welcome. By the way, Detective, you never said what happened. I've given you proof of my alibi. That's what you're asking for, isn't it?" she said shrewdly. "How was my husband killed?"

"Someone shot him at the front door of his house."

She flinched. "There was no love lost between Ben and me, but no one deserves that." She lowered her gaze, seeming to examine the carpet, then a thought must have struck her. Her head flew up as a look of astonishment spread across her face. "I just realized...the house. What about the house? Is it mine now? Mine and my son's?"

"It depends on whether your husband left a will. You'll have to contact his lawyer. Do you know who that is?"

"Yes, it's Mr. Finley."

"Remember, the house is a crime scene right now. No one's allowed inside."

"Do you know when we might go in?"

"If everything goes well, maybe tomorrow morning. Call me after you talk with Mr. Finley, I'll let you know."

"All right. Is there anything else?"

"I need to get in touch with your son. I understand he lives in New York City."

"That's right. But, he'll be here later today."

"He's coming to visit?"

Alice Shipley's face took on a glow as she nodded. "Yes. It was such a wonderful surprise. He was here only two weeks ago. Theo normally comes up once a month, you see. He'll be here this afternoon and he's staying through the weekend," she said excitedly. She held out her hand. "Thank you for coming to tell me in person, Detective. Do you want my son to call you when he gets here?"

"I'd appreciate that." He handed her a small card with the phone number at the station.

Olivia and Jimmy Bou had started down the path and Steven was turning away from Alice Shipley when she said, "Excuse me, Detective. I hope you don't mind my asking but did you live on Chiltington when you were a child? I think the family across the street from us was called Blackwell. The woman was an artist."

Steven smiled. "You have a good memory, Mrs. Shipley. Yes, we moved there in 1912, when I was eleven."

"Ah, I left in 1918." She sighed.

As Alice watched the police pull away from the front of her house, she remembered.

By the end of 1917, Alice knew she had to do something. It wasn't only that Ben sometimes cheated on her. That would have been bad enough, although many wives with powerful husbands accepted that as their lot in life, and she sometimes thought she could, too. It was the feeling of complete and utter abandonment that was taking a toll on her spirit. Her husband was never home. And when he was, he acted as though she were invisible.

At first, Alice tried to explain how she felt. She suggested things they might do together—a drive in the motor car, a summer picnic, or ice skating on the river in winter—but he looked right through her, reacting as if she hadn't spoken, that is, not reacting at all. Ben cared about his work and nothing else.

Alice wondered what had drawn her to him and why she'd married such a cold man. Then she remembered how lonely she'd been after Lillian had left and suspected that was the reason. She'd thought Ben would be her lifelong companion and friend. Had she ever loved him? She wasn't sure.

Unable to confide in or rely on anyone, Alice was alone. She decided to arm herself with information. Before doing anything, she needed to know her rights, so she went to the Village Library in search of books on the New York State legal system. Over time, her Saturday morning visits became a cherished and highly anticipated part of her weekly routine. Alice loved the quiet hush of the library's vast marble-floored rooms, the smell of the oak shelving and the books themselves, and the thrill of being surrounded by all that knowledge. As her own knowledge grew, she became empowered. She was not helpless.

Though she no longer needed to research the legal system, Alice continued frequenting the library to indulge her love of art. She would select a book, study the paintings, and read until lunchtime.

The library also held an unexpected and lovely surprise.

One blustery morning in early January, after Alice had selected her book, she wandered through the massive building, looking for a spot where she could be alone and read. The library was full that day. The radio announcer had predicted the snowstorm would intensify and continue through the weekend. Folks are probably borrowing books to see them through the blizzard, *she speculated. After roaming through the rooms on both floors, Alice happened upon a young boy—he couldn't have been more than nine or ten—lost in a book by himself at a table near a window.*

"Excuse me. Do you mind if I sit here?" she asked.

Big brown eyes looked up at her in a mouse-like face. Alice's heart clenched to see the depth of sadness in that beautiful little face. She felt a lump rise in her throat and had to stop herself from hugging him.

He nodded shyly. "Okay," he whispered.

Alice gave him a big smile, and he returned it with a small, tentative grin.

"What are you reading?" she asked, after settling across the table toward the far end.

"Peter Pan."

"Ooh, that's a good one," she exclaimed.

The next time she saw him, two months had passed, and it was spring.

Chapter Ten

When Steven left for Liverpool, Will signed out one of the department's sedans. Ralph and Pete jostled each other, both trying to grab the front seat.

"What are you two, seven?" Will said. "Just get in."

Moments later, they pulled up in front of Benjamin Shipley's house. Will unlocked the door, stepped inside, and clicked on a light switch. All three officers gasped as they entered the grand foyer. The high ceiling, painted a pale blue, drew their eyes up to an elaborate crystal chandelier glowing in the center of wooden ribs, forming the shape of a dome.

"Wowie," Ralph exclaimed. "I guess it pays to own a five-and-dime. Get a load of this."

"Is Steven's house fancy?" asked Pete.

"No, it's nice, but not like this," Will said. "We've got a lot of rooms to search. Let's get to work. Steven said Shipley had a study on the first floor. I'll start there. You fellas tackle the upstairs."

Ralph and Pete climbed the majestic staircase curving up to the second floor, entered the first room on the left, and saw no one had occupied it in years. The bedroom belonged to a young boy.

"This must have been Theo's," Pete said.

Dark blue wallpaper decorated with toy soldiers and rocking horses covered the walls. A bed draped with a pale green chenille spread sat in front of double windows that looked out onto the street. A matching oak dresser and small desk occupied the space to the left of the closet. To the right towered a tall bookcase stuffed full of books. Evidently, Theo had been an avid reader, as well as a budding writer.

"I'll check the desk, Pete. You do the shelves."

Several minutes later, Ralph closed the final desk drawer. "Looks like Theo took everything when his father sent him off to school. The only things left are a few school compositions." He shuffled through them. "Hey, this is interesting."

Pete turned away from the bookshelf, empty-handed. "What'cha got, Ralphie?"

"It's a report he did back in April 1913. It says *4th Grade - Report on My Trip to New York City*. Get a load of this:

Last week, I took a train to New York City with my mother and father. It was exciting! Grand Central Station is really big. And noisy and crowded. I was glad I was with my parents. I would have gotten lost.

We took a horse and carriage to the Plaza Hotel. When we went in, I thought we were on a tropical island. There were palm trees everywhere. We went up to The Penthouse and met my grandparents. They all went to a fancy restaurant, but I had to stay in the hotel with the maid and eat my supper alone.

The next day, my father had to do business, so my mother took me to FAO Schwarz, the biggest toy store in the world. We had lunch in Chinatown. I saw men in black ponytails and long shirts that looked like dresses with baggy trousers underneath. The waiter showed me how to eat with chopsticks. My mom and I always have lots of fun together. She's my best friend.

This is my report on my trip to New York City. It was a very good trip."

"Must be nice to have a rich family. My parents used to take us to Sylvan Beach for ice cream." Pete smirked. "Well, Ralphie, that's interesting, but does it get us anywhere?"

"We know his mother was Theo's best friend, which would've made it worse when his father took him away. That makes his motive stronger."

Downstairs in the study, Will sat at Benjamin Shipley's mahogany partners' desk, his feet cushioned on a thick Oriental rug. Floor-to-ceiling bookshelves, full of leather-bound classics, lined the walls. Deep crimson damask drapes hung along tall windows and puddled on the oak floor. In one corner, two reading lights illuminated a brown leather Chesterfield sofa and a coffee table covered with neat stacks of magazines and newspapers. Will had already held up and shaken out several issues of *The New York Times* and *The Wall Street Journal*, as well as *Time* and *Newsweek* magazines. No letters, cards, or notes of any kind fell out.

Will turned his attention to the desk. Around the perimeter of a leather insert sat a small lamp, a clock, a double ink well and pen set, and rolling blotter. Will knew nothing about antiques, but he could tell the blotter was old. The bronze top and round knob-like handle in the center were not unusual, but the engraved artwork took his breath away. Intricately carved vines and leaves stretched out across the surface. The edges were fluted, and an ornate scroll was tucked in each corner. Will bet Mr. Shipley had paid a pretty penny for it.

In the shallow center drawer, Will found the usual stash of office supplies, Shipley had saved several back issues of *Barron's* and *The Economist* in a side drawer, and in a bottom drawer, wrapped in pieces of cotton toweling, Will discovered two handguns—a 9 mm German Luger that he recognized as the gun many American soldiers had brought home as a souvenir from the Great War, and a .38 mm revolver. He imagined a wealthy man like Benjamin Shipley had felt the need for protection, both at home and in the store. He made a note of the specifications of each gun, indicated where he'd found them, and put them in a paper bag to bring back to the station for safekeeping.

Will found the calendar in the top right drawer. It was a luxurious leather-bound diary with thick cream pages, hand-cut with a paper knife. He took it out and used the silk ribbon to open the book to Wednesday. In the area marked October 31, Shipley had written *Theo, 8:30.* Under the calendar lay a pale blue envelope the size of a notecard. Will extracted a small piece of linen stationery adorned with Benjamin Shipley's son's initials embossed at the top.

> *Dear Father,*
>
> *I'm still angry at you for taking me from Mother and sending me away, but I'd like to talk. I'll come to your house Wednesday evening October 31ˢᵗ at 8:30.*
>
> *Theo*

Ralph and Pete entered the study.

"What have you got there, Will?" Ralph asked.

Will read the note aloud. "It looks like Theo Shipley was in Knightsbridge last night. Although, according to this, he would have been at the house several hours before the murder."

"He could have come back. Maybe he argued with his father and came back to settle the score," Pete said.

"It doesn't look good for him," said Ralph. "We found out his mother was Theo's best friend. He might have been angrier with his father than we thought."

"Old wounds can fester over time. Maybe he reached a breaking point," Will said.

Instead of turning to go back the way they'd come, Steven drove south on Route 57. As they passed through the village of Liverpool, Onondaga Lake appeared on the right, sparkling with the sun reflecting off its surface.

"Where are we going, Steven?" Olivia asked.

"It's a surprise."

Olivia turned to the back seat. She and Jimmy Bou raised eyebrows and made faces at each other. "Oooh," they chorused.

At a fork in the road, Steven veered to the left, then made a quick right-hand turn into a small gravel area alongside some railroad tracks. He pulled up next to a boxy Ford. "We're here." He cut the engine and engaged the parking brake. A small, ordinary-looking eatery stood at the far end of the parking lot.

"Heid's! I love this place," said Olivia. "There's nothing like a Heid's hot dog."

"Lunch is on me, you two. Jimmy, I've been wanting to show you this place."

"Gee thanks, Steven. This is swell. I sure am hungry."

"Grab a table. I'll bring our food over," said Steven. "Jimmy, I want you to take charge of Alice Shipley's alibi." He handed him his notebook. "While you're waiting, copy these names and addresses. Looks like both women have telephones as well."

After they'd stuffed themselves with hot dogs in soft white buns, potato chips, and garlicky dill spears, they piled into Steven's Chevy and took off toward Knightsbridge.

"All right, Jimmy, let's work on your training. Tell me what we learned from Alice Shipley," Steven said. "And remember the six basic questions."

Jimmy Bou didn't hesitate. "Theo Shipley is making a special trip up from New York City. What if he got here early? What if the visit to his mother is an excuse, and he really came up to kill his father last night? You always say a break in somebody's routine is significant.

"Good, you're thinking like a cop."

"We've gotta find out if anybody saw him last night. Somebody who knows it was really him, I mean."

61

"How's your training going, Jimmy?" Olivia asked.

"Steven's a swell teacher." Jimmy Bou leaned forward and put his forearms on the top of the front seat. He tilted his head toward Steven. "Steven, we should've asked Mrs. Shipley how Theo's getting here. If he's got a car, we need the description."

"You're right. Why don't you call her when we get back? Now, tell me what else we should do."

"Talk to the manager at the five-and-dime to see if anybody at work had it in for Mr. Shipley."

"Very good. Pretty soon, you'll be taking my job," he kidded.

Jimmy Bou tripped all over himself. "Oh, Steven, no! You know I would never...."

"It was a joke, Jimmy. A joke."

Jimmy Bou breathed a sigh of relief. At twenty-three, he still had a lot to learn.

When they arrived at the station, Jimmy went to call Alice Shipley, and Steven and Olivia continued down the hall. When they entered the CID room, Will was setting the telephone receiver in its cradle.

"That was Judge Randolph's office. I sent Charlie back with paperwork for another warrant—for Mr. Shipley's office at the store. It's ready."

"Swell, I'll pick it up on the way over. I want to interview the employees." Steven turned to Olivia. "Are you staying for the rest of the day?"

"Can I sit in on the interviews?"

"Sure. Will, how'd you make out at the house? Find anything?"

Will told Steven about the note Theo had written to his father and the school report.

"Good, we're making progress."

"Oh, I found two guns in Mr. Shipley's desk." He described the wartime souvenir and the one Shipley had owned for protection. "I brought 'em in for safekeeping."

Jimmy Bou popped his head in the doorway. "Steven, Theo's driving up from New York in his car. It's a 1929 Plymouth, light brown, and the top folds down."

Olivia's eyes lit up. "Steven, I bet he wears a cap. A lot of guys who drive convertibles wear caps just like the one the killer was wearing."

Since Shipley's was only a couple doors away, Steven, Olivia, and Jimmy Bou walked to the shopping emporium, stopping to pick up the warrant on the way. The four-story building occupied the entire corner, the words *B. W. Shipley Co. 5 and 10 Cent Store* emblazoned across the front, above large plate-glass windows filled with enticing exhibits of goods for sale. The five-and-dime had been near the top of Olivia's bucket list when she first began spending time in 1934. Curious about the iconic shopping mecca from stories she'd heard as a child, she'd been eager to see the displays of merchandise and shop for her two best friends and herself. Her first visit had lived up to her expectations. Walking into the high-ceilinged store, Olivia had marveled at the sheer variety—hair tonic and parakeets, birthday cakes and paper dolls, Easter corsages and phonograph records. Everywhere she'd looked, there'd been something that fascinated.

Today, Steven had called ahead and Norm Evans was waiting inside when he and Jimmy pulled open the heavy glass doors. The assistant manager stuck out his hand.

"Hi, Steven. What a thing, huh? I couldn't believe it when I heard this morning." He glanced at Olivia, but said nothing as he gestured for them to follow him through the store. "How's life treating you, Jimmy?"

"Good, thanks."

They passed the pennyweight machine—*Your Weight and Fortune*

One Cent—and walked down a long aisle to the back of the store where Evans pushed open a door marked *Employees Only*. Entering the cavernous storeroom, Steven's and Olivia's eyes traveled to the ceiling, taking in the hundreds of cases of merchandise piled on shelf units, secured to the floor with thick bolts through heavy metal plates. They read the labels on the ends of the shelves: stationery, toys, housewares, sporting goods, bath and beauty, and many more. On the left, through a row of windows set in the top half of the wall, they saw two offices, both with paper-strewn desks and boxes stacked on chairs. The assistant manager invited them into his office and settled behind a wooden desk, while Steven and Olivia took the two visitors' chairs and Jimmy Bou stood to the side.

"Let me introduce Miss Olivia Watson, a journalist working on background for a story," said Steven.

"Journalist?"

"She's got the chief's permission, Norm. Don't worry. Nothing we talk about will appear in any story of Miss Watson's. You have my word."

Evans nodded to Olivia. "Nice to make your acquaintance, Miss Watson."

"You, as well, Mr. Evans."

"All right, Norm, like I told you, I need a list of employees and some background information."

Evans handed Steven a sheaf of papers stapled together. "Got this from our bookkeeper after you called."

Steven ran his eye down at the names of some thirty-five people listed in alphabetical order, according to their last name. Next to each was a home address. Few had telephone numbers. A job title and a date were written under the employee's name. "What's the date signify?"

"The day they started working here."

Steven ignored the female names and several men whom he knew were the wrong build. He wasn't crazy about the fact that "slender" didn't eliminate many people, but it was the information he had to work with. Three possibilities remained.

"Tell me about Rudy Hartwicke. He's been in and out of trouble since he was a kid. Nothing serious, nickel-and-dime stuff, but still… how is he as an employee?"

"Yeah, we knew his reputation when we hired him, but he's been okay. He works back here in the warehouse as a stock clerk. Started right after high school. Rudy's an average worker. He's never given us any trouble, but he doesn't do anything extra either, if you know what I mean."

Steven glanced at the list and noted the date Rudy Hartwicke started working at Shipley's. Nearly six years ago. "Has he been doing the same job all this time?"

"Yes." Evans frowned.

"What?"

"Rudy had his annual review last month. I think he was hoping to be promoted to sales trainee out on the floor. Even if he had the qualifications, he wouldn't have gotten the job. Mr. Shipley's nephew is moving here from the Lancaster store. Shipley was preparing to retire, so I'd move up to his position as manager and his nephew would take my place after getting familiar with our operation. Rudy Hartwicke was never going to get that salesman job."

"What was his reaction when he realized he wasn't going to be promoted?" Steven asked, guessing the answer.

"Upset. Angry. Not only did he lose the prestige a promotion carries, but Mr. Shipley didn't increase his salary either. Like I said, Rudy's an average worker. He's not a go-getter, and that kind of attitude doesn't lead to promotions or pay raises."

Ever conscious of his position as Jimmy Bou's mentor, Steven always gave the young officer a chance to ask questions. He gave Jimmy the signal.

"Did Rudy ever threaten Mr. Shipley?" asked Jimmy Bou.

"Not that I know of."

"Who are his friends here at work? Is there someone he pals around with? Anybody he might confide in?"

"Not really. He's a bit of a loner. Spends his coffee breaks and lunchtime on his own."

Jimmy scribbled more notes.

"Does Rudy still live with his aunt, Norm?" Steven asked.

"Yeah, Miss Salem."

Steven consulted the list. "Tell me about George Wise and Clyde Moore? Can you describe them? Physically, I mean. I don't know either of these men."

"George is middle-aged. He's average height and build, not as hefty as me. There's nothing special about him except his limp. I guess that counts as physical description, doesn't it?"

"Yes, it does. How pronounced is the limp?"

"It's pretty bad. He sways from side to side when he walks."

"All right. That's all I need on Mr. Wise. What about Clyde Moore?"

"He's our bookkeeper. I'd say he's close to seventy. Tall, skinny, thick white hair."

"Okay, that'll do it for now." Steven closed his notebook and stood. "Is Rudy here? I'd like to speak with him."

"No, he called in sick this morning."

Out on the sidewalk, Steven checked his watch. "Jimmy, it's nearly four. We've got time to walk over to Rudy Hartwicke's house. Let's see if we can get a preliminary interview with him." He turned to Olivia. "We always want to get an impression of a suspect as soon as possible. Do you want to come with us?"

Olivia turned away from Jimmy Bou and lowered her voice. "I'd like to, but I need to get started on my new project for the Fashion Institute. And I want to get a second run in before dinner. That marathon's next month, remember?"

"All right, I'll meet you at six-thirty, right? Pizza and a movie?" he whispered.

"It's a date." The words slipped out before she could pull them back. Steven smiled and wiggled his eyebrows.

"Jimmy, it was fun spending time with you. I've got to go."

"Bye, Olivia. See you tomorrow."

"Enjoy the rest of your day." She gave him a warm smile. Olivia knew Jimmy Bou had a crush on her.

They parted company at the corner, Steven and Jimmy going left along the baseball park towards Maple Avenue.

Rudy's aunt's home resembled many of the houses in this part of town. It was a small Arts-and-Crafts style cottage set back from the sidewalk on a quiet tree-lined street. Steven and Jimmy Bou climbed two steps to the front porch and Steven rang the bell.

A plump woman with greying blond hair answered the call. Noticing Jimmy's uniform, the first words out of her mouth were: "Police? What happened?"

Steven introduced himself, showed his badge and ID, and said, "There's no reason to be alarmed, Miss Salem."

"What's this about?"

"Rudy's boss was killed last night."

"Yes, I heard. How awful." Gleaming eyes told Steven she was more fascinated with the gossip than saddened by the news.

"We're talking with all the store employees, ma'am. We need to get some background information. I hope your nephew'll be able to help us."

"I'm sure Rudy will be happy to help you, Detective." She absently fluffed her hair and gave Steven a coy smile. "But, he isn't here. Did you try the five-and-dime?"

"He's not there."

"Then, I'm sure I don't know where he is."

"When did you see him last?"

"At the Halloween Party at the Elks with George. He was gone this morning when I got up."

"George Ferguson?"

She nodded.

"What time did he return home last night?"

"He was still out when I went to bed around ten-thirty. I woke up going on midnight and went to the kitchen for some water. I heard him snoring when I went past his door. Rudy has a hard time falling asleep, so he probably went to bed around eleven."

Not wanting to spook a potential suspect, Steven simply said, "Thank you, Miss Salem. When you see Rudy, please tell him to stop by the police station. He's not in any trouble. We just have some routine questions."

As Steven and Jimmy Bou headed back to the station, Jimmy took out his notebook and, while they walked, read aloud a couple of items he'd written earlier. Steven listened as he watched him read. Jimmy finished the notes he wanted to discuss, and both men looked up. Ten yards away, a slender young man had turned the corner and was heading toward them. He caught sight of Jimmy Bou's uniform, gasped, and halted, then spun to his left and took off across the grass along the side of Herb Steadman's house.

"It's Rudy Hartwicke," shouted Jimmy, shoving the notebook in his pocket and breaking out in a run.

"I'll go right, Jimmy," Steven yelled as he crossed the front of Herb's house and ran toward the back.

Stretched along Herb Steadman's backyard stood a tall wooden fence. Steven arrived in time to see Jimmy fly over the pointed wooden slats. Seconds later, he, too, reached the barrier, jumped onto a nearby tree stump to get leverage, and vaulted over the fence. When he landed, he saw Jimmy Bou chasing Rudy toward the sawmill.

The Mohawk River Sawmill stretched out along the southwestern edge of town between the river and the railroad tracks. It was a large two-story, rectangular building constructed of roughly hewn logs whose natural coloring had darkened over the years. A mechanized chute led from the back of the mill down to the river at a 30-degree angle. A group of men using iron poles guided logs onto the deck of a waiting barge. Another group was loading cut lumber onto a second barge.

Rudy Hartwicke sped over the railroad tracks in front of the mill and disappeared down a line of boxcars. Steven raced to the property on the far side, nearly colliding with Jimmy Bou. They saw Rudy leave the tracks and dart into a maze of open-sided sheds filled with bundles of lumber stacked ten feet high. Steven and Jimmy split up, taking parallel paths. As he ran, Steven breathed in the smell of freshly cut wood and was vaguely aware of the wail of saws in the background. He sped past heaps of two-by-four studs, two-by-tens, and four-by-eight plywood sheets.

Two things happened simultaneously: Rudy Hartwicke appeared on the far side of the labyrinth of lumber, and Steven's friend Artie Sinclair exited a shed near the river.

"Artie," Steven yelled. "Grab him. He's getting away."

Artie jerked his head up at the sound of Steven's voice. He threw a scrap of wood on the ground and spun to his right. Rudy was closing in on a truck with the engine running. He put on a burst of speed. With the advantage of being a dozen feet closer than Steven or Jimmy Bou, Artie reached him first. He flew into the air and tackled Rudy Hartwicke. They hit the ground with a thud, then rolled over several times. Rudy thrashed about, struggling to get free from the vise-like hold of Artie's arms around his middle. Jimmy Bou jumped into the fray. The two men stilled Rudy's resistance, then forced him face down. Steven pulled a pair of handcuffs from his pocket and immobilized the young man.

"You just made things a lot worse for yourself," Steven panted, dragging him to his feet. "Rudy Hartwicke, I'm taking you in for questioning regarding the murder of Benjamin Shipley."

Chapter Eleven

Olivia stopped at the Village Drugstore to buy the morning edition of *The New York Times* on her way home.

Negotiating her way around Steven's Knightsbridge was now routine. When she'd begun spending time outside the house, she'd had to pay attention to where she was going every minute. Everything looked so different from her time: some roads weren't paved, many buildings didn't exist yet, and certain buildings that did exist no longer stood in her time. Luckily, there were a few familiar landmarks—the Village Green, The Three Lords, Bailey's Diner, the Village Library, and, of course, the house in which she and Steven lived.

If finding her way around town had taken time, what had taken longer was monitoring what she said and controlling her reactions to what others said. Part of it was the way people talked—she had to be careful not to let 21st-century slang slip, and part was the difference in social mores—people were friendlier in some ways and more formal in others. Men were more polite, tipping their hat and calling her Miss Watson, but often overlooked her as a person. The trickiest pitfall in adapting to life in 1934 was when someone mentioned a name or recent event in the news. She'd had to learn the names of congressmen, the governor, and the mayor. She'd studied old newspapers and magazines online to learn what had happened in national and world events since the beginning of the year.

Now, she was at home with the language and the way people thought and acted in 1934. She no longer slipped up or acted confused or surprised when she should have known better.

Olivia let herself into Steven's house and went upstairs, glad she didn't need his help to return to her own time. They'd discovered early on that it was necessary to touch in order to travel back or forward into a different century, but they could always return home without assistance. Olivia's theory was that they belonged in their own time, so it was a natural move, something like putting the universe right.

PRESENT DAY

As Olivia stepped over the threshold, Evangeline's room became hers. Her sleigh bed and flat-screen TV emerged. Steven's mother's midnight blue chair and caramel-colored leather Moroccan pouf disappeared, replaced by her reading nook with the coffee table piled high with newspapers and magazines.

Olivia kicked off her shoes, set her bag on the bed, and padded into her office to start her latest research commission—Women's Clothing during the Depression Years. Martine LaFayette at New York's Fashion Institute of Technology needed a photo file to accompany a book she was writing and had heard of Olivia's skills in unearthing hard-to-find materials. Olivia couldn't wait to talk with Liz and Sophie; in her mind, they'd already volunteered to be models. She knew they'd be delirious with joy at the chance to wear Evangeline's stunning wardrobe for the photoshoot. Liz, as the curator of the local history museum, loved all things vintage. Sophie had been a fashionista since they were ten years old.

Olivia always began with a plan. For this project, she decided to organize the file in categories—At Home, Daywear Out and About, Eveningwear, and Sportswear—and illustrate each one within the framework of the four seasons. She also decided that, if asked, she would tell her client the vintage clothes came from a collector who wished to remain anonymous. To get the right atmosphere, she planned to shoot the photographs in varying degrees of shadow and, if she needed to tweak anything, her digital skills were up to the task.

Olivia did the math: four categories times four seasons with four to five outfits or accessories in each one meant seventy to seventy-five photographs. Thank goodness Evangeline had left an extensive wardrobe and she, Liz, and Sophie would fit in most of the clothes. She'd use photos sourced online for the rest.

Olivia ran down to the cellar to grab a clothes rack that held seasonal items. Leaving her winter jackets and coats in a pile on a chair, she brought the rack up to her bedroom and spent the rest of the afternoon sorting through high-end clothing, creating outfits, deciding what to include.

Shortly after five, she changed into a long-sleeved t-shirt, hoodie, leggings, and her running shoes, grabbed a bottle of water, and left the house for her second run of the day. She headed north toward the Mohawk River Road to a new path dedicated for walkers and joggers and was turning the bend to access the running path when she nearly collided with a good-looking Asian American man. She skidded to a halt.

"Ken!" she exclaimed.

"Olivia! Holy smokes!"

Ken Liang looked as sexy and fit as when he'd been Olivia's first high-school boyfriend nearly twenty years ago. She hadn't seen him since graduation, and no one knew what had happened to him. Studying him now, she thought he resembled Tim Kang, the actor who'd played Cho in *The Mentalist* and acted in one of the *Rambo* movies.

Ken reached down and pulled Olivia into a hug. He wore the same cologne and was still the best hugger. Olivia's stomach did a somersault. *Oh my.*

He let her go. "Do you still live here? What have you been doing? Are you married?" Questions tumbled out.

She laughed. "I worked for the *Post-Standard* in Syracuse after college. I came back to Knightsbridge six years ago when my dad got sick. I own a research agency and I write travel articles freelance." She smiled up at him, the auburn highlights in her brown hair glimmering in the setting sun.

"How is your dad? I always liked him."

"He's fine, thanks. He and my mom moved to California after he got better." Olivia took a swig of her water. "What about you? You disappeared after graduation."

"After my grandparents died, I wanted to know my ancestry. I've been living and working in Seoul, South Korea. I came back to the States a few years ago and got my degree in physical therapy. I work here at the hospital with in-patients." Ken took her in from head to toe. "You didn't answer my question. Are you married, involved with someone?"

"No, I'm not married. There is someone but I'm not sure where it's going."

"Ah. Well, if you want to get together sometime and catch up, call me at the hospital. We'll go to the pub." Ken leaned over and kissed her cheek. "Enjoy the rest of your run." And he was gone.

Olivia's feet had cemented to the sidewalk. *Move, Olivia. Go.* She forced herself to continue her run. She hadn't thought of Ken Liang in decades. These days it was Steven who filled her mind.

It was true what she'd told Ken. She had no idea where it was going with Steven—or *if* it was going. How could it go anywhere? He was certainly dead in her time, after all, he'd been born in 1901, and she hadn't been born yet in his. It was ridiculous to think she could ever have a relationship with him.

But there it was. Since she'd first spied him in the doorway, Steven had become the central figure in Olivia's life. She didn't have to announce it out loud, but she couldn't deny it to herself anymore.

Now Ken was back in town, and Olivia was stunned to find her heart racing and her palms sweaty.

Chapter Twelve

THURSDAY, NOVEMBER 1, 1934

While Olivia was running into her old boyfriend, Steven and Jimmy Bou were escorting Rudy Hartwicke into the police station.

"Whaddya think yer doin'?" protested Rudy. "I don't know anything about no murder. Yer settin' me up!"

Steven ignored the complaining. At the back of the building, he opened a cell door and, removing the handcuffs, nudged his suspect inside and slammed the grill shut, rattling the bars to be sure it had locked. Rudy whirled around and rushed Steven. "I ain't done nothin'. You can't keep me here."

"We'll talk after you've settled down, Rudy."

Steven headed to Chief Thompson's office, stepping aside as two officers exited. They said hello then continued their conversation as they disappeared around a corner. Steven heard one say, "...that's a real specific list."

"They sound excited," Steven said. "What's going on, Chief?"

Thompson regarded him from behind the mountain of paperwork covering his desk. Bushy eyebrows extended over tired hazel eyes, his wild mane in need of a cut.

"Keller's liquor store was robbed."

"Oh! That makes, what, five in the past few weeks?"

"Yup, Rome, New Hartford, a couple in Utica, now us."

"I suppose it was inevitable. I want you to know we've got our first suspect in the Shipley murder in one of the cells. Rudy Hartwicke."

"I thought we were looking at the son. What's the connection with Hartwicke?"

"He works at the five-and-dime. He was angry when he didn't get a promotion and a raise. Honestly, I wouldn't have thought that was enough reason to kill a man but when Jimmy and I went to talk with him, he ran."

"That tells us something." Thompson leaned back in his chair, which squeaked as he came dangerously close to toppling over. "What's your plan?"

"I want him to calm down before I question him. Right now, he's yelling that he didn't do anything and doesn't know anything about the murder. If he sits there for an hour, he'll be more forthcoming. While he's cooling off, I'm going to see if there are any outstanding warrants on him in case we want to keep him overnight."

"Good. Let me know if you need anything." Thompson looked down over his paperwork and sighed.

Steven slid a pad of paper across his desk and began listing the questions he wanted to ask Hartwicke. He wouldn't use the list during the interview, but the act of writing them down cemented them in his mind. He got through a half dozen when the phone rang.

"Blackwell."

"Detective, this is Alice Shipley. Theo arrived a little while ago."

"Did you tell him I need to talk with him?"

"Yes, I also called our lawyer. Ben never changed his will, so the house belongs to me and my son."

"I'm glad to hear it. My men are searching the house as we speak.

You should be clear to take possession tomorrow. I'll let you know if that changes."

"Thank you. We plan to arrive early. Mr. Finley is meeting us at the house with a key. I imagine I'll stay for some time. I'll need to decide what to do about the house."

"I see. Can you put your son on the phone?"

"Hello, Detective. This is Theo Shipley. How can I help you?"

"Would you come to the station after you drop off your mother?"

"How about eight-thirty, nine o'clock?"

"Thanks, I'll see you then."

Will entered as Steven was hanging up. "Who was that?"

"Theo Shipley, he'll be here in the morning."

"Good. How'd it go at the five-and-dime?"

Steven gave him a quick run-down. "I'm going to question Rudy after he cools down. Would you watch from behind the mirror? I'd like your take on him."

"Sure, what do I need to know?"

Steven repeated what he'd told the chief, then added that there were two outstanding warrants on their detainee. "So, even if he doesn't tell me anything now, we can keep him overnight."

"That's a break."

Steven thanked his lucky stars that Sergeant Will Taylor had signed up with the Knightsbridge Police Department six years ago. He was the best partner he'd ever worked with. Will could read people like they were wearing signs and had honed his tracking skills to a fine art.

The brawny police officer hung his Chesterfield and fedora on the coat tree. Steven admired the dark brown trim on both hat and coat. Will had class.

Will positioned himself behind the one-way glass to observe Steven's interview with Rudy Hartwicke.

Steven entered the room with Hartwicke in tow. Rudy's clothes were dirty and his hair stuck out in odd places, as though he'd been running his hands through it. He brought his hand to his mouth a couple of times, then dropped it, evidently realizing there was no cigarette.

"I got nothin' to say," Rudy grumbled as Steven deposited him in a chair, then went around to the far side of the table.

"Would you like some water?" Steven said, pouring a glass and setting it in front of Hartwicke.

Rudy frowned. "I'm gonna have bruises from you and your thugs tackling me in the lumberyard."

"I doubt that. But you ran away. Want to tell me why?"

"I always run from the cops. They never did me no good." He glared at Steven, his eyes like storm clouds.

"You know the drill, Rudy. You break the law, you deal with the police."

"That's not what I mean. I didn't have nothin' to do with Shipley gettin' killed."

"What *do* you mean then?"

"Hit-and-run accident that killed my mother. You creeps never made it stick. Everybody knew it was Shipley."

"I'm sorry, but I don't know anything about that. When did it happen?" Steven wondered if the tragedy explained Rudy being in and out of trouble for the past decade.

"Fifteen years ago. I was ten."

"Do you remember the date?"

"You think I can forget?" Hartwicke sneered. "It was nighttime. Me and my little brother was getting ready to go to bed. My mother was late, and I was getting worried. The cops came to the door and told us. It was March 28th, 1919."

"I'm truly sorry. Where was the accident?"

"On the Mohawk River Road. 'Bout five miles out of town."

"Why do you think it was Mr. Shipley who killed your mother?"

"There was a witness, said it was the same kind of car he had. Bastard just drove off and left her in the street."

"What was your mother's name?"

"Emily."

Steven reached across the table but didn't touch Rudy's hand. He held him with his gaze. "I promise I'll look into it, Rudy. You have my word."

Hartwicke's bluster evaporated. He took the glass of water and drank. "So, can I go?"

"Tell me where you were last night."

"Georgie and I went to the Halloween party at the Elks around seven-thirty."

"I didn't see you."

"We had masks on. We had some cider and a couple'a donuts. Left around eight."

"Then what?" Steven asked.

Rudy shifted in his chair and looked around, as though the answer were printed on the walls. "Don'know. Drove around."

"Where?"

"No place special. Looked at the Halloween decorations and stuff. We stopped at one of my friends but he wasn't home."

"You still have several hours to account for, Rudy."

"I guess we went to see a friend of Georgie's."

"You guess? Who? What's his name?"

"I don't know. They call him Tappo. Looks like a fire hydrant," he snorted.

"Where does Tappo live?"

"Over near Utica." Hartwicke scowled. "I don't know where.

Georgie was drivin' and it was dark. I didn't pay attention."

"When did you get home?"

"Around eleven. You can ask my aunt. She'll tell you."

"I will." Then to keep Hartwicke off-balance, Steven asked, "If you think Mr. Shipley killed your mother, why do you work for him?"

A glimmer entered Rudy Hartwicke's eyes. "Keep your enemies close."

"I see. I understand you were angry with Mr. Shipley because he didn't give you a promotion or a raise."

"Yeah, I do a good job. I should'a got a raise, at least."

"How angry were you, Rudy?"

"Not enough to kill him," Hartwicke sneered.

"You're going to have to do a lot better than that. You've got a motive. You say you were driving around town last night, but you ran when you saw Officer Bourgogne and me. It doesn't look good for you."

"I got nothin' to say."

"Well then," Steven said. "I'm afraid I have bad news. You're going to be our guest a while longer. In the meantime, we'll talk with George to see what he has to say for himself."

Shutters closed down on Rudy Hartwicke's eyes. "Tell my aunt so she don't worry. And I'm hungry. You got any food in this joint?"

Steven instructed a patrolman to inform Rudy's Aunt Celia of his whereabouts for the night and to bring the detainee some hot coffee and a couple of sandwiches from Joe's Sandwich Shop. "Have Joe put it on the station's account. And get Rudy more water, too."

Will was updating the information on the murder board when Steven returned to the CID room. He'd added Olivia's earlier observation that the killer was right-handed and had written:

SUSPECTS

<u>RUDY HARTWICKE - employee at Shipley's 5 + 10</u>
Motive - Thinks Shipley killed his mother
Angry didn't get raise/promotion
Opportunity - Alibi - George Ferguson. Not verified yet
Other - History of trouble with the law
Ran away from police (Blackwell/Bourgogne)
<u>THEO SHIPLEY - estranged son</u>
Motive - Angry father took him from mother
Opportunity - Was in KB night of murder
Evidence - Theo was at house with his father
letter from Theo to BS
note on BS's calendar

Will turned at the sound of footsteps. "Well, that's one for the books. I don't know anything about the hit-and-run, but if he believes Shipley killed his mother, that's a powerful motive."

"I agree, but why wait fifteen years? Besides, all his arrests have been for petty theft or vandalism. It's a big leap to go from throwing a bucket of red paint on somebody's car to killing a man in cold blood."

"True. I'll see what I can get out of George Ferguson tomorrow," Will said.

"I think Theo's a more likely suspect," said Steven.

"I do, too. He was here and he's got a strong motive."

"Right, and how many times has it turned out to be someone in the family? That's where I want to concentrate first. I'll have Jimmy look into the accident, though."

Will joined Steven at their desks, facing each other for easier discussion.

"This isn't bad for our first day, Steven. We've got two viable suspects."

"So far, so good."

Chapter Thirteen

PRESENT DAY

Olivia met Steven at her bedroom door. He'd put on a pair of soft corduroy trousers, a flannel shirt, and his slippers. He called them *house slippers*, which always tickled her. She noticed his collar was wet. He'd splashed water on his face.

"Hi." She beamed at him. "Ready for pizza and a movie?"

"You bet!"

Olivia reached out into the middle of the threshold and felt the warmth of his hand as he gripped hers. She stepped back slowly, bringing him into the 21st century.

Steven grinned like a kid. "No matter how many times we do this, I still get a thrill out of it. I hope I don't ever take it for granted."

Olivia nodded. "Me, too. Every once in a while when I'm in your time, I have to remind myself how epic this is. I've gotten so used to being in 1934 sometimes I forget what we're doing."

Still holding hands, they turned around in a small circle, then Olivia led him out the door and down her 21st-century hallway. As they reached the bottom of the stairs, the doorbell rang.

"Here's our pizza!" she said.

The mouth-watering aroma of the pizza swirled around their heads as they walked down the hall and into the kitchen, where Olivia had set plates and napkins on the table. Steven enjoyed spending time in her kitchen with its cheerful red-and-white decoration. He felt happy there.

"That smells delicious. I'm starving," Steven said. "Can I do something?"

"What would you like to drink?"

"Do you have any beer?"

"Sure, they're in the fridge."

Plates full of sausage-and-mushroom pizza, Steven and Olivia concentrated on eating at first.

"So, how did the rest of your day go after I left? Did you make any progress?" she asked.

"Some." He told her what he'd learned from his interview with Rudy Hartwicke. "I'm more interested in Theo Shipley, though. I'm interviewing him in the morning."

"Maybe this'll be an easy case and you'll solve it quickly."

"Wouldn't that be nice?"

Feeling like she could never hear enough about Steven's past, Olivia changed the subject. "Tell me about some places you lived when you were a kid."

For the next half hour, he regaled her with stories about living in San Francisco, Norfolk, and Pearl Harbor. "When I was eleven, my dad was shipping out and knew he'd be at sea for a long time. He wanted my mother and me to settle someplace permanently, so he sent us here to his hometown. It was a few years before the Great War."

Every time anyone mentioned the *Great War*, Olivia's stomach knotted up, and a lump rose in her throat. She knew that conflict as *World War I*—she also knew that in a few short years the world would be plunged into a second global war. In 1941, Steven would be forty.

Surely that was too old to be drafted.

Knowing something catastrophic was coming and not being able to say or do anything was the hardest thing for Olivia to deal with in her time-travel adventures. It was also why she'd never googled Steven's name. She did not want to know when he was going to die. The mere thought sent her heart into overdrive.

"That was the best pizza I ever had," Steven said, polishing off his last slice. He stretched out his legs and raised his glass. "Cheers. And thank you for supper."

"You're very welcome. Are you ready for the movie? It's called 'Gravity.' It's about a couple of astronauts who go out into space."

"Science fiction? Swell!"

"Well, no…it's not as fictitious as you think it is. Some day when you want to hear about it, I'll tell you about our space program and what's happened in the past fifty years. You'll be amazed."

"Don't tell me we sent a man to the moon," he laughed. "That'd be a good one."

"Uh…."

"What? You're kidding? Did we really?" He gaped, his eyes like saucers.

"Let's keep that for another night, okay?"

"Just when I think I'm getting used to the future, you tell me something like that." He shook his head in amazement. "You know something? When we met, I used to wonder what programs you listened to on the radio. Then, when we figured out how to come into each other's time, I thought *Wow, this is swell. We can sit in the front room after supper and listen to President Roosevelt's fireside chats, or George Burns and Gracie Allen, or The Shadow.* I never imagined that we could *watch* things. I really underestimated the future."

They settled in Olivia's living room, where a mix of modern and classic styles blended comfortably. She'd splurged on a navy blue velvet sofa with a tufted back, chosen an ottoman upholstered in a red tartan plaid, and hung framed vintage London transport posters on the walls. Like the kitchen, it was a happy room.

An hour into the movie, Olivia's cell rang, and she picked it up without thinking, pausing the DVD at the same time.

"Hello."

Steven raised his eyebrows at her.

"High school friend," she mouthed.

"My friend Steven is here…Yes, he's the one I meant…We're watching a movie…No, no problem…Yes, as a matter of fact, we are. You'll get to meet him Saturday…Okay, see you then."

"So, who were you talking to about me?" Steven asked in a kidding sort of way.

"When I was out running this afternoon, I ran into somebody I haven't seen since graduation. His name's Ken and he's moved back here. When we were catching up, he asked if I was involved with someone and I said *Yes, sort of.*"

Steven saw the heat rise in Olivia's face. Why was she blushing? Was she embarrassed that she'd let it slip that she thought they were involved? Or was she embarrassed about the "sort of" part of her answer?

Another thought struck him. Had this fella been important to her? Was he still someone special? *Wait! This is ridiculous. You're jealous. Ask her, for heaven's sake. You've always been able to talk with her. Don't stop now.*

Steven slid over on the couch and put his arm along the top of the back behind her. He could smell her perfume and feel her breathing. "You called me a friend, but you also said we're sort of involved. I don't know what all that means to you."

"Oh, Steven." She put her palm on his chest. "Let's not talk about it tonight, okay? Can we just finish the movie and enjoy our evening?"

Steven felt his insides twist into knots. His throat closed and for a moment he couldn't speak. What was going on? Didn't the past eight months mean anything? Look at all the time they spent together. Practically every evening, and now some of their days, too. Hadn't they formed a bond?

But, wait. Maybe when she'd told Ken they were *involved*, she was thinking of their time-travel experiments. Steven felt crushed. He'd thought they'd become a part of each other's lives in a way that was more than friends. He wanted to be a part of Olivia's life. When he really thought about it, he wanted to be the most important part of Olivia's life. No matter how hard that would be.

Steven sighed. Obviously, she didn't want to talk about it tonight. Well, he'd meet this Ken fella Saturday night, and maybe then he'd know where he stood.

Chapter Fourteen

SPRING 1918

Alice closed the heavy door and paused as the peace and quiet of the library enveloped her. This glorious edifice had become her refuge, her solace and hope. Long past researching her rights under New York State law, she now came to feed her passion for art. Each Saturday morning, when Theo had his chess and piano lessons, she got lost in oils, watercolors, pen-and-ink sketches, and gouache. She would choose an illustrated volume of the works of an individual artist and pore over each painting; she'd even purchased a magnifying glass to examine the artwork closer. Then, she would read the accompanying text, thrilled to learn about the painter's style, use of color, choice of medium, and approach. Thus far, she had enjoyed the watercolor landscapes of J. M. W. Turner and Thomas Girtin, choosing Turner's "The Grand Canal-Venice" as her favorite. Today, Alice was excited to learn about John Constable, one of England's foremost landscape artists.

She selected her book and headed toward a table near an open window, thinking the warm breeze would be a welcome addition to her morning. As she reached the end of a long aisle of book stacks, she saw him—small in stature, light-brown hair falling over his forehead, sweet face. He was so engrossed in his book that he was unaware of her until she set her large *tome on the opposite side of the table.*

He looked up. "Oh. Hello again." He smiled.

"Hello to you, too. I've missed seeing you."

"I couldn't come. I had to help my uncle. Well, he's not really my uncle, but that's what I call him." He made a face. "But, I'm still reading. I've been borrowing the books and reading them at home."

"What is it today?"

"Treasure Island. Pirates!" His face lit up.

"Oh, isn't that a hard one to read?"

He shook his head. "Not for me. I'm a good reader."

"My son likes that story, too. We read it together last winter. He's about your age."

"I turned ten in January," the boy said proudly. "Double digits."

"Ah, yes," she smiled. "A turning point. My son's a year behind you. His name is Theo. Theo Shipley."

"I don't know him." He hesitated for some time, seeming to struggle whether to say what was on his mind. Finally, he whispered, looking up at her from under long lashes. "I don't...I don't have many friends."

"I see. Well, that's all right. I'm in the same boat, you know. My best friend moved away a long time ago. I miss her."

"I'll be your friend."

She reached across the table and extended her hand. "That would be lovely. I'm Alice."

He shook. "I'm Leon. It's nice to meet you, Alice."

Chapter Fifteen

FRIDAY, NOVEMBER 2, 1934

S nowflakes drifted against a gray sky outside the window as Steven and Olivia faced each other across the breakfast table ill at ease for the first time, but trying to act like nothing had happened.

"I'm happy we change our clocks back tomorrow night. Being eighty years off is hard enough, but the hour difference feels like you're living in Chicago," Olivia said.

Daylight savings had already ended in 1934. Until it was over in Olivia's time, communication continued to be a challenge.

"I'll be glad, too. It's been confusing. Where are you meeting Liz and Sophie tonight?"

"The Red Lantern for Chinese. Yum." She attempted a smile, but it felt fake. "Listen, about the Halloween party tomorrow, are you still coming with me?"

"Yes, but do we have to wear costumes? I don't have time to put anything together, especially now."

"I don't know how you're going to react to this but I have an idea." Olivia knew she often spoke or acted without thinking things through and was making an effort to stop. She never wanted Steven to feel insulted by something she said that would be normal in the 21st century but could push some of his Depression-era buttons.

Steven made a face. "Why is it I feel like I should hold my breath when you start out like that? Go ahead. If I don't like the idea, I'll tell you."

"You could go as a guy from the 1930s. Wear your normal clothes and slick your hair back like you always do. I'll wear one of your mother's outfits."

He burst out laughing. "*That* would be a costume? You're kidding."

"No, eighty years in the future that *is* a costume. Imagine if someone from 1850 was going to a party now. They could wear their normal clothes and look like they were in costume."

"Yeah, you're right. Can I wear my new hat?"

"Yes, definitely wear your fedora. By the way, you're not going to believe the research job I just contracted for."

Steven finished his bowl of cereal and poured more coffee for both of them, the rich aroma drifting out of the percolator's spout.

"What is it?" he said, setting the pot back on the stove.

She explained her plans for the fashion project. "Would you mind if I moved the rest of your mother's things into my closet? I won't keep all of them, but I'd like to get everything together so I can sort through and pick out what I'm going to use. I could work on it at home without going back and forth into your time."

"Of course, that makes sense. Listen, Olivia. I think you should keep everything. My mother's gone. She doesn't need her clothes anymore." He swallowed hard, and a brief shadow of sadness touched his face. "I've been holding on because I couldn't face throwing out her things. In January, it'll be a year since she died. I have to let go."

Olivia wanted to reach out and squeeze his hand and, if it had been yesterday, she would have, but instead she said, "I know how much she meant to you. I wish I could have met her. I would have loved to talk with her and get to know her."

"You would have gotten along swell. You're a lot alike–your curiosity to find out about things and the way you want to experience everything you can. I think the quality I admired most was her kindness. She never judged people. She listened and tried to understand how they felt and why they thought the way they did."

"You're like that, Steven. It's one of the things that makes you so good at your job."

"Thanks. Wowie! Look at the time. We better make tracks. Get one of my mother's jackets from the closet. I'll go warm up the car."

Without thinking, this time Olivia did grab his hand. "Hang on a minute."

Steven stopped halfway out of his chair. "Come on. We've gotta go."

"No, wait, please. This probably isn't very good timing but I have to tell you something."

Seeing the look on her face, Steven lowered himself onto his chair again. He turned his hand in hers and squeezed. "What is it? What's wrong?"

"I haven't said anything because I wasn't sure. And I'm still not, but I can't get it out of my head. I want to tell you and let you decide what to make of it."

"Okay, now you've got me worried. Just tell me."

"I'm not sure if the killer saw me the other night."

Steven's jaw dropped. He stared.

Olivia couldn't tell if she had shocked him or made him angry. She hurried to explain. "While you were in the house making sure no one was there, I was doing some tricks that I use to fix details in my memory. When I finished, an image of the killer glancing up at me flashed through my mind. I don't actually remember it, Steven. It was subconscious, or maybe unconscious. I don't know if I imagined it or if he really did look up. If he did, it was super fast. And he couldn't have seen my face because of the light behind me." Her face became pinched, her brow furrowed. "I hope you're not mad."

Steven exhaled forcefully. "No, of course not. I understand why you didn't say anything. But, Olivia, the entire town knows you're staying here. The killer will know it was you." He looked away for a moment. "Maybe you should go home. If he thinks you can identify him, he could come after you." Steven leaned across the table and took both of her hands in his. "I couldn't live with myself if something happened to you. We should play it safe. You can come back after I arrest him."

Olivia's face crumbled. "No. I understand what you're saying. And I appreciate it. I really do. But, I can take care of myself. You know that. I won't go anywhere alone. I'll make sure there are always people around. And if I get into a situation where, for whatever reason, I'm alone, I'll run back here and go back to my time." She squeezed his hands. "Please, I want to stay. Remember, I might have imagined it."

Steven let go of her hands and stood up. He walked to the sink and stood with his back to her, gazing out the window. After a long minute, he turned around. "All right. I know you can take care of yourself. You've proved that. But, you have to promise me you won't take any chances. None, Olivia."

Steven had never sounded so serious. Olivia rose from the table and went to him. She reached up and put her hands on his shoulders. "I swear I won't take even the smallest chance. I'll either be with you or in a crowd. I promise."

Steven nodded and went outside to start the car. Leaving the gearshift in neutral with the parking brake on, he returned to the house while the engine warmed up. He washed his breakfast dishes and set them to dry in the rack, then threw a couple of sandwiches together and poured the remainder of the coffee into his Thermos.

"Olivia, after I talk with Theo Shipley this morning, I'd like your help to figure out the killer's height. When do you have to go back to your time?"

"As long as I'm home before eleven-thirty, twelve o'clock, I'm okay. I want to work on the clothing project all afternoon."

Out of respect for Steven's neat habits and routine, Olivia washed and dried her own dishes, then went to the hall closet for a jacket. The thrill she'd first experienced wearing Evangeline's fabulous clothes hadn't gone away, and she hoped it never would.

She slipped on a short wool jacket over the skirt and sweater outfit she'd chosen for today. The brown plaid wool skirt was fitted and flared out below her calves and although she was still getting used to the feel of the garter belt and stockings, especially when sitting, she loved the rustle the skirt's silk lining made when she moved. Steven had told her most women only owned a few outfits—she would stand out if she wore something different every day—so this morning, Olivia had donned a creamy silk blouse and the same tangerine cardigan she'd had on yesterday. The pièce de résistance was the chocolate brown béret that she angled in a rakish manner. *You're killing it, Olivia.*

Steven joined her in the hallway. "Come on. We need to leave. The car should be warm enough now."

The patrol room in the Knightsbridge Police Station was smoky and crowded. As Steven, Will, and Olivia walked by Ralph and Pete, Ralph jumped up and offered his chair to Olivia.

"Here, Miss Watson. Take my seat."

Olivia thanked him and said hello to Pete.

"Morning." The wiry comedian grinned, doffing his cap, revealing a shiny bald pate. He and the stocky blond patrolman were the station's comic duo. Like Laurel and Hardy, you never saw one without the other.

"Good morning, men." Steven got everyone's attention, and the chitchat died down. "Today's our second full day on the Benjamin

Shipley investigation. We're looking at two suspects: Shipley's son Theo and Rudy Hartwicke. We have Rudy in custody because he ran from Jimmy and me. He thinks Benjamin Shipley killed his mother in a hit-and-run accident fifteen years ago, which gives him a powerful motive, even if it isn't true. Jimmy, I want you to investigate. The accident occurred on March 28, 1919, sometime in the evening. The victim's name was Emily Hartwicke. Get the key to the records room from the chief."

"You got it."

"We searched Shipley's home." Steven told them what Will, Ralph, and Pete had found, as well as the news about Alice Shipley and her plans. "After he drops his mother off, Theo's coming here. I led him to believe it was for a casual conversation. So far, he's been pleasant and is cooperating. Check the board later for updates."

Steven walked across the front of the room to Ralph and Pete. Next to Pete, Olivia was writing in the black-and-white marble notebook she'd bought at the five-and-dime; she'd begun taking notes before the briefing started and was still scribbling.

"How'd you two make out tracking the killer's path? Anyone see our suspect?"

"Nothing yet," Ralph said. "We went backwards from Judge Randolph's. We're making a map and checking off places. So far, we covered Hickory. The only choices there were The Three Lords and the Elks. Cooper Lewis was tending bar at the pub. He said it was slow because a lot of folks were at the Halloween party but it got busier around nine-thirty."

"Coop told us he didn't notice anyone who matched the description Miss Watson gave us, but people took their coats and hats off," Pete said. "I asked him about Theo because he knows him. He thought he saw him Wednesday but, when the fella turned around, it wasn't him."

"Who was it?" Steven asked.

"Leon Quigg."

Steven looked at Olivia. "What do you think? Could it have been Leon?"

Olivia gazed off, trying to picture the killer, then Leon, whom she'd seen twice. "Same build, but I'm not sure. Maybe."

Steven made a note then said, "Ralph, go ahead."

"We talked with members of The Elks who were at the club finishing the clean-up. They agreed it was impossible to tell from the description we had. If the killer was at the party, he would have taken off his jacket and cap, same as the pub."

"Plus, he could've been wearing a mask," Pete said. "So, we don't know if he was at the Halloween party or not."

"All right," Steven said. "Let's give it one more day. If you're still at a dead end this afternoon, we'll go at it from another angle."

Ray reported no additional information on his team's efforts to track the killer's route after the murder. Steven told him to keep at it.

"Steven," called out a young officer, "about the five-and-dimes. I have an answer for you on who owns the Shipley stores now."

"Swell. What did you find out, Charlie?"

"I talked with Christopher Koschnick, at the County Clerk's Office. According to the records, all the stores belong to the family. Mrs. Shipley and Theo each own fifty percent."

"Theo's motive just got stronger," Will said.

"Yes, it did," Steven agreed. "Good work, Charlie. Today I'd like you to put Benjamin Shipley's background together. I imagine there's a lot of information out there and it should be readily available. When you write it up, keep the business-related material separate from the personal."

Charlie gave a sharp salute.

Steven wrapped up. "I have a final piece of information. Theo drives a 1929 Plymouth. It's light brown, and the top folds down. I want everybody to get a good look at it when he gets here. Although we know the killer walked up the street, at least from the corner, it's possible he parked a vehicle nearby. Be on the lookout for anybody who saw a car matching that description.

"One last thing before you tackle your assignments for today, I need several men to go to the Shipley house with Miss Watson and me for an experiment. We're going to figure out the killer's height. Olivia will position herself upstairs in my house and look out the window like she did Wednesday night. We're going to re-create the scene when he ran down the steps and across the front of the house. Olivia said he'd be an inch or two shorter than the hedges." Steven pointed to the left side of the room. "I want everybody to get up and go over to the wall. Arrange yourselves in a line with the shortest man to the far left and the tallest here at the front."

All the police officers grinned as they rose. There was the scraping of chairs as they pushed them out of the way and headed to the wall.

"Feels like we're in kindergarten again," quipped Pete. "Do we get milk and cookies later?"

Everyone laughed. Several younger patrolmen jostled each other and there was a moment when a husky patrolman elbowed Jimmy Bou, who spun him around and pretended to slap cuffs on him.

"Oh ho," exclaimed Ralph, clapping loudly. "That'll teach you to mess around with Jimmy Bou."

After a minute, everyone focused on the task at hand and organized themselves against the wall. Steven called out several names. "I want you fellas to meet us at the Shipley house after I talk with Theo. Stay here and get some of your paperwork done so I can find you when I'm ready. It won't be long."

Olivia chuckled and shook her head. *What a great bunch of guys.* Steven had told her how dedicated the men on his team were and how lucky he was to work with officers who could also lighten the mood. Police work could get them down, and he was glad to have fellas like Ralph, Pete, and Jimmy Bou around.

Realizing this was a good time to get more information for her *Gazette* article, she approached them as they walked away from the line-up.

"Can I ask each of you a question for my article?"

"Sure," said Ralph, as he straightened his tie, spit in his hand, and flattened his hair.

"Yes, ma'am," Pete said, adjusting his jacket and smoothing the front.

"I'll give you the lowdown, Olivia," said Jimmy Bou.

Olivia laughed. "Wow, thank you." She faced Ralph and Pete. "I have the same question for both of you: what do you like most about being a cop?"

"Helping people," Ralph said, without missing a beat. "I like knowing that anybody in Knightsbridge can come to the station with a problem and we'll help them. It feels good."

Olivia wrote his answer in her notebook. "Pete?"

"Getting justice for people who've been wronged. I like it when we catch the killer or the thief or the person who broke the law and hurt somebody."

Olivia gave him a warm smile. "Jimmy, where do you see yourself in five years?"

"Right here with the department but I'll be a detective by then!" Jimmy Bou's face glowed in anticipation.

"This is swell. Thanks very much, guys. I want to catch Chief Thompson before he leaves. See you later." Olivia hurried toward the door where Thompson was about to exit. "Excuse me, Chief Thompson. Can I ask you a question for my article?"

"Sure. I was wondering when you were going to get around to me."

"Can you tell me what's better about police work now compared to when you started?"

"Oh, that's a good one," he exclaimed. "I've been doing this job for about 30 years and there've been plenty of changes for the better. We have more ways of knowing that what we think is evidence really is. We've got the forensics lab and Hank Flynn does a bang-up job. Verifying fingerprints is routine and accurate. The department cars are faster and more reliable, so when we're chasing somebody, we usually catch him. HA! How's that?" The chief raised his bushy eyebrows. "Is that enough?"

Olivia smiled. "That's perfect. Thank you. And thanks again for letting me do the article. Sam wants it by the end of next week. Can I give it to you for approval maybe Monday or Tuesday?"

"Sure, that's fine."

Steven had waited for Olivia, and they returned to the CID room together, though walking farther apart than usual. Olivia checked the information on the murder board and sketched Steven's set-up, smiling at how much it reminded her of the way she approached her research projects. As she worked, thoughts of last night assaulted her. She was furious at herself for handling things the way she had and felt she owed Steven some kind of explanation, but she didn't want to embarrass him by talking too much.

It wasn't common for men in the 1930s to talk freely about their feelings—she'd already been surprised the few times he'd shared something private with her.

Why hadn't she simply answered his question when he asked what her words meant? She couldn't bear this uncomfortable atmosphere with him. It had been less than twenty-four hours, and already it felt like days since they'd acted normally with each other.

Steven was sorting papers when the telephone rang. Hearing the old-fashioned ring tone, Olivia glanced at the chunky black Bakelite phone with a dial connected to the wall with a cord.

"Hello. Detective Sergeant Blackwell."

"Morning, Steven. It's Doc. I've got your autopsy results."

"Any surprises?"

"Nope. Benjamin Shipley was shot at close range, in the center of his forehead with a .38 caliber gun. There's stippling around the wound, which confirms what Miss Watson saw. There's no exit wound. As you'd expect, there's damage from the bullet bouncing around inside the skull and, of course, internal bleeding."

"What shape is the bullet in? If we find the gun, do you think we'll be able to match it?"

"It ricocheted around but, yes, you'll have a good chance. We know the time of death because of our witness. Other than the fatal gunshot, Mr. Shipley was healthy and fit for a man of his age, which was sixty-six."

Olivia and Will listened to the one-sided conversation. After several minutes, Steven thanked the medical examiner, then shared the information.

Tommy Forester entered. "Detective Blackwell, Theo Shipley is here. Where do you want to talk with him?"

"I'll get him in a minute, Tommy." Steven turned to his partner. "Will, would you observe from behind the mirror?"

Will nodded and rose from his seat. "Olivia, come with me. We'll be able to see and hear what's being said, but our suspect won't know we're there. This is a swell new invention."

Steven stepped into the vestibule and approached a young man reading notices on the bulletin board. Theo Shipley was lean and fit-looking. "Good morning, Theo. I'm Detective Sergeant Steven Blackwell," he said, reaching out to shake the man's hand.

"I think we knew each other when we were kids, Detective. My mother told me we lived across the street from each other for a short time."

"I'm sorry we're not meeting under better circumstances." Steven led him to the far end of the hallway.

Theo Shipley read the sign on the door, the pleasant look on his face turning sour. "Interview 1? Detective Blackwell, I thought I was here for a chat."

"You are. This is the only place we can talk privately. I have a few questions, that's all."

Theo looked skeptical but entered anyway.

Believing it gave the police a psychological advantage if the suspect faced a solid wall rather than the exit, Steven continued to the far side of the table, leaving Theo to sit with his back to the door.

"Would you like a glass of water or a cup of coffee?" he asked, taking in Theo's dark green corduroy trousers, brown-and-green plaid flannel shirt, and short brown jacket. He also wore a cap like the one Olivia had described.

Theo thanked Steven but declined.

"This is an informal interview, Theo. Most of what I need is background information on your relationship with your father."

"All right."

"I understand you had been estranged since you were a child but you recently contacted him about meeting. Can you tell me about that?"

Theo's lip curled and he shook his head. "My father was a real SOB. He treated my mother terribly—even as a kid I could see that. I never blamed her for leaving him. He dragged me back here then abandoned me. He was gone when I got up and didn't come home until late at night when I was sleeping. He finally shipped me off to the Manlius School." Theo Shipley winced at the memories. "It was brutal—up before the sun, long runs in all kinds of weather, cold showers, boxing lessons. I hated every minute. Thank God, I had a teacher who saw what I was going through. He told me to toughen up, and, even better, he recognized my interest in writing, nurtured my ability, and encouraged me. I owe everything to him."

"I understand why you were angry. I think I would have felt the same way," Steven said. "So what happened? I saw the note you wrote. Why see him now, after all this time?"

"Our relationship has been gnawing at me. I've wasted energy being angry and I'm sick of it. I wanted to confront him and also see if he'd changed, although I knew that was unlikely. I figured if I saw him one more time, I'd be able to shut the door on the past, maybe just pretend he was dead."

"Interesting choice of words, Theo."

"Don't make something out of it that isn't there, Detective. I didn't kill my father. I'll tell you something, though. My mother always says, 'You made your bed, you lie in it.' I agree. We're responsible for the things we do. My father abused a lot of people. He paid the price."

"Tell me about Wednesday," Steven said.

"I left New York about noon, made good time to Poughkeepsie then stopped for gas and something to eat in a town called Fishkill."

"Did you keep either receipt?"

"Not the restaurant receipt. The one from the gas station's probably in the glove box. I'll look when we're done."

"All right. And after you stopped to eat?"

"I ran into snow after Albany, so I had to slow down. Somehow, I arrived in Knightsbridge around seven-thirty. I was sure the weather was going to make me late, but it didn't." He shrugged. "I was meeting my friend Joe later…"

"Who's Joe?"

"Joe McMillan. We kept in touch after I left…" Theo Shipley raised his brows, evidently looking for a signal from Steven to continue.

Steven nodded.

"Joe had told me about the Halloween Party so I went to the Elks to kill some time." Theo scowled. "My father was a stickler for punctuality. Arriving early wouldn't have been acceptable."

"Did you talk to anyone at the party?"

"No. I thought I might see someone I knew, but I didn't. It was a bit provincial, cute, but not really my style. I had a cup of cider then went to my appointment at eight-thirty."

"You drove to your father's house?"

"Yes, of course." Theo's eyes narrowed.

"How did your father greet you?"

Theo reached for the pitcher, poured a glass of water, and took a drink before he answered Steven's question.

"He hadn't changed one damn bit. If anything, he was colder and more remote than I remembered. He invited me in. It was already dark. Lamps were lit in the living room. There was a light in the back, too. The kitchen, I think. He led me down the hall to his study, poured us both a drink then asked me what I wanted."

Benjamin Shipley settled comfortably behind the desk in his big leather chair. He took a swig of the twenty-year-old scotch and eyed his son. Theo sat on an upholstered chair in the corner, appreciating the symbolic distance between them.

"So," began the elder Shipley, "I suppose you need money. Is that it?"

"No, sir. I make enough money writing for The New Yorker. *I thought it was time we buried the past."*

"Why? I haven't heard a word from you since you left the Academy. I had to listen to rumors from the lousy gossips in town to find out what my own son was doing."

"With all due respect, Father, you did a terrible thing to me. Can you really say you were surprised I never came back?"

"A boy needs discipline. That's what the Academy did for you. I'm sure you're a stronger man for it. You should thank me." He took another swig of his drink.

"I won't bore you with the details of that place. Suffice it to say, it scarred me for years. I never would have survived the treatment in that place if it hadn't been for my writing and for Mother's letters."

"Don't talk to me about your mother. She walked out on me. Me! And if you took a minute to think about it, she walked out on you, too. Your precious mother. Nothing but a traitor."

Theo hadn't imagined the interview with his father would try his patience to this extent. It took everything he had to remain in his chair and not leap upon the old man and strangle him.

Why am I bothering? *he thought.*

"Father, I came here with good intentions. I thought we might bury the hatchet. After all, you might have grandchildren someday."

Benjamin Shipley threw back the remainder of his drink, stood up, and sneered at his son. "Some things are the way they are. There's nothing we can do about it. You've wasted your time, Theo. I have no interest in any grandchildren. You remember the way out?" He turned his back on his son and poured himself another scotch.

"So that's that. It's over now," Theo said.

"Let's finish up here and you can get back to helping your mother."

"Sure."

"You left your father pouring another drink. What time was that?"

"About nine. I didn't look at my watch, but I got to Joe's a few minutes after. We talked with his folks for a while. His mother has always been good to me. She wanted to know about living in Greenwich Village, writing for a famous magazine, and my writer friends at the Algonquin."

There was a shadow of a smile, and Steven thought he saw a glimpse of the sensitive young man Theo Shipley had once been.

"Where does Joe live, Theo?"

"404 Second Street."

"Did you stay at Joe's Wednesday night?"

"Yes, but we went out for a few hours."

"Tell me about the rest of the evening."

"We talked with Mr. and Mrs. McMillan, then walked to Pinky's. It was crowded. If you're looking for my alibi, there are plenty of people who saw us there around eleven."

"How do you know the time your father was killed?"

"Mr. Finley told my mother. I think everybody knows by now."

"You're probably right. Go on."

"We stayed a couple of hours, drank too much, got back to Joe's around midnight."

"One last thing, Theo, can you give me the names and telephone numbers of some friends and also your boss at the magazine?"

Theo Shipley took two small books from his jacket pocket, paged through the address book, and wrote several names and telephone numbers in the notebook. "Character references?" he asked wryly. He tore out the page and handed it to Steven.

"Something like that." Steven smiled. "Thank you. We always need to know where everyone was and what they were doing. You may have seen something even though you're not aware of it. Let's go out to your motor car and see if you can find that receipt."

Chapter Sixteen

OCTOBER 1907 – SYRACUSE, NEW YORK

I n the beginning, Lillian grieved the loss of her old life—so much so that she didn't know how she would make it from one day to the next. She missed laughing and talking with Alice and longed for their walks by the river in all the glorious New York seasons. She lay in her narrow bed at night, waiting for sleep to take over, replaying happy memories in her mind. She smelled the sweet scent of lilacs in the spring and felt the warmth of the summer sun on her face, heard the crunch of fallen leaves under her feet in autumn, and tasted the bite of cold air in the winter. There was no river to walk along on Tipperary Hill, and she could not afford the fare for the electric trolley in order to walk along the shores of Onondaga Lake.

Lillian missed her mother so badly she felt genuine physical pain. Most nights she cried herself to sleep, but the weekly letters from Mam, filled with love and longing, kept her going during the day. Although her mother maintained a cheerful tone, Lillian sensed a falseness about it. She could tell her mother yearned to see her, too, and knew she was only trying to keep her spirits up. Mam rarely mentioned her father. Lillian took that to mean he was still hurt and disappointed in her.

Well, she had disappointed herself, too. This was certainly not what she'd thought her life would be. When she was younger, she had dreamed of *falling in love with a wonderful, kind, handsome man. They would marry and have a houseful of children. There would be fun, laughter, and years filled with love. Naturally, Alice would make the same kind of life. They would raise their children as one family. They'd play together and grow up to be best friends, like their mothers.*

One foolish night had destroyed all that. Now she was alone, and her dreams were dead.

One day Lillian felt the strange sensation of a flutter, and everything changed.

The first time it happened, she was at work. She had no idea what it was and hoped she wasn't coming down with something, since she couldn't afford to be sick. As the days and weeks went by, the flutters became stronger and increased in frequency, and Lillian realized her baby was moving inside her. The sheer wonder of it stopped her in her tracks. Understanding the miracle that was taking place, she began to pray again and embraced her new life.

Lillian forced herself to forget about Alice and about being a daughter to Mam and Da. She would be a mother herself soon, and the life growing inside her would need everything she had to give.

She didn't know why she always thought he when she dreamed of her baby. Did expecting mothers know these things? Lillian allowed her imagination to run wild. She pictured teaching her son the alphabet and counting on his fingers and toes, and imagined taking him for walks in the neighborhood in a fine perambulator. All the ladies would stop and admire him. He would be smart, clever, and, of course, beautiful to behold. She thought he might have her fine, brown hair, but she imagined her mother's rich brown eyes. She hoped he'd have her brother's laugh. Lillian wondered what he would be when he grew up and prayed he would be happy above all else.

The first time she felt him kick was September 22nd, her 18th birthday.

Chapter Seventeen

FRIDAY, NOVEMBER 2, 1934

After interviewing Theo Shipley, Steven returned to the CID room. Entering, he saw Olivia watching as Will updated the murder board. Will wrote Theo's motive, the explanation for his visit with his father, and the alibi he gave.

"I've got his gas receipt, Will. Tommy's calling the station to see if they remember Theo or his fancy-schmancy Plymouth. You ought to get a load of his motor car. It's got black trim and red spokes in the tires. There's a rumble seat and he can put the top down in nice weather." Steven whistled. "I doubt anyone could forget seeing that baby."

"That's a lucky break for us," Will said.

Tommy Forester poked his head in the detectives' room. "The owner at the gas station in Fishkill remembered Theo's car, Steven. He's sure."

"That was fast, Tommy, thanks." He turned to Olivia. "I'd like to go to the house now."

"I'm ready when you are."

Steven gathered the half-dozen officers he'd selected earlier. Two climbed in the back of his Chevy and a patrolman signed out one of the department's Fords to take the others.

When they arrived, Steven pulled the car into his driveway and crossed the street to explain the experiment to his team, then joined Olivia upstairs, stationed as she'd been Wednesday night. He opened the window and signaled for his officers to start.

The first man walked up the path, climbed the steps, and stood at the door. He pretended to take a gun from his pocket and shoot an imaginary victim, then he turned and ran down the stairs and across the front of the house. As he passed in front of the hedges, Olivia could tell he wasn't the right height. She shook her head.

"Nope. Too tall."

Steven stuck his hand out the window and gave a shrill whistle to signal the next man. They hit the right combination with the fifth patrolman.

"That's it!" Olivia cried. "He's perfect. A similar build, too."

"This is good. It gives us one more piece of information. Thank you." Steven closed the window and took a step into the hall.

She grabbed his arm. "Wait, I don't want to forget this. I've been waiting until we were alone. Did you notice Theo Shipley's hands this morning?"

"His hands?"

"He's got a murderer's thumb."

Steven stared. "I never thought you, of all people, would accuse a man of something so serious without evidence."

"No, no, Steven. It's a physical condition. I'm literally talking about his thumb."

"What do you mean?"

"The thumb on his left hand looks more like a big toe than a thumb. It's short and stubby. The nail was short and broad, too. It's a condition called a *murderer's thumb*. They also call it a *clubbed thumb*."

"Oh, I saw it, but I didn't think anything about it. Why? Are you saying it's important?"

"Only that his father probably had it, too. It's genetic."

"Genetic? Like hair and eye color?"

"Exactly. You inherit a murderer's thumb from one of your parents. I noticed Alice's hands. She had long graceful fingers so it can't be her. I'll bet Benjamin Shipley has a murderer's thumb."

"*That's* what Doc was talking about."

Olivia raised her brows, waiting for the explanation.

"Doc mentioned a deformed thumb in the autopsy report. I was going to ask him about it later."

"I thought you should know, but it doesn't really help your case, does it?"

"No, we already know Benjamin was Theo's father. But thanks, I'll file the information away. Who knows? Maybe someday it'll be important. Are you going home now?"

"Yes, I need to work." She paused at the threshold to Evangeline's bedroom. She wanted to say something but now wasn't the time. Instead, she said, "Have a good evening tonight."

"You, too. Enjoy your supper with the girls."

Olivia accompanied Steven downstairs. As they walked onto the front porch, Leon Quigg was climbing the steps, his mailbag hanging off his shoulder, his hand filled with envelopes of different sizes.

"Miss Watson, I have a package for you," he said, handing her a large manila envelope.

Olivia read the return address. "Ooh! My copies of *The American Girl.*" She tore open the end and slid out one of a half-dozen complimentary copies. In the center of the bright orange cover, a young woman dressed in a pilgrim-style outfit held a turkey on a platter in front of a full moon backdrop. Steam wafted from the huge roasted bird.

Steven peered over her shoulder and read aloud. "*The American*

Girl. For All Girls–Published by the Girl Scouts. Open it. Let's see your article."

Olivia scanned the table of contents. "Here it is: 'How Teenaged Girls Are Living During the Depression by Olivia Watson, page 36.' I can't wait to give the girls their copies. I'd like to invite them to breakfast tomorrow. Steven, would you do me a favor and call Annie for me tonight?"

"Sure, I'll tell her you had something to do, but you'd like to meet them at Bailey's at eight. How's that?"

"Perfect. Thank you." She wanted to hug him, but kept her arms at her sides.

Olivia was thrilled to discuss the article with Annie, Molly, and Lilly. The girls looked up to her like a big sister, and she enjoyed the growing friendship with these interesting young women. She turned to the mailman. "Leon, thanks so much."

"I didn't realize you were a writer, Miss Watson. Congratulations." He handed the rest of the envelopes to Steven and doffed his hat. "Enjoy the rest of your day, Detective, Ma'am." The mail carrier descended the stairs and walked on to the neighboring house.

Olivia went inside to return to her own time, and Steven rejoined his team across the street. After a quick debriefing of their experiment, the patrolmen left to help Ray canvas the northern side of town–they still needed to figure out where the killer went after he ran away.

Steven had one leg in his car when he noticed Leon at the house next door. The mailman was bent over, slowly walking up and down the front walk, his head moving from left to right and back again.

"Leon, did you lose something?" Steven called out as he approached.

"My mother's medal. I've been looking for it for two days."

"What does it look like? I'll keep an eye out."

"It's a small silver medal of the Virgin Mary. I wear it on a chain around my neck. When I changed my clothes for the party Wednesday night, I realized the chain had broken. The medal must have fallen out someplace along my route. I'd hate to lose it. It was the last thing she gave me before she died."

It surprised Steven to learn so much personal history at once. Leon Quigg was a private person.

"I'm sorry to hear that."

Steven thought of the medal he'd found in front of Benjamin Shipley's house the night of the murder, but kept the information to himself. If it was the same one, Leon certainly could have dropped it on his route, like he said, but he also could have lost it after killing Shipley.

Steven frowned. Why on earth would Leon Quigg want to kill Benjamin Shipley? They barely knew each other.

After Steven and Olivia had left, Will got on the telephone. Armed with the names and numbers Steven had given him, he began with Harold Ross, Theo Shipley's editor at *The New Yorker* magazine. It took less than a minute for the operator to put him through to New York City.

"Hello, Mr. Ross. My name is Will Taylor. I'm a sergeant with the Knightsbridge Police Department in the Mohawk Valley."

"What can I do for you, Sergeant?"

"We're investigating the murder of Theo Shipley's father."

Ross gasped. "When did that happen?"

"Wednesday night."

"Theo's up in your neck of the woods now, Sergeant, visiting his mother."

"Yes, we spoke with him this morning. He gave us your name and telephone number."

"How's he taking it? I know they weren't close, but even so. I mean murder…."

"As you'd expect. Listen, Mr. Ross, I know you're a busy man so I'll get right to the point. I'd like your assessment of Theo's character. We have to do this for everyone involved and Theo hasn't lived here since he was a child."

"Of course, I understand. He's very smart, one of the best writers I've worked with. He has a brilliant career in front of him. I don't think Theo would risk everything he's worked for to kill someone, even his estranged father."

"What if I told you we were positive he did it? Can you imagine the circumstances that would push Theo to take that risk?"

"I assume you're speaking hypothetically. In that case, I'd say it would have to have something to do with his mother. He adores her. If someone hurt her, maybe." Ross was silent a moment. "You should talk with some of our friends. There's a group of us who meet at the Algonquin–they call us The Round Table in the papers." He chuckled. "I can give you their names and phone numbers."

"Theo gave us Dorothy Parker, Robert Benchley, and George Kaufman. Are they the people you're thinking of?"

"Yes, they're good choices. They'll be honest with you. Did Theo remember to give you Dottie's number in L.A.? She moved to California a while ago."

"Yes, that's the one I have. Is there anything else you think I should know, Mr. Ross?"

"Only that if Theo is a suspect, I'd hope you have the wrong man. He does have a dark side, but murder? It's hard to imagine."

After writing a quick summary, Will stood and stretched. Glancing at the clock, he realized it was too early to call Dorothy Parker on the West Coast. He'd do that later. Now, he wanted to get out in the community and talk to people face-to-face.

Will donned his hat and coat, slipped his notebook into a pocket, and stuck his head in the patrol room. "Jimmy, how are you coming with the hit-and-run case?"

"I found the file. From what I read so far, the investigation was thorough. All the reports are arranged chronologically. Everything's neat and in order. And the file's thick. They played it by the book, Will."

"That sounds good. You'll get there. Listen, I'm going to check Theo Shipley's alibi with the McMillans. Can you come with me?"

"Sure!" Jimmy grabbed his outer gear and followed him out of the station into the sunshine. "Where are we going first?"

"Let's start with Mrs. McMillan at home, then Joe at the sawmill."

They strode down Hickory and turned onto Second Street, greeting folks enjoying the crisp, sunny day. They found number 404 in the middle of the second block. The McMillans' home was typical of many houses in town, a two-story clapboard structure with a wide front porch gained by a short staircase. Will rang the bell.

They waited, and Will rang again.

"The drapes are pulled shut," Jimmy said. "Looks like nobody's home."

"We'll come back. Let's go to the mill. You do the questioning," Will said. "You need to keep practicing."

Jimmy's face lit up. "Right!"

Will was pleased to see that Jimmy Bou was going to be a good detective. He was as sharp as they came. His mind absorbed information then he sorted it into neat little packets. He had the ability to ignore what was irrelevant and zero in on the bottom line. It seemed Jimmy Bou had a knack for police work.

Some twenty minutes later, the two policemen entered the Mohawk River Sawmill. The mill was crowded and noisy. The air was thick with sawdust, and it covered every visible surface. Men in flannel shirts and heavy work boots were lifting, carrying, or cutting logs into lumber. The vast room resonated with the shrill sounds of chain, band, and circular saws.

Steven's friend Artie Sinclair spotted them and came over. He yelled above the noise. "What are you fellas doing here?"

"Looking for Joe McMillan," Jimmy Bou yelled back.

"He's outside helping load a barge." Artie jerked his thumb toward a side entrance.

"Thanks," they shouted.

Outside away from the noise, Jimmy Bou said, "Phew! Those fellas must be deaf by the time they go home." He led Will along a path to the river.

Several men were loading a barge moored to a long wooden dock. They had formed an assembly line stretching from a stack of rough-cut lumber up on the river bank down to the water. A worker hoisted a heavy-looking piece of lumber and gave it to the next man who passed it on to the person below him. In the middle of this assembly, Joe McMillan was handing over a twelve-foot long four-by-four when Will and Jimmy Bou arrived.

"Hi, fellas. What are you doing here?"

"We need a quick word, Joe," Jimmy Bou said. "Can we go over there where we can keep it private?"

"Sure." He stepped out of line. "What gives? Is this about Mr. Shipley?"

"Yes, we have to know where everybody was Wednesday night, Joe. Can you tell me when Theo got to your house?" Jimmy Bou said.

"Close to nine-fifteen. I was listening to 'The Town Crier.' That comes on at quarter past and it had just started."

"What did you fellas do when he got there?"

"We sat and talked with my folks, then went to Pinky's. Got back around midnight."

"Did Theo leave Pinky's at any time?" Jimmy asked.

"Leave?" Joe frowned. "No."

"How did he seem when he got to your house?"

"What do you mean?"

"Was he tired from the long drive? Glad that he'd seen his father?"

"We don't talk about stuff like that."

"What do you talk about?"

"He asked me about work and if I was stepping out with someone. I wanted to know what it was like living in a big city and working for the magazine. We talked about old times."

"You're sure he never left the bar? Did he go to the john?"

"Well, yeah, but how long does that take? Besides, Bobby put one inside a few months ago, so you don't have to go out back anymore. Sure is better in the winter." He grinned.

"We need to talk with your mother, Joe," Will said. "She wasn't home when we stopped."

"My parents went to Saratoga to visit my grandmother for the weekend. They'll be back Sunday night."

On their return to the station, Will quizzed the young officer.

"What do you think, Jimmy?"

"I think your best friend would lie for you. But I know Joe. I don't think he was lying."

"I agree. If you were in charge of this case, what would you do next?"

"I'd talk with Pinky's regulars and find a couple who can say for sure Theo never left, then go back to the McMillan's and check with Joe's mother."

"That's exactly right," Will said. "When we get back to the station, why don't you update the murder board? Then take your time with your report. We got a good deal of information from Joe. What he told us counts as a preliminary confirmation of Theo's alibi and that's significant."

Chapter Eighteen

Steven returned to the station and poured another cup of coffee before settling at his desk. He leaned back and studied the murder board from a few feet away. Two good suspects. Both Theo and Rudy had strong motives, and they hadn't confirmed either alibi yet.

Steven considered the estranged son, who had reappeared with the excuse of settling the past with his father. Steven didn't buy it. He believed many of the controversial theories postulated by well-known psychologists, but this didn't make sense. Theo Shipley was a successful New York City writer with a sophisticated lifestyle and philosophy of life. Why would he care about the father who had treated him so badly when he'd been a kid? He was smart enough to bury the past on his own—he didn't need a face-to-face with his old man. *Although*, Steven switched gears as he thought it through, *Theo had admitted he was in Knightsbridge Wednesday night and someone living in a big city like New York would have plenty of ways to get a gun. That's three out of three. Means, motive, and opportunity.* He had to find out more.

And what about Rudy? The man had two good motives, and it was possible for a delinquent to graduate from petty crime to something more serious.

Maybe Benjamin Shipley had been the driver of the car that killed

Rudy's mother. If so, Steven couldn't imagine what it would be like working for him. How could you go to work and see your mother's killer every day, never getting justice? How long could you smile and pretend to be polite to the man who had ruined your life? But if the hit-and-run accident was the motive, why wait fifteen years and why Wednesday night? Surely Rudy'd had chances before now.

Rudy's second motive was weaker, but strong enough to consider. Although Steven didn't really think losing a promotion and raise constituted enough motivation for murder, he reminded himself they were in the midst of a depression that had been going on for five years, and it had hit some people harder than others. Steven thought that for someone like Hartwicke, two dollars a week could mean the difference between being comfortable and warm or cold and shivering on a winter's night.

Steven checked his notes. Rudy had slipped up in the interview yesterday. He'd mentioned a name.

He grabbed the phone, asked the operator to connect him with the Utica Police Department, and, after a moment, said, "Can I speak with Lieutenant Schiaparelli, please? This is Detective Blackwell with the Knightsbridge Police."

Enzo's accented greeting boomed over the phone line. "Steven! *Come stai?*"

"I'm fine, Enzo. How are you?"

"*Bene, grazie.* How can I help my friends in Knightsbridge?"

"Do you know a fella called Tappo?"

"*Ma certo.* Of course. He was a bootlegger during Prohibition. Not sure what he's doing now. Could be more of the same. We got plenty of people who'll buy cheaper stuff and don't ask questions. They don't want to know where it came from. We've had Tappo in and outta here for years, but we can never make a case stick. What's he done now?"

"I'm not sure yet. Do you know if Tappo has a job?"

"He works at his father's restaurant. Sicily's Best Pizza."

"What's his father's name?"

"Eugenio Grasso. What's your interest in Tappo?"

"Someone shot Benjamin Shipley Wednesday night. A suspect told me he and his pal were visiting Tappo around the time of the murder."

"Ah. Are you coming over to talk with him?"

"I'll have to. Probably tomorrow morning."

"Call before you leave and I'll go with you. Mr. Grasso knows me well. *Capisci?*"

Steven chuckled. "Oh, yeah, I get it. By the way, when are you going to come here for supper at Giovanni's? It's been a while."

"Mmm. That sounds good, my friend. Soon, maybe soon, eh? *Ciao.*"

"Bye, Enzo. Thanks for your help. See you tomorrow."

Over the years, Steven noticed some investigations made linear patterns. They were straightforward, one thing leading to another, eventually revealing the identity of the perpetrator. These cases held little surprises. Others were more complicated and created elaborate patterns. In the past twenty-four hours, this case had fallen into the second category.

The investigation had unearthed a twist. Leon Quigg was now in his sights.

Cooper Lewis had made a mistake when he thought he'd seen Theo, only to realize it had been Leon. Did they really look that much alike? Steven closed his eyes and tried to picture the two men. He shook his head and frowned. He didn't see it. Maybe if he got them together, the resemblance would be apparent. Then there was that business of the lost medal. He reminded himself that it might not be the same one, but even so.

So, what *did* he know about the mailman?

Leon Quigg lived around the corner from Jimmy Bou. He had moved to Knightsbridge to live with a relative, Marvin Quigg, when he was a kid. Steven made a note to find out when, why, and where he'd lived before. Leon had worked for the post office for as long as Steven could remember. He was a quiet man, Steven had once thought shy, but in recent years, he'd become an active member of the Elks Club. He seemed devoted to the local children. Every year, it was Leon who organized the Easter Egg Hunt on the Village Green, the July 4th Picnic with games and prizes for the kids, and the Halloween Party. Leon's biggest and most challenging undertaking was the annual Christmas Party. For the past five years, he'd collected donations and made sure that every child in town received a gift from Santa Claus. To accomplish all that in the middle of a depression was nothing short of miraculous. On the surface, Leon seemed like a good person. But Steven had been doing this job for a long time, long enough to know that appearances were too often misleading.

Time to learn more about Leon Quigg. He donned his coat and hat and left the station.

When Will and Jimmy Bou returned from the mill, Tommy Forester informed them they'd just missed Steven, who was on his way to the high school.

"High school?" Jimmy scrunched up his face. "What's he doing there?"

"We'll find out later," Will said. "Now, take time with your report."

"Will do. See you later."

They parted ways, Jimmy entering the patrol room and Will continuing to CID.

Will grabbed up the phone, provided a number, and asked the operator to connect him to Los Angeles, California. A woman picked up on the second ring, and he identified himself.

"I'm looking for Miss Dorothy Parker."

"That's me. Where's Knightsbridge? I haven't heard of that place."

"We're in Upstate New York, ma'am. I'm calling about the death of Theo Shipley's father."

"Hmm. There's a lot of that going around these days. Another one ruined in the stock market?"

Will was glad she couldn't see his stunned face. "I should have said his murder, Miss Parker."

"Oh, well, that's different. Why are you calling me?"

"I'm looking for some insight into Theo's character."

"What do you want to know about J & H?" She chuckled.

"J & H?"

"That's what I call him, you know Jekyll and Hyde. Two personalities."

"Can you elaborate?"

"Theo's a tough cookie. That military school his old man stuck him in got him ready for the real world, and then some, I'll tell you that. For someone so young, he's pretty jaded. He looks out for himself. You don't want to get on his bad side, that's for sure."

"Would he harbor a grudge?"

"Probably, but he wouldn't necessarily act on it, especially now. His career is going really well. I doubt he'd risk it. His father was cruel, but murder him? I don't think he'd bother."

"What about his other side?"

"His soft spot is his mother. He adores her, he'd do anything for her."

"Including murder?"

At the other end of the line, Dorothy Parker shrugged. "That's a good question. Maybe."

"Thank you for your candor, Miss Parker. I wish you a good day."

Will updated the murder board, left Steven a note saying he was going to Keller's to follow up on Rudy's alibi, and signed out one of the department vehicles.

A small bell tinkled when Will pushed open the door to the liquor store. He strode to the counter where a man with salt-and-pepper hair stood behind a gold-toned cash register. Next to the register sat a pile of paper bags and a revolving display of bottle openers and corkscrews.

"Hello, Mr. Keller. I'm Sergeant Will Taylor." He showed his badge and ID. "I'd like to speak with George Ferguson. I understand he works here."

"Is this about the robbery?"

"No, sir. What robbery?"

"I reported it this morning when I came in and found some of my stock missing. A couple of your fellas came over and said they'd look into it."

"I haven't heard about it yet. When did it happen?"

"I don't know. I was out of town from Wednesday afternoon until late last night. The officer thought the thieves broke in the back door because there's splintering on the frame and somebody jimmied the lock. He figured it happened at night."

"What about an alarm system?"

"I'm too small a business for that. Can't afford it."

"Do you know what they took, Mr. Keller?"

"I can tell you exactly. Two bottles each of scotch, rye, and gin; one bourbon; and three vodka. That's ten in all. That's a fortune for me. It'll wipe out any profits I had for weeks."

"How can you be sure of the amount and how did you discover the theft so quickly?"

"I did my monthly inventory this morning so I know how much stock was in the back room. And I found a scrap of paper on the floor that looked like a shopping list. The items on it matched what I discovered was missing. I gave it to the officer."

"I'll check with my colleague and follow up. In the meantime, where can I find George?"

"Today's his day off. He'll be in tomorrow at nine."

"Okay. One more question, sir. Why did you hire George?"

The businessman grimaced. "I know his reputation." He shook his head. "He's my nephew. I couldn't say no to my sister."

Will thanked the store owner and turned to leave, but Keller's next comment stopped him. "Oh, I should tell you that if you find the bottles, I can identify my merchandise." He explained what he'd done.

Will listened, then a smile crept over his face. "Very clever, Mr. Keller. Good for you. I'll be sure to pass on that information."

Steven opened the door and entered the high school's main office.

"Hello, Mrs. Stoner," Steven greeted the secretary. If anyone knew about Leon Quigg, it would be Betty Stoner, a middle-aged woman who had spent the past thirty years working in the high school office. Not only that, Betty Stoner had practically invented the town grapevine.

"Steven, how nice to see you. How are you?"

"Fine. And you?"

"Can't complain. How can I help you?"

Steven had brainstormed several excuses he could give so as not to alert the secretary that Leon Quigg was a potential suspect in a murder investigation. The last thing he wanted was gossip going around town.

"We're thinking about organizing some basketball games for the kids this winter. A couple of volunteers aren't members of the police department so I need to get some background information on them for our files." He thought this sounded extremely thin and mentally crossed his fingers, hoping it would pass muster.

"Oh, of course," she beamed, obviously thrilled to be a source of information for the police. "Who are they and what do you want to know?"

Steven gave her two names, one was Leon's.

"Let's start with Leon Quigg," he said. "Do you remember when he moved to Knightsbridge?"

"Hmm, let me see. He graduated with my son. That was in 1926, so he was here then. If you can wait a minute, I'll get his student records, then I can tell you for sure."

"That'd be swell, Mrs. Stoner. Thank you."

The secretary disappeared into a large closet at the back of the room. A few minutes later, she reappeared with a manila folder. She set it on the counter and dusted it off. "That room could do with a cleaning." She opened the folder and ran her finger down the first sheet of paper. "These records should be in chronological order, the earliest papers on top, the most recent in the back." She paused as she read over the paper.

Steven forced himself to be patient.

"Here we go. Marvin Quigg—he was his guardian—enrolled him in the fifth grade in January 1918." She lifted the sheet of paper. "Here are the records from his school in Syracuse."

"Mrs. Stoner, I'd like to read through this file if you don't have any objections."

The secretary shrugged. "You're the police, Steven. You probably shouldn't keep it too long, though."

"How about if I bring it back to you by Tuesday? Or Wednesday at the latest."

"I'm sure that would be fine. Leon's my mailman, you know," the secretary added.

"Mine, too. He's a nice fella." Steven hoped these comments would inspire Mrs. Stoner to embellish.

They did. The resident gossip couldn't resist sharing personal insights.

"Yes, he is. Shy, though. Even when he was in school, he spent most of his free time alone."

"By the way, Mrs. Stoner, do you know why he moved here? What happened to his parents?"

"They died," she stated, sounding as though that was obvious. "Such a shame, to lose one's parents at such a young age. Can you imagine how devastating that would be for a child?"

"It must have been hard for him to fit in and make new friends."

"Yes," she mused. "I'm not sure he ever really did fit in. Poor kid."

After returning from a thus-far failed investigation, Ralph and Pete were pouring over a map of Knightsbridge still attempting to plot the killer's path.

"Okay, Petey," Ralph said, frustration filling his voice. "We know where he *couldn't* have been."

"Right, all the businesses close by six. The bars and eating places are the only things open later than that. I still think it's a good bet that he went someplace for a drink first. You know? Fortify himself."

"Yeah, me, too. Give himself the courage to do the deed."

"So, we've got The Three Lords, Pinky's, the bar in the hotel, and that dive bar down along the Mohawk River Road."

"Coop didn't see anyone matching our description, so the pub's out. The bar in the hotel's too fancy and that dive down by the river's too far away. Let's go to Pinky's and ask Bobby," Ralph suggested.

"I like it," Pete said, giving a decisive nod.

It was late afternoon and already getting dark when Ralph and Pete arrived at Pinky's Bar and Grill on the north side of town. The clapboard building was a depressing sight, in need of a coat of paint and shutters hanging crooked. A floodlight should have illuminated the sign with the name of the drinking establishment, but the bulb had burnt out. Instead, it was lost in shadow and simply looked sad.

Pete pushed open the wooden door and the two policemen walked into clouds of smoke. They strode to the bar in the middle of the room and waved the barman toward them on the quiet, unoccupied end.

"Hi, Bobby," Ralph said, leaning over the polished oak counter, keeping his voice low. "Pete and I need to talk to you. Officially, I mean."

"Sure, Ralphie. What gives? Is this about Benjamin Shipley's murder?" said the tall, gangly proprietor, reaching across the bar to shake hands.

"Yeah, it is. Were you working Wednesday night?" Pete asked.

"I work every night. Except Sundays."

"Do you remember who was here around eleven?" Ralph asked.

"Sure, that's easy. On weeknights, the place empties out by ten, ten-thirty. We started out slow Wednesday, then around nine-thirty there was a bit of a rush. Lasted an hour or so and that was it. By eleven, there were only a half-dozen people left."

"Who, Bobby?" Ralph asked again.

"Mostly regulars."

"Who are your regulars?" Pete asked.

"Larry Castleman, Marty Carpenter, Hank Flynn, and Joe McMillan. Joe had an old friend with him." Bobby's jaw dropped. "That was his father!"

"Whoa, you lost me," Ralph said. "What are you talking about?"

"Joe McMillan's friend was Theo Shipley. He's Ben Shipley's son, isn't he? That was his father who got killed Wednesday night."

Pete had been taking notes throughout the conversation. "Wait a minute, Bobby. You're saying Joe McMillan was here with Theo Shipley Wednesday night?"

"Yeah, they got here about ten and drank themselves silly for a couple hours."

"You're positive?"

"Sure."

"This could be important, Bobby," said Ralph. "Are you a hundred percent sure Theo Shipley was here the whole time? Could he have left for twenty minutes or a half-hour and you didn't notice?"

"Well, sure, it's possible. I wasn't looking at him all the time. Why's this a big deal? You don't think Theo Shipley killed his old man?" The bar owner gasped and stuck out his neck turtle-like. Big brown eyes grew bigger and his dark brown hair flopped over his forehead. He pushed it back with a broad hand.

"Now, don't go starting a rumor, Bobby," said Pete. "We're not saying anything like that. You know how it works. We have to account for everybody. So, would it be fair to say you think Theo was here from about ten to midnight, but you can't be positive he didn't leave at some point?"

"Yeah. And I'll tell you something kind of funny. At first, I thought it was my mailman who came in with Joe. And I thought, *Well, this is a first. I didn't know these two even knew each other.* Then, when they got up here to the bar and the light was better, I could see that it wasn't Leon."

Ralph and Pete exchanged a look. Ralph raised his eyebrows. Pete answered with a shrug.

"You thought it was Leon Quigg with Joe?" said Ralph. "Does he come in here?"

"No, that's why I was surprised." Bobby turned to the far end of the bar, where a customer was calling his name. "Excuse me, fellas."

When the barman was out of earshot, Pete asked his partner, "What do you think, Ralphie?"

"That's twice somebody made the same mistake. I don't know if it's important, but we've gotta tell Steven first thing in the morning. He'll know what to do." He scrunched up his face. "It's gotta mean something, don't'cha think, Petey?"

"Maybe, maybe not. Look at Bobby here. He's Jimmy Bou's cousin. They're both tall and skinny, brown hair. Maybe Leon and Theo are cousins, too." Pete frowned. "But, I don't see where it gets us."

The station had emptied, and a peaceful hush enveloped the darkened building. The night-duty officer worked quietly at the front desk. Chief Thompson sat in his smoke-filled office finishing paperwork. Steven remained the lone occupant of the CID room.

He rose from his chair and walked to the large chalkboard. Gray Wilson had dropped off photographs from the crime scene, and Steven had tacked them around the wooden frame. He leaned in with his magnifying glass, scrutinizing the photos of the victim lying in his foyer. He wasn't sure what he thought he was going to see now in a picture that he hadn't seen the other night at the crime scene, but he looked anyway. You never knew. Maybe the camera had caught a glint of light reflected on something he hadn't noticed Wednesday night. He shook his head. *Well, it was worth a try*, he thought, and returned to his desk to write his report.

Twenty minutes later, Will walked in.

"Hi, have you been gone all day?" Steven asked.

"Just about. But I got a lot accomplished," Will said, dropping onto his chair. "I'm beat."

"Me, too. What do you say we touch base first thing in the morning and swap information?"

"Sounds good. I'll write my report and head home."

Shortly after, Steven left his partner finishing his paperwork, and stuck his head in the office at the end of the long, dark hallway. "Chief, here's my report. I'm going home if there's nothing you need from me."

Andy Thompson looked up with bloodshot eyes and a sagging face. "Nah, go on. I'm almost done too. I'll be following you out in a few minutes." He lifted his arms, stuck out his chest, and pushed his shoulders back in a long stretch.

"See you in the morning, Chief."

"Enjoy your evening, Steven."

As he drove the short distance home, Steven looked forward to putting his feet up and doing nothing the whole night long. It was unusual to spend an evening without Olivia, but she'd made plans with Liz and Sophie, and that was all right by him. He didn't have the energy for an uncomfortable evening with so many unsaid things hanging in the air between them. He was dog-tired, hungry, and could already taste the cold beer and leftover meatloaf and gravy he planned to warm up. He was looking forward to listening to some of his favorite radio programs–"The Lone Ranger," "Tarzan," "True Stories of the Sea," and "Death Valley Days"–stretched out on the sofa with nothing that he had to do. He might even take a nap before he went to bed.

Chapter Nineteen

SPRING 1918

*S*aturday mornings at the library had become the highlight of the week for Alice and ten-year-old Leon. He would tell her about the book he was currently reading and she would show him some of her favorite paintings, explaining why she loved them so much. Alice praised him on his story-telling skills. Leon expressed his appreciation for a variety of artists and styles—he liked the watercolors best. They would sit opposite each other at the big oak table, reading, studying art, and talking. One day, Leon confided his dream for the future to Alice.

"I've decided what I want to be when I grow up," he said, nodding his head as if it were a punctuation mark.

"Oh," she said, eyes twinkling. "What have you decided?"

"I'm going to work with kids, maybe a teacher or a librarian. I want to help them love books like I do."

"Wonderful! You'll be perfect. I always enjoy the way you tell me about the stories you're reading."

"I haven't told my uncle yet. Do you think I should? I'll have to start saving money for college. I think it's probably expensive."

"Yes, that's true. Although I believe where there's a will, there's a way," Alice told him. "You'll figure out something. But, yes, it would be a good

idea to talk with him about it." It was a testament to the closeness that had developed between them that Alice felt able to ask a delicate question. "Did your parents leave you any money?"

Leon's face dropped. "No. Alice, can I tell you something?"

"Of course," she said softly. "What is it?"

"I don't think I had a father. Either that or he ran away. My mother told me he died, but I think she didn't want me to feel bad that he abandoned us. I heard her whispering one night with my Aunt Cathleen. I didn't really understand all of it but I don't think he's dead."

Alice reached across the table and squeezed his hand. "There's nothing to be embarrassed about, Leon. Sometimes things happen. From what you've told me about your mother, I know how much she loved you. She sounds like the most wonderful mother a son could ever have. Don't let that other stuff get in the way of the beautiful memories you have of her. That's what's important." Alice squeezed again, then let go. "Your mother would want you to be happy. Believe me, I know. Because that's what I want for my son... and for you, too." She gave him a smile that reached deep into her clear gray eyes.

Leon felt the warmth envelop him like a hug. He loved Alice with a fierce devotion.

Chapter Twenty

FRIDAY, PRESENT DAY

I t was growing dark by the time Olivia finished her run and returned home. Streetlights glowed, and in houses up and down the block lights were coming on. She, too, turned on lamps in the living room, then climbed the stairs to get ready. As she was going to her bedroom, she experienced a rare moment of disconnect. Momentarily disoriented, Olivia stopped dead in the middle of the hallway. *Where am I?* The sensation only lasted a few seconds, but it was enough to disquiet her, and she wondered if she was going back and forth to Steven's time too often. *Maybe I should cut back on the time I spend in 1934 and stay here for a while.*

Oliva peeled off her clothes and took a steaming shower. After blow-drying her hair and putting on some make-up, she went into her bedroom to dress. Always happy to get back into her own clothes, Olivia put on a pair of jeans, a black sweater, and short leather boots. When she stood up, she glimpsed the framed black-and-white photos she'd taken in Paris, London, Venice, and Prague. A smile crept over her face. *Yep, it's time for a 21st-century trip.*

Olivia wondered what it would be like to go overseas with Steven. She knew he enjoyed traveling. When he was a kid, his family had lived in a half-dozen places because of his father's Navy career. He'd told her he wanted to go to Paris first. His beloved mother was French. She and his dad had met in the City of Light, in Montmartre. Olivia adored Paris. Maybe they could go together someday.

Her thoughts skidded to a halt. *What are you thinking? Exactly how would you manage that? You haven't even stayed overnight in 1934 yet. And after the disaster you caused last night, we'll be lucky to have a relationship left.* She sighed. *I have to fix this. I can't let him slip away because I hesitated.*

Olivia had time before meeting Liz and Sophie, so she went into the kitchen to organize her notes for the *Gazette* article. She kicked off her boots, fired up her laptop, and settled at the table with her feet on a chair and the laptop resting against her legs.

The first thing that struck her from shadowing Steven was the way a police officer approached an investigation. It was how she'd been trained as a reporter to go after a story. In the car on the way home from Liverpool, when Steven quizzed Jimmy, he'd made him list the key questions: who, what, when, where, how, and why. *When* did the crime happen? That was obvious for alibis, but there was also a bigger *when*. Steven reminded Jimmy Bou that many murders began in the past. The police needed to find out when the victim had met each suspect and what the relationship had been like. *Who* was another obvious interrogative. Who were the people in the victim's circle of family, friends, co-workers, and neighbors? Officers had to check out those who had played a part in the victim's life, whether good or bad. She worked on her notes until it was time to leave, then saved everything on a flash drive and closed the laptop.

Olivia parked in the farthest corner of the lot, then strolled under the extended awning to the double front doors of The Red Lantern. Charlie Finch greeted her, adding that Liz and Sophie had arrived, and pointed toward the far side of the dimly lit dining room, where Liz was pouring two glasses of red wine from a crystal carafe. Not a fan of red, Sophie was already sipping her Chardonnay.

"Hey, guys." Olivia gave Liz a hug and slid into the booth next to Sophie, giving her a one-armed squeeze. She shrugged off her jacket and rubbed her hands together. "Boy, it's getting cold out."

In the light of a pagoda-shaped lantern hanging over the table, Olivia saw the concern on her friends' faces. Sophie was paler than usual, and Liz looked strained.

As if reading her mind, Liz leaned across the table and whispered, "What the heck happened? You actually saw a murder?"

"I knew you shouldn't be going back and forth with this time-travel stuff," Sophie said.

Olivia could see it in her face and hear it in her voice—Sophie was scared. She put her arm around her shoulders and gave her a second, hopefully reassuring, hug, then reached across the table to squeeze Liz's hand.

"I'm okay. Please, don't worry. The guy never saw me. He doesn't even know I exist."

Olivia hated lying to her friends. *But it isn't really a lie*, she told herself. She wasn't positive the killer had looked up at her. The most important thing was that her best friends didn't worry.

"How do you know that?" Sophie's brow creased, her lips trembled. She looked like she might cry.

"I was looking out the bathroom window upstairs." She explained what she'd witnessed. "When Steven came back outside, I helped him start the investigation. It was really interesting."

"Wait. How do you know the killer didn't see you?" Sophie persisted. "Weren't you even a little scared?"

"No, he shot Steven's neighbor, then ran away. I was only alone when Steven chased after him and when he checked inside the house.

Four minutes tops. He was with me the rest of the time."

Liz and Sophie frowned at each other, shaking their heads. They knew she tended to do what she wanted and rarely heeded their advice to be careful.

"How did your interrogation go?" asked Liz, rolling her eyes. "I can't believe I just said that."

"Aren't you worried the police'll find out about your time-traveling?" asked Sophie.

"No, the interview went fine. When Steven and I had breakfast, he briefed me, so I knew what to expect." She took a drink of her wine.

"Did he tell you what Will was going to ask?" Liz asked.

"No, he said I should describe only what I saw and use his address when Will asked where I live."

The waitress, black-haired and stunning in a red silk dress, took their order and left dishes of raw mustard, sweet-and-sour sauce, and fried noodles.

Olivia swiped a noodle in the mustard and crunched before she said, "I think I helped Steven's case. I described the killer pretty well."

"Do you think he's someone you've met? Did he look familiar?" asked Liz.

"No idea. It was too dark."

With an unspoken agreement, they moved on to safer topics and enjoyed their dinner. Liz confided that she and Joe were ready to try for a baby again. Sophie told them things were getting serious with Luc.

As they sipped their green tea and laughed over the fortunes they'd pulled out of the cookies, Olivia said, "You're not going to believe who I ran into today."

"Who?" Liz and Sophie chorused.

"Ken Liang."

"Ohmygod!" Sophie always said it as though it were one long word.

"What?" Liz's jaw dropped.

"Yeah, I literally ran into him when I was out running. He looks as good as ever."

"Where's he been all this time?" asked Liz.

"Seoul, South Korea." Olivia explained what Ken had told her about finding his roots. "He asked if I wanted to get together to catch up."

"What did you say?" Sophie gasped.

"I didn't have a chance to say anything. He said to call him if I was interested. And he mentioned it *after* he asked if I was married or had a guy in my life. I told him sort of but that I didn't know where it was going."

"Wow," they whispered.

"Yeah, and he's causing trouble already," Olivia added.

"What do you mean?" Sophie asked.

Olivia told them how Ken had called during the movie last night and how she'd reacted. "I totally screwed up. And I don't know why. Steven asked me who it was because, of course, he heard me mention his name...."

"Totally normal," Liz said.

"Right, and I froze. I didn't know what to say. Steven is so much more evolved than most of the 1930s guys I've met but he's still in that generation. They don't talk about their feelings or relationships."

"I know what you mean," Sophie said. "I remember my grandfather. I know he loved me but he never said it."

"Me, too," said Liz. "So, what are you going to do?"

"Tomorrow night at your party, somehow I'm going to make it obvious to Steven that I'm interested in him, not Ken."

"Ken was always a bit creepy," Sophie said.

Olivia's jaw dropped. "You never said that."

"I don't mean creepy like a horror movie. Possessive, like if you were a couple he'd keep you from seeing your friends out of jealousy."

"I hated his arrogance. He acted like he was God's gift," Liz said.

"Why didn't you guys ever say any of this to me?" Olivia was stunned.

"Get in between you and your first love? No way," Sophie said.

"Besides, we knew it'd never last. You deserve better than Ken Liang," Liz said.

"I'm so annoyed with myself. The tension between us is terrible. We've never had that before. Tomorrow night I'm going to make sure he knows where he stands—no matter what I have to say or do."

Chapter Twenty-One

SATURDAY, PRESENT DAY

Olivia awoke Saturday morning feeling unsettled, the unresolved situation with Steven still on her mind. She dressed quickly and took off for a run, hoping to clear her mind. The weather had done one of those strange shifts and it was a beautiful, almost balmy, day.

One of the things Olivia liked about her friendship (*relationship?*) with Steven was how easy and natural it was. They had clicked right away, and it had been smooth sailing ever since. They always managed to understand each other, even if it took some discussion to get there. She knew Ken's phone call had upset Steven. She had wanted to tell him how she felt about him, but what would be the point?

Every time she allowed herself to think about it, the same question popped into her mind. How would she and Steven manage a relationship? What could they possibly do to make it work? It always came back to that, and she always ended up deciding to leave things as they were.

Olivia showered and changed into a casual outfit for a Saturday morning breakfast in 1934. She chose the dark brown corduroys she'd worn the other day, a silk camisole, enjoying the sensation as it slid over her body, and her cream-colored wool pullover since a cold day was forecast in Steven's time. She commandeered a beautiful leather tote bag of Evangeline's and filled it with the *American Girl* magazines and some necessities. Finally, she added a touch of make-up and double-checked herself in the mirror.

Satisfied there was no trace of the 21st century, Olivia went downstairs into the kitchen to feed Mr. Moto. She found him sitting on the window seat, looking out at the waking neighborhood, his little head turning back and forth as if at a tennis match. The sun shone on his inky black fur, and suddenly he looked different. When had her kitten turned into a cat? She set the can of cat food on the counter and approached him in the dining-room alcove, scooped him up, and hugged him tightly. "Have I been neglecting you spending so much time with Steven?" Emerald green eyes flashed. He wiggled out of her arms and flew back onto the cushion. "I'll try to do better." She grabbed him again and kissed the side of his face. This time Mr. Moto purred, then complained loudly that he wanted breakfast.

Olivia dished out his food and set the bowl on the floor next to his water. The tea kettle sang, and she filled her French press. While the coffee brewed, she retrieved *The New York Times* and *The Gazette* from the front porch, where they were delivered every day. Although Olivia was firmly planted in 2014, she didn't want to let go of the print copies–there was something about holding those big sheets of newsprint that thrilled her.

Forty-five minutes and a second cup of espresso later, she was up to date. Even though she hadn't worked as a reporter for several years, Olivia was still a news junkie. She fired up her laptop and skimmed *The Washington Post* and *The Huffington Post*.

The timer on her cell sounded—time to meet Steven. When Olivia returned to her bedroom door to wait, she still hadn't decided whether she should say something about last night.

SATURDAY, NOVEMBER 3, 1934

As he soaked in the hot bathwater, Steven replayed the events of Thursday night. Frowning, he pushed the bar of Ivory under the surface, then watched it pop back up. He couldn't afford to be distracted today. These next steps in his investigation could be critical, and he needed to concentrate. As he washed his hair, he reminded himself that he'd decided to trust the relationship he believed he had with Olivia and not say anything about the call or her friend Ken. If there was something between them, he'd see for himself tonight. After all, he was a trained detective. If he couldn't figure out what was going on in his own life, he'd better hang up his hat.

At seven-thirty, an anxious Steven met Olivia at her bedroom door.

"Good morning," Olivia said, smiling.

"Morning." Steven sensed a hesitation in her voice. Her smile looked strained, not the usual Olivia, who sparkled with happiness and the sheer joy of being alive. He reached out and took her hand. He noticed the warmth and a bit of moisture as well. Was she nervous, too?

"Ready?" Steven stepped back into the hallway, bringing Olivia into 1934.

"You called Annie last night, right? Our breakfast is on?"

"Yes, she practically damaged my hearing for life with the scream she let out. They'll be there with bells on, all three of them."

As they left the house and prepared to go their separate ways, Olivia wished him luck with the investigation.

"Thanks. If I can find out more about our suspects, it'll be a good day's work."

"Fingers crossed. I'll see you tonight at eight, right?"

"I'm looking forward to it," he said. "Enjoy your breakfast. And remember to make sure there are always people around you. Just in case it was a real memory."

"I will. Don't worry."

Steven entered the CID room and found Will at his desk. He'd hung his suit coat on the back of his chair and rolled up his shirt sleeves. Will was concentrating so deeply he hadn't heard him, giving Steven the opportunity to study his partner. Will had lost a little weight over the past few months, and it showed in his face. The chiseled cheekbones and jawline reflected the Mohawk ancestry he was so proud of. He'd slicked back his dark hair, revealing a widow's peak touching his high forehead. It struck Steven that Will looked like a matinée idol.

"Morning." Steven bent to stow his lunch box, then poured a cup of coffee from his Thermos. "So, how did you make out yesterday?"

"Good. I talked with Theo's editor and one of his friends, then Jimmy and I questioned Joe McMillan. I'm making a timeline of Theo's movements Wednesday."

"Swell. That'll give us an idea of where we stand with him. What did everybody say?"

"His boss said Theo wouldn't risk his career by committing murder. Evidently, he's a rising star. His friend Dorothy Parker thinks he has an evil side." Will shared her nickname for Theo. "They both thought he'd do anything for his mother."

"That's damning."

"When I asked Miss Parker if Theo had it in him to kill his father for his own reasons, not for something connected with his mother, she said…and this is a quote…'he wouldn't bother.' How do you like that?"

"He wouldn't bother? That's an odd way to put it."

"Yeah, we should keep him on the list until we've verified his alibi. That Jekyll and Hyde reference makes me uneasy."

"I agree. I wonder which side came out Wednesday night. What about McMillan?"

"Joe confirmed what Theo told us. We should have somebody go to Pinky's and check. Mrs. McMillan's out of town so I'll talk with her Monday." Will set down his pen and stretched, his muscles rippling under his shirt.

"One step closer," said Steven.

"Right. Now here's something interesting." Will told him about the liquor store robbery.

"I heard about that. You think it's connected to our investigation?"

"Maybe. Guess who works at Keller's."

"Who?"

"George Ferguson, Rudy's alibi."

"Funny you should say that. I was wondering about something that slipped out when I questioned Rudy. He mentioned a fella in the Utica area named Tappo. I called Enzo…."

"Enzo? We haven't seen him in a while."

"I'm going to see him this morning." Steven relayed what the Utica cop had told him. "He's taking me to the restaurant to talk with Tappo's father."

"So, we've got small-time punk Rudy, who says he's driving around with his pal when Shipley is murdered but he can't tell you where. And we have his alibi, George, who happens to work at the liquor store that was robbed around the same time. Hartwicke drops the name Tappo who's connected to illegal booze-running…."

"Yup, I see a picture emerging, don't you, Will?"

"Well, we sure don't believe in coincidences. By the way, why did you go to the high school yesterday?"

"I'm putting information together about Leon Quigg," Steven said.

"Why Leon?"

Steven told him about the mailman searching for a lost medal. "And I can't get it out of my mind that Coop mixed up Theo and Leon. If they do look alike, maybe it was Leon that Judge Randolph saw. I talked with Betty Stoner." Steven gave Will the rundown. "It looks like Leon is coming into his own now that he's involved with The Elks. I wonder if Jimmy Bou is his first real friend."

"Could be. It takes some people longer than others to find their way."

Steven stepped to the murder board. Under Theo's name, next to *Motive*, he wrote: *Harold Ross (boss) says murder unlikely. Dorothy Parker (friend) describes evil side, says motive relating to mother possible.* Under *Opportunity* he added: *Alibi - Joe McMillan - almost confirmed.*

Steven thought: *Theo Shipley? Rudy Hartwicke? Leon Quigg? Which of you killed Benjamin Shipley?*

"I know we have to look at Leon, but why would he want to kill Mr. Shipley?" As far as Steven was concerned, *motive* was the most important part of an investigation. No motive, no murder. Three days into the investigation, and all he knew for sure was that he needed more information on the mailman.

Jimmy Bou, Ralph, and Pete came in laughing, no doubt at one of Pete's jokes.

"Steven, we've got great news," said Pete.

"We went to Pinky's yesterday. Bobby told us Theo and Joe were there Wednesday around eleven," Ralph said.

"How certain was he?" Steven asked.

"Not good enough to confirm Theo's alibi, but pretty sure. His regulars were there and we've got the list," Pete said.

"There's a funny coincidence though," said Ralph. "Remember how Coop thought Leon was Theo? Bobby mixed them up, too. He thought Theo was Leon. Weird, huh?"

Steven and Will looked at each other.

"We hit a dead end tracking the killer, Steven," said Pete. "We can question Bobby's regulars today. What do you think?"

"Yes, do that. I'm going to Utica this morning to follow up on Rudy

CHAPTER TWENTY-ONE

Hartwicke's alibi. It shouldn't take too long."

"While Steven's in Utica, I'll question George Ferguson," Will said. "Jimmy, why don't you come with me?"

"Sure! Hey, what about pitting Rudy and George against each other? If they think the other person ratted on them to get a deal, we might get the truth out of 'em," said Jimmy Bou.

"That's a swell idea," Steven said, turning to his partner. "Will, let's use Tommy to coordinate."

"Right," said Will. "I'll hold off leaving for Keller's until you call in to say you're on your way back from Utica, Steven. I'll interview George at the liquor store, then bring him in, ostensibly for more questions. Jimmy can call the station to let you know when we're headed back."

Sal's News, a long narrow shop packed with magazines, newspapers, and tobacco products, was next to the diner. Olivia stopped to buy the 1934 editions of *The New York Times* and *The Gazette.* She paid Sal three cents, marveling at the change in prices in only eighty years.

"Thanks, Sal. Have a good day," said Olivia, who had become a regular face in the shop.

Sal gave her a brief salute and grinned. "See you tomorrow, Miss Watson."

As Olivia entered Bailey's, the tantalizing aroma of frying bacon and percolating coffee filled her senses. Bacon and eggs in Steven's time had become a treat, the kind of breakfast she never ate at home. Regulars crowded the popular eatery. Smoke filled the air, and Olivia appreciated once again that it was illegal to smoke in public places in her time.

She made her way down the narrow aisle, past the shiny chrome stools topped with red seats lining the counter to a booth in the back. Her excitement building, Olivia extracted four brand new copies of *The American Girl* magazine from her tote and set them on the table.

As she sipped a cup of coffee, she paged through her copy. Articles about autumn, stories about Thanksgiving.

Hearing excited chatter, Olivia looked up as Annie Sinclair, Lilly Coffin, and Molly Silverstone approached.

"Hi, Olivia," said Annie, dark blonde hair pulled back in her trademark plait, eyes glittering like topaz. She gave Olivia a lopsided hug as she plopped down next to her.

"Good morning," chimed Molly and Lilly, sliding onto the wooden bench on the other side of the table.

"Oooh," all three chorused, as they spied their copies of *The American Girl.*

"Page 36." Olivia grinned.

While they were turning the pages, the waitress arrived and took their orders for eggs, bacon, toast, and home-fried potatoes.

"Listen to this," Molly gasped. "Fourteen-year-old Molly S. hopes to have it all. A talented artist, Molly plans on a career in either design or advertising and says she would also like to marry and have children." She looked up. "Olivia, you called me a talented artist. Gee, thanks!"

"You are. I'm still impressed by the sets you painted for the school play last spring."

Molly finished reading. "This reporter believes Molly *will* get everything she dreams of." Eyebrows forming a dark line across her forehead, Molly stared at Olivia. "You've said that before. Do you have a crystal ball or something?"

Olivia forced a laugh. Little did Molly know that years from now, she and her current boyfriend George Talbot would marry and eventually become Sophie's grandparents.

"Here I am," cried Lilly. She read: "Lilly C., her auburn hair circling a delicate face, is wise beyond her years. Interested in the world and people who live in foreign climes, she is determined to travel and learn how others live. 'I think that no matter what their culture, language, or religion is, people are basically the same all over,' says Lilly. 'Mothers and fathers want the best for their children.'" She stared at Olivia. "You made me sound amazing!"

Olivia laughed. "You are."

"My turn," declared Annie. "When Annie S. talks about her dreams for the future, it's easy to believe her. Passionate about history, she wants to teach so she can share exciting stories of kings and queens, presidents and revolutionaries. When Annie talks, one can imagine how thrilling it will be to sit in her classroom as she brings the past alive." She turned to Olivia. "Wow! Do you really think that?"

"Of course. All three of you are remarkable."

Their waitress returned with juice for the girls and four plates of food.

"Bon appétit," Olivia said.

"Ooh, it's like being in France," swooned Lilly.

The conversation turned to school, boys, and the Halloween party.

"Molly got her first kiss, Olivia," whispered Annie.

"Hey, I wanted to tell her." Molly blushed.

"Let's hear it." Olivia smiled.

Bubbling with excitement, Molly leaned across the table. "We were still in our costumes and we had our winter coats on, so we couldn't get that close." She smirked. "We managed though."

"Tell her how you almost got caught," said Lilly.

"Oh, it was nothing. Just the mailman."

"The mailman? What do you mean?"

"We stayed after the party to help clean up. Anyway, George was walking me home. The long way, of course." She grinned. "We got to The Green, and he said, 'Let's sit for a while.' So, we sat on a bench. That's when…you know…he kissed me. Then, all of a sudden, we heard screeching brakes. A car came out of nowhere and nearly hit my mailman." Her eyes grew wide. "He was running across The Green toward the street and he wasn't looking where he was going. He almost got killed, Olivia."

"How awful. Who's your mailman?"

"Leon Quigg."

"When was this?"

"Right after eleven. The clock had just chimed."

"And you saw him clearly? You're sure it was him?"

"Yeah, why?"

"Oh, nothing. I met him at the Halloween party. He seemed nice." Olivia changed the subject.

Jimmy Bou returned to the patrol room to finish reading the case file on the hit-and-run accident, and Steven got ready to leave for Utica. He went to the bookcase on the far wall, hoping to find what he needed.

Some years ago, at his suggestion, the department had begun collecting all manner of items with potential resource value: telephone directories from all over New York State; local high school yearbooks; a book on poisons; and one on general medicine that Doc had donated. They used the yearbooks most often since they couldn't always obtain a photograph of people involved in a case, and a senior picture often did the trick. Steven knew Rudy was twenty-five years old. He did a quick calculation.

The yearbooks were thin and piled in a corner of the middle shelf. He grabbed the stack and flipped through until he reached the one from 1927. Returning the rest to the shelf, he opened it and paged through to the senior pictures. There they were grinning like they owned the world–Rudy Hartwicke and George Ferguson. Steven noticed there were no sports, no clubs, no extra-curricular activities of any kind listed under the two names.

It was a beautiful morning for a drive. As he drove down the

Brighton Road on the way to pick up Route 5, Steven realized he was alone in his car. It felt strange. He couldn't remember the last time he'd gone someplace on his own. If he was working, Will or Jimmy Bou usually went with him. Outside of work, Olivia had become his constant companion. Too bad she had plans with the girls this morning. She would have enjoyed the ride, and she would have loved the surprise awaiting Eugenio Grasso.

When Steven arrived in Utica, Route 5 became Genesee Street, and he had to pay attention to his driving–streetcars, automobiles, and motorcycles crowded the main thoroughfare, all vying for limited space. He passed the Munson-Proctor-Williams Institute, the renowned fine arts center. A few blocks later, he drove by the spectacular baroque-style Stanley Movie Palace, whose marquee read: Coming November 9 "Evelyn Prentice" with William Powell and Myrna Loy. *That ought to be good,* he thought. *I'll bring Olivia next weekend.* He continued crawling down Genesee Street, passing churches, hotels, shops, and office buildings. At last, he pulled up in front of the Utica Police Department. As he exited his Chevy, a short stocky man dressed to the nines in a dark wool suit, crisp white shirt, and burgundy tie waved and hollered from his perch on the side of the concrete staircase. Enzo Schiaparelli blew a lungful of smoke up into the air, threw a cigarette over the edge, and approached Steven with both arms held out wide.

"*Buon giorno, amico mio. Come stai?*" He kissed Steven on both cheeks.

Used to Enzo's European ways, Steven mimicked his friend, then answered, "*Bene, grazie. E tu?*"

"*Molto bene.* Excellent."

"Actually, Enzo, I have a gift for you."

"Oh?" said his friend, looking around and seeing nothing.

"You told me you suspected the Grassos were still involved with illegal booze but you haven't been able to make a charge stick."

"Yes, this is true."

"Well...." And Steven told him about the robbery at Keller's Liquor Store.

"How does that help me?"

"When Mr. Keller first heard about the rash of liquor store robberies, he was afraid he might be next. So, he secretly marked all the bottles of liquor and wine in his store."

"*Madonna mia!* Is it my birthday? *Fantastico.*"

"Yup, he wrote his initials DK on the label on the back of every bottle, in ink, of course. So, if George Ferguson sold Grasso merchandise stolen from Keller's store, you can prove it."

Enzo reached over and grabbed Steven's shoulders for a second time in five minutes, then gave him two more kisses on the cheeks.

"Okay, okay," Steven said. "Let's get going. I'll follow you."

Enzo poked his head inside the front door and gave a piercing whistle. Two uniformed officers hurried out. "Back up," he told Steven. "The restaurant is on Bleeker, less than five minutes."

Enzo commandeered a black police sedan then led Steven to a busy neighborhood, where he parallel parked along the sidewalk in front of N. J. Flihan and Company. Next to the restaurant supply store was a one-story, nondescript pizzeria with a sign above the door that read Sicily's Best Pizza.

Enzo pointed a couple doors down. "See that *pasticceria*? Swell cannoli but they gamble in the back. We arrest them at least once a week." He sighed. "I wish they'd stick to pastries."

The front of the pizzeria was dark. Steven tried the door and found it locked.

"He's here. Probably in the back getting ready to open." Enzo banged on the glass.

Steven shaded his eyes, peered in, and spied a tall, black-haired man peeking around a corner in the back. When he crossed the restaurant to let them in, Steven saw a man dressed in an apron reaching his knees and a dusting of flour covering his hairy arms.

"Well, look who's here. What can I do for you, Lieutenant? Who's your friend?"

"Detective Sergeant Blackwell is with the Knightsbridge Police Department. He has a couple of questions for you if you have a minute, Eugenio." Enzo gave a false smile.

"*Ma certo.* Of course. Always glad to help the *polizia*." His smile matched Enzo's.

These two are used to this dance, Steven thought.

"I can see you're busy, Mr. Grasso. I'll make this quick."

Grasso's brows rose, and he pursed his lips–the look clearly said *So you say.*

Steven opened the yearbook to the page of senior photos and pointed to Rudy Hartwicke and George Ferguson. "Can you tell me if these two fellas were here Wednesday night?"

Grasso took the yearbook and stared at the pictures. "*Sì*, they come to see my boy."

"Can you remember what time they got here and when they left?"

"I don't know when they arrive but they leave at quarter to eleven."

"That's very specific. How can you be so sure?"

"I close at eleven. I yell at them 'You got fifteen minutes and I throw you out.'" He chuckled. "They're good boys."

Steven immediately understood the implications of this news: Rudy didn't kill Benjamin Shipley. He couldn't have returned to Knightsbridge in time for Judge Randolph to observe him strolling up Chiltington, and it would have been impossible for Olivia to look out the window minutes before eleven and see him walking up the path to Shipley's house. Rudy Hartwicke was in the clear.

"Thank you, Mr. Grasso," Steven said with a nod. "Now, I believe

Lieutenant Schiaparelli has something to discuss with you."

While they'd been talking, the two Utica police officers had casually moved toward the bar across the room. At a nod from Enzo, they went behind the counter; each grabbed a bottle of liquor and checked the label on the back.

"DK, Lieutenant," said the beefy blond.

"Same here, boss," said the other, holding a bottle of scotch high in the air.

Uncertain what was happening, but sensing it wasn't good, Eugenio Grasso made a move for the door. Steven grabbed the restauranteur, spun him around, and pushed him face down onto a table. Enzo rushed over and slapped a pair of cuffs on him.

"Eugenio Grasso, I'm arresting you for buying stolen goods. Let's go." He pulled him up, passed him off to one of his officers, and turned to Steven. *"Evviva!* That was a good morning's work, eh?"

By the time Olivia waved goodbye to Annie, Molly, and Lilly, people filled the sidewalks doing errands, grocery shopping, getting books from the Village Library, or simply enjoying the fresh air. *Lots of people around,* she thought. *I'm safe today.*

She walked around the corner to Shipley's Five-and-Dime. Excited to bring Liz some Depression-era Halloween noisemakers, Olivia first indulged in a stroll up and down the aisles. She chose a set of aluminum cookie cutters with red handles for Sophie and treated herself to a box of pale blue linen stationery and envelopes, then picked up a copy of *Astounding Stories*, a science-fiction comic book she thought Steven would enjoy, and the latest *Black Mask* for herself because she'd heard Jimmy Bou raving about the detective stories he always read in the magazine. At last, Olivia reached the Halloween display. She selected a dozen black-and-orange noisemakers—bells, ratchets, rattlers, and tambourines—and took her purchases to the cashier.

Not ready to go home, she decided to walk to a section of town she hadn't visited yet. She headed down the crowded Margate Road to Tulip Street, then turned by the bustling Farmers' Market, where local housewives, their children trailing along, snatched up potatoes, squash, apples, and other fall goodies. As houses replaced businesses, Olivia passed families raking leaves and burning them along the edge of the road, the smoke from the fires transporting her to Saturday afternoons at her grandparents' house when she was young.

Olivia hiked several more blocks, then turned around to head back home. As she approached the corner, she saw a familiar silhouette striding toward her–slender, average height, dark brown jacket, cap. *Oh, no!*

Suddenly, she realized she'd left the crowds behind and had been walking alone for the last three blocks.

Stay cool, Olivia. Stay calm. No matter what you do, you can't give yourself away. It might not be him.

The distance between them was shrinking, then they were feet apart.

"Hello, Miss Watson. We haven't formally met, but I've seen you across the street at Detective Blackwell's house. I'm Theo Shipley."

"It's nice to meet you. My condolences on the loss of your father."

"Thank you," he said, then noting her packages, added, "Out doing a bit of shopping?"

"Yes, a few errands and a walk. It's such a beautiful day."

"Well, I won't keep you then." He nodded and moved on.

Olivia realized she was sweating. She needed to get off these empty streets and back to the safety of the house. *Now!*

She increased her speed. Nearing the corner, she heard footsteps. Glancing back, she saw Theo hurrying toward her. *No!* Heart pounding, Olivia began to power walk. She heard him call out to her. *Faster.* Olivia was almost running now. She stepped off the curb, ready to run across the road, when a large delivery truck careened around the corner. Olivia skidded to a stop, then backed up onto the sidewalk. She spun around, her back to the truck that was now speeding away, its driver oblivious to the drama unfolding, and set her packages on the ground. Arms loose at her sides, legs slightly bent, ready to use her kickboxing skills to defend herself, Olivia faced her pursuer.

Theo Shipley caught up with her, then stopped a foot away. Breathing hard, he bent over and placed his hands on his knees. Olivia stayed alert and poised.

"Gee, Miss Watson. Are you getting ready for a marathon?" He reached out his hand. "Here. You dropped this."

Feeling like an idiot, Olivia took the proffered receipt from her five-and-dime purchases. "Oh, thank you. Yeah, sorry about that. Sometimes I just like to run."

Chapter Twenty-Two

Will pulled the police car alongside the curb and they got out two doors down from the liquor store. "In case he's looking out the window, Jimmy."

Jimmy fingered his nightstick. "What if he runs, Will?"

"I'll go in the front. You go 'round the back. We'll have both exits covered."

"Right!" Jimmy inhaled, then blew the breath out. He shook his shoulders, hit his palm with the truncheon, and gave a determined nod. "Let's go."

Mr. Keller looked up from the counter when Will knocked on the window, then hurried to open the door. "Good morning, Sergeant. Do you have news about the robbery?"

"Not yet, sir. I need to talk with George. Is he here?"

Keller was about to answer when the stock room door opened and George Ferguson stepped into the store. He caught one look at Will, spun around, and flew back through the opening, slamming the door shut. Will took several long strides and reached the door in seconds. When he jerked it open, he saw what he had expected, but it gave him a secret thrill, and he grinned.

Jimmy Bourgogne stood at the threshold of the back entry, arm raised, nightstick about to come down on his quarry's head. The lanky officer towered over short, stocky George Ferguson. In a move taken straight out of *The Black Mask*, Jimmy whispered, "Give me a reason, George. Make one move and you won't know what hit you."

"This is a set-up," George yelled. "I didn't do nothin'."

"We'll see about that. Sit down," Will said, indicating the table and chairs that served as the store's lunchroom.

Will stood behind a chair, rested his hands on the back, and faced Ferguson. Knowing that intimidation was the best approach with a two-bit hood like George, he put on a slightly threatening, serious face. George must think there was no leeway to lie.

Ferguson shifted his gaze, refusing to look at Will. "I can't tell you nothin' about the robbery, Sergeant. I wasn't workin' Wednesday."

"I haven't asked you about the robbery. And why mention Wednesday?"

"Isn't that when the store was robbed?"

"Was it? Tell me what you did on Wednesday?"

"When?"

"After supper."

"Me and Rudy went to the Elks for the party."

"What time did you leave?"

"Who's the stoolie in the corner?" Ferguson cracked his knuckles and smirked in Jimmy Bou's direction.

"You're talking with me, George. The party. When did you and Rudy leave?"

"I don't know. We was there a couple hours."

"That's not what I asked."

Ferguson shrugged. "Nine, nine-thirty."

"Then where did you go?"

"No place special. Drove around a while then went to see a pal of mine."

"What's your friend's name?"

"I don't know."

"You don't know your friend's name?" Will looked at Jimmy Bou. "Have you ever heard of anything so ridiculous, Officer?"

"No, I have not." Jimmy kept a poker face.

"Try again, George."

"Tappo. Everybody calls him Tappo."

"What's Tappo's real name?"

A bead of sweat appeared at George's hairline.

"How should I know?"

Will's eyes bore into George's. "Where does Tappo live?"

"I don' know. Somewhere in Utica. We went to his old man's pizza joint."

"Name?"

"What's it to ya?"

"Tell me the name." Will's gaze intensified to the point where George rubbed an imaginary spot on his forehead.

"Sicily's Best," he said, frowning.

"Where were you at eleven o'clock Wednesday night?"

"Why? What happened then?"

"That's when Benjamin Shipley was gunned down." Will leaned across the table, close enough to feel George's breath on his face. "I wonder what you can tell me about the murder, eh, George?"

Ferguson jumped up so fast that his chair went flying and hit the wall behind him. He scrambled back from the table as though he'd been electrocuted. "Now, wait a minute. You're not pinning that on me. I wasn't anywhere near old man Shipley's house that night. I didn't have nothing to do with that. I don't know nothin' about no murder," he shouted. "You're not putting that on me."

Will smacked the table so hard that George jumped at the sound. "George Ferguson, you're wasting my time. I think spending the weekend in a cell ought to help your memory."

George put his hand up. "Whoa! Okay, okay. I was just havin' a little fun. I'll tell you what you want to know. You don't have ta do that."

"Too late." Will took the handcuffs from his back pocket. "George Ferguson, I'm taking you in for questioning about the murder of Benjamin Shipley and the robbery of Keller's Liquor Store. Hands behind your back." Will snapped the cuffs on him, spun him around, and marched him out the back door.

Jimmy re-entered the store to call the station and let Tommy know they were on their way. Then he informed Mr. Keller that George wouldn't be back to work today.

Steven stood outside the cell chatting with Rudy Hartwicke through the iron bars. "You're going to wish you'd talked to me, Rudy. Your pal George has been spilling his guts to my partner for the last half hour. He's making a deal. If you want to get in on it, you've got to help us out."

When he heard activity at the front entrance, Steven unlocked the cell, took Rudy by the arm, and prepared to walk him two doors down to Interview 1.

In the lobby, Will removed George's handcuffs. They took several steps down the hall toward Interview 2, Will holding George's arm, Jimmy Bou walking behind them to block the exit in case the prisoner decided to run for it. Ralph and Pete stuck their heads out of the patrol room to get a look at the action they suspected was coming.

Rudy Hartwicke took one look at George. "You bastard!" He jerked away from Steven so violently that Steven's grip loosened. Rudy hurled himself at George, shot out his fist, and smacked him square in the face, then pulled back and did it a second time. A crack resounded in the narrow hallway and blood gushed over the front of George Ferguson's jacket. George lunged at Rudy, pushing him to the floor and pummeling his face. Rudy grabbed George's hair and yanked. George screamed. Rudy yelled expletives at the top of his lungs.

Steven and Will dove for their prisoners. Jimmy hurried to give Will a hand pulling George off Rudy. Pete ran into the hall to help Steven subdue Rudy and drag him out of the way. Will grabbed George by the shoulder of his jacket and half-walked, half-dragged him into Interview 2, George all the while complaining about his bloody, broken nose. Steven held Rudy by the collar of his shirt and propelled him into Interview 1.

Steven sat across the wooden table from Rudy Hartwicke. They'd spent the past five minutes staring at each other. The fear in his eyes betrayed Rudy's defiant pout, while Steven's steel-cold glare nailed the prisoner to his seat.

"It's time to talk, Rudy. Right now, you're looking good for the murder of Benjamin Shipley. You've got nothing to lose. George already told us everything. If you tell me where you were, what you did, and when you did it, maybe you'll be the one to supply me with a detail your pal left out. If that's the case, you'll get the deal," Steven said dispassionately. In his years on the force, he had learned a bluff like this was best delivered casually, as though he really didn't need Rudy to talk at all, like he was doing him a big favor. "Frankly, I wouldn't worry about the robbery if I were you. Murder carries the death penalty."

"I told you I didn't have nothin' to do with Shipley. Didn't you ask the mailman?"

"What? What are you taking about?"

"Quigg. I told you how George almost hit him."

"No, Rudy, you left that out. Now would be a really good time to tell me about that."

"Can I have a drink?" Rudy nodded toward the water pitcher. He rubbed the knuckles on his right hand with the palm of his left.

Steven guessed they were sore from the punches he had thrown. "Sure." He poured a glass and pushed it across the table. "So, what am

I supposed to ask the mailman?"

"When me and George got back to Knightsbridge, Georgie almost hit Leon Quigg."

"Where was this?"

"On Victoria near the tower." Rudy beamed. "I can tell you when, too."

"I'm listening."

"Couple minutes after eleven. The clock rang when we was driving up to the corner." He gave a decisive nod and looked straight at Steven, as if to say *so there*.

"Where was Leon coming from?" asked Steven.

"Somewhere on The Green. He was running towards Victoria. It was dark. That's why Georgie almost hit him. One minute the street was empty, the next minute here comes Leon Quigg running smack in front of the car. He never even looked."

"Then what?"

"Nothin'. Georgie slammed on the brakes and swore at him. Leon kept running down Tulip. Georgie dropped me off at my house."

"What was Leon wearing?"

"His cap and a jacket."

"You're positive it was him? And you're sure about the time?" Steven asked.

"Yeah, I told you."

"All right. I'll talk with him. We'll see what he says. Now, tell me again what you did after you left the Halloween party. All of it this time. I want details."

Rudy slumped in his chair. "Why not? I'd rather go down for robbery than murder. We robbed the liquor store where Georgie works. Then, we drove to Utica to meet Tappo."

"Why Tappo?"

"He's one of George's contacts." He laughed. "Georgie's got contacts all over the place. You'd be impressed," he added in admiration. "Tappo gives George a list of what he needs. We…," Rudy raised his eyebrows and made a face, "*procure* what's on the list. His old man buys the stuff for the bar in his pizza joint. He gets a good deal on the booze. Me and Georgie split the money. Everybody wins."

"Except Mr. Keller."

Rudy shrugged. "We don't always take the stuff from Keller's. We go all over." He took a drink of water. "So, what kind of deal can I get?"

"I'll need information about how you robbed Mr. Keller. How did you get in? Exactly what did you take? You know, Rudy, details. Spell it out for me. Every. Single. Thing." Steven held his gaze, not blinking.

Rudy Hartwicke spilled. When he finished, Steven slid a pad of paper and a pencil across the table. "Write it all down. Then, we'll see what kind of deal the D.A.'s willing to make. And don't forget to write what you told me about Leon Quigg."

Steven rose and opened the door. "Officer McGrath," he called. Pete materialized at the doorway. "Stay here with Mr. Hartwicke while he writes his statement. Then take him back to the cell and bring me the statement."

The conversation in Interview 2 was going about the same as that in Interview 1. Will called for some towels, and George put them against his nose, then tilted his head back.

"Try to pinch your nose, George. It'll slow down the bleeding."

"My damn nose is broken! I need a doctor."

"And we'll get you one. But not right now. The faster you tell me what I need to know, the quicker you can see the doc. Like I said, your pal Rudy already squealed on you. I only want you to confirm what we know."

"Whadda'ya want to know?"

"Start from the time you left the Halloween party and take me to when you got back here from Utica."

George told the same tale Rudy had shared with Steven. He paused now and then to wipe a spot under his nose and check his finger for blood. Finally, he said, "That's it. I don't know nothin' about no murder. We wasn't anywhere near Shipley's place. I *swear*. I steal booze. I don't kill people."

Will gave him a pad of lined paper. "Write everything down. Be sure to put the times when you got to each place and when you left. Then sign it. I'll have someone call the doc."

Will called to Jimmy Bou from around the corner. "Stay with him, Jimmy. When he's done, take him to the other cell and call Doc Kranken. See if he'll come over and look at George's nose."

"You got it, Will."

Steven and Will met back in the CID room to plan their next move. When Will saw the new piece of information his partner had written on the murder board, his face lit up. Under *SUSPECTS*, Will read:

LEON QUIGG - Mailman
    Relationship to victim - Unclear.
    Motive - Unclear.
    Opportunity - Seen by Rudy H. running across The Green minutes after 11. Nearly hit by car driven by George F.
    Why was Leon there? Where did Leon go after the party?
    Other
    1. LQ resembles Theo. Are Leon and Theo related? Did Judge R. see Leon, not Theo?
    2. Seen Fri. by S. Blackwell searching for religious medal near Shipley's house. Is the Virgin Mary medal his?

"What? Rudy saw Leon Quigg running from the direction of the crime scene? George never mentioned it." Will looked stunned. "Why didn't he tell you that before?"

"Says he thought he had."

"Talk about one door opens. We eliminate Rudy and find a reason to investigate Leon. I didn't see that coming," Will said.

Steven drew a large X across Rudy Hartwicke and wrote *Alibied*.

Jimmy Bou entered, already talking as he walked in. "I finished the hit-and-run file. Mr. Shipley didn't kill Rudy's mother." He noticed the board. "Wow, and Rudy didn't kill *him*!"

"Nope, Rudy and George were in Utica selling booze they stole from Keller's."

"So, it was them. That takes care of two things at once," Jimmy said.

"What did it say in the file, Jimmy?" Steven asked.

"A salesman named Brown was passing through town on his way home to Albany. Wasn't paying attention and driving too fast. The detective on the case tracked down a witness who got a good look at the registration plate. It was enough, and Brown's been in jail for years."

"I'll make sure I tell Rudy before he's transferred."

Jimmy approached the murder board. "Leon? You're not serious?"

"We have enough questions to warrant looking into him, Jimmy. I'm sorry. I know he's your friend," Steven said.

Chapter Twenty-Three

SUMMER 1918

*A*lice was dreading Saturday morning. She'd spent days agonizing over her decision and had put off telling him for weeks. If there had been any other way, she would have seized on it, but she couldn't wait another day. The time had come, and it broke her heart to do this to him.

He was sitting by the window at what they had dubbed "their table," and, when she saw him, she realized how much he'd grown since they first met. He was taller and was getting some meat on his bones. And there was something else. What was it? Suddenly, he looked familiar—not because she had grown to know him, but familiar in a different way.

It hit her like a physical blow. Alice nearly stumbled and grabbed onto a shelf as she felt the breath catch in her throat.

Oh, my God. How did I never see this before? Can it possibly be?

He must have heard her sandals on the wooden floor because he looked up from his book. A big grin spread across his face. He gave her a little wave, then looked around to be sure no one had seen.

"Hi," he said excitedly.

"Good morning." She forced herself to smile. "How are you?"

"Good." He must have sensed something because his smile faded and was *replaced by a look of concern. "What's wrong? Are you all right? Are you sick?"*

"No, I'm not sick. But, I need to ask you something then I have something to tell you as well."

Leon placed a scrap of paper in his book, marking his spot, and closed the cover. He sat up straight, as though bracing himself for what was coming. Alice knew this child had already faced more loss in his life than most adults her age. Oh, how she hated to tell him. But, first, the happy news.

"Leon, I think the most extraordinary coincidence has happened. Do you mind if I ask you what your mother's name was?" Alice held her breath as she waited for the answer she knew was coming.

"Lillian. Lillian Quigg. Like me. Didn't I ever tell you?"

"No, but I have something wonderful to share with you."

He cocked his head, waiting for her to continue.

"Do you remember the first time we met I told you my best friend had moved away, and I was sad?"

"You said you missed her a lot." He had a serious expression on his face.

"Her name was Lillian Quigg."

Leon's jaw dropped. He stared at her. "You knew my mother? You were friends with my mother?"

Alice saw tears fill his eyes, threatening to spill over. "Yes," she whispered. "I only realized it today. You're starting to look like her. I can see Lillian's face in yours."

He did nothing to stop the flood, his thin shoulders shaking as he silently wept.

"I'm so very sorry about what happened to your mother, Leon."

He thanked her with a nod. "She had consumption. Nobody could help her."

Alice rose from her chair and went to his side of the table. As she put her arm around his shoulders, she caught the fresh scent of soap mixed with that little-boy smell.

Leon leaned into her as he sobbed. Neither of them moved for some time. Leon took a handkerchief from his back pocket, dried his eyes, and blew his nose.

"You said you had something to tell me, Alice."

Oh, Lord. How can I tell him now?

"Leon, I know this is terrible timing, but I have to tell you today. It's a little bit of bad news but I hope we can look at it as more of a change. I don't want you to feel sad because I have a solution and that's good news."

He sat up and looked her in the eye. "Just tell me." He sniffed.

"First of all, it's a secret. Can you promise not to say anything?"

"Of course. Friends keep secrets, don't they? I never had a secret before. I promise, Alice. Don't worry."

"I have to move away..." She hurried to continue as his face crumbled and fell. "Wait, it's only to Syracuse. And remember I have a solution." She handed him an envelope. "These are for you. Go ahead, open it."

Leon untucked the flap and slowly extracted several paper rectangles. He read, "Greyhound Bus Line - Round trip. Knightsbridge - Syracuse. What does it mean?"

"The bus is a new way to travel. It's like a big automobile with seats for a lot of people to ride together. You can come to Syracuse. I'll meet you at the depot and we can go to the Syracuse library together. Wait until you see it! It's beautiful. We can still spend our Saturday mornings together, Leon."

Leon's face was full of wonder. Clearly, this was an adventure to excite a young boy. "They have children's books?"

"Yes, lots of them. And I'll tell you how the bus works so you won't be afraid. Okay?"

"I'm not afraid. How long will it take for me to get there?"

"A couple of hours. Look behind the last ticket. I put a schedule in for you."

He pulled out a piece of folded paper, opened it up, and read. "Two hours and five minutes. I can leave at seven-thirty in the morning and I'll arrive at nine thirty-five."

Alice handed him a second envelope. It was much thicker than the first one. Leon opened it and his jaw dropped. Inside was a stack of dollar bills.

"I've never seen this much money. What's it for? Why are you giving me money, Alice?"

"After you use all the bus tickets, you'll have the money to buy more. I'm giving it to you now because, while I'm here in Knightsbridge, I have access to money. I won't when I leave, at least not right away."

She gave his shoulders a tender squeeze before removing her arm and returning to her seat. Leon was reading the bus schedule when she settled again.

"So, what do you think?" Alice asked. "Will you come?"

"It'll be a grand adventure, Alice."

Chapter Twenty-Four

SATURDAY, NOVEMBER 3, 1934

Jimmy's face fell. "Steven, there's gotta be an explanation. Leon wouldn't hurt anybody. He's a good person."

"That may be true, but remember, Judge Randolph said the killer reminded him of Theo. We can't ignore the fact that two people have confused Leon and Theo. You know we need to pursue it, if only to eliminate him."

"I understand," Jimmy said, slumping onto the extra chair.

"Jimmy, how long has your family lived next to the Quiggs?" Will asked.

"Forever. My dad was born in the house we live in."

"I'd like to interview your father to see if he can tell us anything about Leon's past," Steven said.

"He's at the store today."

"Okay, now listen. We need your help. I want you to think about all the times you and Leon talked. Is there anything you can remember that would give us a line on his parents or his life before he came to Knightsbridge?"

Jimmy's brow furrowed as he cast his mind into the past. As much as he liked Leon, he'd like it even more to be the one who provided

Steven with the clue that broke the case.

After a minute, his face lit up. "Yeah! He never said anything about his father but, last year on Mother's Day, I ran into him in the backyard. I said something about taking my mom out to Bailey's for breakfast. He looked real sad and told me he'd lost his mother when he was a kid. I said I was sorry, and I hoped he had nice memories of her."

Leon's face fell. He looked like he was in pain. Jimmy knew it had been more than a decade since Leon had come to Knightsbridge to live with his guardian. Like everyone else in town, he'd always assumed Leon's parents had died, and it shocked him now to see Leon's grief looked as raw as if his mother had died yesterday.

"My mother was beautiful," Leon said. "She was gentle and kind. She always encouraged me. She told me I could do anything I set my mind to." He allowed a small smile. "She smelled like lilac. She was a hard worker. Even after she got sick, she worked long hours six days a week."

"I'm really sorry, Leon. That's tough breaks. What was her name?"

"Lillian. And she talked with an Irish lilt."

"I never heard Leon talk so much," Jimmy Bou said. "Something got him going that day."

"That's exactly what I needed to hear, Jimmy," Steven exclaimed. "I know where to go to find out more. Since it was your information that showed us a new way into this case, you're coming with me."

"Sweet." Jimmy Bou loved being in on the action. "Where are we going, Steven?"

"There's a neighborhood on the west side of Syracuse called Tipperary Hill, settled by Irish immigrants. They're close-knit, so there's a good chance someone will remember Leon's mother. I'll call Fred Schultz."

Steven dialed the operator. "Syracuse Police Department, please."

After leaving a message for his friend, he shrugged into his coat and adjusted his fedora. "Let's go."

An hour and twenty minutes later, Steven pulled up to the curb near the corner of Clinton and Willow Streets, and he and Jimmy Bou entered the Syracuse Police Department. They identified themselves to the desk sergeant, who waved them in, then climbed the wooden staircase to the second floor and entered a door on the left, where they spied Fred Schultz at his desk toward the back.

"Steven," his deep voice boomed. "And Jimmy Bourgogne. How are you?" He stood and shook hands, then gestured for them to sit.

"Fine, thanks. And you?"

"Can't complain," said the tall, husky policeman. "So, what can the Syracuse PD do for Knightsbridge?"

"We're working on the murder of Benjamin Shipley."

"Yeah, I heard about that. Tough break, huh?"

"I'm trying to trace a woman named Lillian Quigg. She had a son called Leon. We think she lived on Tipperary Hill, and she died before 1920, probably between 1915 and 1919. I don't know who her son lived with after her death or where, but eventually the boy moved to Knightsbridge to stay with a relative. A fella named Marvin Quigg. He died last spring, so I can't question him."

A young officer with copper-colored hair and bright green eyes entered the room and sat at the desk butted up against Schultz's. "Did I hear the name Quigg?"

"This is my sergeant, Sean O'Callaghan." Fred performed the introductions.

"Yes, you did, Sergeant. Do you know someone with that name?" Steven asked.

"When I was growing up, a family named Quigg lived behind us. Not a name you can forget. It's not very common, even on Tipperary

CHAPTER TWENTY-FOUR

Hill."

Steven took out his notebook. "Tell me everything you can remember about them, Sean."

"There was a boy around my age. I don't remember his name. Lionel. Leonard." He shook his head. "Something like that. A skinny kid. He used to sit under a tree in the backyard in the summer and read. My brother and I tried to get him to play with us but I think he was shy."

"Parents? Grandparents?"

Sean gazed off, the right side of his face becoming pinched. He scratched his cheek. "Sorry, I'm not sure. I was a kid, I didn't pay attention. I know there was a man in the house but I don't think it was his father." His face lit up. "Leon! That was the kid's name, Leon. My mother would probably know who the man was. She was friendly with one of the women in the house."

"There was more than one woman living there?"

"Sure, a lot of Irish families live with two or three generations in the same house."

"Is your mother home, Sean? Do you think she'd mind talking with us?"

"She loves talking about the old days. I'll call her and let her know we're coming." He looked at Lieutenant Schultz. "If it's all right with you, sir."

"Of course. Take one of our cars. It'll be easier."

"Fred, one other thing if we have time, we need to verify Mrs. Shipley's alibi." Steven told him about the Women's Trade Union League meeting and said they wanted to question two women who had attended Wednesday night. "Jimmy's been calling but no luck reaching them yet."

"Sure, that's fine. Good luck."

Steven immediately recognized the woman who answered the door as Sean O'Callaghan's mother. She had the same coppery hair and emerald eyes, the same pale complexion and dusting of freckles across her nose.

"Hello," she said, her voice sang with the Irish lilt. "I'm happy to be meeting you. Come in."

Sean introduced Steven and Jimmy Bou.

"Mrs. O'Callaghan, I appreciate you giving us your time today," said Steven.

"Oh, and why wouldn't I?" She laughed. "You just ask your questions and I'll do my best, Detective." She set a kettle on a gas burner and got out a teapot, cups, and a bottle of milk. The sugar bowl was already on the table.

"We need to find out everything we can about a young man named Leon Quigg and the family he lived with. Your son tells us they used to live behind you."

"Oh, my! I haven't thought about the Quiggs in donkey's years. They're all gone now, though." She looked sad.

"Can you remember when Leon and his parents first came to live here?"

"It was the summer of 1907. But, it was only his mother. Lillian was all alone."

"How can you be so precise? What do you mean she was alone?"

"She was carrying him when she got here. Lillian and I were both due to have our babies about the same time." She looked at Sean. "That's your brother."

The kettle whistled. Mrs. O'Callaghan rose from the table. She splashed boiling water inside the teapot, let it sit for a moment, then swirled it around, warming the pot, and dumped it out. She dropped in a couple of teabags, poured the steaming water over them, and regained her seat while the beverage steeped. "Where was I? Oh, yes. Lillian was younger than me, only seventeen or eighteen. She said her husband had died, and she'd come to live with her aunt and uncle."

"Do you remember their names?" Steven asked.

"Brian and Cathleen Quigg. Truth be told, I don't think Lillian had a husband. She was too young, even for those times. But mostly she didn't act like a widow. Didn't seem to be grieving. I think she got herself in trouble and left home. Leon was born the following January, a few weeks after my Danny." She got up again and poured milk, then the strong tea, into four cups, which she handed round, and slid the sugar bowl across the table. "They were a normal family, had their ups and downs like the rest of us. Lillian and her uncle both worked. Cathleen stayed home with the baby. The years went by. Then, everything started going bad." She took a restorative drink of tea.

"First, Lillian got the consumption. The poor lass fair wasted away. It was pitiful to watch." Her face became pinched. "Lillian died in the spring of 1917. I'll never forget that day. I felt like I'd lost my sister. We were that close. Leon had always been a quiet child. Can you imagine what that did to him?" She leaned over and pointed outside. "I want you to look out the back window here, Detective. Tell me what you see."

"All right." Steven peeked through the green-and-yellow plaid café curtains. "I see a small backyard, a fence, then another small yard and your neighbor's house."

"I hang my wash out there. See how close my clotheslines are to the fence?"

Steven nodded.

"I wait until later in the evening to bring 'em in, gives the clothes plenty of time to dry and to pick up that fresh smell." She raised her brows at him.

Steven smiled. "I know what you mean."

"That was Leon's room, the one on the left, on the first floor. Only a few yards away from me when I was taking in my wash. I could hear everything coming from the open window, Detective, although I wished I couldn't. For months after his mother died, that child cried himself to sleep. Night after night after night. Fair broke my heart." She lifted a corner of her apron and wiped her eyes. "Leon was shy before his mother died. After, he was in a world of his own. Sometimes when I saw him out in the yard and went over to the fence to say hello, he acted like he didn't even hear me." She shook her head. "I'm afraid I'm going on too much, Detective Blackwell."

"No, no. This is exactly what I want to hear. I need to understand what Leon was like. Go on, please."

Mrs. O'Callaghan took another drink of tea. "That family seemed destined for tragedy. You'll remember, of course, that spring President Wilson declared war. Brian Quigg signed up and went off to fight in Belgium. He was killed in the Battle at Ypres in '17. A few months later, Cathleen died." She paused to catch her breath. "In less than two years, that boy's entire family was wiped out."

Once in the car, Jimmy Bou exclaimed, "I feel awful about what Leon went through. He never let on about how hard his childhood was."

"Most people don't. You just get on with your life the best you can."

"Yeah, but still...."

"Detective Blackwell, I'm happy to take you to wherever you need to go now. Did you say something about checking an alibi?" Sean asked.

"Yes, thanks. Jimmy, read off those addresses."

At the mention of Tompkins Street, Sean said, "That's right around the corner."

"Swell, let's go."

Sean made a couple of turns, then stopped at a red light.

"Hey, get a load of that traffic light!" Jimmy exclaimed. "It's upside down. What gives?"

The Syracuse officer laughed. "The folks in the neighborhood refused to have the English red over the Irish green, so they destroyed the first light. The City Council put another one up, and the locals threw rocks until it was demolished, too. This happened over and over until the council gave in and changed the lights. Now, the green of the Irish is on top."

"I'll be darned," Jimmy Bou marveled.

The light changed and, a minute later, they pulled up in front of a small house. Jimmy hopped out of the back seat and went to the front door. He rang the bell, waited, rang again, then knocked. He shaded his eyes and peeked in a window, then turned to the police car and shrugged. An idea must have occurred to him because he held up a finger and went around the side to the back.

"Looks like nobody's home. I'll have to keep trying to get her on the phone, Steven," Jimmy said on his return.

"Where's the other address?" Sean asked.

Jimmy checked his notebook. "Old Liverpool Road."

"That's an easy detour. We can stop on our way back," Steven said. "Thanks for all your help today, Sean."

As they circled around the end of Onondaga Lake, Steven asked, "Jimmy, what's Leon really like?"

"He lived behind us for about ten years before he even said hello. We started talking a few years ago. One day, I told him about The Elks. That's when he came out of his shell. He's nice, and he works hard to put on all those holiday events for the kids."

Shortly after, Steven pulled into a dirt driveway in the hamlet of Galeville. "Number 417," he read off the mailbox. "Let's see if Irene Flint is home."

They got out and climbed wooden steps to the front porch of a tall house with a dormer projecting from the roof. Jimmy rang the bell, and they heard it peal inside. A chubby woman with a square-shaped face came to the door, smiling. She had a bowl of batter in her arms and was holding onto a big spoon. Evidently, they'd interrupted her baking.

"Hello, can I help you?"

"I'm Officer Jimmy Bourgogne from the Knightsbridge Police Department, Mrs. Flint. This is Detective Sergeant Steven Blackwell." They showed their IDs and badges. "Can we speak with you a moment?"

"About what?"

"We're investigating a murder and we need to know where everyone connected with the victim was at the time."

"My!" Eyebrows lifted. "Well, yes, all right. Ask your questions."

While Steven remained quiet, allowing Jimmy Bou to take the lead, he took a moment to appreciate the efficiency of this woman and thought how unusual she was. She was calm and seemed unconcerned by the appearance of the police on her doorstep.

"Where were you last Wednesday evening from seven to midnight?" Jimmy asked.

"Wednesday." She stirred as she considered. "Ah, yes, home. I was supposed to be at a meeting but I didn't feel good so I didn't go."

"What meeting was that?"

"The Women's Trade Union League. I'm president this year."

As Irene Flint stirred—her hand gripping the wooden spoon, slowly going round and round in the bowl—Steven caught the scent of apples, cinnamon, and vanilla. *Mmm.* He wondered if Olivia knew how to bake.

"Have you spoken with anyone who attended?" Jimmy asked.

"No."

"Do you know if Rose Flanagan is out of town? I need to know if Alice Shipley was at the meeting."

"She'd know about Alice. I called when I knew I wouldn't be able to attend because Rose had to lead the meeting." Irene Flint stopped stirring. "You know, now that I think about it, she said something about visiting her daughter in Buffalo this weekend. Maybe if you tried calling Monday morning?"

Shortly before five o'clock, Steven pulled up in front of the A & P Food Market. The rain had stopped, but a fierce wind cut through them. Both men pulled their coats a little tighter and pushed their hats farther down over their ears.

"Steven, what do you want me to do while you talk with my dad? Are we breaking any regulations having me there?"

"No, your father isn't a suspect. He's going to provide us with information. There's no reason why you can't stay."

"If I think of something while you're interviewing him, can I ask?"

"Yes, of course. Our goal is to get as much background on Leon as we can. If you think of something that'll trigger your father's memory, that'd be swell," Steven said, as they entered the grocery store.

Jimmy saw his father right away. "There he is." He pointed and waved to catch his attention.

Louis Bourgogne strode down the aisle and greeted them. "Hi, son. Hello, Detective Blackwell." He extended his hand to Steven, and the two men shook. "Come back to my office."

They entered a small room with *Manager* stenciled on the door's window. When they had settled, Steven and Jimmy facing Mr. Bourgogne behind his desk, Steven began.

"First, I want to make it clear that we're only here to get information about Leon and the Quigg family. I don't want you to draw any conclusions. And I'd like you to keep this interview confidential."

"Certainly, Leon's a good kid. I wouldn't say anything to harm him." Louis Bourgogne lit a cigarette. "What do you want to know?"

"Jimmy tells me you've lived your whole life in the same house and you knew Marvin Quigg. Is that right?"

"Yes, Marvin and I were the same age. He was my great boyhood friend. We did everything together." Bourgogne smiled, evidently recalling fond memories.

"I need some background on the family. Whatever you can remember."

"Sure, now let's see…Marv had an older sister named Lillian. I can't tell you much about her. The three of us didn't play together, and she left town when we were in high school. I don't know why. I think it was something about a better job."

"Where did she go?"

He shook his head and shrugged. "No one ever said."

"Do you know if she was married?"

"Married? No, she was only seventeen or eighteen when she left." He turned his head and exhaled a stream of smoke toward the wall. "Maybe later in life but I never heard anything about her after she left."

"Do you mean neither Marvin or his parents mentioned how she was doing in her new job or her new life? Didn't she ever come back to visit? Even on holidays?"

"Nope, never saw her again. It was kind of odd, now that you mention it. Like she didn't exist anymore."

"All right. What about Leon? Can you remember when he moved here and what Marvin may have told you about him?"

"Sure, 1918 is a year I won't forget. He came in January, a few months before the influenza pandemic broke out. Marv said Leon was his cousin's son from Syracuse, and he was going to live with him because his parents had died."

"Leon was lucky to get out of Syracuse. I heard they had an especially high number of deaths," Steven commented.

"It was because of the Recruit Camp at the State Fair Grounds.

178

Soldiers came from all over the country getting ready to ship out to Europe for the Great War. They brought the influenza with them." He stubbed out the cigarette.

"Did Lillian work in Knightsbridge before she left?"

A big grin appeared on Louis Bourgogne's face. "She sure did. She worked at the lunch counter in Shipley's. Marv and I used to go there for ice cream sodas once in a while. She'd put in extra ice cream for us. On the sly, you know." His raised brows told of the grand adventure it had been for two young boys.

Steven grinned back at him. That would have been a real treat for a kid. "Was Lillian a popular girl? Did she have a lot of friends?"

"A couple of girls used to come to the house, but no boys."

"Was she old for her age?" Steven asked.

"What do you mean?"

"Do you think she may have been stepping out with someone older than the high school boys? Maybe a fella from work?"

"Oh, I see. I don't have any idea. All I cared about in those days was playing baseball, going fishing, and, in the winter, ice skating on the river."

Steven rose and thanked Jimmy Bou's father for his time and information.

Back in the car, Steven said, "We learned something important, Jimmy. Do you know what it is?"

Jimmy Bou was lightning quick. "We got the connection between Leon Quigg and Benjamin Shipley. His mother worked for him."

"Take it one step further, Jimmy. Connect the dots."

Jimmy Bou sat straight as a poker on the bench seat next to Steven while he thought. Steven stayed quiet and let him work his way through to the conclusion he had come to moments before.

Jimmy's jaw dropped, and he gaped at Steven. "Lillian had an affair with Mr. Shipley! She left town because she was expecting a baby.

DEATH RANG THE BELL

His baby–Leon. Holy mackerel!"

Steven nodded. "Now we have to prove it. And of course, the question is does Leon know Benjamin Shipley was his father?"

Chapter Twenty-Five

Steven was meeting Olivia at her bedroom door at eight o'clock for the party. Although he had visited what he thought of as *the future* several times during the past few months, he'd only been at a large gathering once. When they got together with her friends, it was always Liz and Joe and Sophie and Luc. He felt comfortable and safe with them because, except for Luc, the others knew who he was and where he was from. He knew they'd grown to like him, as he had them, and, if necessary, they'd cover for him. So far, there had been no danger of exposing his secret—until tonight.

He had no idea who would be at this Halloween party. A journalist looking for the story of the century? The professor for whom Olivia had done research on *time* last year? A scientist looking for the next big discovery?

Steven thought of another party guest and felt the knot in his stomach return. Ken, the fella who made Olivia blush.

He splashed water on his face and under his arms, brushed his teeth, and grabbed his bottle of Hair Slik. He selected his Sunday best–a gray suit with a double-breasted jacket and full-cut, cuffed trousers, coupled with a white shirt and burgundy tie. He dusted off his new fedora–a darker shade of gray with a black band folded on the side like a ribbon–and set it on his head in a jaunty position. It felt strange to dress normally to travel into the 21st century.

PRESENT DAY

A few minutes before eight, Steven saw Olivia come into view, appearing like she was walking through a magical otherworld.

Unable to bear it one moment longer, and wanting to relax and have fun with her tonight, Steven said, "Listen, Olivia, I didn't mean to interrogate you the other night."

"No, please. It was my fault, Steven. I was embarrassed that I said you were a friend, and we were sort of involved. The truth is I didn't know what to say."

"You felt like you had to explain to him?"

"Well, when you put it that way, no."

"Olivia, I spend more time with you than anybody. Of course, we're involved."

Olivia's smile was genuine this time, her eyes sparkled, and she looked like herself again.

"I'm so sorry, Steven. I didn't mean to make a big deal out of it."

For a moment, they simply looked at each other, then Steven whispered, "You look beautiful."

"Thank you. So do you."

They both laughed.

"You know what I mean," she said.

Olivia reached out and took Steven's hand. They were like a well-oiled machine now in their time-traveling routine: through the doorway, turn in a circle then walk back across the threshold, Olivia leading him into the 21st century.

As they got into Olivia's car, she exclaimed, "Wow, look at the sky. This is the perfect night for a drive with a view." She pushed a button and the moon-roof cover slid out of sight, revealing a star-studded expanse.

"Wowie! We're like the actors in the movie the other night. It's like we're out in space." He laughed in pure delight.

A few minutes later, Olivia turned onto Mulberry Lane and, after passing dozens of cars parked on both sides, they reached the end of the road. "Yikes! They must have invited half the town."

She pulled in a driveway, reversed, and headed back to an open spot she'd noticed. They got out, and she hit a button on the key fob, Steven no longer jumping at the sound.

Olivia led him up the sidewalk to the wide porch fronting Liz's and Joe's two-story home. Steven could hear the noise—what Olivia and her friends called music—and conversation through the closed door. Olivia pressed the doorbell and walked in without waiting. Liz, her razor-cut blond hair flying as she hurried to greet them, enveloped Olivia, then Steven in a hug.

"Are you a good witch or a bad witch?" Olivia asked with a grin.

"You guys look awesome. Wait a minute." Liz leaned back and eyed Steven. "Is this how you normally look?" she whispered.

He grinned and nodded.

"Cool. I like it." She looked at Olivia. "Is this the way you dress when you go there?"

"Yup."

Olivia was wearing one of her favorite outfits—a form-fitting, black-and-white silk dress that hugged her slender curves and stopped mid-calf. She'd found a pair of red pumps in Grace's Dress Shop, a popular clothing store in Steven's time. To complete the effect, she wore a pair of stockings with a black seam up the back and a thin red leather belt. Olivia twirled for Liz to see the entire outfit.

"Holy cow! Where'd you find those stockings?"

Olivia leaned close and whispered, "In a shop in 1934."

"I want your life," she sighed.

Olivia handed Liz an orange-and-black gift bag, the handles tied with colorful ribbon streamers. "Here. I got you something at Shipley's this morning."

Liz gasped as she peeked in at the vintage noisemakers. "They're for me?'

"Of course."

"Good. I don't want to give these to the museum."

A wave of people swept into the house, filling the foyer.

"Come on," Liz said, taking Steven's hand, leaving Olivia trapped in the crowd. "I'll show you where the food and drinks are. Everybody helps themselves. Don't be shy, Steven, there's plenty of everything."

They entered the dining room, where a buffet covered two long tables. Someone called out to her and Liz disappeared, leaving Steven on his own. He saw several people taking bottles out of a large plastic box. He walked over and watched a fella raise the lid, take a bottle, then reach for an opener on a nearby table. As the man cleared the way for Steven, he raised his beer, said hi, and walked away. When Steven lifted the top of the box, the choices of beer, ale, lager, and stout amazed him. He rummaged around and spied a Newcastle Brown Ale lying on a layer of ice cubes toward the bottom. He used the opener and took a long swig. Ice cold and delicious.

Steven moved aside to make way for the crowd behind him and sauntered over to the food table. Olivia had told him not to eat supper because there would be food at the party. He gazed upon platters of sliced meats and cheeses, several kinds of bread and rolls, a variety of salads, some he recognized, others he'd never seen before. There were relishes, dishes of pickles and olives, bowls of potato chips, and, on a smaller table nearby, trays of cookies and his favorite—chocolate brownies with dark chocolate frosting. *Wowie. I remember when food was abundant. I wonder how long the depression's going to last.*

A tall, black-haired man with East Asian features sidled up next to Steven, grabbed a small cookie, and popped it into his mouth. "Great costume!" He stuck out his hand, and they shook. The fella's grip was firm. "I'm Ken. Don't think we've met before."

"Steven. Nice to meet you." *Is this THE Ken?*

"Are you a friend of Liz and Joe's?"

"My friend Olivia is a friend of theirs. I came with her." Steven raised the bottle of ale and drank.

"Ah, you're the boyfriend." Ken eyed Steven from head to toe, blatantly analyzing every detail.

"I don't remember Olivia telling you I was her boyfriend. I was there when you called."

Ken shrugged. "I know Olivia. I could tell." He took a swig of his beer.

"How long has it been since you've seen each other?"

"Last time was at our high school graduation. What's that, fifteen, sixteen years ago?"

"We were all kids in school, Ken. People change." *He's sure of himself. Talk about arrogant.*

"So, how long have you guys been together? How did you meet?"

"We met last winter. What kind of work do you do, Ken?"

"I'm a physical therapist at the hospital. What about you?"

"I'm a cop."

Ken snorted derisively. "A cop? What do you do, walk the streets all day?"

"Not exactly. I'm a detective." Steven decided he'd had enough of this condescending snob. "Well, nice to meet you, Ken. Enjoy the party."

Olivia had lost sight of Steven when Liz pulled him out of the hallway. As she tried to spot him through the mass of people, Sophie grabbed her arm and drew her into the living room.

"You look awesome, Olivia."

"Thanks. You, too, Marie Antoinette." Olivia chuckled and twirled around to give Sophie the full effect. "Check out my stockings."

"Ooh, sexy! Where's Steven?"

"Liz took him to the dining room. Is Luc here?"

"Yeah, he's in the kitchen talking with some guys. He's the one in the Bugs Bunny outfit." She rolled her eyes. "I couldn't talk him out of it."

"Oh, dear." Olivia laughed. "I'd better go find Steven in case he needs rescuing. See you later."

Olivia edged her way through the crowd toward the spot where she'd last seen Steven and peered down the long hallway towards the kitchen. Nope. She stepped into the dining room and froze. There they were. Steven and Ken together. *Oh, no!* They were facing each other, their profiles toward her. Olivia had no idea what they were talking about, but she knew Ken Liang. He had an ego and was competitive. Whether or not he wanted her back, he was the kind of guy who could make trouble for the sport of it. *Why was I attracted to this guy? Talk about dumb choices.*

As she approached the spot where the two men stood—Steven looking classy in his suit, Ken obnoxious in his Superman costume—Steven said something and turned to leave. Olivia couldn't hear what it was but saw Ken bristle. It wasn't obvious unless you knew him. What could Steven have said? He had too much class to start something, especially in someone else's home.

She reached them in a few steps. Steven was still turning away from Ken, the two of them engulfed in an atmosphere so thick you could cut it with a knife. Olivia gazed from one to the other. Ken had raised his head so that his chin stuck out. Olivia had forgotten his superior look until now.

Steven took one look at her and broke into a smile that reached deep into his eyes. "Hello there."

Olivia filled with joy. Steven was in her life now, not Ken. She acted without thinking. "Here you are," she exclaimed, throwing her arms around his neck and giving him a big hug.

Steven's arms closed around her instinctively. "Well, I'm glad to see you, too," he murmured, breathing in the scent of her. "Where've you been?"

"Talking with Sophie," she mumbled into his shoulder. She stepped back from him. "Hi, Ken. How are you doing?"

"Great. Having a good talk with Steven here." He looked from one to the other.

"Well, enjoy the party." Olivia turned away from Ken, from her past, and placed her hand on Steven's arm. "Let's find Joe. He wants to show you something."

The rest of the evening passed in a happy blur for Steven. Why had he doubted Olivia? He knew her. He knew what they had together. Maybe he couldn't define it, but it was *something*. He felt everything inside him settle into place.

Chapter Twenty-Six

SUNDAY, PRESENT DAY

Olivia stretched and poured her second cup of espresso. Still in her pajamas and robe, she was enjoying her Sunday morning ritual. Piled high on the table, the thick Sunday editions of *The New York Times*, *The Washington Post*, and *The Gazette* nearly blocked Mr. Moto, who was snoozing on the bench in the bow window across from her. A crack of thunder shook the house, and she jumped. *Yikes, I hope this weather doesn't keep people away from Liz's exhibit this afternoon.* She rose and turned up the heat a notch. It was a cold damp day, perfect for staying in with her newspapers, then spending time in a museum.

When Olivia was eleven, a new friend had invited her to go to the Everson Art Museum in Syracuse with her and her family. Olivia had never been to an art museum before. Her parents, being lovers of the outdoors, had always taken her on camping and hiking adventures in the Adirondacks. That Sunday had been a cold, wet autumn day as well. The Everson had occupied an old building with creaking wood floors and lots of enticing nooks and crannies. As Olivia and her friend roamed from room to room, exploring secluded corners and tiny hidden spaces, thunder boomed and lightning split the sky, flashing in the windows set high on the walls. From that moment on, Olivia had associated Sunday afternoons with museum exploration.

Around one, the phone rang. As she expected, the caller ID declared it was her mother calling from California.

"Hi, Mom."

"Are you done with your newspapers yet?" Paige laughed.

Olivia chuckled. "Yes, I'm getting dressed. Sophie and I are going to Liz's new exhibit at the museum in a while. How are you and Dad?"

"We're good. So, listen, your father and I were talking about Christmas this morning. We'd like to fly back and spend time with you. What do you think?"

"I'd love it. Do you know when you'll come?"

"Depends on when we can get tickets. But, ideally arrive on the 23rd and stay until the 28th. We want to spend New Year's in New York City. And before you tell me you're going to rearrange a lot of furniture, we're going to stay at Gina's. That'll give me a chance to visit with her, too."

"How is Aunt Gina?"

"She's fine. The B&B is always busy this time of the year with people coming for the leaf peeping, and pretty soon Thanksgiving. So, what do you think?"

"That sounds great. Whatever you want to do is okay with me. You know you can always change your mind and stay here."

Olivia and her mother spent the next half hour catching up on each other's news. Her father came on the phone for a bit, and Olivia was happy to hear his voice. Finally, she said, "Mom, I've got to go. I need to get ready to leave. It's pouring out here. I told Sophie I'd swing by and pick her up."

"Okay, sweetie. Take care of yourself. Your dad and I love you. I can't wait to see you in a few weeks."

"I love you too, Mom. Email me your flight info. I'll pick you guys up at the airport."

Shortly before two, Olivia and Sophie hurried up the steps and out of the rain into the Knightsbridge History Museum. Inside the door, a poster announced: *CHRONICLERS OF OUR PAST, An Exhibit of Newspapers and Personal Memorabilia from 1915 to the Present. Open through JANUARY 4.* They left their umbrellas and dripping jackets at the coat check and entered the exhibit room, handing their engraved invitations to the docent at the door.

Liz was talking with some dignitaries at the other side of the room and waved. Moments later, she ascended the small dais and addressed the crowded room.

"Good afternoon and welcome. And thank you for coming out in this deluge." That got some laughs. "I won't take your time with my words when we have the wonderful words of others waiting for you to read. I only want to say that on behalf of the museum staff and myself, we are grateful to all the families who donated diaries, journals, scrapbooks, and letters so that future generations can see for themselves what it was really like living through the Great Depression...," Liz raised her eyebrows at Olivia. "...World War II, the baby boom era, the psychedelic sixties, and more. Please help yourselves to refreshments and enjoy your journey into the past."

Olivia made a beeline to the glass-front cases displaying newspapers and immediately got lost in an article encouraging Americans to buy Liberty Bonds to help support the Great War, an op-ed making a case for the United States to join the Second World War, and a piece welcoming servicemen back from Korea. She moved on to the next case where the headlines of a yellowed *Gazette* screamed, "LOCAL COP KILLED." *Oh, no!*

Olivia gripped the edge of the case, fear for Steven's safety tearing through her.

Officer James "Jimmy" Bourgogne was killed in an automobile accident last night on Chiltington Road while walking his dog. Detective Sergeant Steven Blackwell, who was first on the scene, told this reporter that by the time he reached "Jimmy Bou," it was too late. The beloved young officer was dead.

When? When did this happen? Olivia frantically scanned the top of the page for the date. Tuesday, November 6, 1934. *Oh, my God. It's going to happen tomorrow night.*

Olivia read on.

"Jimmy Bou was loved by everyone in the department. He was like the little brother I never had," Blackwell said. "Jimmy loved being a cop, and he was exceptionally good at it. He was quick to see things that others sometimes missed. He was invaluable on a case. I will miss him more than I can say."

A lump rose in her throat. Olivia had grown to love Steven's protégé. He was sweet and full of excitement and enthusiasm for police work. *Karma be damned. There's no way I'm letting this happen.* She read the rest of the article, memorizing what little detail there was.

Olivia didn't care that she was about to break every single time-travel rule that existed. And she blocked out all thoughts of the ripple effects and repercussions her act would have on the future. *I don't care. Not Jimmy Bou. No way.*

Her hosting duties fulfilled, Liz wove her way through the crowd and found Sophie.

"Where's Olivia?" Liz asked.

"She'll be wherever the newspapers are."

"Across the hall."

They approached the display case where Olivia stood, gripping the edge of the case.

"Hey, what's wrong? You look like you've seen a ghost," Liz said.

"Look at this article. That's Jimmy Bou. I've told you guys about him."

"Oh, no," they chorused.

"Come on. There's an empty room back here." Liz took Olivia's arm and led her and Sophie into a small storage space nearby.

"Olivia, I'm so sorry. I remember you telling us about Jimmy. He's the one with a crush on you," Sophie said.

"I didn't notice the date on the paper," Liz said. "When was it?"

"Tuesday. It happens tomorrow night!" Her voice shredded with anguish.

Liz and Sophie gave each other a meaningful look.

"No, Olivia," said Liz, shaking her head slowly, a grave expression on her face. "You can't. This already happened. We've talked about this before. You can't change things when you go back. You can't."

Sophie paled. "Olivia, what if you try to save him and you get killed instead?"

Olivia's forehead rippled as her brows drew together, and she squeezed her eyes shut. She felt sick. "After what Steven's been through this year, I can't let him lose someone else. I just can't. And I can't let Jimmy Bou die knowing I did nothing to save him. Look, there weren't many details. All it said was a car accident on Chiltington when he was walking his dog. It doesn't say what time."

Liz and Sophie watched her grapple with her emotions, the taboo of changing the past, and her will to save one young man's life.

"What do you think about this?" Olivia asked after a moment. "I'll find out when he walks his dog and the route he takes, and think of a reason to keep him from doing it. I'll invite him to dinner at Steven's or out to the pub for a beer. Maybe I can't save him. Maybe I'll fail. If that's the case, I'll have to accept it was meant to be.

"*But*," she nailed them with a stare, "what if I was *meant* to see that article and I'm *supposed* to save him? What if that's the *real* past?" Olivia looked from Liz's skeptical face to Sophie's worried countenance. She pressed on, needing her two best friends to be with her on this. "Remember what happened to Isabel last winter? The way everything ended was the way it was *supposed* to end. All the newspaper accounts and her memory changed after." She exhaled deeply. "I *need* to do this. I know it's the right thing. I *know*."

"What about Steven? Isn't he going to think it's weird you asking this guy to dinner or out for a drink?" Liz asked, her brown eyes looking darker than usual. "I don't see how you're going to pull it off."

"Olivia, all I care about is you," Sophie confessed. "It never mattered to me whether or not you changed history when you went back, as long as you always came home. If you interfere in this, you could be the victim instead of Jimmy. How would Liz and I ever know?" She sounded panicky. "You could get hit by the car and be lying in a hospital in a coma. How would we find out what happened to you? Your parents would never know. We'd spend the rest of our lives wondering. *We* don't know how to time travel." When Sophie finished what was for her a very long speech, her entire body was tense.

"I promise both of you. I *swear* I'll be careful. I won't put myself in danger or risk getting hurt and putting you through that. I *will* come home tomorrow night and I'll text you the second I get back."

"Olivia, this breaks all the time-travel rules," said Liz. "What if there's a law you don't know about yet? What if you save Jimmy but you're trapped in the past as a punishment?"

Silence blanketed them as all three contemplated the possible outcomes of Olivia's plan.

"I never imagined I would say this," Liz went on. "But we've got to come up with a way, something we can do, if the worst ever did happen. If someday you didn't come home."

Sophie started to cry, softly, quietly. Her face crumbled. "Liz, don't say that. Don't put the thought out into the universe. Everything's been okay up to now. Don't jinx it. *Please.*"

Olivia squeezed their hands. "Hey, you guys are my family. I would never make you wonder. I'd find a way to let you know what happened. Come on. Let's go back out there and celebrate Liz's exhibit." She turned to Liz. "It's wonderful, by the way. You did a great job." Olivia reached out and hugged her, then pulled Sophie into a long, tight embrace. "I'll be careful, Sophie. I promise."

Olivia had no idea what she was going to do or how she was going to do it, but she knew she had to save Jimmy Bou. And she had to do it without telling Steven. She hated that she was going to keep a secret from him, especially one as big as this. But he'd always said he didn't want to know about the future. As uncomfortable as it was to deceive him, she had no choice. Olivia was on her own.

Although Olivia had told Steven she'd go to Benjamin Shipley's wake with him, she wished she could crawl back into her PJs and stay home, where it was warm and cozy. There was nothing like having supper in your pajamas, curled up on the couch with a glass of wine, watching TV when it was miserable outside. But she had promised, and she couldn't back out at the last minute. Steven had told her the killer often attended his victim's wake or funeral. Olivia was going to see if she could spot him.

At five-thirty, Olivia climbed the stairs and waited at the doorway. A minute later, Steven appeared in the hall. They grinned at each other, both happy to be back to normal.

"Hi, are you ready?"

"I sure am," he said, reaching out.

Olivia grasped his hand. It was warm and felt familiar. She stepped back into her room, leading him into the future.

"Something smells good. What are you making?"

"Good old American comfort food," Olivia answered as they turned, then walked through the doorway and descended the stairs to her kitchen.

"Comfort food? What's that?"

"Just what it sounds like." She gave him a brief explanation. "Tonight, we're having mac 'n' cheese." Seeing a brief frown, Olivia added, "Macaroni and cheese."

"Swell."

As they entered the kitchen, the timer on the stove buzzed. She grabbed a mitt and pulled the casserole from the oven. Steven leaned over and inhaled.

"Mmm, I love cheese," he exclaimed. "I got that from my mother. We had cheese after every meal—brie, Camembert, chèvre—with bread, of course. She never lost her French habits." He smiled, then pointed to a bottle of wine next to the bright red toaster on the countertop. "Would you like me to open this?"

"Yes, please."

Olivia filled their plates, and they sat at the table, covered in a black-and-white checked cloth with witches flying on broomsticks. A small carved pumpkin sat in the center of the table, a tiny tea light flickering inside.

"I see you're still enjoying your Halloween decorations." He chuckled as he picked up his wineglass and reached out. They clinked.

"I found out something that could be important but I forgot to tell you last night."

Steven stopped eating, fork in mid-air. "What's that?"

"When I was having breakfast with the girls, Molly said she saw Leon Quigg almost get run over by a car a couple of minutes after eleven Wednesday night." Olivia related the story the teenager had told.

"She was sure about the time?"

"Yes, she said the clock on The Green had just chimed."

"How did you react? What did you say?"

"She called him the mailman, so I made sure she was talking about Leon. I said I'd met him and thought he was nice. That puts Leon near the crime scene at the time of the murder, doesn't it?"

"Yes, it does. Thanks. I found out this morning that Rudy Hartwicke saw him, too. It always helps to have two people say the same thing. It makes our case stronger. We're looking at Leon seriously now."

"You'll get there. You always do."

"So, how was the exhibit? Did you have a good time this afternoon?"

Olivia swallowed hard. She'd done a good job pushing that newspaper article to the back of her mind, as well as the questionable, and risky, decision she'd made. Not wanting to let on that anything was wrong, she banished all thoughts of Jimmy Bou and told Steven a couple of stories about townspeople who had attended the exhibit.

Lying to Steven sickened Olivia, but she remembered her reasons why and pushed the feelings aside.

Chapter Twenty-Seven

SUNDAY, NOVEMBER 4, 1934

There wasn't a single parking spot open within two blocks of Gettman's Funeral Home when Steven and Olivia arrived. He had told her to dress warmly and, as they hurried along the sidewalk, Olivia was glad she'd worn a winter coat. As usual, he had on his Sunday suit, and she'd chosen a crêpe-de-Chine dress in a dark golden yellow with fancy stitching down the front, brown suede pumps, and a small leather bag.

"Listen, Steven, how do you want to do this? Should we stay together?"

"Let's play it by ear. But, stay within view of everyone in case he really did see you. And just so you know, I'll be keeping an eye on you."

Olivia swallowed hard. By now, everyone in town knew she was staying with Steven. It wouldn't take a rocket scientist to know she'd been the silhouette at the window. What if the killer had decided to attend the calling hours, or had no choice and was obligated to be there? Would he be able to get her alone and silently stab her without anyone noticing? The wake was being held in the main viewing room, but there was a coat check off to the side, isolated alcoves with chairs for quiet conversations, and a long hallway where the restrooms were located. Olivia wasn't taking any chances. She had no intention of wandering off to any of these areas.

Mourners packed the large room. Upon entering, Olivia registered an assault on her olfactory senses. The closed-in space reeked with a mix of cloying sweetness from the flower arrangements—she blamed all those lilies—and choking cigarette smoke. She nearly gagged and dug out a mint. She'd focus on that until she acclimated and no longer noticed the smell. Steven led her to the receiving line. With an unspoken agreement, they refrained from conversation until they reached Alice and Theo Shipley. Steven shook Theo's hand, and they expressed their condolences.

Olivia spotted Will across the room and gave a little wave. He nodded, allowing her a small smile. When Steven wandered off to talk with his partner, Olivia moved to an empty corner where she could see everyone, and everyone could see her. From her vantage point, she scrutinized the men, mentally discarding the short, fat ones and the tall, skinny ones. She paid attention as they walked from place to place and noticed how they moved, their gestures, and if they were right- or left-handed. As she eliminated them one by one, she wondered how accurate her memory of the killer was.

Suddenly, he was standing right in front of her.

"Hi, Olivia," Jimmy Bou said.

"Jimmy, I'm so glad to see somebody I know. Can you keep me company while Steven's talking with people?"

"Sure," he exclaimed, grinning ear to ear.

"In the briefing the other day, I heard you say Leon Quigg was your neighbor. Do you live with your family?"

"Yeah, my mom and dad, and my little sister, Adeline. We call her Addie. And my dog, Waffles."

"I like dogs. What breed is Waffles?"

"She's a cocker spaniel. I got her last year."

"Was she a puppy?"

"Yup." He pulled a worn leather wallet from a back pocket and extracted a family photograph. "There's me holding Waffles. My parents gave her to me on Christmas day."

"She's beautiful. I like the red bow around her neck. I bet you're teaching her all kinds of things."

"I am! How to sit and fetch and shake hands and lie down."

"Do you walk her every day?"

"Every night after supper. We always take the same route, up Tulip and across Victoria to The Green. She likes running on the grass. I chase her and throw sticks. After that, we turn onto Chiltington and walk up past Steven's, then home."

"Wow, that sounds like good exercise for her."

"For me, too." He laughed, then noticed a clock on the wall. "It's almost eight. I'm late tonight. I better get home so I can take her out. Are you coming to the station in the morning?"

"I'm not sure, probably. Enjoy your walk, Jimmy, and thanks for keeping me company."

"My pleasure. Hope I see you tomorrow." His caramel-colored eyes sparkled.

Olivia settled back into her corner and mulled over the information she had gained. Jimmy left his house every night before eight, and she knew the route he would take. Now she had to come up with a plan.

A few minutes later, another young man approached her. "Hello, Miss Watson." He doffed his wool tweed cap, then put it back on. As he adjusted it, pulling the back with his left hand and holding the visor with his right to settle it in place, Olivia noticed his thumb. He had a murderer's thumb.

"Leon, hi," Olivia said, trying not to stare. "How are you?"

"Not bad." He smiled shyly.

"Did you know Mr. Shipley?"

"Only to say hello. He was always working when I delivered the mail, so I never saw him. I'm surprised to see you here. You couldn't have known him, did you?"

Is he looking at me funny?

"No, I never met him. He was Steven's neighbor, so I came to pay my respects."

"That's nice of you. I can't believe someone would shoot him at his own front door. And with Detective Blackwell living right across the street," Leon exclaimed.

Could it be him?

"Yes, it was risky."

"Did you and Detective Blackwell see anything?"

Does he know it was me at the window?

"We were in the kitchen when we heard the shot," she lied. "I thought it was a car backfiring but Steven knew right away it was a gun."

"I suppose being a cop he went outside to check, right?"

"Yes, but he missed him. Whoever it was ran away."

"They'll get him. Say, did you enjoy the Halloween party? Being from a big city like Syracuse, it probably seemed awfully simple to you."

"No, not at all. You did a wonderful job, and the kids were sure happy."

"Thank you. I try to do something special for them on holidays. Childhood should be fun, don't you think? Kids should laugh a lot."

Olivia thought that was an unusual comment for a young man to make, but before she could respond, Steven appeared over Leon's shoulder.

"Olivia, are you ready to leave? Hi, Leon."

"Hello, Detective. Well, I'll be seeing you." He crossed the room to the entrance and disappeared from view.

CHAPTER TWENTY-SEVEN

"Have you seen enough?" Steven whispered.

"Yes."

"So, what did you think? Did anybody look familiar, ring a bell?" Steven asked when they were in the car.

"No," she groaned. "I can't believe it was only a few days ago. I'm sorry."

"That's all right. Did you have a chance to observe Theo and Leon, especially now that we know Leon was nearby at the time of the murder?"

"It could be both of them or neither one. I didn't talk with Theo, but Leon came over to say hello." Olivia repeated their conversation. "When he asked if we saw anything, I lied through my teeth. I hope I was convincing."

"I bet you were. You're good at getting information out of people without giving anything away."

"There was something strange, though. Is Leon related to Theo?" Olivia asked.

"Why?"

"He's got a murderer's thumb, too. I noticed it when he was fixing his cap."

"That's good to know. I found out Leon's mother worked for Mr. Shipley in the five-and-dime."

Olivia made the leap in a flash. "Are you saying you think Shipley was Leon's father?"

"It's a strong possibility. It's time I talk with Leon Quigg. And I've got to send Jimmy back to his father with a couple more questions."

They reached the corner, then crossed Victoria to drive the last block home.

"If only the dead could talk, huh?" Steven said.

"Oh, my God," Olivia exclaimed.

Steven's arm flew out to protect her as he slammed on the brakes. "What? What is it?"

"I remembered something."

"Jeez, Olivia, don't do that. I thought I was about to run over someone."

"Sorry."

"Okay. What did you remember?" He chuckled. "This had better be good."

She grimaced in the dark. "I remembered the expression on Mr. Shipley's face when he answered the door and saw who was there."

"Ah, the dead speaking. How did he look?"

"Surprised at who it was. *Very* surprised."

"So, he knew his killer."

Chapter Twenty-Eight

It was freezing when he left the wake. It wasn't over, but he'd had enough. He'd wandered around Gettman's for more than an hour, greeting people, smiling, and listening in on their conversations. Occasionally, he made small talk.

For years after he'd lost his mother, his only desire had been punishment for the man who'd ruined his life. Eventually, he realized he didn't know when he'd be able to carry out the sentence, and justice would wait. He threw the hatred into a dark corner at the back of his mind and moved on.

It was over now and he really could move on.

His anticipation of curling up in the armchair near a crackling fire with a hot drink and Mark Twain's *The Mysterious Stranger* at its peak, he reached the house and let himself in. He turned on lights, got a fire going, and went up to change, chuckling at himself. He hadn't gotten into his pajamas this early since he was a kid. Maybe he should make hot cocoa instead of tea. Sure, why not? And a cheese sandwich. That sounded good. He hadn't eaten much for supper.

Chapter Twenty-Nine

Alice Shipley walked up the path to the house she'd lived in so many years ago—it was strange being there. She didn't know if she wanted to move back and live in Knightsbridge or not. She had to consider her work with the Women's Trade Union League in Syracuse. That was the most important thing in her life, except Theo, of course. She was so proud of him she wondered how her heart could hold such joy. And Leon. That sweet boy had grown into a lovely young man. For a long time now, Alice had felt like he was every bit her son, too.

Coming back to the League, if she was honest, it wasn't only the work they did but the friendships she'd made as well. Alice had become an active member in that female fraternity and enjoyed the company of the women who worked alongside her.

Her cousin Edith was a fierce feminist. Edith had been active in the suffrage movement and had convinced Alice to join the suffragettes. Once she'd met those passionate women and had learned what it was all about, Alice had caught the spark. She'd dedicated her life to improving the lives of women. Alice supposed she could start a chapter of the league in Knightsbridge. That would help grow the movement.

Putting the Women's Trade Union League aside, did she want to live here on a permanent basis? Knightsbridge represented her old life, and she hadn't been that person in a very long time. Well, she had plenty of time to think about it and decide.

Alice pushed open the front door and entered the grand foyer. She hung her coat and hat on a brass hall tree, checked her hair in the black-and-gold-framed mirror above the mahogany table, and went into the living room. Theo was sitting in one of the big leather chairs near the fire, navy bathrobe tied closed over his pajamas, reading. She had to smile—like Leon, her son loved to read.

Theo looked up at the sound of footsteps and set his book on the side table. He got up, reached Alice in two steps, and pulled her into a warm embrace. "Are you all right, Mom?"

"Yes, I am. Thank you. And thanks for letting me take your car. It's freezing out." She stepped back from the hug and examined his face. "What about you?" Her brows met in the middle.

"I'm fine. I'm sorry I left you there, but I couldn't take it anymore. I suppose things were meant to work out this way with Father. I'd hoped we could make peace, but it wasn't in the cards." He grabbed her hand. "Here, come sit by the fire. Would you like me to get you a drink? I made hot chocolate."

"I think we can both use a real drink, Theo. There's something I need to tell you."

"Uh oh. That sounds ominous. I'll get a bottle."

Alice kicked off her shoes and tucked her stockinged feet under her in the roomy club chair. The heat from the fire felt wonderful—she reached out and warmed her hands.

Theo returned with a bottle of scotch and two cut-crystal tumblers. As he poured generous portions into each glass, the glow from the fire lit up the amber liquid, making it look alive.

Alice waited until he set the bottle on the table and settled in his chair before she began. She had decided on the way home she would be calm and objective and would relay the facts as she knew them.

205

Theo had the right to his own feelings and to make up his own mind. She took a gulp of whiskey. "I wasn't sure I'd ever tell you this, but given the circumstances we find ourselves in, you deserve to know." Alice took a deep breath. "Theo, you have a brother, a half-brother actually."

Theo slowly nodded. "I can't say I'm surprised. I know he cheated on you. The odds were there might have been a child out of wedlock somewhere."

"I'd like to tell you about it because there's something I want to do."

"Tell me."

"There was a girl who worked at the lunch counter in the store."

"Our store?"

"Yes, the one here in Knightsbridge. She was my friend, the best friend I ever had. I want to make this very clear, Theo. Lillian was a good person. She got involved with your father before he and I began stepping out together. She wasn't the kind of person who'd spend time with a married man. Never. She was Catholic and believed deeply in the sanctity of marriage."

Spring 1907

Alice practically skipped through the aisles of Shipley's, her new cream-colored trumpet skirt brushing her ankles as she moved, her weekly treat tucked in her draw-string bag. It was turning into a warm day, perfect for an ice-cream soda and a walk along the river with her best friend, Lillian.

Friday was Alice's favorite day of the week. Alice's father adored her and every Friday morning at breakfast gave her two crisp dollar bills and a quarter. Practically a fortune! Some weeks she went to a fancy dress shop and purchased something new for her closet. Other times, she wandered through the new five-and-dime emporium picking up cologne, powder, hankies, or stationery. Occasionally, she bought a big bouquet of flowers or new sheet music for the piano. This afternoon she'd bought a package of beautifully embroidered handkerchiefs, a box of pale blue linen writing paper and matching envelopes, and a stick of sealing wax.

Alice's path would never have crossed the path Lillian was on if it hadn't been for the lunch counter in Shipley's. From the very first minute of that very first day when Alice sat down and ordered an egg salad sandwich and coffee, she and Lillian had become friends. Alice learned Lillian had had to leave school in the eighth grade and had worked various jobs before being hired at the five-and-dime. Although Alice had never worked a day in her life, somehow, something magical connected the two young women. Alice always tried to arrive shortly before Lillian's shift was over. Then they would go to the park and feed the ducks or go for a walk along the river. Sometimes Alice treated Lillian to an ice cream, but it usually took some convincing. Lillian was proud and didn't like accepting what she called charity. But, always, every time they met, they talked and talked and talked.

Which was why this day was about to be so devastating for Alice.

When Alice sat at the counter, Lillian grabbed her hand and squeezed it warmly, as she always did, but when Lillian placed the tall glass filled with ice cream, soda, and whipped cream in front of her, Alice knew something was wrong. Lillian wasn't making eye contact. Raised to keep her thoughts to herself until the appropriate moment, Alice said nothing until she'd finished her soda, Lillian had hung up her apron, and they'd left the store.

They chose to walk along the Mohawk River on this glorious May day. As they strolled arm in arm, sunlight glinting off the rushing water, Lillian said the words that changed Alice's life.

"Alice, my dear, I have some bad news."

"I knew something was wrong." She stopped walking and faced her friend. "What is it? Can I help?"

"I'm leaving Knightsbridge. I have to go away."

"Why?" In her despair, Alice nearly screamed, her eyes filling with tears. Lillian was everything to her.

"I'm going to live with my aunt and uncle. They found me a job where I can make more money. I can't stay with my parents any longer. They need to take care of my brother. It's too much for them to have an extra mouth to feed."

"Nooo," Alice cried. "You can't. What will I do without you?"

"One of these days, you'll meet that special boy and he'll sweep you off your feet. You'll get married and have lots of children." Lillian swallowed hard.

Alice stared at her. As she studied her friend's face, she knew with sudden clarity that Lillian was lying to her. But she also knew that no matter how many times she asked, Lillian would never tell her the real reason she was moving away.

Alice leaned back in the chair, aware that the room had become chilly. "Would you put some more kindling on the fire, Theo?"

Her son rose and placed another log on the grate, causing a small burst of sparks that filled the hearth. "Are you all right? You look exhausted. Maybe you should go to bed. You can finish telling me in the morning. Even though you didn't have feelings for Father anymore, I think this has been an ordeal for you. I don't want you getting sick."

"Yes, you're right. The rest can wait until breakfast." She kissed her son good night and went upstairs.

Chapter Thirty

DECEMBER 1916 – SYRACUSE, NEW YORK

I*t wouldn't be long now. Lillian didn't need a doctor to tell her this would be her last Christmas, and she probably wouldn't see her tulips bloom in the spring. Determined to savor every moment she had left, she filled her lungs with the scent of the pine boughs decorating the stores, felt the bite of cold air on her cheek, and relished the sound of birdsong at their kitchen window feeder.*

Lillian had scraped together enough money to buy three special gifts to put under the tree for her son. This morning, she'd stayed in bed an extra hour to get as much rest as possible before heading downtown. After forcing herself to eat a poached egg and little bit of toast, she'd caught the trolley from Tipperary Hill to Salina Street in the center of Syracuse. Lillian knew what she was going to buy—a scarf and a new pair of pajamas. She'd purchased the book Leon wanted two weeks ago and was still debating about the inscription she would write. She couldn't be dramatic or too obvious because she didn't want him to panic, but these would be the last written words she would ever say to him, and they had to be special.

It had taken her a long time to decide on the scarf and pajamas. Like the words, these final gifts must be chosen with care. While struggling home one evening in the snow and icy wind, it hit her. She would buy something that would hug him and keep him warm after she was gone.

Lillian knew it would take at least three trips downtown to do her shopping, because her energy had gotten so low. Three short trips instead of an entire afternoon like she used to do. One day last week, when she'd stopped in Chappell's department store to look at children's clothing, she found exactly what she wanted. Yesterday had been payday, and here she was today choosing the last Christmas gifts she would ever buy.

As she was exiting Chappell's, Lillian saw her in the crowd of holiday shoppers. Shocked and shaken to her core, she spun around and headed back inside. But it was too late.

"Lillian! Lillian!" the woman called. "Wait!"

Lillian stopped, closed her eyes tightly, and steeled herself. She turned around. There stood Alice, arms full of packages, joyful wonder painted on her face.

"It is you," Alice exclaimed as she tried to embrace her old friend.

"Hello, Alice. You look wonderful. How are you?"

As Alice studied her friend, her face slowly registered shock. "You're sick. What is it?"

Lillian sighed. She knew Alice would keep asking if she didn't tell her. What difference did it make now? "Consumption."

Alice gasped. "Have you had any treatment?"

"No, it's too late for that." She certainly wasn't going to tell Alice the truth. Like how she had written to Ben for help but had never received an answer. He hadn't sent so much as a dime for the treatment that could save her life. Lillian forced herself to smile. "But, tell me about you. I heard you married. Congratulations. Do you have children?"

"Yes, but it's not going well." Alice looked about to cry.

"I'm sorry." That's Alice, Lillian thought. Why can't I be honest like that?

Alice pointed to the pajamas peeking out of the bag. "Do you have children?"

"A son. He'll be nine next month." She saw Alice glance at her left hand and told the standard lie. "His father died."

"Oh, I'm so sorry. Here," Alice set her packages on the ground, pulled off a leather glove, and extracted a small notebook and pencil from her bag. "This is our new telephone number. If there's anything I can do, call me." She looked close to tears again. "Lillian, I missed you so much. It was awful when you left. Let me help you, please."

"Thank you." Lillian fought back her own tears. The lump in her throat was so big she didn't think she could get the words out. "I missed you, too," she whispered. "But, like I said, it's too late. There's nothing to be done." She reached out and enveloped her old friend in a tight embrace. *It's now or never, Lillian. Tell her or it'll be too late.* "Besides my son, you were the best thing in my life."

She turned and fled.

Chapter Thirty-One

MONDAY, NOVEMBER 5, 1934

S teven entered the CID room, grabbed his phone, and dialed. A deep voice answered on the first ring.

"Knightsbridge Post Office. Duncan Macrae speaking."

"Duncan, good morning. It's Steven Blackwell."

"Steven, what can I do for you?"

"I need to interview Leon Quigg first thing this morning. I want to catch him before he goes out on his route."

"Sure, he won't be leaving for a while. He has to sort all his customers' mail first, and he just started. It takes at least an hour, sometimes two, depending on how much there is. You can use my office if you want to come over."

"Thanks, I'll do that."

"Come to the back and ring the bell. I'll let you in."

Steven went to see Chief Thompson. Through the open door, he saw his boss biting into his first pastry of the day. He knocked on the frame and entered.

"Good morning, Chief."

Andy Thompson said good morning around a mouthful of dessert.

"I'm going to the post office to interview Leon Quigg. He's become a suspect."

"That's a surprise. You're sure?"

"It looks that way. That's what I'm working on today."

"All right. I'll be here if you need anything."

"Thanks. Actually, there is one thing you could do. It would speed things up."

"What is it?"

"While I'm there, would you write up a warrant to search Leon Quigg's house for the murder weapon and have somebody take it over to Judge Randolph?"

"Sure. What's the justification?"

"Several people saw him running from the vicinity of the crime scene after the shot was fired. And I think he's Benjamin Shipley's illegitimate son."

"Holy mother…Well, I can't say I'm surprised. Ben wasn't what you'd call a womanizer, but he did stray. I'll do it now. As soon as the office opens, I'll send Charlie over and tell him to wait for it."

"Thanks. Let's add a search for correspondence linking Leon to Benjamin Shipley, too."

"You got it."

Steven went looking for Ralph and Pete, catching part of a conversation when he entered the patrol room.

"I'm waiting until the rain lets up. I don't feel like getting drenched before we even start the day."

"I'm with you, Petey," Ralph said.

Steven approached them. "I'm afraid I've got bad news, Pete."

"Uh oh. What is it?"

"Looks like you're going to get wet after all. I have a job for you two."

Both patrolmen groaned.

"I need you to stand guard at Leon Quigg's house while I go to the post office to question him. We're getting a warrant to search and I don't want him to go home and remove anything before we get there."

"Sure, Steven, we understand," Ralph said.

"We'll get some rain gear out of the supply closet," said Pete.

"If everything goes smoothly, you won't be out there long." Steven checked his watch. "I'm leaving in a few minutes. I want you to be at Leon's by seven-thirty. Charlie should be back here with the warrant by the time I'm finished at the post office. I'll have a quick briefing, then Will and I'll search the house."

"Okay. What do we do about the briefing, Steven?"

"Jimmy Bou'll update you. Have you questioned Pinky's' regulars yet?"

"Not yet," Ralph said.

"All right, I'm going to have Ray follow up on that so you can do something else. Jimmy will explain later."

When Steven returned to the detectives' room, Will was leaning over his desk, reading the morning paper. Black hair fell onto his high forehead, brawny arms rested on strong thighs. Steven said he was going to interview Leon Quigg and asked if he'd accompany him.

"Sure, I can finish this later."

"Before we leave, I want to tell you what I found out Saturday. It makes a difference in how we listen to Leon." Steven told his partner about Leon's childhood, the tragedies he'd survived, and the murderer's thumb, raising the question of his relationship to Benjamin Shipley.

Will whistled. "That puts a new perspective on things. Suddenly he has a motive. If Shipley was Leon's father, and he abandoned him and his mother, Leon could have built up resentment for years. Maybe something triggered it and he took revenge."

Icy rain poured down and snuck inside their coat collars as Steven and Will ran across the lot behind the station to the back door of the Knightsbridge Post Office. They crowded together under the tiny awning while Steven rang the bell.

"Where did fall go? It's too early for this," Will commented, shivering.

The heavy door swung open and Duncan Macrae's voice boomed, "Come in. Come in. What a day, huh?"

Steven and Will slapped their fedoras against their legs to shake off the water, then hung their coats and hats on nearby hooks.

"Before we talk with Leon, I'd like to ask you a couple of questions," Steven told the burly manager.

"Sure." He led them into a cramped room in a back corner. Two wooden file cabinets stood against one wall, a small table piled with papers and file folders sat between them. The tiny window needed a good cleaning, blinds with a broken slat hung crookedly.

"How would you describe Leon Quigg, Duncan?" Steven asked.

"He does a good job. He's reliable, always on time. Never complains about the weather like some of the fellas. A bit quiet but he's a good worker."

"What's his work schedule?" asked Will.

"Gets here at six to sort the mail for his route. He's finished and out the door by eight at the latest. He stops back around eleven-thirty for his lunch break and to pick up his second bag. He's usually done with his afternoon route around three or four. The job is Monday through Friday and one Saturday a month."

"Is he especially friendly with any of the other employees?" Steven asked.

"There aren't many opportunities for that. The sorting takes concentration and the mail carriers are gone all day on their routes. Leon's pleasant enough but, like I said, he spends most of his day out on the streets."

"What about lunch?" said Will. "Does he eat with anyone in particular?"

"No, all the men come back at pretty much the same time. There's only one table in the lunchroom, so they eat together, then go back out."

"Thanks, Duncan. Would you get him now?" Steven said.

When the post office manager went to get Leon, Steven looked out into the sorting room. Several men worked in their shirt-sleeves, ties loosened, jackets and caps hanging on nearby hooks. They stood behind tables, putting piles of envelopes and magazines in order, evidently according to the way they walked or drove their routes. Behind them, covering the entire wall, was a system of shelves and cubbyholes. Steven could see writing on the edges of each section, but he was too far away to read it. When he saw a man take a handful of mail from a cubby and distribute the envelopes onto his table, he guessed the compartments made up a preliminary sorting scheme.

Oblivious to his surroundings, Leon Quigg stood at the far table with his head down and his hands flying, concentrating on sorting piles of mail. He must have heard footsteps on the concrete, because he looked up as his boss approached. Steven saw Duncan speak, then Leon peek around him, peering toward the office. He spied Steven and gave a friendly wave.

Duncan Macrae deposited the mailman in his office, left again, and Steven got down to business. "Leon, we need to ask you some questions."

"Sure, Detective."

"We have several witnesses who saw you running across The Green around eleven Wednesday night. I'd like to know what you were doing."

"Going home after my walk."

"The information we have is that you were coming from somewhere

216

in the middle of The Green. It's pitch black there late at night. Why were you walking on The Green in the dark?"

"Normally, I don't. I was going up Chiltington, but it was cold and I didn't have a heavy jacket on. I decided to cut my walk short and head across The Green. Then, I thought if I started running I might warm up a little." He grimaced. "It didn't work. I was freezing by the time I got home."

"You were there around the time Benjamin Shipley was shot."

Leon's jaw dropped. "Is that what I heard? I thought it was a firecracker. You know, for Halloween."

"Where were you when you heard it?" Will asked.

"Probably around the middle, like you said. I'm sorry, Detective. If I had known, I would've told you. I never heard a gunshot before. I didn't realize that's what it was."

"Did you see anyone? Especially walking up Chiltington," Steven asked.

"No, the only thing I was thinking about was getting home as fast as I could. I didn't have gloves on either."

"You were running so fast that you almost got yourself killed, Leon," Will said.

Leon grimaced. "Yeah, I know. That was dumb. But the streets were empty, and everything was so quiet it never occurred to me there'd be cars out that late. I didn't look."

Steven shifted gears. "Do you own a gun, Leon?"

"No, why would I have a gun?"

"What time did you leave the Halloween party?"

"About quarter to ten."

"Where did you go after you left?"

"I stopped in The Three Lords for a drink."

"Did you talk to anybody?"

"No, I stood at the bar."

"Then you went for your walk?" Steven asked.

"That's right. I took the long way home. I like to walk."

"Leon, I have to tell you that right now Judge Randolph is signing a warrant for us to search your house."

"Why?"

"We're going to look for the murder weapon."

"I told you I don't have a gun."

"Would you like to be there while we search? You have that right."

"No, I'd rather do my route. There's nothing in my house, Detective. Go ahead and look. The front door's unlocked."

"All right. The warrant also gives us permission to look for any correspondence between you and Mr. Shipley."

Steven thought he saw a flash of something in Leon's eyes, a sort of standing to attention. What was it? Surprise that the police knew there was a connection between him and Benjamin Shipley? Fear that they'd guessed his motive?

"I never got a letter from Mr. Shipley."

"Then I'm sure our search will prove that. Leon, are you sure there's nothing you want to tell us that could help find the person who killed Mr. Shipley?"

"No, Detective, there isn't."

As he watched Steven and Will leave the post office, Leon thought of the letter he'd hidden in his dresser.

It was Leon's Saturday to work. He was alone in the back room of the post office. It was pouring outside, and he wished he was at the library in Syracuse with Alice instead of having to trot around Knightsbridge delivering mail in the rain. He'd almost finished sorting all the bills, notices, letters, cards, and magazines when he came upon an envelope. A small piece of paper attached with a paper clip covered the recipient's name and address. Leon read:

Please extend our most sincere apologies to Mr. Shipley for the long delay in sending this letter. It was found behind a cabinet Thursday night when we painted and the furniture had to be moved out of the way. Evidently, when the post office employee was sorting the mail, the envelope slid to the back of the counter and fell to the floor, where it's been for all these years trapped between the cabinet and the wall. We hope this hasn't caused any difficulties for Mr. Shipley.

The manager of the Syracuse post office branch had signed his name and dated the note two days ago.

Leon removed the paper clip and note and gasped. The writing on the envelope was in his mother's hand. He stumbled to a wooden chair and dropped. Taking deep breaths so he wouldn't pass out, Leon read the postmark, November 22, 1916. Oh, my God! His mother had written this letter just months before she died. It had been lost in the post office for nearly eighteen years.

Leon didn't hesitate. He could always tell Mr. Shipley the envelope had been damaged. He tore it open and extracted two pages of pale blue stationary. His mother had written:

Dear Benjamin,

I'm writing this second letter because I haven't heard anything from my first one. I know you are busy, but I am running out of time. In case you've forgotten what my first letter said, I will tell you again.

I am dying. I have consumption, what they are calling tuberculosis. I only have six months left to live. This concerns you because we have a son. Did you ever wonder why I left Knightsbridge? Before you even think the thought, yes, Leon is your son. You know full well that you are the

219

only man I have ever been with. There is no question. Leon is your son, Ben.

I have been working hard since I moved to Syracuse but I don't make very much. There is a treatment they give to patients at a place called The Little Red Cottage, in Saranac Lake. They've had a lot of success with it. The man who runs the clinic is called Dr. Trudeau. He is my only chance, Ben. I need some money to pay for the treatment. My uncle will drive me there in his motor car. I don't know for sure what the cost will be but my doctor told me probably between $50.00-$75.00, depending on how long I have to stay there.

I have never asked you for anything. I am asking you now to help me so I can live and raise our son. I cannot leave him an orphan. Please, please, anything you can spare will help me. In the memory of our lovely time together and in the hope for our son's future, I beg of you to help me.

Yours, Lillian

Leon felt the wind knocked out of him, as if someone had punched him in the stomach. Reading his mother's words and seeing her handwriting reignited her memory, bringing her back to life. Leon felt as though he could reach out and touch her, hear her Irish lilt, and smell the lilac she wore.

Even more earth-shattering than finding this missive was learning its contents. For nearly two decades, Leon had wondered who his father was. Now he had a name.

Leon felt dizzy. He bent over, put his head between his knees, and tried to control his accelerated breathing. This was so much worse than he had ever imagined.

Benjamin Shipley—his father—could have saved his mother's life.

But he didn't.

The richest man in town could have bought the Little Red Cottage, but he refused to send his mother fifty lousy dollars.

The sadness that had lurked around the edges of Leon's life turned to anger and filled him with a rage threatening to explode.

The weather hadn't let up. Icy rain drenched Steven and Will on their dash back to the station.

"Tell me we don't have to go out again today," Will groaned.

"Ha! You wish," Steven exclaimed. "You don't think I'm going to Leon's house without my partner, do you?" Steven chuckled.

Someone had turned on the heat and the CID room was toasty warm. They hung their dripping outer gear on the coat tree. Steven poured a steaming cup of coffee from his Thermos and faced his partner across their desks.

"I don't need to ask what you thought of that," Steven said.

Will shook his head, looking perplexed. "This is a tricky one. I have to admit, I thought we were going to eliminate Leon. I don't read him as a killer. He sounded genuine. He was relaxed, not at all threatened by our questions, but–and here's why I'm changing my mind–his reasoning didn't make sense to me. I didn't believe the walk late at night and his excuse for running across The Green."

"I agree, but, take me through your thinking, will you?"

"All right. First, he was in charge of the Halloween party. He worked all day delivering the mail, then he worked all evening at the Elks Club and stayed to help clean up. By that time, you'd think he'd be tired. A late-night walk seems like a flimsy excuse."

"Plus, it was a work night," Steven observed. "He'd have to be up early the next morning to get ready and be at the post office by six."

"Right. And second, if he walked up to The Three Lords from the Elks Club, he knew how cold it was. This business about running to warm up…." Will shook his head. "It's something a child would say.

He could have gone home to put on a heavier jacket if he wanted to go for a stroll. Besides, who goes out walking at eleven o'clock at night?"

"I can't believe he never heard a gunshot before," Steven said. "He must have walked past the shooting booth at the county fair at least once in his life."

Will pursed his lips. "I suppose it's possible he never went. Seems unlikely, though."

"He had motive and opportunity, Will."

"It's only motive if he knew Shipley was the father who abandoned him."

"True."

At eight o'clock, the officers on Steven's team crowded into the smoky patrol room, exchanging stories about what they'd done over the weekend. Chief Thompson walked in and lit one of his ubiquitous Camels as soon as he sat down. Steven and Will entered on the heels of the chief.

"Good morning, men," Steven began. The room quieted immediately. "We've got a lot to accomplish today, so the briefing's going to be short. If you've checked the board, you know we've eliminated Rudy Hartwicke. Theo Shipley has a strong motive, would probably do anything for his mother, and, according to a friend of his, has a dark side. We know he was here the night of the murder. We're close to confirming his alibi, but we still need to talk with Mrs. McMillan and some regular customers at Pinky's who were there Wednesday night. Ray, I'd like you to take care of those interviews." He gave him the list of names.

"Right, Steven."

"We're keeping Theo on the board until we're sure he wasn't involved. Now, Leon Quigg has become our strongest suspect." A buzz went around the room.

CHAPTER THIRTY-ONE

"Leon?"

"The mailman?"

"What's he got to do with it?"

Steven explained that four people had seen Leon running from the general direction of the Shipley home moments after the shot was heard.

"We haven't considered him because there doesn't seem to be a motive or connection between him and Mr. Shipley. But Coop and Bobby Pinkerton confused Leon and Theo, so it's possible Judge Randolph saw Leon when he thought he'd seen Theo. And there's more than a superficial resemblance between them. They both have what's known as a murderer's thumb. Now, don't go off on the wrong track," Steven hurried to add, as several patrolmen voiced indignation. "A murderer's thumb is the name of a particular kind of deformed thumb. It's a condition that someone is born with. It doesn't mean either of them is our killer.

"Listen and picture this." Steven described the thumb. "Here's the important part, fellas. You get a murderer's thumb from one of your parents. You know how some people look like their mother or their father? How a child might have brown hair or green eyes like one of their parents? This is the same thing. Now...Benjamin Shipley had a murderer's thumb." Steven paused for the information to sink in and the implication to register. "We know that's where Theo got his because I've met Alice and she doesn't have the deformed thumb. We need to find out where Leon got his. Mr. Shipley cheated on Alice, so we have the possibility of illegitimate children."

The buzz got louder. Steven let it hum for a minute, allowing the adrenalin to surge, then he pulled his officers back.

"Will and I are going to search Leon's house for the murder weapon and evidence of communication between him and Mr. Shipley. And, since Leon seems to like reading so much, we need to talk with Miss

223

Cartwright at the Library to see what she can tell us about him. Jimmy, I'd like you to tackle that."

"You got it."

"We're going to build a picture of Leon's life. Ralph and Pete will talk with the members of the Elks to see if anybody knows what Leon does and where he goes when he's not working."

"There's about a dozen of us this year, Steven," Jimmy Bou interrupted. "Talking to everybody could take all day."

"Why don't you help after you've finished at the library? You can ride over to the house with Will and me, talk with Ralph and Pete, and make a plan."

Jimmy gave the thumbs up. "Okay."

"That's it, men. You've all got your assignments. Be sure to keep checking the murder board for updates. I expect there'll be quite a few today."

Chapter Thirty-Two

Early Monday morning, Alice and Theo Shipley sat at the kitchen table, still dressed in their nightclothes and warm bathrobes, enjoying the treat of having breakfast together, neither wanting to talk about the funeral taking place later that day.

"The omelet was delicious, Theo. You're a wonderful cook." Alice beamed at her son's culinary skills.

"Eggs are easy, Mom. Wait until you taste my pot roast." He reached for the electric percolator, plugged in at the far end of the table. "More coffee?"

"Thank you." Alice placed her white linen napkin next to her plate. "I think it's time I finish what I started last night."

Theo leaned back and stretched out his legs. "Tell me."

"I was devastated when Lillian told me she was leaving Knightsbridge. And I was even more upset when she wouldn't say why. I knew she was lying when she said it was a better job. If that had been the case, she would have already told me about her interview and what her new boss was like. She would have said who she was going to live with and where. I would have known for weeks. But, she hadn't said anything about it, not one word. I thought we shared everything. It felt like she pushed a knife into my heart.

"But Lillian was tough, and she could be stubborn. I knew there was no point in confronting her. She'd dig her heels in and that would be

225

that, so I had to let her go. She promised she'd write, but I knew that was a lie, too. I never saw her again or had any news about her until nearly a decade later.

"It was December 1916. I wanted to buy some of my Christmas gifts in Syracuse, so I went to Edith's for a few days. One day I was downtown shopping and suddenly, out of the blue, there she was, coming out of Chappell's."

Alice told Theo about the meeting and how distraught she'd been to learn her friend had tuberculosis. "I could tell right away she was ill. She was so pale and thin, I could see the web of blue veins in her cheeks. And it was painful to watch her try to breathe, she was fighting so hard. When she told me about the consumption, that's what they called it in those days, I knew she was dying. I begged her to let me do something, but she refused. I made a vow to myself that if she wouldn't let me help her, I'd find a way to help her son.

"When I got home, I couldn't stop thinking about her. I was still in shock from running into her, and I couldn't believe she was dying–we were the same age. The thought that someone my age had reached the end of their life shook me more than I can say. The hurt I had buried when she left, without telling me why, resurfaced and hurt all over again. So many emotions bubbled up inside of me until I thought my brain would explode."

As she lifted her cup to take a drink, Alice's hand trembled and a wave of coffee splashed up on the rim.

"Eventually, I hired a detective from the Pinkerton Agency. It took two months before he could tell me where Lillian was living. By then it was too late, she died several weeks before." Alice wiped her eyes with the corner of her napkin and cleared her throat. "Then the most miraculous thing happened. A year later, I accidentally met her son." Alice recounted meeting Leon at the library and the ensuing years of friendship. "We've become very close over the years and we're still in touch."

"Who is it?"

"He lives here in Knightsbridge. His name is Leon. Leon Quigg. He took her last name, or, most likely, that's the name she gave him. She certainly couldn't have called him Shipley." Alice looked at her son, thinking how blessed she was that, despite Ben's neglect, Theo had turned out to be a wonderful human being. "But, Theo, that's exactly what he is, legitimate or not. He's a Shipley and that brings me to the discussion we need to have."

"There's no need for a discussion, Mom. I know what you're going to say and I agree. He's entitled to a share in the money. Based on what I imagine his life must have been like, he more than deserves it."

Alice reached across the table and gripped her son's hand. "You're such a good man, Theo. I'm proud you're my son. I'd like to tell him as soon as possible."

Chapter Thirty-Three

After donning their still-damp coats and hats, Steven and Will, with Jimmy Bou hot on their heels, made a mad dash for Steven's Chevy. Moments later, Steven parked in front of number 200 First Street, and they ran to the door. Jimmy stayed in the entry to update Ralph and Pete and form their strategy. Steven and Will entered the house.

"Let's divide and conquer, Will. I'll start downstairs, you go up."

"Okay. While we're here, Steven, we should pay attention to anything that might give us a clue to Leon's activities or whereabouts when he's not at work."

"Right."

Will took the stairs two at a time, disappearing onto the upper floor.

Steven opened drawers and closets in the living room, cupboards, and even the refrigerator in the kitchen. He checked under furniture and on the top of a tall bookcase. No gun. He decided to check the coat closet near the front door. As he approached the hallway, Will thundered down the stairs and skidded to a halt, clutching something in his hand. He waved it at Steven.

"We've got confirmation of Leon's motive."

Steven took the envelope, unclipped a small piece of paper covering the front, then read it. "That's about two weeks ago." He set it aside and looked at the postmark on the envelope. "December 1916!"

"Read the letter."

Steven unfolded a piece of linen stationery and read. "This is it, Will. Benjamin Shipley could have saved Leon's mother, but he didn't. He let her die. I'll bet you money that in Leon's mind Shipley was responsible for her death."

"Leon must have come across this at the post office. Imagine the shock he felt," Will said. "Listen, I checked everything. There's no gun upstairs."

"Same here. Nothing on the main floor. Did you notice access to the attic?"

"Yes, there's a trapdoor in the ceiling of one of the closets. There must be a step ladder someplace."

"Let's look in the cellar. That's where I keep mine."

When Steven and Will had entered Leon's house, Jimmy Bou pulled Ralph and Pete into the vestibule. He told them Steven had asked Ray to track down Pinky's regulars and explained they needed to divide up the members of the Elks and interview them before the end of the day.

"Steven wants to find out how Leon spends his time," Jimmy said. "I have to go to the library first, then I can help with the interviews."

"All right," said Pete. "Let's think about what makes sense so nobody has to backtrack."

"We've got Herb Steadman and Steven's cousin Jim," Ralph began listing the members.

"Artie Sinclair and Marty Carpenter," said Pete.

"Then there's Hank Flynn from the lab, Tim Kennington, and Coop at the pub." Jimmy Bou finished the list.

"There's us," said Pete.

"I don't know anything about what Leon does when he's not working or at the Elks," Ralph said. "Do either of you?"

"Not me," said Pete.

"Me neither," Jimmy Bou said. "We've gone fishing together a few times, but I don't think he goes unless I ask him."

"How about this?" Ralph suggested. "Pete and I can go back to the station and sign out one of the cars. Getting to Hank at the county lab is going to take the most time, so we'll go there first. After we talk with him, we'll come back into town and hit the high school."

"Right. We'll talk with Tim then…where does Jim Blackwell work?" Pete asked.

"The hospital," Jimmy Bou said.

"Okay, we stop at the hospital, then walk around the corner to the bank. After that, we can drive across town and talk with Coop at the pub."

"That leaves Artie and Herb for you, Jimmy. You can walk to the sawmill from the library. Then, up the street and around the corner is Herb's house. He works the night shift at the paper, so he'll probably be getting up by then," Ralph suggested. "Should work out perfect."

"Makes sense." Jimmy nodded.

Ralph pulled the police sedan into the parking area the Oneida County Forensics Lab shared with the medical office building next door. They identified themselves to the security guard, who told them to wait. A few moments later, Hank Flynn, wearing a lab coat and a badge, greeted them.

"Hi there, Ralph, Pete. What are you fellas doing out here?"

"Police business," Ralph whispered as they led him to a private corner.

"First of all, Hank, this is confidential. You can't even tell anybody we were here, okay?"

"Yeah, sure, Ralph. Gee, you sound like you've been reading spy novels." Hank laughed. "What is it?"

"What do you know about Leon Quigg when he's not working? What he does and where he goes."

"Not much. I gave him a ride to Syracuse once."

Pete jumped on it. "When was that? Did he say where he was going?"

"Sometime last summer. He was turning into the bus depot. I honked and stopped to say hello. I asked him where he was going. He said he was catching the Greyhound to Syracuse. I said what a coincidence, that I was going to Fairmount—that's a suburb—to visit my niece for the day. I asked if he wanted a ride."

"Do you know why he was going there?" Ralph asked.

"Said he was meeting a friend at the Syracuse Library. He didn't elaborate, and I didn't want to pry. We mostly talked about the plans for this year's Christmas party."

The two officers thanked the technician and left the lab.

"That was worth the ride out here, wasn't it, Ralphie?" said Pete. "I bet Steven will make something out of that."

"Maybe. You never know the difference one little detail might make. It could solve the case."

Luckily, Ralph and Pete learned something from Hank Flynn, because neither Tim Kennington nor Jim Blackwell could offer any insights into Leon's activities.

By the time they left the bank, it was nearly noon, and they were happy to stop at the pub for a lunch, and, of course, to question Cooper Lewis.

The cobblestone building housing The Three Lords was over two hundred years old. Heavy wooden beams crisscrossed the smoke-stained ceiling, which was supported by dark columns made from real tree trunks.

They spied the publican behind the bar, pulling back on a beautifully crafted fixture with painted porcelain and brass features, then wove around several tiny tables where customers sat on low stools, eating

DEATH RANG THE BELL

and drinking.

"Hey, Coop," Ralph called from the end of the bar.

Cooper Lewis approached them. "Are you fellas eating, drinking, or is this a visit from the police?"

"All the above, except we can't drink on duty." Pete grimaced. "Got a minute?"

"Sure. Come on back." He waved his hand for them to follow.

When they'd settled in a quiet booth at the back, Ralph explained what they were looking for.

"I don't really know Leon," Coop said. "He comes in once in a while. We say hello but there's no real conversation, if you know what I mean. I think he played darts with Jimmy Bou a few times. Otherwise, he's usually alone. I haven't worked with him on any projects for the Elks. Sorry, fellas."

"That's okay, Coop. We'd appreciate it if you wouldn't mention this to anybody, all right?" Ralph told him.

"Sure. Now, what can I get you for lunch?"

Jimmy Bou sprinted through the rain, arriving at the Village Library in no time flat. He ran up the front stairs and stepped between the white Doric columns to the main entrance. The wooden doors were heavy, despite the large glass windows, but Jimmy Bou's skinny appearance was deceiving, and he pulled one open with no trouble. Sitting at the large front desk, a pencil stuck in the white bun on top of her head, Miss Cartwright gave the policeman a genuine smile.

"Jimmy Bourgogne, how are you?" she exclaimed, blue eyes sparkling behind round, celluloid glasses. The head librarian had spent the past three decades working at the Village Library in one capacity or other, and there weren't many people in town that she didn't know.

"I'm good, and you, Miss Cartwright?"

"Fine, thank you. What can I do for you? I doubt you're here for a book." Raising her eyebrows, she hopped off the tall stool and beckoned him to follow. They skirted a gaggle of four-year-olds excited about story hour, a pair of white-haired ladies each with an armful of novels, and a page pushing a cart, re-shelving dozens of books.

Once in her cluttered office, Miss Cartwright closed the door and turned to face him. "What is it? I realize you must be here officially."

"Yes, ma'am, I am. I'm working on the investigation into the death of Mr. Shipley. First, I need to ask you to keep this conversation confidential."

"Of course. How can I help you?"

"We're trying to get a picture of Leon Quigg's life when he's not at work. We know he's a big reader. He must spend a lot of time at the library. Can you tell me how often he comes here and if it's always on the same day?"

"Yes, Leon is one of our patrons with a weekly routine. He visits the library most Thursdays around seven in the evening, returns the books he borrowed the previous week, and checks out new ones. He normally reads one or two books a week."

"How long is he usually here?"

"About a half hour. Sometimes longer if he can't decide which book to borrow. He might sit at a table and read the first few pages of several before he makes his choice."

"Does he come in alone?"

"Now he does, yes."

"What do you mean *now*?"

"When he was younger, he met Mrs. Shipley every Saturday morning."

Jimmy Bou summoned up all his self-control to keep his jaw from dropping, but his eyes grew round in spite of himself. *Leon Quigg and*

Alice Shipley?

"Do you mean Alice Shipley?" he asked in order to be sure.

"Yes. Of course that was years ago, before she moved away. I'd say they met for several months at least, maybe close to a year. The staff got used to seeing them at what we called 'their table.' They always chose the same table by a window. I may be mistaken but I want to say it began shortly after he moved here to live with his guardian."

"Did that seem strange to you? A grown woman meeting a child?"

"Not at all. I knew his parents had died, and I thought it was wonderful that he had someone to talk to like a mother figure. Some days they didn't even talk much. I'd see her showing him pictures of paintings. The books she borrowed were all illustrated volumes of great works of art."

"Do you think she was tutoring him?"

"I doubt it."

"After Mrs. Shipley moved away, did Leon still spend Saturday mornings here?"

"No, and, now that you ask, it seems odd because I know he loved being here. That child was one of those people who truly gets lost in another world when they read. After Mrs. Shipley left, Leon continued borrowing books, but he took them home to read. I don't think he came in at a regular time until a few years ago, when he started his Thursday routine."

"What kind of books does Leon read, Miss Cartwright?"

"What we call popular fiction. Novels, but no particular genre."

"What about murder mystery stories?" Jimmy persisted.

The librarian laughed. "You mean does he read novels about murder so he can commit one of his own, Jimmy? No. I'm sorry to disappoint you."

Jimmy had the grace to blush, but he recovered quickly. "Thank you, Miss Cartwright. You've been very helpful. If you think of anything else, please let me know. And remember not to say anything about this conversation."

The librarian raised her brows and gave him a look. "What conversation?" She chuckled.

Jimmy Bou could hardly wait to get back to the station to tell Steven. He knew he was supposed to interview the Elks members, but this was too important to wait.

When Steven and Will reached the bottom of the stairs to Leon Quigg's cellar, Steven was glad he'd switched on the light before they'd descended. Like every other basement he'd ever been in, this one was dark and damp. There were two additional bulbs hanging strategically from the floor joists above. Will walked ahead and pulled the metal chains, giving them plenty of light to work in.

Along the left-hand side of the cellar, someone had set up an impressive work area. There was a rough wooden bench, cobbled together with scrap lumber but solid enough to hold a heavy toolbox. Steven opened the box and found screwdrivers, wrenches, hammers, a can of nails, a box of screws, and a handsaw. More tools hung on nails driven into the two-by-fours lining the wall behind the bench. Everything looked well-organized, neat, and clean. This was the carpenter's bench of a man who loved and respected his tools.

"This looks efficient," Will said. "I wonder who the builder is—Leon or Marvin Quigg?"

"Probably his guardian. Leon doesn't strike me as a hammer-and-nails kind of fella. Let's see what's in these drawers." Steven bent and pulled the handle of a homemade drawer under the top of the bench. It stuck. He had to wiggle it, then tug harder before it loosened and opened. He peered in. "A book on building birdhouses. A folding ruler. Looks like he used it a lot." He closed the drawer, opened the one below, and rummaged around. "There's a pile of rags in the back.

Uh oh, I think there's something wrapped up here." Steven stopped searching, put on a pair of gloves, then reached into the drawer and carefully pulled out several orange shop towels of the sort mechanics use.

When he set the bundle on the workbench surface, Steven and Will looked at each other. By the heavy clunking sound and shape of the object enveloped within, they knew what it was and what it would mean for the case. The investigation was about to be over.

Steven cautiously took one corner of the rag and peeled it back, then did the same with the others. Shining like a beacon under the bare light bulb lay a Smith & Wesson .38 mm revolver. The murder weapon.

"We've got him, Steven."

Still in the dark about what Steven and Will had discovered, Jimmy Bou ran all the way back to the station. He flew up the front steps, through the lobby—causing Tommy Forester's eyes to pop—down the hall and into the CID room.

It was empty.

"Argh!" Jimmy yelled.

He exited and ran back to the front desk.

"Tommy, have you heard from Steven and Will? Did they come back from Leon's house?"

"Not yet, Jimmy. What's up? You're jumping out of your skin."

"I found out something big for the case."

A whoosh of air being released sounded behind Jimmy Bou, and he turned to see Steven and Will entering the police station.

"Steven, you're not going to believe what I found out!"

"Oh, yeah? Come down to the office. We've got news, too."

As soon as they entered the CID room, and Steven had closed the door behind them, Jimmy blurted out, "Leon knows Mrs. Shipley!"

CHAPTER THIRTY-THREE

"What?"

Jimmy relayed the information Miss Cartwright had provided. "They met every Saturday until she moved away. After that, he stopped going on Saturdays. We have to find out if they met in Syracuse, or maybe Liverpool if there's a library there."

"That's good work, Jimmy, but in light of what Will and I discovered, I'm not sure how important it is, or if it's important at all. I have some bad news."

"Oh, no." He squeezed his eyes shut. "Tell me you didn't find a gun."

"We did," Will said. "There was a .38 hidden in a drawer in the cellar."

"We also found this." Steven handed Jimmy the letter.

Jimmy dropped onto the wooden chair next to their desks and read what Lillian Quigg had written to her former lover in 1916. His face crumbled. "I never would've believed it." He looked up at Steven. "There's his motive—in black-and-white. Mr. Shipley let his mother die. Leon must have felt awful when he saw this."

"I'm sure he did. I'm sorry it had to be your friend, Jimmy." Steven consulted his watch. "We need to make the arrest. Leon might be back at the post office by now. Let's go get him, Will." They stood, and Steven put his hand on his protégé's shoulder. "Jimmy, this is one of those times where I get no pleasure in the arrest. I do think Leon's a decent fella. Maybe it all got to be too much for him. I'm sorry it turned out this way." Steven shrugged into his coat and placed his fedora on his head. "Why don't you get yourself a cup of joe and take some time to write your report. It looks like we can forgo the rest of the interviews with your fellow Elks." He patted him on the back.

For the second time in less than eight hours, Steven rang the bell at the back entrance of the Knightsbridge Post Office. The heavy metal door creaked open and Duncan Macrae poked his head out.

"Steven! Will! What are you doing back here so soon?"

DEATH RANG THE BELL

"Is Leon Quigg here having his lunch?" Steven asked.

"No, you just missed him—he left a few minutes ago. Came back early today, said his morning was light, but he had a lot to deliver this afternoon."

"Do you know his route, Duncan?" asked Will.

"Sure, come in. I'll show you."

Once in his office, Duncan Macrae took a large map from a drawer. Pushing aside a sheaf of paperwork, a stack of envelopes, and some files, he unfolded it and spread it over the desk's surface. Macrae traced his finger along the streets in the southwest part of town, as he explained. "In the morning, Leon's route is all walking. But in the afternoon, he's responsible for this adjacent area. You can see he needs one of the mail trucks to cover the whole thing. He drives up here to the corner of the Embankment Road, then parks while he walks this section. After that, he moves the truck over here to finish the other half."

Macrae looked up. "What's going on, Steven?"

"We need to bring Leon in for more questioning, Duncan. And we need to do it now."

The post office manager raised his bushy brows and whistled. "You're sure you can't wait until he finishes his route and gets back here."

"We'd rather not," Steven said.

"Is there someone who can take over for the rest of the day?" Will asked.

"I'll have to do it. All my men are already out on the street. It's too late to get a replacement."

"Would you excuse us a minute, Duncan?" Steven said as he and Will went into the empty hallway.

"Why don't you take one of the department vehicles, Will? Duncan can help you find Leon, then you can leave him there to finish the job."

"That's a good idea. I'd like to bring somebody with me in case Leon doesn't want to cooperate."

"Good thinking."

They reentered the manager's office and shared their plan.

"How about if we meet in the parking lot in fifteen minutes?" Will said.

"All right. I'll get ready." Macrae shook his head. "I don't like the sound of this, fellas. I like Leon."

Chapter Thirty-Four

After Will left, taking Charlie with him, Steven realized he had been going at full speed since six, and needed to slow down and think.

Over the years, Steven had developed a routine when he reached this point in an investigation. He would sit by himself and go over every aspect of the case: every piece of evidence, every interview, every theory they'd discussed.

He settled at his desk and studied the murder board, analyzing the suspects once again, acting as his own devil's advocate.

What if Will's instincts were right, and it wasn't Leon Quigg? Was there any evidence that could exonerate him? What if his ridiculous story about running across The Green were true, and he didn't kill Benjamin Shipley? What was the relationship between Leon and Alice Shipley, and did they still meet? Maybe she was the best person to ask about him.

As Steven rose from his chair and slipped on his coat, Ray walked in.

"Steven, Mrs. McMillan confirmed Theo's movements Wednesday night, and I talked with Larry Castleman. He was standing near Joe and Theo at Pinky's. He was positive Joe only left once to go to the bathroom."

"So Theo Shipley has a solid alibi."

"Yes."

"Thanks, Ray. Go write it up."

Steven strode to the murder board. *Looks like Benjamin Shipley's son didn't do it.* He grabbed a piece of chalk and, next to *Alibi*, wrote *Confirmed.* Then he put a large X over the area dedicated to Theo.

The murder board now displayed one suspect: Leon Quigg.

Steven grabbed his hat and, on his way out, stopped in the patrol room. Jimmy Bou huddled over his desk looking forlorn, his hand hovering above his report as he gazed off in the distance.

"Jimmy, I'm going to pick up Alice Shipley for some more questions. Do you want to get out of here for a few minutes?"

"Yeah, thanks, Steven. I can't concentrate on this. Maybe some fresh air will clear my head. Looks like the rain stopped."

Theo's snazzy Plymouth occupied the driveway, so Steven parked in the street. Alice Shipley opened the door, wearing a light gray rayon dress with a black collar and belt and small pleats in front at the hemline.

"Detective Blackwell, this is a surprise. Please don't tell me something else has happened."

"No, ma'am, but, I would like to speak with you. Can you come to the station with us?"

"Why, of course. Now?"

"Yes, if it's not an inconvenience. It won't take long."

"Let me get my coat. Come inside if you like."

"Thank you, we'll wait here."

Steven escorted Alice Shipley into Interview 1, while Jimmy positioned himself behind the glass, eager to hear what Mrs. Shipley had to say, hoping it would be something that would let his friend off the hook.

Steven offered a glass of water and set it in front of her.

"I'd like to talk about your meetings at the library with Leon Quigg."

"Leon? My goodness, what does that have to do with anything?"

"We have to know about everybody connected to a victim, no matter how insignificant that connection. There's nothing to worry about."

"I see. Well, it was years ago, before I moved to Liverpool, of course. I had gotten into the habit of spending Saturday mornings at the Village Library. One day, it was so crowded I couldn't find a seat. I wandered around, then saw a young boy alone at a table. I asked if he minded if I sat down. He said no. That's it."

"Could you tell me more? For example, what did you talk about?"

"Books, of course. And art."

"Did you know anything about him? His background? The fact that he'd lost his mother?"

Alice Shipley shook her head and sighed. "That poor child. No, at first, I didn't know who he was. After a few mornings together, he seemed comfortable talking, and he told me his mother had died. My heart broke for him. He was so vulnerable and lost. Over the years, as he grew into a young man, we became friends."

"Did you feel you were in some way replacing his mother?"

"Sometimes, yes, but most of the time, I was just a good friend. Or maybe a favorite aunt."

"Did you continue to meet after you moved away?"

"Yes, there's a beautiful library in Syracuse that actually looks a lot like the one here. Andrew Carnegie donated money to build both of them. That's probably why. Anyway, when I left, I gave Leon several tickets so he could take the bus, and money to buy more after they were gone."

"Do you still meet at the Syracuse library?"

She nodded. "Except when he has to work, but that's only one Saturday a month."

"Leon was lucky to have you growing up."

"Thank you. I was lucky to have met him as well. As you know, my husband took my son to live with him after I left. I'm afraid I spoiled Leon from time to time."

"That's understandable. Can you tell me what Leon's like? He's my mailman but I can't say I know him."

"He's a lovely young man, kind, caring. He has a soft spot for children, as I imagine you know from the work he does with The Elks. He's a bit quiet unless you get him talking about a book he loves. Then, look out." She laughed.

Steven considered asking about her alibi again, but decided to let it go until Jimmy had a chance to speak with the second woman.

After enlisting a patrolman to drive Alice Shipley home, Steven sat at his desk, going over the interview. Something troubled him, but he couldn't put his finger on it.

Jimmy Bou came in and sat in his usual chair next to Steven's desk.

"What do you think, Jimmy?"

"I'm glad she said all those nice things about Leon."

The floorboards creaked, and Will walked in.

"Leon's in Interview 1, Steven. I didn't officially arrest him. I only said we had some more questions, and you'd be with him in a minute. Charlie's standing guard."

"Thanks." Steven frowned. "I'm surprised it took you so long. You just got back?"

"Yeah, Duncan thought Leon started the afternoon where he left off in the morning. But Leon drives out near Route 5 to the far edge of his route then he works his way back into town. It's the opposite of what Duncan thought he was doing. Not that it makes any difference to the post office, but it took us longer to find him."

Steven nodded. "I spoke with Alice." He told his partner what she'd said. "Listen, would both of you observe while I question Leon? Jimmy, you know him best. You might be able to tell if he's lying at some point. And, Will, I'd like you to work your magic."

"Sure."

"You got it."

Steven noticed that Leon Quigg was nervous and seemed to grow more agitated by the minute. He paced the small room, wringing his hands, sat down at the table, then stood up seconds later. He wiped his mouth, ran his hand through his hair, played with his mail carrier's cap.

This is interesting, Steven thought. *Leon hasn't been waiting long. Is this behavior significant? Maybe he wants to get back to work. Maybe anyone would be nervous given the circumstances. Maybe he really did it.*

"Detective Blackwell! Why did Sergeant Taylor bring me here? I should be out doing my route. What about all the questions I answered this morning? I don't have anything more to tell you." Leon's face was a pattern of worry lines, creased brows, and patches of red.

"Please sit down, Leon. Here, have some water and try to calm down. We need to talk about a few things." Steven poured from the pitcher and handed him the glass.

Leon drank half of it in one gulp, then took two deep breaths. "All right. You can tell I'm nervous, but I don't understand why I'm here."

"We went to your house this morning."

Leon nodded. "I know. That's okay."

Steven placed something wrapped in an orange cotton cloth on the table. "Do you know what this is?"

Leon frowned. "It's an old mechanic's rag. My uncle used them."

Steven folded back the corners. The Smith & Wesson .38 shone under the naked bulb hanging over the table.

Leon gasped. His jaw dropped. He looked from the gun to Steven, back to the gun, and up at the detective again. Wide-eyed, he tried to speak, but nothing came out. He cleared his throat. "Where did you find that?"

"In a drawer under the workbench in your cellar."

"But I've never seen it before. It's not mine."

"It doesn't matter whether it's yours or if it was your uncle's. You had access to the same kind of gun that killed Benjamin Shipley."

"Can't you test it? Can you do something to prove I didn't shoot it? I swear, Detective Blackwell, I've never seen that gun in my life. I don't even know how to use a gun."

Steven took out the letter from Lillian Quigg to Benjamin Shipley. He set it on the table, turned around and face-up so Leon could read it.

Leon froze, then his face crumbled and his eyes filled with tears. Sitting quietly as his shoulders shook, he did nothing to stop the flow. A moment later he composed himself, wiped his eyes, then reached out and tenderly touched the blue stationery, the grief on his face as profound as if Lillian Quigg had died yesterday. "She wrote this, my mother. He let her die." Leon looked up at Steven and repeated, "He let her die for fifty lousy dollars. How can somebody do that?"

Steven saw Leon's pain and forced his own emotions away. He knew the grief of losing a beloved mother all too well. "Tell me about this letter, Leon. Where did you get it?"

"It came in with the mailbag from Syracuse about a week before Halloween. It was a Saturday, and I was the only one in the back room. The envelope caught my attention because there was a note clipped to it. I read it. Did you read that too?"

Steven nodded.

"When I took the paper clip off, I recognized my mother's handwriting right away, but I couldn't imagine why she'd write to Mr. Shipley. I *had* to know. She's been gone so long I figured it wouldn't hurt anybody. I tore open the envelope and read it. I nearly got sick.

Detective Blackwell, you can't imagine what it was like.

"I never knew who my father was. My mother told me he died, but I didn't really believe her. To find out it was Mr. Shipley...then to find out she asked him for help and he refused." He swallowed hard. "She wrote him twice...twice! She begged him to save her life so I wouldn't have to grow up without her." His eyes welled up again. "If only he had sent her the money, she might still be alive." Leon bent his head and wept.

Steven waited until he pulled a handkerchief from a pocket, dried his face and eyes, and blew his nose.

"You must have been very angry when you read this, Leon."

"I was."

"Angry enough to kill the man who let your mother die?"

Leon shook his head. "I told you I didn't do it."

"Leon, I'm afraid you're going to have to stay here tonight. You're not under arrest yet, but I'll have more questions in the morning."

"I don't want to stay here. I won't run away. I want to go home."

"Not today. I'm sorry."

After returning Leon to his cell, Steven went back to his office and found Will adding information to the murder board, Jimmy Bou standing at his shoulder. He dropped onto his chair, his head full of facts, innuendos, evasions, truth, and lies. He sensed something didn't add up, but what was it?

Will looked at his partner. "What gives, Steven?"

"I should be jumping for joy this case is over, Will, but I'm not."

"You think we're missing something, don't you?"

"Don't you?"

Will paused before answering. "I admit I misjudged Leon. I didn't peg him as a killer, but sometimes what seems like the most obvious answer is. We've got means, motive, and opportunity."

"Why now, Will? I'd understand it if Leon had rushed over to

Benjamin Shipley's house and killed him that same night after he saw his mother's letter. He would have been crazy with rage. His emotions would have been in chaos—shock, grief, anger. I'd believe it if it had been a crime of passion." Steven nailed his partner with a stare. "But, he didn't. He waited ten days." Steven pushed on. "Someone planned this murder down to the last detail, including the fact that it was Halloween night and everything's chaotic on Halloween. Do we really think Leon Quigg has the nerve to plan a cold-blooded, calculated murder, right across the street from my house when he knew I'd be home?"

Will exhaled, blowing out his cheeks. "No, you're right. We have to look at this again."

"It's been a long day," Steven said. "Let's tackle it in the morning. I don't know about you fellas, but I'm not thinking straight anymore."

Jimmy Bou returned to the patrol room to finish writing his report. Will worked on his while Steven updated the murder board.

LEON QUIGG - Benjamin Shipley's illegitimate son
  Motive - Shipley let his mother die.
  Opportunity - Was seen running across The Green at 11 pm
  Means - .38 found in cellar of his house
  Is it the murder weapon?

Yes, they had some threads to tie up. The final—and damning—evidence would be Hank's ballistics report on the gun, and Steven was sure he knew what those results would be. Like Will had said, when the physical evidence stared you in the face, you had to accept the obvious conclusion. He pushed away his doubts and sat down to write his report.

"Steven, Will," Jimmy shouted, running into the room twenty minutes later. "She wasn't there. Alice Shipley doesn't have an alibi."

247

"What?"

"Mrs. Flanagan just called back. She said Alice never showed up for the meeting Wednesday."

Steven glanced at the clock. "She'll still be at the funeral, and she's not going anywhere. We'll bring her in first thing tomorrow."

"We should talk to the lady she lives with, too," Will said.

"You're reading my mind," said Steven.

The operator put through the call and, when Edith Adams came on the phone, Steven explained who he was and said he needed to speak with her in the morning. After hanging up, he said, "Jimmy, I want you to come with me. We'll leave at six-thirty."

It was dark when Steven finished for the night. As he walked past the patrol room, he noticed a light on. He poked his head in. Jimmy Bou was bent over his desk writing.

"I thought you'd left, Jimmy."

"Almost done. A couple more minutes."

"Listen, you've done really good work on this case. I'd like to treat you to supper at the pub. What do you say?"

Jimmy Bou looked like a kid on Christmas morning. "Really? With Olivia, too?"

Steven chuckled. "Yes. What do you say we meet you at The Three Lords at six-thirty?"

"Gee, thanks, Steven. That's swell."

Chapter Thirty-Five

After freshening up and changing his clothes, Steven met Olivia at her bedroom door.

"Hey! You made it," Olivia exclaimed. "I was wondering if you'd have to work tonight."

"Nope, we've got the whole evening." He grinned. "There's a slight change of plan, though." He told her about inviting Jimmy Bou to supper. "I hope you don't mind."

Wow! That takes care of how I'm going to get together with Jimmy, she thought. *The universe is telling me I made the right decision.*

"Of course not, it'll be fun. I enjoy Jimmy's company. That's really nice of you, by the way. You know he idolizes you, right?"

"He's young. He'll get over it." He laughed.

Olivia suggested they walk. "I love the smell of a winter night," she said when Steven offered to drive. "Come on. It's beautiful out."

In the end, he relented, and they bundled up for the short walk from their house to The Three Lords.

Cooper Lewis stood behind the long polished bar, pulling a pint for Jimmy Bou when Steven and Olivia joined him.

"Coop, put that on my tab. Jimmy's my guest tonight," Steven told the publican.

Jimmy pulled off his wool hat and gave Olivia a little bow. "Good evening, Miss Watson."

"Jimmy, how many times have I told you to call me Olivia? Especially if we're about to have dinner together." She gave him a warm smile.

"All right. I guess I forgot."

Steven ordered his and Olivia's drinks, and they made their way to a booth. Steven slid in next to Olivia. Jimmy sat across the table.

Olivia raised her pint of oatmeal stout. "Here's to closing your case." The three clinked glasses.

A short, plump woman approached their table. "I heard you were in tonight," she said to Steven. "How are you?"

"Swell, Theresa. How's that beautiful daughter of yours?"

"I think she's getting ready to walk. She pulls herself up to the couch and sort of sidles along the length of it. Sometimes she lets go and stands there. Then she seems to realize what she's done, wobbles a bit then plops down on the floor." The young mother radiated joy. "It's nice to see you, Miss Watson. How are you, Jimmy?"

They chatted about the weather and said how it looked like they were in for a long winter.

"That'll be two years in a row," Steven said.

While they talked, Olivia indulged in a moment of pleasure, looking at Steven. Tonight he wore charcoal gray pants, a white shirt, and wool V-neck pullover with pale blue lines worked into the weave. Her heart did a tiny somersault.

"So, Theresa, what's good today?" Steven asked.

"I made a lovely shepherd's pie. Perfect on a night like this."

"Mmm, I like shepherd's pie," Jimmy Bou declared.

"Sounds good to me," Olivia said.

"Looks like three shepherd's pies," Steven told the cook.

After Theresa had left, Olivia said, "We got lucky tonight with the weather. It's a perfect winter evening. I convinced Steven to walk here, Jimmy."

"Yeah, I did, too. Of course, I always walk everywhere."

"You don't drive?" Olivia asked.

"I do, but I don't have a car. I like getting out in the fresh air though, so it's okay."

"Do you walk Waffles even in the winter when it's snowing? Don't her paws get cold?"

"She actually likes the snow. When we get to The Green, she takes off like a bat outta hell." His face froze, his hand flew to his mouth, and his eyes grew big. "Oh, I'm sorry. I didn't mean to curse in front of you."

Olivia laughed. "That's okay. I don't think of *hell* as a swear word. Don't worry, Jimmy."

"I'd love to get a dog, but it wouldn't be fair leaving him alone all the time with the hours I work," Steven said. "I saw an Alaskan Husky once with the bluest eyes you've ever seen. That's what I'd get if I could."

Theresa Covington returned with three steaming plates of shepherd's pie. "Coop's on his way with another round."

"Mmm, this smells great!" Olivia said. "Thank you."

Cooper Lewis deposited their pints on the table and whisked away the empty glasses. "Enjoy," he said.

All three were silent as they dug in to their meal. After a few minutes, Olivia asked, "So, Jimmy, your next event with the Elks is the Christmas party, right?"

"Yeah, it's the biggest thing we do all year. We're already collecting donations. Every kid gets a stocking with two presents, a candy cane, and a treat like a box of Cracker Jacks or jelly beans."

"What toys do you give them?"

"We order these big stockings filled with all kinds of good stuff from the Sears catalog. We open them up, mix everything together, then divide them up. For the girls, there are sewing cards, paper dolls, and tea sets. The boys get toy guns and cars, tops, and watches. Then, there's stuff that can be for both like harmonicas, coloring books and crayons, and disguise sets."

"Where do you get all the stockings to fill?"

"The families give us a stocking with each kid's name on it. We use them every year."

"What an impressive operation! Can I help? Do you need donations?"

"Thanks, Olivia. We never say no."

"How much do those big stockings from Sears cost?"

"A dollar ninety-eight each."

Olivia extracted a brown leather wallet from her purse, took out four dollar bills, and handed them to Jimmy. "This should cover two then."

"I don't know what to say." Jimmy gaped. "This will take care of nearly thirty kids."

"It's my pleasure. I'm glad to help."

"Will you come to the party, Olivia?"

"I'd love to, thanks." She winked at Jimmy Bou. "Can I bring Steven?"

"Hey, just try to keep me away." Steven laughed.

After finishing the meal, they sat nursing their pints.

"Well, I'd better be getting home. Waffles will want to go out for our walk," Jimmy said. "Thanks again, Steven. This was swell."

"Jimmy, after all this food, I could use a walk, too. Would you like some company? Steven and I could come with you. I'd like to meet Waffles."

Olivia avoided looking at Steven because she knew her comment was out of the ordinary and didn't want to explain. She also didn't want to give him the chance to object. Jimmy didn't seem to think anything of it, though.

"Sure, I'll introduce you. She's a great dog."

Phew! Next step done.

The storm clouds cloaking the town all day had drifted away, and the velvety night sky was alight with stars.

The threesome hiked the five blocks to Jimmy Bou's house, talking and laughing. Steven and Olivia waited outside while Jimmy got Waffles.

"What are you up to, Olivia? Why are we taking a walk with Jimmy?"

"Nothing. It's a beautiful night, and I ate too much. I need to walk off some of that dinner."

Jimmy bounded out of the front door, a light brown cocker spaniel with a white muzzle and soft floppy ears running after him. "Olivia, Steven, this is Waffles. Waffles, shake."

Big brown eyes looked up as the dog came to a stop next to her owner, then raised her front right paw. Olivia bent down and shook, then petted her head. "Ooh, you're beautiful."

By the time Waffles tired from chasing sticks on the Village Green, Steven was ready to go home and put his feet up.

"What do you say we head home, Olivia?"

"Sure. Jimmy, didn't you tell me you swing around Chiltington before you head home?"

"Yup, we do. I'll walk with you to Steven's house then go home."

Based on the *Gazette* article, Olivia knew the accident was going to happen on Steven's street. She needed to be vigilant. She needed to succeed. Or Jimmy Bou had only minutes to live.

They left Victoria and turned onto Chiltington, a street with a steep incline. Jimmy was walking closest to the road, allowing Waffles to sniff along the edge of the sidewalk. Steven had steered Olivia between him and Jimmy, and was walking on the lawns to give them all enough space. As they approached Judge Randolph's house, they heard banging on a window and saw the judge's face peek out. He waved to Steven.

"I'll see what he wants. You go on. I'll catch up."

Olivia's heart was in her throat. She knew it had to happen soon and hoped it would be before they reached Steven's house. Otherwise, how would she explain wanting to continue to the corner?

Jimmy stopped while Waffles examined a pile of dried leaves. Olivia paused and waited a step ahead of him, enjoying watching the puppy sniff around the edge of the road, tail wagging. She heard an engine and looked up to see a big boxy car crest the hill.

Is this it?

The Ford began its descent, then took on speed.

The blast of a horn shattered the quiet evening. Olivia froze as the enormous car flew straight at them.

"Jimmy!" Olivia rushed to him, grabbed his arm, and pulled hard, propelling both of them out of the path of the run-away automobile. They fell as one and rolled over onto the lawn.

"Waffles, down!" Jimmy yelled.

As the car jumped the curb, Waffles dropped to the ground, head down. The Model T soared over the dog, slammed into a nearby oak tree, and fell back to the grass.

Jimmy screamed.

Steven had heard the car's horn and looked up as Olivia pulled Jimmy Bou to safety and the cocker spaniel flattened herself on the ground. *Oh, my God, Olivia!* Steven left the judge standing in the doorway and took off running. He skidded to a halt in time to help Olivia to her feet. Jimmy Bou scrambled to the back of the car, threw himself flat on the ground, and peered between the rear tires. They heard a whimper. Jimmy reached under the rear bumper and gently laid his hand on Waffles's back. The puppy was shaking. She moved her head to the side, trying to see Jimmy.

"Come on, Waffles. You're okay. Come on out," Jimmy whispered, crawling around to the side of the vehicle so the dog could see him. Waffles turned and inched forward until her shoulders passed under the running board. "You can do it. You're almost there." When her rump cleared the chassis, Jimmy grabbed her and held her close, running his hand over every part of her, checking for blood. "Are you all right, girl?" She barked, and Jimmy Bou gave her a kiss between the eyes.

Steven realized he was still holding a trembling Olivia and stepped back. "Are you okay?" He scanned her face.

Olivia nodded and tried to speak, but nothing came out. She let out a deep breath, then said, "I'm all right. Maybe a little wobbly."

"Boy, Olivia, if it wasn't for you...How am I ever going to thank you?" Jimmy gasped.

"I'm just happy you're okay. Hey, who's the driver? We need to see if they're hurt."

Steven hurried to the driver's side of the Model T and peered in the window. "It's Doctor Kranken." He opened the door. The GP was sitting still, gazing into the distance. "Doc, are you all right?"

Kranken looked up at Steven, eyes unfocused. "The steering wheel stopped working," he said in a daze. "It just stopped. I tried to turn, but nothing happened. Oh, my Lord. Did I hurt anybody?"

"No, they jumped out of the way. Even the dog is fine. But, I think you hit your head."

Kranken touched his forehead, and his fingers came away with blood.

"We'd better get you to the hospital, Doc. You might have a concussion."

Judge Randolph arrived. "Can I help? Is everybody all right?"

"Judge, would you call an ambulance? I think the doc hit his head on the steering wheel. He's bleeding."

"Right away." Randolph loped across the lawn to his front door and disappeared inside.

"Steven, I'm going to get some water." Olivia turned and headed to their house.

Steven opened the top of Doctor Kranken's heavy jacket. "Try to breathe normally. Help is on the way." He turned as Jimmy Bou approached, carrying the puppy. "Jimmy, are you okay? And Waffles?"

"Yeah, we're all right."

"You'd better take it easy for the rest of the night. I'll drive you home."

"Thanks, Steven, but no. Stay until the ambulance comes. I can walk. I'm not hurt. And I want to get Waffles home right away. She's still shaking."

Twenty minutes later, Steven and Olivia entered their house. They shrugged out of their jackets and hung them on the hall tree. Olivia kicked off her shoes, then turned to see Steven watching her.

"You knew. You knew something was going to happen, didn't you? That's why you wanted to go for a walk with him," he said.

Olivia's face crumbled, and she nodded, her eyes tearing up.

Steven took a step forward and pulled her into a hug. He felt her full weight as she leaned into him and held on tight, giving her the time she needed to release the emotions bottled up inside. Her body shook as she wept. Steven bent his head, pushed her hair out of the way, and kissed her cheek. "I'm not mad. I know you did it because it was Jimmy."

Olivia leaned back. She'd stopped crying, but her eyelashes glistened with tears. She sniffed. "I'm sorry. You never want to know the future. I saw a newspaper article at Liz's exhibit yesterday about a car accident tonight. It said Jimmy died. I couldn't let that happen. Not to him. I just couldn't." She wiped her eyes.

It happened before either of them knew what was going on. Steven's arms tightened around her, her arms slid up around his neck. The kiss seemed to last forever. At one point, Steven broke off and looked into her eyes, finding the joy he wanted to see, but Olivia wasn't ready to stop. She pulled him back to her and they came together in a second endless kiss.

Later, neither would be able to say just who it was that had started it.

Chapter Thirty-Six

TUESDAY, NOVEMBER 6, 1934

Steven awoke at five Tuesday morning, eager to see Olivia, anxious to know what it would be like after their kiss last night. He hoped she didn't regret the step they'd taken, and that it wouldn't be awkward between them. An hour later, he waited at the door, his heart in his throat.

As if by magic, she materialized.

"Good morning," she said, eyes sparkling.

Steven reached into the doorway and took her hand, bringing her into 1934.

"I didn't dream it, did I?" he said.

She laughed. "If you did, we had the same dream." She squeezed his hand.

He poured their coffee, and they settled at the kitchen table. Neither spoke for a few minutes as they munched their cereal and gazed at each other.

Finally, Olivia said, "Should we talk about it, Steven? Are we really going to try this?"

"Yes, why not?"

"You know why not."

258

"I don't care that it looks impossible, Olivia. We'll manage."

"How?"

He reached across the table and took her hand. "Right now, I don't know. But I know if the two of us put our minds together, nothing's going to stop us. We'll figure it out, because we have to. I'm willing to take the risk."

Steven knew she trusted him. Now, if she would only trust *them*.

Olivia looked at him, took a deep breath, and said, "Okay. Me, too."

Steven rose, walked around the table, pulled her up out of her chair, and kissed her long and hard.

"To seal the deal." He grinned when they came up for air.

When they returned to their breakfast, he asked, "How do you feel after your close call last night?"

"I'm fine, although it took me a while to relax and fall asleep, but I slept well. I'm actually more concerned about what I did."

"Saving Jimmy?"

She nodded. "Yeah. I felt like I had to do something. I wanted to save him. I thought it was the right thing to do, but now I'm wondering *what have I done?*"

"I thought about that, too. We need to be careful, especially you, because you're in the past. The things you do here impact the future. We can't even imagine the repercussions one small act might have, to say nothing of saving somebody's life."

Olivia sighed. "I know—ripples in a pond." She drank her coffee. "Well, it's done and, even though I'll never know the effects of what I did, I'm not sorry for saving him."

"Same here."

"Hey, we never had a chance to talk about your investigation yesterday. Are you any closer to solving it?"

"I don't know. The evidence is piling up against Leon." Steven told her what they'd found at his house. "But, my gut tells me he wouldn't have killed Shipley the way it happened. In the meantime, we found out Alice doesn't have an alibi."

"Oh, wow. What do you mean about Leon?"

"The murder was cold and calculated. Leon's not like that. He might have committed a crime of passion, but I can't see him doing all that careful planning."

"Alice is passionate. We saw that the other day."

"That's true, but her motive is shaky, and I don't know how she would've gotten here and gone home so late at night, to say nothing of how she would've got hold of a gun."

"You've been doing this a long time, Steven. If it doesn't feel right, you have to keep investigating. Maybe in the end you'll find out you were wrong, but at least you'll know for sure. No loose ends. Isn't that what you always say?"

"Yup, that's right."

"There's something you haven't mentioned. Did Alice know Leon's mother, Lillian? It sounds like they were around the same age. Maybe they were in school together. They might have been friends. And another thing, did Leon tell Alice about the letter his mother wrote to Mr. Shipley? Does she know he was his father? And would she even care after all these years?"

"You're reading my mind. That's exactly what I'm going to find out today."

"Alice strikes me as a fierce woman, and she's also a mother, which is something you can't discount. Think of a female lion or tiger, Steven, and how they protect their young. They'll go after anyone or anything that threatens their cubs. If Leon showed Alice that letter, it could have unleashed an enormous amount of resentment against her husband. Benjamin Shipley took her son away from her, and now she learns he took Leon's mother from him. I think Alice is capable of a passionate *and* a cold, calculated crime."

"Impressive, Miss Watson! I'm glad you're on my team."

"I should apologize—it never occurred to me the person I saw might be a woman. Now that I think about it, it's possible. I hope I didn't slow down your investigation."

"You didn't." He took their empty bowls and spoons to the sink, then turned. "Don't worry, it's fine. So, what are your plans today?"

"I'm going to stay here and put the finishing touches on my article for *The Gazette*, then take it to Chief Thompson. I promised he could read it before I turn it in. I'll go back home and work after that. What's the scoop on tonight?"

"I don't know how today is going to go. Can we play it by ear?"

"Sure. I got a new client yesterday. I'll work in my room tonight. I can spread out on the bed or in my reading nook. I'll be there when you come home."

"Perfect."

Driving to the station, his heart bursting with joy, Steven couldn't stop grinning. Never in his life had he experienced anything like this sensation. His entire world had opened up, and the future spread out before him with infinite possibilities. He still didn't know how it was going to work, but he didn't care. Somehow they'd figure it out. In the meantime, he had a case to solve.

Jimmy Bou was waiting for him by the front door. He ran down the steps and jumped into the Chevy with an excited *Good morning, Steven.*

They sped toward Liverpool, the temperature dropping with every mile.

"Listen, Jimmy, you've observed Will and me during enough interviews to know how we work together. How about you try it with me today?"

"Sweet! I'm ready."

When Steven pulled up in front of Edith Adams' home, a face appeared in the window, and a moment later, the door opened.

"Detective Blackwell?" asked a short, plump woman with white hair arranged in a knot on top of her head, making her look like a Gibson girl. She was sturdy and seemed planted in the doorway.

"Yes, ma'am. This is Officer Bourgogne."

Both men showed their badges and ID.

"Please come in."

They followed her into the front sitting room, where Steven had talked with Alice.

"I suppose this is about Ben."

"Yes, Mrs. Adams. I hope you understand when someone is killed, we have to consider those closest to the victim, like a spouse," Steven said.

"Yes, of course. You want to know if I think Alice could have killed her husband, right?" She looked at him calmly, as if the police came calling weekly to inquire about her roommate's potential as a murderer.

"Well, I wouldn't have put it so bluntly but yes, ma'am, that's exactly it."

"I feel if one speaks plainly it saves a lot of time. So, yes, my answer is yes. Alice is a passionate woman, something that was lost on that miserable man. When she believes in something, she goes all out. If she thought the world would be a better place without him, she might have done it."

Steven and Jimmy Bou stared at her, unused to such a bold and damning assessment, especially by a sweet-looking old lady.

"Now." Edith Adams sat straighter and laid her hands in her lap. "Having said that, I can't see *how* she would have done it."

"Does Alice drive?" Jimmy asked.

"She knows how, but she doesn't have a license or an automobile."

"Speaking of motor cars, there's a black Model T Runabout in front of your house. I noticed a similar car parked two doors up when I was here the other day. Is it yours or does it belong to a neighbor?"

"It was my late husband's. I'm going to sell it because I don't see well enough to drive anymore. I haven't got around to it yet."

"Does Mrs. Shipley borrow it?" Steven asked.

"No, like I said, she doesn't have a driving license. I've been generous with my cousin, but she knows there are a couple of things that are mine and she's not allowed to use them. So, even if she had a license the Runabout would be off-limits. Alice understands that and respects my feelings."

"Were you home Wednesday evening?" Jimmy asked.

"No, my son picked me up around five-thirty. I stayed with him and his family for a few days. I wanted to see my grandchildren in their Halloween costumes." Her rigid posture relaxed, and she smiled. "Dori's four and Billy turned two last month. Aren't they beautiful?" She reached over to pick up a framed photograph from the piecrust table and angled it to reveal two small children in the arms of a man and woman. Her gray eyes sparkled. "She'll be able to vote when she's older! I was a suffragette," she added, her voice filled with pride.

"Good for you," Jimmy exclaimed. "And about time, too. My grandmother marched."

"It took us long enough, but we did it."

"Let me ask you what might sound like an unusual question," Steven said. "If you found out that Alice had killed her estranged husband, what do you think would have been her reason?"

"Phew! That's a question, all right. Well, I doubt it would have had anything to do with their marriage. For Alice, it was the disappointment of Ben not being who she thought he was and realizing that all her expectations would come to nothing that was hard. She got over the break-up of the marriage within a year. As for Ben taking

Theo away…that almost killed her. For a long time, she blamed herself. She said if she had only known he was going to track them down and take Theo, maybe she would have stayed. But it was too late and, in the end, she survived. She's making up for lost time now that Theo's grown. He comes up for a weekend about every month or so. He turned out to be a good man. Thank God he has none of his father in him." She made a face.

Steven almost laughed at this wonderful woman. She was a character. He liked her and wished she lived in Knightsbridge. She was somebody he would enjoy knowing.

Edith thought for a moment. "I'd say if Alice found out Ben had abused one of his female employees that would probably do it. And before you jump to conclusions, I don't mean in a…personal way…if you get my meaning. I don't think Ben would have stooped to that. I'm thinking of forcing someone to work when she's very sick, or not letting a woman go to her father's funeral if she was supposed to work. Something like that."

"Thank you, Mrs. Adams. We really appreciate your insights. I wish everybody we talked to was so perceptive." Steven rose from the chair.

"You're most welcome, Detective. I didn't like Ben. But murder is just plain wrong."

A half hour into the journey home, the sky darkened so quickly it was like someone had turned off the lights, then they hit freezing rain. Steven turned on the wipers in addition to the headlamps.

These were the worst kind of driving conditions. The wipers left streaks on the windshield, making it difficult to see. The road was slick with the icy downpour, and Steven was sure hidden patches of black ice waited, ready to throw his car into a spin, or worse into on-coming traffic. He slowed to a crawl as they made their way east on Route 31.

Shortly after Rattlesnake Gulch, conditions seemed improved. The precipitation appeared to be more rain than ice, and Steven thought he could speed up a little. He accelerated. *So far, so good.* They approached a dairy farm where black-and-white Holsteins stood huddled in a group. Steven kept his eyes on the road. They passed several acres of grazing field and entered a wooded area. "Keep an eye out for deer, Jimmy."

It happened without warning. The front tire hit a patch of black ice and Steven's beloved Chevy flew out of his control. The heavy automobile spun to the left, the front end reaching toward the oncoming lane, the back shifting sideways and flying along the rough edge of the highway. Gripping the wooden steering wheel, Steven turned it to the left, directing the car into the spin. The movement threw Jimmy Bou toward the dashboard. His hand shot out, preventing the impact, but there was no time to readjust as the powerful rotation propelled him towards Steven on the bench seat. Jimmy grabbed onto the leather strap hanging above the door and, using all his strength, pulled himself back to the passenger side.

Knuckles white from holding on to the wheel, Steven gently let up on the gas. He felt the car slow as it traveled a full circle into the other lane, back to where he started, then onto the side of the road. Taking advantage of the coarse gravel on the shoulder, he slammed his foot down on the clutch and threw the gearshift into first, bringing the vehicle to a crawl so he could ease out of first and brake. The Chevy shuddered to a stop.

Steven pulled on the parking brake and let the engine idle in neutral. Removing his cramped hands from the wheel, he gently shook them to get some feeling back. He exhaled deeply and looked over at Jimmy Bou, still holding onto the strap.

"Are you all right? You didn't hit your head, did you?"

Jimmy Bou's face was pale, his jaw trembled slightly. He shook his head, then turned to Steven. "No, I'm okay. How did you know what to do? It looked like you turned into the spin. I would have gone the other way, trying to stop it."

"My dad taught me. For some reason, it works." Steven blew out his cheeks, exhaling hard, then fell back onto the seat. "I think that's enough excitement for today, don't you, Jimmy?"

"If we weren't so far away, I'd walk home."

When they arrived in Knightsbridge and got out of the car, Steven noticed a metallic scent in the air; it was going to snow.

"Tell the fellas we'll start the briefing in ten minutes, Jimmy."

Wondering when he'd hear from the forensics lab, but sure Hank would confirm the gun as the murder weapon, Steven went straight to the murder board to read through the notes on Leon Quigg. As he stood there, his eyes darting across the board, his mind flying over the details of the case, he knew they needed to take Alice Shipley seriously, and, for the first time in days, he wrote a new name under *SUSPECTS*.

ALICE SHIPLEY - Widow of Benjamin
Separated 16 years.
Lives in Liverpool with Edith Adams.
Motives
1. Get control of stores to improve working conditions for women employees.
2. Revenge for taking son
Alibi - None
Edith says she's passionate.
How did Alice get here?

When Steven entered the patrol room, everyone was talking about Jimmy Bou's escapes from death.

"Jeez, Jimmy, you nearly got killed this morning, and it's not even ten yet," said Pete.

"And you almost got run over last night," Ralph said.

"Yeah, if it hadn't been for Olivia, you'd be planning my funeral."

"You owe her something real good, Jimmy Bou," said another.

"Good morning, fellas," Steven called out. "I've got a lot of information to share, so let's get started. You've probably heard Will and I searched Leon Quigg's house yesterday. We found two critical items: a motive for murder and a gun. We discovered a letter that proves Leon was Benjamin Shipley's illegitimate son, and, even worse, Shipley let Leon's mother die without trying to save her. We also found a .38 hidden in a drawer in the basement. Hank's got it at the lab now and he's running tests. We'll know soon if it's the murder weapon."

Excitement filled the room.

"I never would've pegged Quigg for a killer."

"I can't believe it. I like Leon Quigg."

"This is a record! Solving a case in less than a week. Wowie."

"We haven't solved it yet, fellas," Steven interrupted. "I hate to throw a wrench into the works, but I'm not convinced Leon's our killer. I know the evidence points that way, but look at the man. This was a cold, calculated crime, and I don't think Leon's like that. While we're waiting for confirmation on the gun, I want to look into Alice Shipley."

Several officers protested they were looking for a man. Steven reminded them a woman could easily disguise herself. "All she had to do was put on a pair of men's trousers and jacket, and stuff her hair under a cap. Her son probably leaves clothes at her house. It was dark, nobody saw her up close, and she fits the description.

"We've also learned Mrs. Shipley does not have an alibi for Wednesday night. The one she gave us was a lie, so we have to ask *if she lied about her alibi, what else is she lying about?* This morning Jimmy and I learned more about her character and possible motivation." He shared what Edith Adams had told them. "Alice has believable motives. The sticking point is opportunity and, of course, means, but we'll tackle that later.

"If Alice Shipley was our killer, how did she get here? She knows how to drive but doesn't have a license or a car, so she would've had to take the train or a bus from Syracuse. Ralph and Pete, go to the train station and bus depot this morning and find out if anyone saw her arrive on Wednesday or leave later that night. She might have been dressed as herself or already in disguise."

"You got it, Steven," Ralph said, and Pete gave the thumbs up.

"By the way, how did you make out on your interviews with the Elks yesterday?"

"Hank Flynn told us something interesting," Pete said. "He gave Leon Quigg a ride to Syracuse once. Leon was going to meet somebody at the library. Ralph and I thought maybe he was meeting Mrs. Shipley."

"It was last summer, so we figure they still get together," Ralph said.

"You're right, when I talked with her yesterday, she mentioned they do." Steven explained their next steps, then wrapped up with a caution that everyone stay in touch throughout the day. "I don't know when or what I might need from you today. If you're out on patrol, check back with Tommy at least once an hour. If you're in and out of the station, check the murder board as often as you can. Thanks, fellas."

His phone was ringing when Steven entered the CID room with Will and Jimmy Bou.

"Steven, I've got news for you," said Hank Flynn. "The gun you found in Leon Quigg's house hasn't been fired in a very long time, and the bullet Doc extracted from Mr. Shipley didn't match the barrel. This is not the murder weapon."

Steven's jaw dropped. "You're kidding! I was sure you'd find a match."

"There's no question. I checked and double checked. The killer did not use this gun."

Steven thanked the forensics technician and strode to the board. Under Leon Quigg's name, he wrote: *Gun found in house not murder weapon.*

"It wasn't Leon after all," Jimmy exclaimed.

"He's not out of the woods yet, Jimmy," said Will.

"I want to go through Alice Shipley's life with a fine-toothed comb," Steven said. "Will, I'm sorry. I made a mistake this morning. I should have foreseen this possibility and asked Edith Adams about any guns in her house."

"You can't think of everything. I'll go."

"Thanks. Today's her day off, but call first, just in case." Steven looked at Jimmy Bou. "Jimmy, I want you to talk with your father again. We never asked him about Mrs. Shipley. Find out what he knows about her, especially if she knew Leon's mother, Lillian."

Jimmy Bou whistled as he strode through town. The weather had made one of those odd shifts in the past hour—the temperature was rising, and the sun was out. When he arrived at The Great Atlantic and Pacific Tea Company, he saw someone had propped open the front door, letting in the fresh air.

On the way to his father's office, Jimmy glanced at the familiar signs posted high on the back wall, advertising butter, cheese, eggs, milk, and cream. He passed several housewives pushing small carts, two-tiered rolling metal frames, each level holding a small wire basket. One woman set a large cardboard container of Quaker Oats in her basket.

The door was closed, so Jimmy knocked first, then entered. His father was on the telephone and waved him onto a chair.

"All right, Mr. Jenkins, I'll get that invoice out to you right away." Louis Bourgogne put the receiver in its cradle. "Well, this is a treat, son. What can I do for the Knightsbridge Police this morning?"

"Dad, I need to find out if Mrs. Shipley–Alice–knew Lillian Quigg. Do you have any idea?"

"Yes, she did. They were great friends."

Jimmy's jaw dropped. "Really? You're sure?"

His father pursed his lips and raised one eyebrow. "Is that the way you'd conduct an interview if it wasn't with me, Jimmy?"

"Oh, sorry, Dad. You're right. Um, yes." Jimmy looked down and wrote something in his notebook, giving himself a moment to gather a professional attitude around him. "How can you be sure they were friends, sir?"

His father hid a small smile. "Do you remember when I told you and Detective Blackwell how her brother Marvin and I used to go to the lunch counter in Shipley's for ice cream?"

"Yes."

"Well, whenever we went, if it was time for Lillian to quit and go home, Alice was always sitting at the counter waiting for her. They were like two peas in a pod, those two. You rarely saw one without the other."

Inside Jimmy's head, he was shouting *Wowie!* but he forced himself to remain calm.

"It's interesting they'd be friends. I read in Alice's background that her family was wealthy, and it seems Lillian's parents didn't have much money. She had to work a low-paying job." *Steven would be proud of that observation,* Jimmy silently complimented himself.

"Yes, that's true. And it would be a barrier for many people. Evidently their parents raised them the way your mother and I raised you. You don't judge people by how much is in their wallet."

"Do you remember when Alice started stepping out with Mr.

Shipley?"

"No idea. But, it was after Lillian left. I do recollect that."

"Did Alice go to the Quiggs' house to play with Lillian when they were kids?"

"I never saw her there. I think they became friends when they were older. In high school maybe."

Chapter Thirty-Seven

Chief Andy Thompson had his back to the open door when Steven knocked on the frame. He slipped a file folder into a cabinet, slammed the drawer shut, and turned. "Morning, Steven. Tell me you've got something. I had to put off that annoying reporter again. Told her I missed the briefing this morning and she should talk to you." He dropped onto his chair, which squeaked in protest.

"We're getting closer, Chief." Steven updated his boss with the latest details. "I've got to ask you something but I don't want you to get upset."

Thompson screwed up his face. "Here we go. Is this going to cost me money? You know there's a depression on. We've gotta watch the budget."

"No, it's nothing like that. We're at the point where we're considering Alice may have killed her husband."

Thompson's jaw dropped. "What?" He stood up so quickly that his chair flew against the back wall and tipped over, crashing into the metal wastepaper basket that rolled over, spilling papers all over the floor. "You can't be serious. Crap!" He leaned over and struggled to reach across his belly in an effort to upright the chair. He fell back onto the wooden seat and lit a cigarette. "Why?"

Steven explained Alice Shipley's motives, lies, and how easy it would have been to disguise herself.

"The question is how she would have got here. I need more information, especially about her character. I'd like to talk with Mrs. Thompson if that's okay. Your wife can fill me in on Alice's childhood, what she was like growing up."

"I know you believe in all that mumbo jumbo these psychologists are coming out with, but, don't forget it's hard evidence that nails the conviction. From what you've told me, you don't have any of that yet, do you?"

Steven grimaced. "No, but you know I'll get it."

"Yeah, you always do." Thompson sighed. "I'll let Gloria know you're coming over."

"Thank you. Tell her I'll be there as soon as I can. I have a couple stops to make first."

While Steven was talking with the chief, Ralph and Pete were pushing through a pair of swinging doors into the waiting room at the DL&W Railroad Station. They heard the roar of a train leaving the platform, then Pete wrinkled his nose.

"Smells like they just painted."

"Looks like it, too," Ralph said.

The patrolmen approached a skinny, white-haired man behind the ticket window.

"Good morning, officers," said a high, squeaky voice. "What can I do fer ya?"

"How are you, Mr. Ferguson?" Ralph said as they identified themselves and flashed their badges and IDs. "Were you working last Wednesday?"

"Sure, I work every day except Sunday."

"Do you remember if a slender man, probably wearing a short dark jacket and cap, came in from Syracuse?"

"No, I don't think so. It was a slow day." Ferguson named a couple of Knightsbridge citizens who had returned from Albany and a group of churchwomen who'd come back from Syracuse.

"Do you know Alice Shipley?" Pete asked.

"Yup, seen her a few times."

"Did she pass through the station Wednesday?"

"Not that I saw."

"When does the last train leave for Syracuse?" asked Ralph.

"Eight-forty during the week. Nine-thirty Saturdays and Sundays."

They thanked the railroad man and left.

A large blue-and-white box on wheels idled in front of the bus depot. The sign on its roof read Greyhound Lines, the words chased by the picture of a sleek greyhound. Ralph and Pete elbowed through a swinging door into a shabby waiting room. A middle-aged man sat on a stool in the ticket window.

"Hi, Nate."

"Well, if it ain't the dynamic duo. What can I do for you fellas this morning?"

Ralph repeated their questions about a slender man arriving or departing via the bus last Wednesday.

Nate hopped off the stool and disappeared behind the counter, bending to retrieve something. He popped up with a ledger in his hand. "Lucky for you, the main headquarters is keeping track of our passengers for a few weeks, some kind of study on the bus routes. I have to make everybody sign this—coming and going." He chuckled, pushing the register over.

Ray flipped through the pages until he reached Wednesday, October 31. The answer to his question was clear: the page was empty until one in the afternoon and they knew the man who'd signed.

"When does the last bus leave at night?" Ralph asked.

"Monday through Saturday ten-oh-five, Sundays six p.m.."

"That takes care of that. Thanks, Nate," said Pete.

When they arrived at the station, Steven was out.

By the time Steven finished discussing the investigation with the chief, it was after eleven. He grabbed his hat and coat, and had one foot out the door, when Jimmy Bou rushed in.

"Steven, Alice Shipley knew Leon's mother. My dad said they were really close. He saw them together all the time." Panting, he paused to catch his breath.

"That confirms an idea I have, Jimmy. Keep your coat on. I want you to go over to the five-and-dime." Steven handed him a sheaf of papers, pointed to a name, and told him what he wanted to know. "I'm going to the Shipleys' to ask Alice a few questions, then the chief's house to talk with Mrs. Thompson. If you get back before I do, stay here. I might need you later."

Alice Shipley answered the door with a book in her hand, as Steven had first seen her.

"Good morning, Detective. Is there news?"

"Not yet, ma'am, but I do have a question if you have a minute."

"Of course, come in," she said, leading him across the foyer into a sitting room, where she placed her glasses and book on a small table, then sat in a large club chair, motioning him to take its twin.

"You gave me the names of two trade union league members as your alibi for Wednesday evening."

"Oh, yes, I know what you're going to say. I didn't go that night."

"That's right. Mrs. Flanagan said you never miss a meeting but last week you weren't there. Can you explain that?"

"Of course, it was silly. I've had a lot on my mind lately, and I was so shocked at the news you brought that day, I simply got confused. I *always* go to the meetings. I'm the secretary and they rely on me to take the minutes. It's important that we have a written record of everything that's discussed, the plans we make, and, most of all, the voting on our projects."

"Why didn't you attend last week?"

"I had planned to, but I must have eaten something for supper that didn't agree with me. I spent the evening being sick in the bathroom."

"Can your cousin confirm that?"

"No, Edith's son picked her up earlier that day. She spent a few days with him and his family."

"So, you have no alibi for the time your husband was killed."

"No, but I don't have a motive either, Detective." She raised her brows and tilted her head as if to say *you see?*

"You're passionate about the rights of women, Mrs. Shipley. Now, along with your son, you have control of all the Shipley five-and-dimes. You're in charge of the employee salaries, promotions, the hours they work, in fact, every single aspect of their working conditions. All of it. You can make a difference in a lot of lives now that your husband is gone."

"And you think I would kill someone to accomplish that?" She looked like there was a bad smell in the room. "That's appalling. You must have a very low opinion of human nature."

"Unfortunately, I've seen worse than that, ma'am."

"I had absolutely no reason to remove Benjamin from the operation of the Shipley stores. The issue of women's rights in the workplace is much larger than that. I want to improve working conditions for female employees all over New York State, not just the stores we own. The Women's Trade Union League is a powerful organization and we're making progress. We're fighting to make an eight-hour workday the law, to establish a minimum wage, and most especially to abolish child labor. We're proposing legislation that will affect all women, in all kinds of jobs, and we're training women for better jobs and protecting them at work with new safety regulations. I'm not going to break the law to get better laws on the books."

"I see. That's an honorable cause. It must be a lot of work."

"Well worth it, wouldn't you say?"

"Yes, I would." Steven consulted his notebook in order to restore the balance in the interview. "Do you have a driving license, Mrs. Shipley?"

"No."

"So, you wouldn't own a motor car."

"There wouldn't be any point, would there?"

Steven studied Alice Shipley while she spoke. She hadn't hesitated, and most of her answers seemed straightforward. He knew she'd lied about Halloween night, but sensed she told the truth about her feelings on women's rights and the law.

His instincts told him this case hinged on the relationship between Alice Shipley and Leon Quigg, but how?

Steven decided to check back at the station before talking with Mrs. Thompson, in case Will had called in. He hadn't, but before Steven could leave again, Ralph and Pete hurried in, talking over each other, followed once again by Jimmy Bou.

"Slow down, fellas, one at a time," Steven said. "Jimmy, are you back already?"

"No, I haven't left yet. The chief asked me to do something. I'm going in a minute."

"Steven, we talked with Mr. Ferguson, who's got a mind like a steel trap. He said nobody who looked like the killer came in or left the train station on Wednesday," Ralph said. "And he knows what Mrs. Shipley looks like, she didn't come in either."

"Nate over at the bus depot has a register with all the passengers' names in it. The killer didn't take a bus either," said Pete.

"What about the last train or bus out at night?" Steven asked.

Ralph explained how both options would have been impossible.

Jimmy took the opportunity to tell Ralph and Pete about the friendship between Alice and Lillian.

"Coming back to Wednesday night," Steven said. "If Alice killed her husband, arriving by car is our only option. Maybe somebody gave her a ride, and she went back by train Thursday morning, but I say Edith Adams is naïve thinking Alice wouldn't borrow her car because it was off-limits and because Alice doesn't have a license."

"Yeah, if you're going to kill somebody, who cares if you're driving without a license?" Ralph snorted.

"What if she took her cousin's car, drove here, and parked it someplace where nobody would notice, then left in the middle of the night after the heat died down?" Pete suggested.

"Or maybe she stayed in Knightsbridge until morning," Jimmy Bou said. "What if she went back to the house?"

"Steven left a patrol there all night," Ralph said.

"Yeah, but all she had to do was wait until the patrolman was walking around the perimeter, and she could have snuck in. Alice Shipley seems like a smart lady. I bet she kept a key," Jimmy said.

"Wouldn't that be risky with Steven living across the street?" Pete said.

"She probably didn't know who lived there," Jimmy Bou replied.

"These are good ideas," Steven said. "I've got questions I intend to answer today, too. Does Alice know her husband was Leon's father? Does she know her best friend was Leon's mother? And the biggest question of all...does Alice know Benjamin Shipley let Lillian die when he could have helped her live?"

Steven stopped abruptly. Familiar with his methods, the others stayed quiet while he thought. A moment passed.

"What if we're looking at this all wrong? What if the murder has to do with the death of Leon's mother?"

As soon as Steven said it out loud, he knew.

It was as if pieces of a giant jigsaw puzzle took flight, rocketing through the air, then coming together in an orderly, logical fashion to form the picture.

This murder was all about Lillian.

After sending Jimmy Bou on his way and instructing Ralph and Pete on what he wanted them to do, Steven left for Chief Thompson's house.

Gloria Thompson answered the door with a feather duster in her hand and a kerchief around her hair.

"Detective Blackwell, I'm afraid you've caught me in the middle of my housework, but come in. Andy told me you'd be stopping with some questions about Alice." She led him into a crowded living room. "Mind the vacuum cleaner. Don't trip on the cord." She pushed a pile of newspapers to one side on the couch, indicating he should sit, and plopped down on a sagging chair across from him. "Now, what can I do for you?" She set the feather duster on a side table. "Oh, forgive my manners. Would you like a cup of coffee or a sandwich? Have you had lunch?"

"No, thank you, Mrs. Thompson. I have a few questions, then I'll let you get on with your work. If I told you your cousin Alice needed to spend a night here in Knightsbridge, who do you think she might stay with?"

"What a strange question. I assume you mean before Ben's murder since the house is hers now?"

"Yes. Has she stayed in touch with any friends or relatives other than you?"

"I'm her only family here. She knows she can always stay with us, although she hasn't. I don't think she has any friends left in town. She was close to one girl when they were in school, but I don't know what happened to her."

"What about a neighbor or a former nanny, babysitter, or tutor?"

"No, not that I can think of. Is there a particular date you have in mind?"

"Mrs. Thompson, this interview is confidential, all right? I need to ask you not to talk about it to anyone, except the chief, of course."

"All right." Gloria Thompson's eyes narrowed, and she leaned forward. "You think Alice killed him, don't you?"

"You know I can't say."

"Right, of course. What date do you need to know about? Halloween night?" she asked shrewdly.

Steven nodded, admiring her attitude.

The chief's wife scooted to the edge of her seat. "Alice is no dummy, Detective Blackwell. Where's the last place you'd ever think to look for her if she did kill Ben?" She raised her eyebrows so they disappeared under her bangs.

"You don't mean here?"

"No. The house, Detective, her house. Ben's house."

"But, she hasn't lived there in nearly twenty years. How…."

"Like I said, no dummy. She kept a key," Gloria Thompson said, as if it were the most obvious thing in the world. "My guess would be she waited someplace until you and your team left, then she went back. Probably let herself in the back door. The rear of the house is in complete darkness at night. She would have been invisible."

The last piece clicked into place.

Steven remembered something Will had told him after he'd searched the Shipley house. He stood and reached out to shake her hand. "Yes, I see. Thank you very much, Mrs. Thompson. I appreciate your thoughts and your time. And remember…."

"We never spoke." She touched her nose, raising her brows and giving him a sly smile.

Driving back to the station, Steven's mind was buzzing. He was sure he knew what had happened, and if he was right, he had the wrong man behind bars.

Jimmy Bou knocked on the frame of Norm Evans' open door at the back of Shipley's Five-and-Dime. The assistant manager looked up from his paperwork. "Come on in, Jimmy."

Evans removed a box of Thanksgiving decorations from a chair and motioned for the policeman to sit. "What can I do for you? I assume it's about the murder."

"I'd like to talk with Gladys Pekoe. On the paper you gave Steven the other day, it looks like she's been working here since 1904."

"Yes, she'll be manager of the lunch counter now, if I have anything to say about it. Good worker. Smart, dependable, always on time. She's getting ready to open, prepping some of the food, putting coffee on."

"Swell." Jimmy stood, and they shook hands. "Thanks, Norm."

There was something about the lunch counter in Shipley's that Jimmy Bou had always loved. He still remembered the first time his mother brought him here for ice cream. It was summer, and they were shopping for school supplies. After they'd purchased his pencils, erasers, a ruler, tablets of lined paper, and two black-and-white marble notebooks, she steered him to the far side of the store. It was a sweltering August day, and they were both sweating. They perched on red-topped stools, and his mother clearly and efficiently told the girl behind the counter they wanted two tall glasses of ice water and chocolate ice cream sodas. Jimmy had never heard his mother command anyone before. His chest had swelled with pride.

A thin gray-haired woman wearing a hairnet and apron stood next to an industrial sink with her back to him.

"Excuse me, Mrs. Pekoe?"

She turned around, a loaf of Wonder Bread in her hand, the product's name in bold red ink, with yellow, red, and blue polka dots covering the package. "Yes?"

"I'm Officer Jimmy Bourgogne," he said, showing his badge and ID.

"Yes, I've seen you around town."

"Mr. Evans tells me you've been with the store for a long time. Do you remember a girl named Lillian Quigg?"

"Oh my, Lillian. I sure do. We worked behind the counter together. I trained her. Sweet thing. Very hard worker."

"I understand she was a friend of Alice Shipley's."

"Oh, yes. They were great friends. Of course, that was before Lillian left and Alice married Mr. Shipley."

"Can you tell me anything about their friendship? Were they close?"

"Like sisters."

"Do you know why she left?"

Gladys Pekoe shook her head. "No, one day she was just gone. I missed her. She was a good person to work with. Made the time go by fast."

"What was she like?"

"Smart, funny, kindhearted."

"Can you tell me anything about Mrs. Shipley?"

"She never came back to the lunch counter after Lillian left. I'd catch a glimpse of her in the store shopping, but she didn't look like the same person anymore. Like the life had gone out of her, if you know what I mean, no spark."

Ralph and Pete entered the DL & W Railroad Station for the second time that day and went directly to Mr. Ferguson.

"Yer back," the elderly man quipped.

"Yeah, we have a couple more questions. We need to know about last

Thursday. Do you remember if a slender man—or possibly a woman wearing man's clothing, a short jacket and cap—bought a ticket to Syracuse? It would've been early. A train that would get to Syracuse no later than ten or ten-thirty," Ralph asked.

"Nope. That'd be the seven forty-five. Gets in at nine-fifteen."

"Are you sure you didn't see anyone matching that description?"

"Positive. Place was a ghost town till noon."

"All right. Was there anything unusual about Thursday morning?"

Stuart Ferguson squinted and scrunched up his weathered face. He bent to the side and spat a wad of chewing tobacco into a can on the floor. "Well, yeah, now that you mention it. There was a motor car in the parking lot when I got here, but there wasn't anybody waitin' for me to unlock the station door."

"Don't people leave their vehicles in the lot sometimes?"

"Once in a while, somebody might leave their car for an hour or two during the day. While they're doing some shopping, you know? But I've never seen one left overnight. The car was wet so I know it was here all night."

"And you didn't see anybody around who looked like they owned it?"

The rail employee shook his head.

"Can you remember what the automobile looked like?"

"It was an old black Ford. I'm amazed it was still runnin'. I can tell you the numbers on the registration tag."

"You can?" Pete's face lit up. "What were they?"

"J-0716."

"How can you be so sure?"

"That's my birthday. July sixteen." Ferguson grinned, revealing two missing teeth. "I turned eighty-six last summer," he said proudly.

"Good for you. That's a real accomplishment, Mr. Ferguson. Did you see the car leave?"

"Nope."

Ralph and Pete thanked him, tipped their hats, and left the station.

Cutting through an empty field near the hotel on the way back to the station, Ralph and Pete chattered like magpies about what they'd discovered. Both officers felt that familiar tingle from uncovering an important clue.

Steven grabbed the phone without even removing his hat and coat, and when he heard a woman's voice, said, "Mrs. Adams, is Sergeant Taylor still there?"

"Yes, Detective, he's looking for the gun. My husband owned a .38mm revolver which he kept in his bureau. I could never face cleaning out all his belongings, and I left several drawers and part of the closet untouched. Would you like to speak with Sergeant Taylor?"

"Yes, thank you."

"I won't be a minute."

While Steven waited, he paced back and forth behind his desk, wishing he had one of those cellphones from Olivia's time so he could walk around the room while he was waiting.

"Steven, it looks like the gun is gone." Will's deep voice boomed over the telephone line.

"Will, find out if her husband's gun was registered and if she has the paperwork. We need everything you can find. I'll explain when you get back"

"Got it. I'll be back as soon as I can."

Ralph, Pete, and Jimmy Bou entered the CID room, all speaking at once.

"Jimmy, you go first," Steven said.

Jimmy shared what Gladys Pekoe had told him about Alice and Lillian. "It sounds like Alice changed after Lillian left. Mrs. Pekoe said she was like a different person, and real sad."

Steven nodded, weighing the implications of this news. "Ralph, Pete?"

"Nobody fitting our description took the train to Syracuse Thursday morning, but Mr. Ferguson noticed a car left overnight in the station's parking lot. It was a black Ford, registration number J-0716."

"I saw a Ford Runabout in front of Edith Adams's house the other day. I wonder if it was the same one," Steven exclaimed. "Jimmy, call the Tax Commission in Albany. Have them look up the owner. Tell them it's part of a murder investigation and ask if they can put a rush on it."

"What do you want us to do, Steven?"

"We can't arrest her yet, but I don't want Alice Shipley slipping through our fingers. Take one of the department cars and go sit in my driveway. I want you to keep an eye on the house. There's a call box near the corner by Dr. Kranken's house. Call if you need anything."

"We're on our way," said Ralph.

"Take some sandwiches with you. You might be there a while," Steven added.

"We'll swing by Joe's, and get some coffee, too," Pete said.

Steven's stomach was growling, but he didn't want to stop now. Things were happening too fast. He retrieved the keys to the cell, went to get Leon Quigg, and escorted him into Interview 1.

Leon appeared calmer than he'd been yesterday, and that wasn't all. An inner strength that Steven hadn't seen until now struck him, and he realized Leon would have to be incredibly strong to have survived the tragedies he'd faced as a child. The man must have a core of steel.

"Are they treating you okay, Leon? Someone brought breakfast and coffee, and lunch?"

"Yes, Detective, thank you. Did you test the gun? Could you tell it hasn't been used?"

"We're working on that." Steven lied, then leaned forward and spoke in earnest. "Listen, Leon, I'm going to lay my cards on the table. I need you to help me with some things. I think you can help yourself at the same time." Steven caught his gaze and held it. "I need you to trust me."

Leon regarded Steven for several long seconds, seeming to take the measure of the detective.

"All right. I will."

"You have to tell me the truth."

"I have told you the truth."

"Good, I'm glad to hear it. Now, I want you to tell me about the day you found the letter your mother wrote to Mr. Shipley."

"I already told you everything, Detective. There's nothing else to say."

"Tell me again, please."

"I found it in the mailbag from Syracuse."

"Do you remember exactly when? The date?"

"It wasn't the Saturday before Halloween. It was the Saturday before that."

Steven took out his wallet and extracted a small card, *The First National Bank and Trust Company* printed across the top, and below a calendar for 1934. The day Leon was referring to was October 20th.

"All right. Go on."

"I read the note, took off the paper clip, and saw the envelope. I recognized her handwriting immediately. It felt like somebody hit me on the back with a baseball bat. When I read her letter, I thought the floor fell out from under my feet. My knees buckled, and I had to sit down. I read my mother's words, Detective, but I had a hard time taking in the meaning. All my life, I wondered who my father was. But I never imagined I'd find out anything like what was in the letter.

At first, I couldn't understand it, then after a few minutes, it sunk in. I couldn't believe somebody could act like that."

Steven could see Leon was fighting to stay in control. His jaw trembled ever so slightly. His eyes glistened but radiated purpose. He seemed to will Steven to understand and to believe him. This was the kid who survived the death of his beloved mother, his uncle, then his aunt—the only family he had ever known—all in less than a year. At the age of ten. Steven thought that, for the first time, he was seeing the real Leon Quigg.

"If it hadn't been for that man, she might still be alive," Leon whispered. He leaned back in his chair and put his hands in his lap.

"What did you do after you read the letter?"

"I put it in my pocket and went out on my route."

"It must have felt like it was burning a hole in your pocket."

Leon nodded slowly. "I didn't have much choice, did I?"

Steven wondered if that statement summed up Leon Quigg's life. *Not much choice.* Leon had been the victim of so many tragic circumstances.

"Why were you really running across The Green Wednesday night?"

"I wasn't lying. I just didn't tell you everything." Leon dropped his head for a moment, a flush creeping onto his cheeks, and, when he looked up, Steven saw courage and determination.

"I was going to confront Mr. Shipley with the letter and ask him why he didn't save her. I wanted to look him in the eye and let him know what he'd done to her and to me. After I left the pub, I thought, *Okay, it's now or never.* I started walking up Chiltington and thought I saw somebody ahead of me, so I slowed down because I didn't want to run into anyone. I almost got to Judge Randolph's house when I heard the shot. I really thought it was a firecracker. But it didn't matter. I didn't want to be anywhere near whatever was going on. I took off between two houses and ran across The Green. I didn't see anybody until I tried to cross the street and almost got hit. Then, I kept going and went straight home."

This is the truth. Now, we're getting somewhere.

"Tell me about your friendship with Alice Shipley."

A transformation took place before Steven's eyes. Leon completely relaxed. His shoulders dropped, his face took on a glow, and he smiled. "Alice," he whispered, as his eyes closed for a second. "She's wonderful. She helped me more than I could ever explain."

"Can you tell me about it?"

"You know I'm a private sort of fella. I don't like talking about myself. But I do trust you, Detective. If you say this is going to help me, I'll tell you." He took a deep breath and sat up a little straighter.

"I met Alice when I was ten. It was a few months after my Aunt Cathleen died and I had to move here. I'd never met my guardian before. He was nice to me, but I was lost and desperately unhappy. The only place where I felt okay was the library. I love to read. You can get lost in a book, you know. That winter, I started going to the Village Library on Saturday mornings. One day, it was really crowded. Alice came to the table where I was reading and asked if she could sit down. There weren't any other empty seats. I said sure, and that was it. We didn't even talk that first time."

"When did you get to know each other?"

"A couple of months later, in the spring, I went back and Alice sat with me again. That's when we introduced ourselves. We got talking, and we just kept it up every Saturday. Later, I found out the most amazing coincidence, Alice and my mother were friends." Leon's eyes grew wide.

"That is something! I imagine it brought you closer."

"Maybe. I never thought about it like that."

"How long did you meet at the library?"

"Here in Knightsbridge, till August. That was when she left Mr. Shipley and moved to Liverpool. We met at the Syracuse Library after that. They have a beautiful library. Alice couldn't come back here, so I took the bus to Syracuse every weekend. It was a real adventure for a kid."

Steven imagined that the grin that had appeared on Leon Quigg's face was a reflection of his exciting boyhood journeys to what he probably thought of as *the big city*. "I bet it was. You weren't scared? Going so far all alone?"

"Nope."

"Leon, do you think Alice felt she was acting on your mother's behalf? I certainly don't mean she could ever take her place, but maybe looking out for you the way a mother would?"

"She didn't know who my mother was when we met. It was months later that she saw a resemblance to her in my face and we figured it out." A tender smile appeared again. "But, when I was younger, sometimes she did things a mom would do. She remembered my birthday every year, and she gave me a present at Christmas. I always showed her my report card and sometimes I made her things in art class. We've been friends for a long time."

"Do you and Alice still meet?"

"Yes, but not every week because of my job."

"She must seem like family after all those years."

"She's the only family I have now."

"Leon, when you found the letter your mother wrote, did you show it to Alice?"

"Of course. I took it with me the next weekend."

"What was her reaction?"

"Upset. Angry." Leon dropped his head.

Steven almost didn't hear what came next.

"She cried."

Chapter Thirty-Eight

S hortly after two-thirty, Will walked in with a smile on his face. "It took a while, Steven, but I've got the paperwork from the gun registration. Mrs. Adams found it in a box in the cellar." Will extracted a sheaf of papers and joined his partner at their desks.

"Hang on a minute. I've got a surprise for you," Steven said.

In less time than it took Will to get a glass of water, Steven was back. He was holding a revolver in his gloved hands.

"This is the gun you found in Shipley's desk drawer, Will. Let's see what we've got." He turned the gun upside down and looked under the butt, then read off the numbers while his partner checked the registration confirmation that Smith and Wesson had mailed back to Mr. Adams.

The numbers matched.

"What did I miss, Steven?"

Steven related his conversation with Chief Thompson's wife and shared the information the team had uncovered in the past few hours.

Will whistled and shook his head in amazement. "Well, I'll be darned." His brow furrowed. "But we don't have her yet, do we?"

After lunch, Alice Shipley donned a jacket and went out on the porch to remove the Halloween decorations. Jolly pumpkins marching up the front steps didn't seem appropriate under the circumstances. After throwing them in the trash, she got a broom to sweep the porch and steps. Alice loved autumn and hated to brush away the beautiful colored leaves that had drifted onto the wooden planks, but she liked a neat house.

This was her house again and, until she decided what she wanted to do, she would take pride in keeping things picked up and presentable. Theo had told her last night he needed to get back to the city. He had a deadline at the magazine, and he missed his life. Her son had made a life for himself in New York, and that was where he was going to stay. He didn't want the house, but said that if she decided to sell, he'd return to help take inventory, clean out the sizeable dwelling, and sell or donate things. Theo was leaving tomorrow morning.

"Good morning, Mrs. Shipley."

Alice looked up from her sweeping. The mailman was walking up the front path with a handful of envelopes, mostly sympathy cards she imagined, maybe some bills.

"Good morning...," she stopped herself. "Where's Leon?" she asked, frowning. "I thought I saw him leave the mail yesterday."

"Oh, Mrs. Shipley, you haven't heard?"

Alice held her breath. "Heard what?"

"They arrested him. The police locked him up in jail yesterday. The rumor is he killed Mr. Shipley."

Alice's hand flew to her chest. There was an intake of breath and she swayed. One arm shot out to grab the railing so she wouldn't topple off the porch.

"You're sure? You're sure he's not just home sick today?"

"Yes, ma'am. I'm sure." He took a step up and reached out to give her the stack of envelopes. Then he tipped his cap and was gone.

Alice leaned the broom against the wall and dropped onto the top step. *So this is it,* she thought. She had known since she'd first formulated the plan to kill Ben that if someone else was blamed, she would own up to it. Most importantly, she would never ever let her beloved Leon take the blame for something she had done. But there was something she needed to do first, and she needed time. She wasn't ready to turn herself in yet.

Alice rose, brushed off the seat of her trousers, and re-entered the house.

"Theo, where are you?" she called out.

"Upstairs, Mom. In my room."

Alice climbed the grand staircase and entered her son's former bedroom. "What are you doing?" she asked when she saw him sitting at his old school desk. How had he managed to fit in there?

"Writing some notes for my next *New Yorker* article."

"Listen, dear, I need to go out for a while. Can I borrow your car?"

"Of course." Theo got up from the chair and walked to the closet. He reached into his jacket pocket and retrieved his keys. "Here you are. Where are you going? Are you going to be long?"

"Probably most of the day. Don't wait dinner for me."

"Okay. Be careful on the road, Mom." He leaned over and pecked her cheek. Something must have seemed odd, because he grabbed her hand. "Are you all right? Is something wrong?"

Alice patted his hand. "Nothing for you to worry about, Theo. Just a few things I need to do."

Alice Shipley backed out of the driveway, then headed east down Hickory. As she drove past the police station, she had to force herself not to look. Leon was confined inside that innocent-looking building, flung into a cell with bars on it, cold metal bars robbing him of his freedom. He must be confused, and maybe angry. She prayed he wasn't panicking. Her heart clenched. What had she done to him? Locked up for something he hadn't done.

Alice knew how much Leon loved to be outside walking. This must be hell for him. She wondered if he had anything to read. If he didn't, that would make the nightmare even worse. *Only a short time to go, my dear. I won't let you stay there a moment longer than I have to. I promise.*

Alice made her way out of town, eventually reaching Route 12, where she began her journey north into the Adirondack Mountains. She would have loved to simply walk down the street to the library and find a quiet corner, but she didn't know how long this would take, and she didn't want any interruptions. She also wanted complete privacy; she couldn't risk anyone peering over her shoulder.

As she drove along the narrow twisting road, the thick tree growth blocked much of the sunlight, and she felt the temperature drop. It was always colder in the mountains, especially ones as massive as the Adirondacks. Alice loved being here—she was at peace in the calm of the forest. This was the perfect place to do what she had to do.

Alice rolled down her window. The cold air bit her face, but felt good. It wouldn't be long before she would no longer be able to enjoy this luxury. She pulled the car onto the shoulder and let the engine idle with the parking brake on. She slid over on the bench seat and rolled down the passenger side window. Two tiny chipmunks chased each other along the verge, running like the devil was on their tails. She heard a muffled snort and several deer roamed just inside the tree line, one behind the other, their white tails flicking the coded message: *It's safe here.* Alice breathed in, leaned back on the soft upholstered seat, and closed her eyes. The familiar scents of balsam fir, Scotch pine, and white spruce smelled like Christmas, and made her smile, though she knew she had celebrated her last Christmas. There would be no more tree-decorating for her. Memories would have to be her solace.

As she lay back against the seat, Alice felt a tear trickle down her cheek. She brushed it away. Now, where had that come from? She didn't regret shooting Ben. If she hadn't acted as an avenging angel, who would? There was no doubt in her mind the universe had demanded vengeance—for cruelly snatching Theo from her, causing her to beg God on her hands and knees every night for years to bring her son back to her, or put her out of her misery and take her life; for robbing sweet Leon of the happy childhood with his adored mother that he had richly deserved; and for ignoring her beloved Lillian's pleas for help, thereby condemning her to an early and painful death. Yes, no one had needed to be killed more than Benjamin Shipley, and Alice had accepted the role of executioner.

Enough. She had things to do. There was no time for indulgence. Fixing the scent of the pine trees in her mind, Alice took her last deep breath of the wonders of the forest, slid back onto the driver's side, and continued on her way.

She turned right after Kayuta Lake, heading northeast on Route 28. She drove through the small town of Forestport and passed White Lake. Shortly after, she spied Otter Lake on her left.

Many New York moneyed families owned property in the Adirondacks—hunting lodges, fancy fishing cabins, or summer homes referred to as "Great Camps." The Shipleys had none of these, but, years ago when she was a child, Alice's father had taken her and her mother to The Inn on Otter Lake. It had been an idyllic week and now seemed the perfect spot. It was remote and quiet. No one would bother her here. Alice could concentrate on writing the most important letters of her life.

She pulled into the gravel drive and headed down a small incline toward the lake, around to the back of The Inn. Since she had no idea how long her tasks would take, she had come prepared to stay, if necessary. She would book a room and register for one night. If everything went quickly, she'd simply leave. If she had to spend the night, she'd call Theo so he wouldn't worry. She could easily get back to Knightsbridge tomorrow before he needed to leave for the city.

Alice took her overnight case from the rumble seat, closed the top, making sure the latch was secure, and locked Theo's car. The wooden planks creaking as she stepped onto the porch, Alice pulled open the door and stepped to the registration desk.

"Hello, I'm looking for a room for the night. I didn't have a chance to telephone," she told the manager.

"Yes, ma'am," he said, looking behind her toward the door as if expecting someone to follow her in. "How many guests will there be?"

"Just me."

Thick black eyebrows shot up to the salt-and-pepper hair. "Of course. We have a room with its own private bath. Would you prefer that?"

"Yes, thank you."

"That'll be two dollars and fifty cents."

Alice extracted her change purse and set the money on the counter. The manager turned the guest register around and she signed her name and address. He handed her a large metal key adorned with a loop on the top end.

"Number four. It's at the top of the stairs. We serve dinner at six. Would you like me to reserve a table for you?"

"Yes, thank you."

Alice dropped her case on the bed, walked to the window, and threw open the sash. Inhaling deeply, she cataloged more scents into her memory for the years to come. She smelled worms—it must have rained earlier—fish, and the lake, with its faint smell of decomposing plant life. Turning away from the window, she opened her case and extracted a packet of blue linen stationery and her pen, then settled at a small desk fashioned from birch tree branches. Enjoying a moment's delight at her temporary office, she turned on the lamp and began her first letter, the one to her son.

My darling Theo, when you receive this letter, I will be in jail accused of murdering your father. It's true. I want to explain why I did it and I pray you will understand and not judge me...

Alice explained in great detail why she had felt obliged to end Benjamin Shipley's life. She described how she had wanted to die when he took Theo away from her and how enraged she had been when she'd learned that he'd sent Theo away to the military academy. She told him about the letter Lillian had written pleading for her life and how Benjamin had ignored it, sentencing her to death and leaving Leon an orphan.

When we spoke about your half-brother, you said you wanted Leon to share in the family fortune. I hope you will still feel the same way. Before you go back to New York, go to him, Theo. Reach out to him, please. He's going to need you. And perhaps you will need him too. Leon's very shy. It may take him a while to want to know you and to embrace you as his brother. He has also inherited his mother's sense of pride. You might have to be clever in order to persuade him to accept the money. You are more sophisticated than Leon is. I think you will understand all of this and proceed cautiously and thoughtfully. He will likely be angry with me. Not for taking your father's life, but for creating the circumstances which force me to be away from him. I hope they will let him visit me, wherever I end up. And you too, of course. I love you with all my heart, Theo.

Please forgive me.

Alice next wrote a short explanatory note to Edith, with an apology for borrowing the car. She described where she kept all her notebooks and the papers for the Women's Trade Union League, asked her to telephone Theo and have him pick up her clothing and belongings, and told her where she'd hidden some cash. She said Edith should keep the money for any trouble she had caused and in thanks for her generosity over the years.

Finally, Alice was ready to write her letter to Leon. She had left this one for last because she knew it would be the most difficult.

Alice stretched to relieve her aching hip. All this sitting wasn't good for her. She closed her eyes for a moment in order to gather her thoughts. As she had with Theo's letter, she would write this one from her heart and pray that he would understand and forgive her.

Chapter Thirty-Nine

After Will left to deliver the gun to the lab for confirmation that it was indeed the murder weapon, Steven updated the murder board. As he was setting the chalk down, his phone rang. Hoping it was the news they were looking for, he rushed to his desk and grabbed the receiver.

"Detective Sergeant Blackwell," he answered.

"This is Bill Edwards at the Tax Commission. Officer Bourgogne asked me to call you. I have the information he requested."

Steven said a silent prayer. "Yes?"

"The license registration number J-0716 belongs to a Mr. Robert Adams of 403 Cypress Street, Liverpool."

Steven silently mouthed, *Yes!* "Thank you, Mr. Edwards. You made my day."

Edwards laughed. "Glad to hear it. Call us anytime, Detective."

In a serendipitous moment of perfect timing, Jimmy walked in the door.

"We've got her, Jimmy! Will's taking the gun to Hank for ballistics testing." Steven explained their findings on the presumed murder weapon. "And the car belonged to Edith Adams' husband. That's how she did it. Alice Shipley drove here on Wednesday then drove back to Liverpool Thursday morning."

Jimmy Bou's face lit up. "Wow! Let's go get her."

"I want to tell the chief first. I'll be right back."

Steven hurried to Thompson's office and walked in without knocking. "It's Alice Shipley, Chief." He updated his boss and said he and Jimmy were leaving to pick her up.

"Good work, Steven. I was hoping it wouldn't be her, but there's nothing I can do about it. My wife will have to accept what her cousin did, that's all there is to it."

Steven and Jimmy Bou pulled into the empty driveway of the Shipley house.

"Uh oh, Theo's car is gone," Steven said. "I hope the two of them haven't legged it. Ralph and Pete are still in my driveway. I wonder what's going on."

Steven rang the bell. They waited. He rang again. They looked at each other. Steven frowned, shaking his head.

Theo Shipley wrenched open the door. Panting, he said, "Sorry, I was upstairs, Detective Blackwell. What can I do for you?"

Steven noticed he appeared relaxed, almost jolly.

"We need to talk with your mother, Theo. Is she home?"

"No, you just missed her. She had some errands to do. Is there something I can help with?"

"Thanks, but no. Where did she go?"

"She didn't say."

"Do you know when she'll be back?"

"Later this evening. She told me not to wait for dinner."

"Looks like she took your car?"

"Yes."

"All right, thank you. We'll check back later."

Jimmy followed Steven across the street to where Ralph and Pete sat in a black Ford. Steven knocked on the window and Ralph cranked it down.

"What's up, Steven?"

"That's what I want to know. Why didn't you call in? Alice is gone."

"What?" the two officers shouted.

"The car was already gone when we got here, Steven," Ralph said. "We figured Theo was out. We've been watching the house. We saw a curtain move, and a light go on. We figured it was Alice inside."

"Come back to the station. We need a plan," Steven instructed.

In the car on the way, Jimmy said, "Theo didn't seem to be lying for her."

"I agree, but we're not taking any chances. We're going to look for her now."

Will was at his desk when Steven, Ralph, and Pete entered the CID room.

"Did you get her?"

Steven told him what had happened. Will groaned. Jimmy came in with a large map that he spread out on a worktable.

Years ago, someone in the department had divided Knightsbridge into zones and marked the perimeters with a thick black line. Each zone was assigned to a pair of patrol officers who would walk the streets every day and evening.

"Let's see." Steven traced his finger along several lines. "We're looking for Theo's Plymouth. We'll use the map to divide up the town. Everyone who's already out on foot will be checking in with Tommy soon. I'll give them instructions through him. Will, would you take Charlie and cover the outskirts to the east from the knitting mill around to St. Joe's church? Ralph and Pete, take the other car and check the woods and fields around the high school. Go all the way over to Route 13. Jimmy and I will cover the rest of the perimeter and check the farms out on Route 5."

"We'll find her, Steven. She won't get away." Jimmy punctuated this pronouncement with a firm nod. "What about Leon? Are you letting him go?"

"Not yet. I'm holding him until we have Alice. We may need him to give us information that nobody else can. Grab your jacket and let's go." He paused. "Actually…wait here, I'll be right back."

Steven hurried to the cell where Leon Quigg was lying on the cot, reading.

"Leon, I have a question for you."

Leon laid the open book face down on his stomach. "What is it, Detective?"

"Besides the library, does Alice have a favorite place? Somewhere she might go to be alone?"

"She loves the mountains. Her father took her to Otter Lake when she was little. She has happy memories of that place."

"Okay, thanks."

On the way out of the station, Steven updated Tommy Forester. "When they call in, tell everybody I want Alice Shipley found and brought in. Remind them what Theo's motor car looks like." He paused so Tommy could write the description of the roadster. "If she's on foot when they see her, they're to tell her she's urgently needed for questioning, and they're to escort her back here. If she's driving, I want them to flag her down. She should park the car wherever they are, and they can walk her back to the station. Theo can pick up his vehicle later."

"Got it, Detective. Where will you be?"

Steven told him. "I'll stop and call in every half hour. Do you have all that?"

Tommy gave a determined nod. "Yup, you can depend on me."

"Okay, and tell everyone not to listen to any excuses from Mrs. Shipley. They're to bring her in."

For the next two hours, Steven and Jimmy Bou circled Knightsbridge, driving along every road, street, and pathway marking the town's perimeter. They went up and down the lanes of the sawmill's enormous parking lot and the lot at the railway station, searching for the abandoned car. They drove along every inch of the banks of the Mohawk River. They bounced down rutted dirt driveways, connecting farms to the main route.

Every half hour, Steven waited in the car while Jimmy Bou made telephone calls from the hotel, the DL & W Railroad Station, and two gas stations. Tommy Forester reported that the members of Steven's team were calling in at regular intervals, but no one had seen Alice Shipley or Theo's car.

At six o'clock, they returned to the station to implement the next step in Steven's plan. While Jimmy waited in the car, Steven dialed the local office of the New York State Troopers. He explained that he needed an All-Points Bulletin put out for Alice Shipley, told the officer why, and provided the relevant information. He also explained what he and his team had already done and emphasized that Otter Lake was a favorite spot of Mrs. Shipley's.

At seven, Steven and Jimmy Bou headed back to the police station in defeat. Tommy told them each team of patrolmen was still out looking, but Mrs. Shipley continued to elude them.

While he waited for the results from the APB, Steven updated the chief, then began a long, detailed report on the day's activities, the evidence they'd discovered, and what he'd learned. As he wrote, he realized it would be cruel to detain Leon any longer. He retrieved a set of keys and an item from his desk drawer, then walked to the end of the hall.

"Leon, you're free to go," he said as the young man sat up and set his book on the edge of the cot.

"Really? You believe me?"

"Yes, and I'm sorry we had to put you through this. I hope you understand that we have to investigate every line of inquiry that we get. When we make an arrest, we have to be sure."

"You've made an arrest?"

"Not yet, but soon. Would you like someone to drive you home? Jimmy can sign out one of the department vehicles."

"No, I want to walk. I've missed walking. It seems like I've been here a long time."

Steven handed him his jacket, cap, and belongings. "I truly appreciate the help you've given us, and I think we found your mother's medal." He held out the silver Virgin Mary medal found on Halloween night. "Is this it?"

Leon's face lit up. "Yes, it is! Thank you. Where did you find it?"

"You must have dropped it on your route." Steven held out his hand. "I wish you all the best, Leon. Thank you for your help."

Leon Quigg shook Steven's hand, returned his wallet to his pocket, donned his outer gear, then picked up the book. "Goodbye, Detective."

Steven escorted him out of the police station, then stopped at the front desk.

"Tommy, still no word?" Steven asked after Leon had left.

"Nothing yet, Detective."

Steven got a cup of coffee then, glancing at his watch and hoping Olivia would be awake when he got home, he returned to his paperwork. Will arrived shortly after, disappointment on his face, frustration in his voice.

"She's still out there, huh?"

Steven nodded,

"You don't look very upset," Will said. "Why not?"

"I remembered something Theo Shipley said last week. He told me his mother always takes responsibility for her actions. Maybe I'm clinging to straws, but I don't think she's run off. Besides, everybody's out looking, and I called in an APB."

At that moment, they heard Tommy Forester shout, "Ma'am, you can't just go down there. Wait. Please."

Steven jumped up and rushed out into the corridor.

To his amazement, Alice Shipley was striding down the hallway, heading right toward him.

"Detective Blackwell, I must speak with you immediately."

"Come with me, Mrs. Shipley." Steven called to Will. "Sergeant Taylor, if you and Officer Bourgogne have one."

Recognizing the coded message, Will grabbed his notebook and got Jimmy Bou. They positioned themselves behind the one-way mirror in Interview 1.

After settling at the table, Steven said, "I've been looking for you, Mrs. Shipley."

"I understand you have Leon Quigg in one of your cells. He didn't kill my husband." She took a deep breath and said, "I did."

"I know you did."

Her mouth gaped and her eyes grew large. "You do?" She sat up a little straighter.

"Yes, ma'am. I realized it today. And we have the evidence, but I'd like to hear everything from you. Would you tell me about it?"

"Have you seen the letter Leon's mother Lillian wrote to my husband? The one where she begged for her life?"

Steven nodded.

"It was the straw that broke the camel's back," she said calmly. "You know how I met Leon. The first time I saw him sitting in the library reading, all alone at that enormous table, he looked so small and helpless. When he told me his mother had died, I wanted to hug him and tell him everything would be all right. Shortly after that, I lost my son. Ben ripped my life apart when he took Theo. There were times when I thought I'd kill myself because of the pain. Leon and

Edith saved my life. It's as simple as that. Edith got me involved with the suffragettes. Once I saw what those women were fighting for, I stopped thinking about myself. And Leon gave me someone to care for, if you know what I mean."

"Yes, I do."

"I'd lost my son. He'd lost his mother. We formed a bond. Later, when I realized he was Lillian's son, I vowed I would do everything I could to help him through life. I wanted to do all the things a mother would do, things I couldn't do for my own son, and things Lillian had been robbed of doing."

Alice Shipley reached toward the pitcher of water, but Steven lifted it and filled a glass for her. After drinking half in one gulp, she continued.

"To tell you the truth, Detective, I hadn't thought of Benjamin in years. In a personal way, I mean. It was the letter that did it."

"Tell me about that."

"Leon and I met at the Syracuse Library like always. It was the Saturday before Halloween. As soon as I saw him, I knew something had upset him. There was a book open on the table, but he was staring off into space. I sat down and asked him what was the matter. He explained how he'd found the letter then showed me."

Steven watched the color drain from her face and noticed the hand holding the glass shook. She closed her eyes a moment, regaining control, then glared at him. "Lillian was the best friend I ever had. I loved her like a sister. There were times when we thought the same thoughts, felt the same feelings, and said the same things. We joked that we must be the same person. She was sweet and gentle and kind and funny. The treatment she needed to save her life would have been a pittance to Benjamin. And he couldn't be bothered." She looked incredulous.

"I just snapped. Like a rubber band that's pulled to the limit of its endurance. Something inside me broke. I knew he had to be punished.

He took Theo from me. He took Leon's mother from him. And he took the most precious thing from Lillian–her life. So, I took his."

Steven looked into her eyes and saw no anger, no fear, only truth and acceptance.

"I don't regret it. I'll take the punishment for what I did, Detective Blackwell."

"Tell me exactly how you managed it, Mrs. Shipley, how you got here and got back to Liverpool, where you got the gun and what you did with it after."

Although Steven was sure he knew the answers to these questions, this preliminary confession would form the basis for her written statement.

"Certainly. I'm afraid I took advantage of Edith. She'll have every right to be angry with me. I wouldn't blame her for that. I've written her a letter and can only hope she'll understand and forgive me. Do you think you could make sure she receives it?"

Steven nodded.

"Thank you. I knew Edith's late husband had a gun, and that she hadn't been able to face throwing away all of his things. It didn't take long, one evening when she was out, to find it. She kept the keys to his automobile on a hook in the kitchen. When she told me she was going to spend a few days with her son and his family, I decided I would do it that first night she was gone–just to be sure she didn't come home early and find I had taken the motor car, you see. When I realized it would be Halloween, I thought it was perfect timing because that night's always chaotic. After Edith's son picked her up, I gathered a jacket and cap that Theo keeps at the house, and an old coat and fedora of Edith's husband. I drove to Knightsbridge and left the car parked in the lot at the train station. I made sure I arrived with just enough time to do what I needed to do. I didn't want to have any extra time to kill. I got lucky because it was an exceptionally dark night. It was quite cloudy.

"I wore the jacket and had the cap in my trousers' pocket. I put the overcoat on over the jacket and stuffed my hair under the fedora. I left the train station and cut through the field next to the hotel, then went up the Brighton Road to Victoria. The only place where I was a bit nervous was when I had to walk past The Three Lords. I didn't want somebody to come out and run into me, but I was lucky again because the streets were empty. I hurried to the gazebo on the Village Green, left the coat and fedora there, then ran back to Victoria. I thought of cutting through to Chiltington between a couple of houses, but I couldn't take a chance that a neighbor would come outside with their dog or take out the garbage. I thought it would be safer to use the sidewalk out front. I put my collar up and pulled the cap down. I figured anyone who saw me would think I was a young man trying to stay warm on a cold night."

Alice Shipley caught her breath and drank more water.

"After I'd done it, I ran around the house and back to the gazebo. I put the coat on over the jacket, stuck the cap in the pocket, and put the fedora on again. I crossed The Green and walked up Victoria to School Hill Road, then I hid behind the school for about two hours. When I thought it was safe, I returned to the house. I'd kept a key to the back door when I left Ben. It was easy to let myself in. I knew Ben kept a gun in his desk that his father brought back from the Great War. I wrapped the gun I used up with that one. I spent the night in the guest room and left town before the sun came up."

When she looked at him, Steven saw her eyes were clear, and she no longer shook. "That's it," she said.

"Where did you go today, Mrs. Shipley?"

Alice told him about the letters she wrote in the inn at Otter Lake. "Would you see they get them? I'm not sure how Theo's going to feel, but Leon will be devastated. I tried to explain everything. I told him he can probably visit me wherever I end up." Her face became pinched. "Please," she pleaded.

Steven nodded. "I'll make sure they receive your letters. Thank you for telling me everything, Mrs. Shipley. I'll tell the district attorney you cooperated." Steven pushed a pad of lined paper across the table. "When you're ready, I need you to write it all down." He stood. "Alice Shipley, I am charging you with the murder of Benjamin Shipley. You will be held in custody overnight. I'll speak to Judge Randolph and the D.A. first thing tomorrow morning."

Steven met Will and Jimmy back in the CID room. They all looked exhausted. Steven handed Alice's letters to Jimmy Bou.

"Jimmy, give this one for Edith Adams to Tommy to put with the mail going out tomorrow morning. He has stamps at the front desk. And I want you to hand deliver the other two right now. Theo should be at the house, and if Leon's not home, wait until he gets there. He's been through enough. I don't want him finding out about Alice before he reads her letter. Go home after that, it's been a long day." He patted his protégé on the shoulder. "Rest tonight. Get some sleep."

"Okay, Steven. Thanks."

As Jimmy Bou shuffled out of the room, Steven turned to his partner. "It's over, Will."

"We got there in the end."

"I'll go tell the chief."

Will nodded, then sat at his desk to write his final account of the case.

Exiting his Chevy, Steven looked up at a velvety black sky dotted with thousands of brightly shining stars and smiled. His house was dark, but he knew that in Olivia's time there would be a light in the window upstairs overlooking the front porch.

He took the stairs two at a time, then slowed as he approached the bedroom door. He stood just beyond the threshold, watching his mother's room fade away and Olivia's sleigh bed come into view.

"Hi," he called out.

"Ooh, you're home."

"Sorry I'm so late," he said as she took his hand, bringing him into the room. "But, we got her."

Olivia wrapped her arms around his neck, and Steven leaned into her.

"So, it was Alice."

"Yes, she turned herself in and confessed."

"An existential woman."

"I don't know what that is, but tell me tomorrow, okay? I'm beat."

"I saved you some supper. Why don't you take a hot bath and change while I warm it up?"

An hour later, Steven and Olivia snuggled together on her couch, her back to his front, his arms around her. He leaned over and kissed her cheek.

"What's that for?"

"Because I can do that, now…right?"

"Yes, and it goes both ways." She turned in his arms and kissed him back.

The remainder of the evening passed in a most pleasant way.

Not…the end.

Acknowledgements

I offer my heartfelt thanks to the following people who helped me in so many ways.

To Beta Readers Mickey Hunter, Karen Lasher, Marylou Murry, and Sue Scheeren Watchko who took their time to read the manuscript and give me fantastic feedback.

To Lt. Jon Anderson (ret.) for offering insightful comments and suggestions and for keeping me true to police procedures both now and in the 1930s. Any errors are my own.

To Mary Ann Shovlowsky who listened to me read the entire manuscript and offered great feedback.

To Bruce Coffin, Anna Cotter, Arthur and Marni Graff, Belinda King, Dan Luca, John Mullins, Lissa Redmond, and Hal Wood who offered their expertise to help in my research.

To Nancy Quigg for letting me use her name.

To my fellow Sleuths and Sidekicks Tina deBellegarde, Jen Collins Moore, and Lida Sideris who have become my book family.

A special shout-out to Sue Watchko for a list much too long to mention.

To Shawn Reilly Simmons for her continued enthusiasm and interest in Steven and Olivia, and for her insightful comments that helped make this a better book.

To Everyone at Level Best Books for their work on behalf of Steven and Olivia.

To Ella Smith for her fabulous cover. I love it!

To my Friends and Family who always encourage and support me in my writing. I hope you know how much it means that you listen as I ramble on about the "book stuff" and that you're still genuinely interested. Tons of love to you all.

To All the Readers who enjoyed meeting Steven and Olivia in *Doorway to Murder* and continue to read about their adventures and to spread the word about the books. A special thank you for the wonderful reviews you've posted.

About the Author

A former language teacher and translator, Carol Pouliot is the author of The Blackwell and Watson Time-Travel Mysteries, which include *Doorway to Murder* (#1), *Threshold of Deceit* (# 2), *Death Rang the Bell* (#3), and the upcoming *RSVP to Murder* (#4). When not writing, Carol can be found reaching for her passport and packing a suitcase for her next adventure. Sign up for Carol's newsletter and learn more at http://www.carolpouliot.com

CPSIA information can be obtained
at www.ICGtesting.com
Printed in the USA
LVHW031738261121
704539LV00008B/784